Praise for *The Game* series:

'Flawless' The Book Lovers blog

'Perfect for summer' ...rts **Service**
...ill Dara

'I devoured this book in the span of hours.
As in: could not put it down' Lovin' Los Libros blog

'An emotional rollercoaster' The Three Bookateers blog

'A series you don't want to miss' Paperbook Princess blog

'Romantic, fun . . . perfect summer reads' Bookcrush blog

WITHDRAWN FROM
KILDARE COUNTY LIBRARY STOCK

D0234612

By day, *New York Times* and *USA Today* bestselling New Adult author Emma Hart dons a cape and calls herself Super Mum to her two children. By night, she drops the cape, pours a glass of juice and writes books.

She likes to write about magic, kisses and whatever else she can fit into the story. Sarcastic, witty characters are a must. As are hot guys. Emma likes to be busy – unless busy involves doing the dishes, but that seems to be when all the ideas come to life.

You can find Emma online at:
emmahart93.blogspot.com
🐦 @EmmaHartAuthor
📘 /YAAuthorEmmaHart

In The Game *series*:

The Love Game
Playing for Keeps
The Right Moves
Worth the Risk

EMMA HART

THE RIGHT MOVES
&
WORTH THE RISK

LEABHARLANN
CO. CILL DARA

HODDER

The Right Moves first published in ebook in 2013 and *Playing for Keeps*
first published in ebook in 2014 by Hodder and Stoughton
An Hachette UK company

This omnibus edition first published in paperback in 2014

1

Copyright © Emma Hart 2014

The right of Emma Hart to be identified as the Author
of the Work has been asserted by her in accordance with the
Copyright, Designs and Patents Act 1988.

All rights reserved. No part of this publication may be reproduced,
stored in a retrieval system, or transmitted, in any form or by any
means without the prior written permission of the publisher, nor
be otherwise circulated in any form of binding or cover other than
that in which it is published and without a similar condition
being imposed on the subsequent purchaser.

All characters in this publication are fictitious and any
resemblance to real persons, living or dead, is purely coincidental.

A CIP catalogue record for this title is
available from the British Library

ISBN 978 1 444 79721 3

Typeset by Palimpsest Book Production Ltd, Falkirk, Stirlingshire
Printed and bound by CPI Group (UK) Ltd, Croydon, CR0 4YY

Hodder & Stoughton policy is to use papers that are natural,
renewable and recyclable products and made from wood grown
in sustainable forests. The logging and manufacturing processes
are expected to conform to the environmental regulations
of the country of origin.

Hodder & Stoughton Ltd
338 Euston Road
London NW1 3BH

www.hodder.co.uk

Contents

THE RIGHT MOVES

Abbi

You just need one.

One thought. One second. One impulse. One touch. A lot of little things – little *ones* add together, snowballing and spiraling into something bigger. A big one. But one all the same. And one thing is all it takes to change your life.

Irreparably. Inexplicably. Irreversibly.

It's been two years since those little ones added together for the first time and I fell in love with Pearce Stevens. It's been two years since I felt that sweet fluttering of a first crush followed by the gentle thump of falling head over heels in love. Two years since the things that meant everything would fall apart, leaving me plunging headfirst into the dark abyss of depression.

If I knew then what I know now, I would have made different choices. Ignored the thoughts as the wishful musings of a teen heart, passed the time, fought the impulses, and shied from the touch. If I knew how the next months would unfold and the direction my life would take, I would have hopped on the next plane outta here and hunkered down in the Caribbean.

But I didn't know – and there was no way for me to. How could I know? I never imagined those little ones would grow into a big one, and I never imagined they'd come back just months after I felt them for the first time.

But the second time was a darker thought. It was a black second, a swallowing impulse, a deadly touch. The first time I watched the blood drip down my ankle from my accidental shaving cut, the newly bare razor blade flat between my fingers, was a moment that changed my life just as much as falling in love with Pearce did. It was a moment I can never change. I can't take it away and I can't pretend it never happened.

It's a part of me, just like Pearce is. A part of my past, and they are the two defining moments in my life. If you ask me where it all went wrong, I'll tell you – Pearce Stevens and the blade. And I won't be able to explain it for a second, no matter how hard you beg.

I won't be able to tell you why I fell in love with my best friend's brother, or why I didn't run before it was too late. I'll never be able to put into words why I didn't pull off my rose-tinted glasses and see him for what he really was and is.

I will never, ever be able to explain what possessed me to make the first cut on my skin. After all, you can't explain what you don't understand, and sometimes it's better not to understand.

I lean over the bathtub and watch the water run dark from my newly-dyed hair. The dark water swishes around the tub and swirls around the plug, disappearing from view with the same ease my blood did so long ago. I stay here until the water runs clear, shampoo and rinse, and wrap my hair in a dark towel.

Against Mom's wishes I made Dad take me to the store to get the dye. She doesn't understand my need to separate myself from the person I was last year. I don't think anyone does, and it's not something I can explain. I just know I'm not the Abbi I was before; the new Abbi is a different person. By separating the two halves of me, I'm moving forward with the new me. At least that's what Dr. Hausen said. She also said it was a step in the right direction – something positive.

Positive is what I need. That's why my previously pale pink, girly bedroom is now bright blue and purple. It's positive. It's different. It's new.

Just like me. I'm shiny and new.

I sit on my new beaded comforter on the bed and face the mirror. My eyes are brighter than they were before and my cheeks aren't as sunken. I touch a gentle fingertip to the hollow of my cheek and breathe in deeply. A clump of hair falls free from the towel, the almost black color a contrast against my pale skin.

I bend my head forward, roughly dry my hair, and flip it back up. My hand crawls along my bed to find my brush, and I run it through the strands. I don't really focus on anything but the repetitive motion, and I don't think about anything as I start up my hairdryer. It just is.

I don't think about the fact that the corkboard above my desk was once full of pictures of me and Maddie and is now empty. I don't think about the fact all my teenage diaries were thrown out, that three-quarters of my wardrobe was re-bought. I don't think about how much of the past I've thrown away. How much of it I'm running from.

But is it really running if you still have to face up to it every day?

I don't think so. It's not running away if you know where you want to be. It's making the conscious decision to change.

I set the hairdryer down on the bed next to me and focus on the reflection in the mirror, sliding the brush through my new hair one last time. And I smile. I look nothing like the old Abbi, and for just a second, there's a spark of light in my eyes. It's fleeting, but there, and fleeting is better than not at all.

My door opens a crack, and Mom pokes her head through the gap. I hear her sharp intake of breath before I turn to look at her. Her hand is poised over her mouth like she thinks it'll hide the way her jaw has dropped. Like she thinks it'll cover her wide, horrified eyes.

'You . . . Why?'

I finger the dark strands nervously. 'I needed to change it. It reminded me too much of before.'

'Why, Abbi? Your hair was so beautiful.'

My eyes travel back to the mirror. 'Because the outside is all I can change,' I whisper. 'I can't change what's on the inside, not easily, but this I can change. So I did. I needed to, Mom.'

Silence stretches between us as she lets my words sink in. 'I don't understand.'

I shake my head. 'You don't have to understand. You just have to accept it.'

'I . . . I suppose there's not much I can do, anyway.'

I shake my head again. My fingers creep to my arm and under my sleeve, the pads of them rubbing over the slightly raised scars there. The scars I keep hidden from the rest of the world. 'It's better than the alternative. Anything is better than that.'

Mom lets out a shaky breath, and I press my thumb against my pulse point as I always do when I remember. The steady beat of my blood humming through my body reminds me I'm still alive. My heart is still beating and my lungs are still breathing. I'm still existing.

'Yes. It's much better,' Mom agrees and walks across the room before perching on the bed next to me. Our reflections are side by side and the only difference in them is our age. And our hair color. Her blonde hair is the exact shade mine was two hours ago. She reaches over and takes my hand as she meets my eyes in the shiny glass. 'Is there anything else you feel like you need to do?'

'Like what?'

'I don't know, Abbi. I just thought that maybe since you want to change a little we could go to the salon. You know, get a make-over. We both need one. Maybe our nails, too.'

I swallow, her tight grip on my hand telling me exactly how hard it is for her to suggest that. How hard it is for her to finally accept that *her* Abbi isn't coming back this time. That her Abbi is lost forever.

'I'd like that,' I say honestly. 'Maybe that's what I need. Maybe it'll change the last of it. Wipe it away.'

'No wiping away needed. We'll just make new memories to replace the old.' Mom stands up. 'I'll call the salon tomorrow. And Bianca called – you can start in her class tomorrow. A few of her girls just got into Juilliard, and she has a few newbies starting then. She thinks it would be the perfect time for you.

I said I'd speak to you and call her back. Shall I let her know you'll be there?'

Ballet. Juilliard. The ultimate dream. The thing that keeps me going. The thing that saved me when I felt there was nothing left to save. 'Please, Mom. I'll be there.'

'Okay.' She backs out of my room and shuts the door behind her, leaving me to silence once again.

Silence. My best friend and my worst enemy.

I lightly brush my fingers over my wrist again and reach for my iPod. The screen glares back at me, and I click shuffle. Snow Patrol blare out, and I lie back on my bed, curling into my side.

Juilliard chants lowly in my mind as sleep begins to take me under.

~

I clutch the strap of my dance bag to my stomach, and the bag knocks against my knees as I tentatively push open the door to Bianca's dance studio. My stomach is rolling with apprehension, my whole body tense, but I know I'm safe here.

Bianca is one of the few people who truly knows and understands my desire and need to dance. On the day Dr. Hausen suggested using dance as therapy, Bianca arrived in the gym. One private session a week quickly turned to three, both there and here at her studio, and she helped me leave the institution. She reminded me of the freedom that comes with the stretching of a leotard and tying of a ribbon on ballet shoes. And she's the closest thing I have to a friend without Maddie here.

The familiar dance hall stares at me. The mirrors lining the wall, the *barre* on the far wall, the piano in the corner. Dexter, her disabled uncle and pianist, waves at me from the corner. I smile at him, feeling myself relax a little. Only a little, because I know soon the room will be filled with people I've never met.

Two slender hands rest on my shoulders from behind me. 'I can see your tension from the other side of the floor. Breathe and relax, Abbi, because those shoes aren't gonna dance for you.'

'I'm scared,' I whisper as the door opens.

'I know.' Bianca drops her hands and circles me, stopping in front of me and bending down so we're eye to eye. 'You're here to dance, remember that, strong girl, and you'll be fine.'

'To dance.' I let out a long breath, glancing at the growing crowd by the seats.

'And it's something you do beautifully. You're safe here.'

And I know that. I know nothing or no one can touch me here, especially not when my hand touches that *barre* and the music starts. Wherever it is I end up when I dance . . . it's safe.

I pad gently to the corner and remove my sweatpants and top, revealing my dance clothes beneath. I slip my shoes on and run my finger over the satin ribbons. Soft. Safe.

I keep my eyes on the floor in the vain hope no one will talk to me. In the hope no one will even notice me, because like Bianca said, I'm here to dance. Not to make friends, not to build relationships, just to dance.

My shoes reflect back to me in the mirror as I stop. My fingers stretch in anticipation, and I place my hand on the *barre*, letting them curl around the cold metal. Lightness spreads through my body, easing the ever-present suffocation of depression. It's only for a second, but that second is enough. In that second I feel the rush of the girl I could be, and the first easy breath I've taken since I walked in here ten minutes ago leaves my body.

The dull buzz of chatter ceases as Bianca claps her hands once. 'I'm not going to stand here and introduce myself or explain what we're doing here. If you don't know me or why you're here, then you're in the wrong studio, little chicks.

'What I am going to tell you is to forget everything you've ever learned about how dance works. When you slip your shoes on in this studio, you give yourself over to the art of ballet, not the technicalities.

'Ballet isn't about timing, getting that step perfect, or getting the best marks in class. It's about telling a story. It's about taking the feelings and emotions inside you, ripping them out and expressing them with flawless motions of your body. Ballet is a dance that stems and grows from everything we are, regardless of what it means to you, and if you believe any differently, you're in the wrong studio.' Her eyes comb over us all standing at the *barre*, scrutinizing us, like a simple glance can tell her whether or not we believe what she does.

'What you do need to know about how my class works is that you don't stop being a dancer just because you're not on the floor. I expect you to work your asses off. I expect you to be here three nights a week for two hours, then I expect you to work at home. Six hours a week in a studio will not get you to the standard Juilliard expects and demands. Damn, I spend more time than that on my hair each week.

'I don't care whether you dance in a studio, in the shower, in the middle of Central Park – hey, dance on the highway if you really want to – but you must dance. Every. Single. Day. And I will know if you don't. I will know, if for even one day, you forget to dance, because your body will show me.

'I don't want to see any of you in the wrong studio. I want you all to be in the right studio. Some of you I already know and I know you're in the right studio, but the rest of you have to prove it.' She turns and taps the top of the piano, and her uncle begins to play.

'What if we think we are, but we're not? Will you know?' someone further up the *barre* asks.

Bianca turns, her lips twisting on one side. 'Of course.'

'What happens then?'

'Then you leave my studio, because there is someone out there in this city who does deserve to be here. I only teach the best, know that, and I haven't yet had a student who didn't get into Juilliard after attending this class. There's a reason I only teach two classes a week. You are one, and the others are currently seven year olds, and the majority have been with me since they could walk at the age of one. If seven year olds can hack it, I expect young adults such as yourselves to do so.'

'Have you ever asked anyone to leave?'

'Every time I start a new class,' she responds sharply. 'Now warm up before you become the first.'

I fight my smile, training my features into a plain mask, and start my warm-up. I remember hearing the same speech when Bianca walked into the gym hall, and I remember asking her the exact same questions and getting the same answers. It's what endeared me to her so much – unlike most people who know my past, she didn't look at me any differently. To her I was – and am – a girl with a dream, everything else be damned.

The movements of the warm-up are so familiar, and the main door opens as I begin to drop into a *demi-plié.* The feeling of being watched crawls over my skin, prickling at the back of my neck and down my spine. I don't want to, I don't even need to, but I glance upwards and in that direction.

His straight-backed posture and precise steps announce him as a dancer – and a late one – as Bianca approaches him. His dark hair is short but messy, and a distinct British accent floats across the sound of the piano faintly. My eyes roam over his body from his broad shoulders to his defined arms. Dancer's arms; strong yet gentle. The touch from his large hands would be hard yet soft.

You wouldn't know he's a dancer unless you are. His build is closer to that of a football player, but he's far too pretty to do that. *Crap.* Did I really just call him pretty? *What am I even doing?* I shouldn't be standing here trying not to undress the Hot British Guy with my eyes.

He nods once and turns his face toward me. Or the class, but it's me his eyes fall on. Our gazes lock for a fleeting moment, and I almost falter in my warm-up. Even across the studio there's no mistaking the green in his eyes. There's no mistaking the way he looks me over, interest sparking in them as he does so.

And there's no mistaking the apprehension in my chest . . . Or the fluttering inside my tummy when his eyes find mine again. I swallow and look away, telling myself I'm imagining the interest in his eyes and the intensity that kept me looking at him for as long as I did.

I'm not here to eye up Hot British Guy. I'm here to dance, and nothing else.

The dream, Abbi. Juilliard.

Blake

'Shit, shit, shit, shit!' I mutter the curse words under my breath as I climb out of one of the bright yellow taxis that seem to be bloody everywhere in this city. I thought it was all put on for films and stuff, but apparently it isn't.

The strap of my bag catches on the door handle, and I almost trip as I yank it off. Being late to the first dance class is not how I planned on starting my new life in New York. Actually, I never planned on being in a damn class unless it was at Juilliard, but that's not something to think about right now. I can't think about her – if I do I'll get that stupid canary car back here, get in, and go back to my overpriced apartment.

I hoist my bag onto my shoulder and look up at the building in front of me. It's old school and doesn't look right in Manhattan. Instead of the sky high, glass buildings that seem to be the norm, this building is red brick with just a small sign proclaiming, 'Bianca's Dance Studio'. I ruffle my hair with my fingers, sighing deeply, wondering if I've made the right decision. For the millionth time.

But I am late, so there's no damn time left to worry about that. I tuck it into the back of my mind for later – for now I need my head on the dance floor and not in the clouds.

I push the door open and follow the small hallway to a large open room. A *barre* is against the far mirrored wall, and both guys and girls are lined up against it, running through the five positions in time with the gentle music playing. My eyes scan them, noting they all look about twenty or so, except the girl at the end.

Her dark hair is tucked into a pristine bun on top of her head and her eyes are lowered as she bends her knees and moves into a *demi-plié*. She's utterly graceful, and it's plain to see she's completely at peace.

'Blake Smith?' a voice with a strong New York accent says quietly to my side. I turn to face the auburn-haired woman staring at me and nod.

'Yes, ma'am. That's me.'

She smiles. 'I'm Bianca.'

We shake hands. 'It's nice to meet you.'

'And you. You're a little late, but I'd say London is quite different to here.'

I think of the twenty minutes it took me to get a taxi. 'Yeah, you're right there. Sorry – I'm still learning how to get around.'

Her laugh is gentle. 'Yes, I'd imagine it would be tough. Well, if you have any questions feel free to come to me and I'll do my best to answer them. If you put your bag over there in the corner and warm up, we'll get started.'

She silently pads back to her spot, and I look back to the girl at the end of the *barre*.

Our eyes meet.

She almost hesitates in her warm-up, but then carries on as if we're not staring at each other. As if I'm not trying to work out what color her eyes are. They're framed by long, thick lashes that curl toward her eyebrows, and her cheeks pink lightly. I run my eyes down her body, and I can't help but admire the way her leotard and leggings hug her body. She blinks when my eyes lock onto hers again.

Shit. They don't make girls like her in England. And if they do, my mother never introduced me to them.

She pulls her gaze from mine and looks to the front. Something . . . Something tells me I need to know this girl – and it isn't even something in my dick.

I run through the warm-up, half listening to Bianca talking to the class, half watching the girl with the dark brown hair. She's standing slightly back from everyone else, her hands tucked into her sleeves and her head hanging slightly, yet her poise is perfect. Her back is straight and her feet are in position.

Slowly, she moves into the basic positions and moves to Bianca's orders with the elegance of a swan floating along a river in the spring. Every move is perfectly precise – both in positioning and timing. She continues working through the moves at the *barre*, from *plié* and *tendu* to *battements*, oblivious to my eyes following her. Oblivious to my eyes following every curve of her body and every stretch of her limbs. Oblivious to the fact I've never been so attracted to a girl whose name I don't know.

I switch from the warm-up to the basic steps. I know full well Bianca is putting us all through our paces since just over half the class are new. Her eyes flick to each of us, lingering for a second or two as they examine our positioning and posture, but I'm barely concentrating. My thoughts are purely for the girl in front of me; my body is moving fluidly through the instructed steps.

For me, dancing is as natural as breathing. It always has been.

Bianca instructs us to pair off, male and female, and I move toward the brown-haired girl. How could I go to anyone else? As cliché as it sounds, she's the only person in this room I'm really aware of.

I tap her on the shoulder. 'Do you want to . . .'

A pair of startlingly light blue eyes crash into mine. *Blue. That's what color they are.* It's the kind of blue that makes you stop dead and instantly makes you think of a crisp summer's day, complete with beer and a barbecue. It's also the kind of blue that shows everything – the hue too pale to hide shadows lurking beneath – it's the flicker of darkness that makes me pause and stare at her.

I've seen those shadows before.

I know how they linger, barely scratching the surface before pulling you under. And I know the climb is always harder than the fall . . . If you're lucky enough to get a grip on the climb.

'Do I . . .?' she questions shyly, raising her hand to her face then dropping it again.

'Um.' I cough and scratch the back of my neck. Her hesitant smile reminds me what I've actually approached her for. 'Do you want to dance together? Since we have to pair off. You know. Yeah.'

Shit. I sound like an awkward teen boy who has no idea how to speak to a girl.

Her smile stretches a little and her eyes flit around the dance hall. Everyone is paired off and talking to each other quietly.

'I   Sure,' she replies.

'Great. I'm Blake. Blake Smith.'

'Abbi Jenkins.' Abbi's hand slips into my outstretched one. My fingers curl around her smaller ones, but my focus isn't on the silky smooth skin against mine; it's on the gentleness of her tone and the way her lips moved when she said her name.

'Abbi,' I repeat. 'Have you danced long?'

'Since I was eight.' She takes her hand from mine and clasps both of hers in front of her stomach protectively. 'We all need a little something to escape in, right?'

Right. 'Definitely.'

Three sharp claps draw us both from the conversation, and we turn to Bianca. As she instructs us on what we need to do, my eyes trace the line of Abbi's profile. It's dainty and cute – from the way her button nose curves, to the obvious plumpness of her lips. I don't notice I'm smiling until her eyes meet mine again and she raises a questioning eyebrow. I shrug one of my shoulders, and her lips quirk.

'Shall we?'

'Uh, sure.' Shall we what? *Crap.*

Abbi lets the smile break across her face. 'Dance,' she responds with a twinkle in her eyes.

Right. Dance. What we're here for.

Shit. I come thousands of miles to achieve my dream, and what do I do? I get distracted by a pretty face. I need to be thinking with my feet not my damn dick.

For the second time since I walked into this studio, I offer her my hand, and for the second time, she takes it. She moves onto *pointe* seemingly without thinking and closes her eyes. Once again I'm struck by the ease of her movements as I fall into my own . . . With her. It's not until you dance with someone you can truly appreciate the beauty of it.

And it's been only a few seconds, a fleeting moment in the grand scheme of things, but seeing Abbi Jenkins give herself over to the music is to see true beauty.

One moment – one I'll never forget.

Until she opens her eyes as we begin to move, and I'm reminded that even shadows can fall over true beauty.

Abbi looks at me, but I can tell she's not really seeing me. There's a gloss over her eyes, brightening the blue hue of her iris through the pain lingering there. She's somewhere else, somewhere far away, but her steps never falter. She never falls out of time, never makes a wrong move. Even her breathing doesn't change.

Despite the chopping and changing of the music and movements, combined with Bianca's never-ending comments and instructions on arm positioning and timing, my blood is rushing through my body as we move together. I can hear it pounding in my ears and drowning out the music. And I'm mesmerized. I'm mesmerized by the fluidity of her movements, the ease of our dance together. It's like we've always danced together.

The music stops, and Abbi closes her eyes as we come to a standstill. When they open they're clear again, and she smiles shyly. My arms fall from her and she steps back, her fingers lightly brushing across mine. She tugs her sleeves down over her hands, clasping her fingers in front of her stomach again.

'Thank you,' she says, her eyes meeting mine.

My lips curve on one side. 'What for?'

'For the dance.' She smiles as softly as she speaks, turning back to the *barre*. I watch her go. Watch the gentle pad of her feet across the floor, the sway of her hips with each step . . .

'No,' I mutter, never taking my eyes from her. 'Thank you.'

Abbi

'Coffee?' Mom asks, eyeing the Starbucks at the end of the street.

I roll my eyes but I should have guessed she'd ask eventually. I'm sure coffee runs through her veins instead of blood.

'Would I deny you that?' My lips twitch as I look at her. She grins.

'You've tried, honey. You've tried!'

'Only because Dad made me hide all the coffee. I either did it, or he threatened he wouldn't buy Barbie's convertible. I was eight. I *needed* that car, Mom.' I laugh. 'It was a life or death situation, y'know.'

She shakes her head, laughing silently, and grabs the door of Starbucks. 'Life or death was me not getting my coffee that morning, Abbi. Do you want one?'

I look through the tall windows into the coffee shop and shake my head. Most of the tables are full since it's just after lunch, and after making small talk with the manicurist and hairdresser for two hours, I need some quiet.

'No, I'm okay. I'll wait out here.' I smile uneasily at her, my eyes darting between her and the windows. Mom follows my gaze and nods understandingly.

'I'll only be a minute.' She hesitates, sucking the corner of her lip into her mouth, before pushing the door open and disappearing inside.

I sit down on the bench on the opposite sidewalk and sigh. My fingers run through my soft hair, and I realize how tired I am. I can barely believe something as simple as getting my hair and nails done has made me so exhausted. But that's the thing with depression. You never know how or when it's going to strike and it nearly always knocks you off your feet.

It brings a whole new meaning to the phrase 'always expect the unexpected'.

I press the heels of my hands into my eyes and stifle a yawn. The sooner Mom gets her coffee the better.

'Didn't expect to see you anytime soon.'

I haven't heard that voice for a year – maybe more. I can't think of a time when I've wanted to hear that voice again. Jake Johnson.

Pearce's best friend and half of the reason Pearce ended up a drug addict.

'I can't say I *wanted* to see you anytime soon,' I reply, crossing my ankles and staring stonily at Starbucks.

Of course he didn't expect to see me anytime soon. As far as he – and everyone else – knew, I'm still at St. Morris's. The loony bin. The nuthouse. The funny farm. Because I'm *crazy*.

Like they know anything at all. Crazy is hysterical giggles after an hour long pillow fight. It isn't depression.

'Ouch.' Jake laughs huskily, eight years of chain smoking starting to take its toll on his voice. 'I don't remember you having this much fight in you before you went loopy.'

'I didn't,' I say honestly. *You can't have fight for something you don't respect or care about.* 'Aren't you worried about talking to me in public? I mean, what if someone sees you talking to Pearce's crazy ex-girlfriend? Wouldn't that tarnish your perfect bad boy image?'

He laughs again, and it crawls across my skin like slime. I try and fail to repress a shiver. I never liked Jake, and he never liked me; we were civil to each other for Pearce's sake. A lot of things were for Pearce's sake, and not one of them meant anything to him.

'Don't worry, Abbi. There's no chance of Pearce running into us. You don't have to worry about seeing him.'

'I'm not worried about seeing him,' I lie. My throat is dry

at the mere thought of it. I swallow hard. I don't want to think about seeing him.

I'm not sure anything scares me more than that.

A third laugh comes from Jake. 'You won't see him for the next fifteen years, girl.'

My head snaps round, and I look at him for the first time. To look at him, you wouldn't think he was as addicted to heroin as Pearce. You wouldn't think it was what he lived for, the only thing that kept him living. In fact, you'd probably walk past him in the street, look at his gelled brown hair, his clear skin, and his muscular build and it wouldn't even cross your mind.

But I know. I know the devil that lives beneath the surface, and I've met him many, many times.

'What?'

'Fifteen years.' Jake leans against the wall casually, as if he's not talking about the guy he grew up with. 'He lost his job about a month after you went nuts and couldn't afford to keep up with it. He owed money to a lot of people – more than you know, Abbi. A lot of people that wouldn't think twice about breaking his neck, so the jackass made a deal. Said he'd be their runner and deliver the shit to their customers. His dealers got to sit on their asses, and he paid off so much debt that way. He paid less than he would have, because he took some home at the end of the night. It was a win-win for him.'

'And?'

'And he got sloppy. Too confident. He got drunk one night out on his run and the cops got hold of him.' Jake smirks. 'Everyone knows if you're running junk you don't get drunk on the job. No need to draw attention to yourself, y'know? Anyway, he was loaded with shit and had a couple thousand dollars stashed in his back pocket. Took him straight down to the NYPD and had him on possession with intent to supply. He was in court last month. Asshole bagged himself fifteen years in the slammer for a rookie mistake.'

I can't deny the part inside of me that relaxes. I can't fight the relief that floods through me at that news.

I don't have to see Pearce. Maybe ever.

'Well.' I look back toward the door of Starbucks in time to see Mom walking out, her coffee in her hands, and I stand. 'It's nothing less than he deserves.'

I walk away without saying another word. I don't need to. My actions speak louder than my words ever could.

~

I kept my eyes on the floor and wondered why I didn't give in to the screaming voice in my head telling me to grab the door handle and run. Wondered why I was standing here, yet again, while he destroyed himself.

I flinched with every sound he made as he prepared the drug and took it. No part of me wanted to know anything about how he took it. I waited for the inevitable happy sigh that would come as the drug spread through his body.

Still, I kept my eyes on the floor. As if not looking meant it wasn't happening. As if not looking meant I wasn't standing idly by and letting him do it.

But I knew why I was standing there. Fear. Fear of the anger that could erupt from him at any minute, even as he enjoyed his rush. Fear of another bruise or mark to explain away.

The sigh came.

I looked up.

I looked up but away from anything that had anything to do with the drug. His lips twitched into a gentle smile. A satisfied smile. My fingers curled into my palm, my nails cutting into my skin, but I swallowed the urge to speak. I learned early on not to say a word when he was getting that first rush. Don't speak. Don't move. Don't make a single damn sound.

I stepped back, breaking the second golden rule. Luckily, the thick plush carpet masked my footsteps as I backed toward the wall. I reached a hand out behind me, barely glancing over my shoulder.

And I hit a chest of drawers.

I froze, my eyes darting to him. His head snapped up, his blue-green eyes as cold and hard as ice as they met mine across the room. I took a sharp breath as he stared at me, and even as I dropped my eyes and screwed them shut, I could still feel his eyes cutting through me.

The bed creaked as he stood, and my teeth clamped down on my bottom lip. His silent footsteps as he approached were almost more daunting than loud ones. I couldn't see him. I couldn't hear him. I had no idea how close he was until his hand gripped my chin.

Pearce ran his thumb down my jaw almost lovingly before he tightened his grip and yanked my face up to his, forcing my eyes onto his.

'What have I told you, Abbi?'

~

I jolt, and the bath water splashes with the force of my awakening. I grip the sides of the tub so tightly my knuckles are white, and try to steady my breathing. My eyes dart from side to side, taking in the room, as I work to ground myself.

Home. I'm home, in my bathroom. Not at a party. Not with Pearce.

I'm safe.

'I'm safe,' I whisper. 'I'm safe. I'm safe. I. Am. Safe.'

I keep whispering those words, over and over, over and over. Reminding myself of what I know as I struggle to erase the flashback from my mind. I don't need to ride it out – I remember what happened too well. I remember the bruise on the side of my head from hitting the drawers after he shoved me aside and I remember 'slipping on some black ice on my way home'.

I let go of the tub and rub my hands down my face. The water is freezing cold. A quick glance at the clock on the wall tells me I've been in the bath longer than I thought. Much, much longer. I climb out and wrap my body and hair in towels with shaky hands. Adrenaline is still pumping through my blood from the memory, roaring through my body, and it makes me want to forget.

My eyes dart to the cabinet but it's pointless. I know there's nothing in this house that isn't carefully hidden that would hurt me. No razors, no scissors, and the broken mirror in here has been replaced lest I slice my finger along it. There's even a lock on the knife drawer in the kitchen – that's how much my parents trust and believe in me.

But somehow I feel safer this way. Knowing I can't get anything that would hurt me almost makes me feel a little stronger because I have to cope. Right now I have to cope with the memories because my chosen way out isn't an option anymore. I can't escape into the pain or lose myself in my blood swirling down the plug.

I have to feel. I have to remember. I have to live.

Yet it doesn't stop my nails digging harshly into my palms. Even that, the small sting of pain, takes off the edge of the past. It clears my head long enough to make me realize I haven't danced today.

Long enough to realize, I need to dance.

I change into some yoga pants and a tank top, clip my wet hair on top of my head and grab my ballet shoes. The TV buzzes as I pass the front room, and I open the door in the kitchen that leads to the garage.

Dad converted half of the double garage into a mini dance studio when we found out I'd be leaving St Morris's. There are mirrors on the wall and a brass banister that doubles as a *barre*. I'd laughed at him when he showed me it for the first time, but it works surprisingly well.

I take the cold metal in my hand, moving into position, and can't help but think about the last time I danced . . . With Blake.

When Bianca had ordered us to partner off, I was ready to run there and then. Or shout at her for not telling me – either one. I know now she deliberately didn't tell me. And after all, I'd have to dance with someone at Juilliard, so it's better to get that hurdle cleared now. And it was cleared easier than I thought it would be.

When we danced together, I felt nothing but free. I felt like

I could take any steps to any music on any stage in the world and I would get it perfectly right.

The art involved in ballet is like a movie. If the two lead characters don't have chemistry, it doesn't work. If two dancers don't have chemistry, if they don't click, the dance won't work.

I've partnered with more people than I can count, both male and female, and I've never connected with anyone the way I did with Blake. I've never felt so comfortable in someone else's arms as we danced together, and I've definitely never trusted a partner that way. I've also never been as attracted to a partner as I am to him.

And that scares me.

The day I walked out of St. Morris's for the last time I built walls a hundred feet high around every part of me. I topped them with barbed wire and guarded any crack with wolves. I was – am – determined not to feel. I'm determined not to let anyone in. Not until I know I can keep myself up.

Dance is the one thing that keeps me up. It's the one thing I let myself feel; it's the one thing that is truly real to me. It's the only thing that's allowed to get past the wolves and climb my walls. Yesterday, Blake and dance were synonymous. They were one.

Where the dance went, he went, too.

I slowly lower from *pointe* and breathe out. Instead of being at the *barre*, I'm in the middle of the garage. I danced without realizing. Lost in my head, I could have done any dance, any steps, any positions, and I'll never know.

But I did what matters.

I fought the impulse to hurt.

And I danced.

Blake

'Bloody hell.' I mutter as I slam the door to my apartment. 'Takeaway guy needs to get some manners.'

I set the cartons down on the small table in my kitchen and grab a plate from the cupboard. My chef's clothes are in a heap on the floor in front of my washing machine, and I kick them to the side.

I'm a chef and ordering takeaway for dinner. But really, a guy who cooks for ten hours in a shit hot kitchen doesn't want to cook at home as well.

I dump the food onto my plate and take the ten steps into my front room. I sit on the sofa, swing my legs up, and switch the tele on. Just as I'm about to get comfy my phone rings.

'Uhhh,' I groan, leaning my head back. 'Jesus.'

My steaming plate earns a place on the coffee table as I grab the phone – and groan again when my brother's name appears on screen.

'Jase,' I answer. My *favorite* brother. Actually, my only brother.

'Mum was wondering if you were dead. You haven't called her.'

'So she has my barely-legal baby brother calling to make sure her eldest son is still alive?' I snort. 'Save me the sob story, Jase.'

He sighs. 'She's on deadline—'

'And only has however long to get however many designs of her fancy shoes into her office. Yeah, yeah. I've heard it all.'

'Right.' He pauses, and the line cracks a little. 'Well. I think she misses you.'

I snort again. This one full of disbelief. 'I'm her biggest disappointment, bro. I was supposed to follow in Dad's footsteps and go into the firm with him, but instead I decided to "cook fancy dinners", as she puts it. Then I came to New York to do what Tori and I always promised each other we'd do, and she hates that.'

Jase doesn't say anything, and even though he's so much younger than me I know he remembers her. There's no way he couldn't. As usual, the mere mention of her name silences the whole family. Like they won't forget – like I'm the only one who can remember the way her eyes sparkled when she laughed and the way she flicked her hair over her shoulder when she was playing up the daddy's girl act. The way everyone loved her, because she was just the kind of person you couldn't help but love.

'She doesn't like to remember. It hurts her, Blake.' His excuse is lame, and he knows it. I don't like to remember and it hurts me but I still do.

'She's dead, Jase. She existed, as much as our parents would like to believe she didn't. Tori was real and pretending she wasn't and her death never happened won't make it better.'

'It just hurts Mum that you left, and the fact you left to do what Tori wanted to do rubs salt in the wound.'

'Juilliard wasn't – *isn't*,' I correct myself, 'just Tori's dream. It never was. It was always our dream, and you know it.'

'What's wrong with dance school here? You could get into any London school you wanted!'

I swallow as I remember the honest reason I'm here. *That* conversation that the twelve year old me didn't understand.

~

'Blake?' Tori had knocked on my bedroom door softly, pushing it open a crack.

'Yeah?' I looked up from the science homework I was working

*on and into my big sister's wide green eyes. We had the same eyes
– we were the only ones of all six of us that had Mum's green eyes.
Jase, Laura, Allie and Kiera all had Dad's blue eyes.*

'*Can I come in?*'

*I looked at her feet inside my room and laughed. 'You already
are.'*

*She looked down, shrugged, and laughed with me. 'I suppose I
am.' She moved across the room with the grace of the dancer she
was and jumped on my bed. My homework scattered everywhere,
sheets of paper flying onto the floor, and I chucked my pencil at
her.*

'*Dammit, Tori!*'

'*I'm sorry!' Her amused tone said she was anything but. I glared
at her for a minute before breaking into a big grin. I could never
stay mad at her. She was both my sister and my best friend, both
of us the black sheep of the perfect family for our dreams.*

'*I need to ask you something.' Her tone was hesitant and more
serious than it was before. I froze, stopped grabbing my work from
the floor and looked up at her.*

'*What is it?*'

'*Did you mean it when you said you wanted to go to Juilliard?
To dance?*'

'*Of course I did. Why? Did you think I didn't?*'

'*I did wonder.' She chews her lip. 'I wondered if you were just
saying it for me.'*

'*No, Tori. I want to go to Juilliard. We're gonna take on the world,
remember?' I smile at her, and she smiles back almost sadly.*

'*Right. The world.' She pauses. 'I want you to promise me something.'*

'*Anything.'*

*Tori climbed from the bed and knelt in front of me. She pressed
her palms against my cheeks, cupping my face.*

'*Promise me, Blake, that no matter what happens, you'll go to
Juilliard. That you'll go to New York and live our dream.'*

'*What?*'

'*Promise me. No matter what.'*

*I stared at her, not understanding why she was saying that. But
I promised. I always would. I'd promise Tori anything.*

'I promise. No matter what.'

*She stroked my cheeks with her thumbs and pressed a kiss to
my forehead as she stood up. Then she turned and walked away,
pausing for a second at my door. Her head turned slightly, and her
shining, wet eyes met mine.*

'Thank you.'

~

I swallow, wiping at my eyes. 'I promised her two days before
she died I'd go to New York and get into Juilliard. I promised
her no matter what, Jase.'

I'm halfway there, I remind myself. Halfway there.

'Right. Look. I gotta go,' he says in a slightly thick voice.
'Going out. Bye.'

The line clicks dead, and I fight the urge to throw my phone
across the room. Same old response, same old thing every single
time her name is mentioned. No one wants to talk about her,
about the blot on the family name, about the perfect family's
dirty little secret.

No one wants to remember her. If my parents had their way,
she'd be wiped from every family photo she was ever in, our
house would have one less bedroom, and my mother would
have a handful less stretch marks. If my parents had their way,
my eldest sister would have never existed. They would have
had five children, with Kiera being the eldest. As she is now,
by default.

I look at my dinner, still steaming slightly, and chuck my
phone on the sofa instead of at the wall. I glance at the plate
again, shake my head, and walk into the dingy bathroom.

My family may pretend Tori never existed, but they weren't
the ones who spent every spare second with her. They weren't
the ones who knew her hopes and dreams.

And they weren't the ones who found her body.

They can try to forget all they want, but that's the one image I will never, ever be able to erase from my mind. That memory will haunt me forever.

Abbi

The clock ticks steadily in the background. Every tick brings me a second closer to leaving Dr. Hausen's office and entering Bianca's studio. Every tick brings me a second closer to my true therapy.

My psychiatrist clicks her pen in time with the clock. My foot bobs as I stare blankly at a spot on the wall.

'I like your hair,' she says.

My hand goes to the braid hanging over my shoulder. 'Thanks.'

'It's a big change.'

'Yep.'

'Do you think it's a good one?'

I sigh and look at her. Her greying hair is clasped back and her glasses are perched on the top of her head precariously. She stops clicking the pen, instead taps it against her papers. I know this tactic – but I still fall for it. Every time.

I hate pen clicking, tapping, or any variation of a repetitive noise. She knows if she taps long enough, I'll answer just to get her to stop.

'Yes,' I grit out. The tapping stops. 'You know, that's a dirty trick.'

Dr. Hausen smiles, her eyes crinkling at the corners. 'Ah, but it works.' She lets out a small laugh. 'Tell me what made you do it.'

'What made me answer you? The pen clicking and tapping.'

'Abbi.' She tries for stern but the lingering upturn of her lips gives her away.

I shrug. 'Worth a try.'

'What made you dye your hair?'

'The old Abbi was blonde. I'm not that person anymore,' I say quietly.

'So it's the same reason you had for decorating your room before you moved back home.' Statement. Not a question.

'Mhmm.'

'Why do you think that is?'

Because I hate the old Abbi. I hate that she never stood up for herself. I hate that she let Pearce walk all over her, abuse her, defile her. I hate that he made her a shadow of the person she was. I hate the fact she let him ruin her life.

'Because I wanted to separate the past from the present,' I half-lie, scratching behind my ear.

'And the rest?'

'The rest?'

'You're scratching behind your ear.' Dr. Hausen's lips twitch as she relaxes back into her chair. 'Abbi, I haven't been your psychiatrist for a year and not picked up on your habit. You scratch behind your ear when you're keeping something from me. Usually I let you keep it inside, but this time, I want to know. I want you to tell me the whole reason.'

I push myself from the plush armchair I'm so accustomed to and walk over to the large window. Her office overlooks St. Morris's gardens, and I look toward the apple trees filling with tiny apples.

'I don't know what you mean.' I fold my arms across my chest so I don't scratch my ear. Damn. I'll have to remember that.

'So unfold your arms and sit back down.'

I swallow, silently counting the apples I can see on the tree. 'I . . . I didn't want anything to do with the person I was. What happened – what he did to me, what I did to myself – it changed me. I don't like the person I was. I don't want anything that reminds me of her, so I changed it. Moving on. Going forward. You know. Isn't that why I was released from here? So I could move on and forget everything?'

'There's nothing good in forgetting. Remembering, although it hurts, is what you need to do. You need to take all the memories no matter how much they hurt and force them out. Even if it means reliving every single time he hurt you and every single time you hurt yourself, you must remember. Forgetting isn't the key to moving on. Remembering is, because only once we've remembered can we forget.'

'That makes no sense.'

'You can't forget what you don't know, Abbi. You can't forget what you haven't allowed yourself to know. All holding it back will do is keep you stuck in a limbo you have no control over.'

I glance over my shoulder at her. 'I have control. I haven't cut for months. I've wanted to, but I haven't. *I have control.*'

My hands are shaking frantically as I look back out of the window. I blink to clear my eyes of the tears forming there. I feel like a frustrated toddler trying to get their point across without the necessary words.

I hear the shuffle as Dr. Hausen puts her papers down and the click of her heels on the hardwood floor.

'Abbi,' she says softly, laying a hand on my shoulder. 'I know you have control. *That* is the reason you were allowed to leave St. Morris's. Many people come here and never leave; for some reason some people don't have the fight in them to push the darkness away. Some people will never get better, they'll never fight their demons.

'But you? What you suffered was horrendous. Disgusting. I wish with every part of me you didn't have to go through what you did, but I know you're not one of those people. I know you have the fight in your body to push that darkness away. You are strong enough to remember everything you went through and still keep a hold on that light.

'Yes, I could have kept you institutionalized here. I could have kept you in your bland white room, kept your strict meal times, your group activities, your daily counseling sessions. But why? That wasn't benefitting you. Not even I'm perfect, Abbi. I didn't realize what you needed until you asked to dance – I didn't realize how strong your desire to dance was until I saw you in the gym the first time. That's why I let you leave.'

'But why? Bianca was happy to keep coming here. Why not keep me here where you had an eye on me? You know I still feel like I want to cut when it gets bad. You know how hard it is.' Tears stream down my cheeks, and Dr. Hausen turns me to her gently.

'Because, Abbi, you have something many of the others here don't.'

'Which is?'

She bends down an inch or two so we're face to face. 'A dream. You have something to live for, something you *couldn't* live for while you were locked up in here.'

'Why does that make such a difference?'

'Because you can only truly live for something once you've stared death in the eye. You've been close to death, close enough to touch, but you can still hold onto life because of your dream. You cannot appreciate everything until you've had nothing. *That* is the difference.'

~

The silence of the studio wraps around me, cocooning me in a blanket of security. Here is where I'm at home, with my foot on the *barre* and my head against my knee as I stretch out.

The studio is empty because I'm half an hour early – before the ten minutes early Bianca demands of us. After seeing Dr. Hausen, I need to let off some steam before the class starts. Her room is so constricting, so suffocating, and I just need to feel free. Even if it's for just a moment.

So I twist my braid into a bun, and I dance.

I leap and twirl and spin my way across the studio floor, dropping from *pointe* and raising back up again. My toes take a beating as I lose myself in the piece, my leg muscles tighten and my back arches when I stop for two seconds. Then I'm back into it. I'm back flying across the studio, the heaviness of my discussion with Dr. Hausen lifting a little more with every step, every *plié*, every turn.

And then, for one blissful second, I can't feel a thing. All I can feel is the music. And in that second, I find a small piece of myself.

I find a tiny part of the fight Dr. Hausen told me was there. And I hold onto it as tightly as I can before the heaviness comes crashing in, weighing me back down again.

'Wow.'

My heart jolts into my throat as my body jumps back. I somehow stop myself from falling over by grabbing the *barre*, and look toward the piano. Blake is standing by the great black piano with his bag at his feet and his awe-filled eyes fixed on me.

I shift uncomfortably. 'Uh, wow?'

'Yeah. You can dance, huh?'

'Really? I thought I was lost on my way to a take-out.' I tilt my head to the side slightly and my lips twitch.

'That came out kind of dumb.' He laughs at himself and grabs his bag and sits down in a corner. 'Obviously you can dance, that's why you're here, and I've danced with you so I *know* you can dance, but yeah. I'm just going to shut up, because I'm really digging myself a hole here.'

My hand covers my mouth and I giggle into it. 'Well, I'm glad we cleared that up.'

He looks at me with a striking pair of green eyes, and smirks. 'Okay, not only is she a beautiful dancer, she has a smart mouth, too. I'm pretty sure that's a recipe for my perfect girl. Hey, this could be fate, you know.'

I feel my cheeks redden slightly and grab my water bottle. 'If that was a line, it was a terrible one.'

'Really?'

'Really terrible,' I clarify.

'Worth a shot though?'

I sit on the bench and look at him, grinning. 'Definitely worth a shot.'

'Then it was worth completely and utterly embarrassing myself.' He smiles at me. 'I meant it, though.'

'What, the fate thing?'

'If I said "maybe", would it work this time?' he asks hopefully.

'No.'

'Damn.' Blake pauses, and I raise an eyebrow. 'In that case, I meant what I said about you being a beautiful dancer. I don't know what it is about you, but when you dance it's like you're in a whole other place. I noticed it the other day when we danced together. It's like you weren't even here.'

I smooth my hair back unnecessarily, looking toward the open door as the rest of our class starts to filter in. 'I wasn't,' I admit. 'We're all allowed to get a little lost sometimes, because life sucks. This happens to be where I get away from all the sucky stuff.'

'Right,' he says softly. 'I get that. I feel the same, I guess. Just sucks we have to come back.'

'Exactly.' I turn back to him and our eyes meet. Something flashes in his, something indiscernible. An understanding, almost. Something that connects us in a way I've never connected with anyone. After a beat I pull my gaze away and stand.

Chatter picks up around us, and I approach the *barre*. The cold metal is grounding to me, as always, and I hold onto it like it's what's keeping me standing.

'I feel like I should apologize for my bumbling speech when I came in and the really, really shitty chat-up line I inadvertently used,' Blake's voice says lowly from behind me.

'Hey, like you said it was worth a try, right?' I drop my head a little and fight my smile.

'Well, it was. But that doesn't mean I shouldn't apologize. Honestly, I'm twenty-one; you'd think that by now I could bloody well talk to a girl without making a complete and utter twat of myself.'

I lift my head and glance round at him. 'Twat? What the hell is that?'

He groans, dropping his head back for a second. 'Bloody Americans.'

'Freakin' British,' I respond, amused.

'Touché.' He laughs. 'A twat is pretty much a . . . Well. It's a glorified idiot.'

I let my lips form a tentative smile as his eyes find mine. 'In that case, I feel like I should tell you, you really did make a complete and utter twat of yourself.'

Blake grins as Bianca steps into the studio and claps her hands twice. He winks as I turn my head to the front.

I feel his eyes on my back as Bianca's uncle begins to play our *plié* music. I feel him watching my every move like he's memorizing every inch of my body, memorizing the shapes my limbs make. His gaze is hot on me and it burns into my skin in a way that makes me inhale sharply. Facing the front and keeping my concentration is near impossible when a part of me just wants to turn my face and meet that searing gaze. It's thrilling and disconcerting simultaneously, but there's nothing I can do. I'm here to dance, not have a wary session of eye-sex with Blake the Hot British Guy. I have to grit my teeth and bear it.

Besides – if he was in front of me, I can't say I wouldn't be doing the same thing.

I might not want to feel. I might have walls built around me that rival any prison's, but I am still human. And that means I can still appreciate a hot guy.

And, if I'm honest, Blake is about the hottest thing that's appeared in my life since my aunt dropped half a pack of chili powder in her chili con carne.

Blake

'The spiced prawn risotto, Blake! I need the damn risotto!' Joe yells across the busy kitchen. With the constant swinging of the doors and clashing of pots and pans, it's a wonder I can hear him at all.

'Right. Risotto.' I pull open the heavy fridge door and walk into it. Shelves of pre-cooked meals wrapped in cling film stare back at me, and I look side to side, holding in my groan. 'Risotto. Risotto. Where's the fucking risotto?'

'Where's the fucking risotto?' Joe yells, punctuating his words with a bang of a saucepan.

Good question. 'There's none here, Chef!'

'Then get your ass out here and make me some fucking pronto! I need it in one hour for the party coming in – they're Friday night regulars and always order the damn meal!' The doors bang open. 'For the love of beer, Jackie! How many of these goddamn tickets are you gonna pin on my board?'

'As many as I'm given!'

'Forty-five minute wait for food!'

'But—'

'Get out the kitchen before he throws the salmon at you, Jackie!' Matt, a trainee chef fresh from high school, yells at her.

The doors slam again as she walks out. I grab the prawns from the freezer compartment and leave the bag running under some water to defrost while I gather the rest of the ingredients like there's a rocket up my arse. When Joe says he wants something now, he means yesterday afternoon. It's busier here than anywhere I worked in London – but I guess that's what I get for taking a job in one of the most popular restaurants in the center of Brooklyn. So Brooklyn is no Manhattan, but it's close enough and big enough to be busy as hell.

I cut the carrots, slice the olives, and finely chop an onion and a red chili pepper. The onion and rice cook in a huge pan, turning a golden brown color before being drowned in white wine. When the chicken stock has soaked into the rice, I add the rest of the ingredients, including pine nuts, and give it a good stir. A touch of black pepper, a few more minutes, and it's ready to go.

The spicy smell of the chili wafts up to my nose, and my stomach rumbles quietly. Damn. The biggest problem with being in a kitchen that makes the best seafood this side of Brooklyn Bridge is I want to eat it. There's only so many take-outs and quick-fix meals a guy can eat before he starts missing finer food.

And God knows there was plenty of fine food in my childhood. With my parents' high profile jobs, they were always dragging us kids to functions and dinners and expensive charity nights that probably cost more to organize than was raised. And of course, the dinner parties with business associates that all happened to have good-looking, well-mannered sons and daughters that were pushed on Kiera and me. For a second, I feel a twinge of regret that I've left her to that by herself – and now Allie will be subjected to it, too. Even if Allie is a carbon copy of Mum, happy to marry a rich man and let him fund her lifestyle while she draws pictures of pretty dresses or whatever.

'The fucking risotto!' Joe bellows.

I shake off the lingering thoughts of my life in London and spoon the risotto into a large glass dish, ready to cover and whisk into the fridge after it's been plated up. I carry the dish across the busy kitchen and place it in front of Joe.

'Least it smells like risotto,' he mumbles, grabbing a spoon. He puts some in a small bowl and tastes it – he doesn't yet trust my ability to cook. It's written all over him, and proven by the look of surprise currently plastered on his face.

'Damn, kid.' He nods. 'This is good. Plate it up and get that damn Jackie in here to take it out.'

A breath I didn't realize I was holding leaves my body, and I grab some clean plates from the shelves behind me.

Maybe now he'll stop doubting me.

I press the button to alert the wait staff there's food waiting and take the risotto dish to the back.

'You can take off once that risotto is away, Blake,' Joe calls. 'It's under control here and already half an hour over your shift. You did good tonight, kid.'

I shut the fridge door behind me. 'Thanks, Chef. I'll see you Monday.'

'See ya. Damn it, Matt! Stop that fucking pan boiling over!'

I scoot out of the kitchen and grab my coat before he decides he'd rather send Matt home instead of me, and get the hell out of Double Bass Restaurant. Downtown Brooklyn on a Friday night is busy – not as crazy busy as I'm sure it is on the other side of the East River – but enough that the ten-minute walk to my apartment is at least mildly amusing.

As I think this, a group of three girls round the corner in front of me. One of them stumbles into my side, and I grab her arms to steady her.

'Oh! I'm so sorry.' She giggles, putting her hand to her mouth.

'No problem.' I smile at her and drop my hands.

One of her friends gasps. 'He's British!'

Oh God. I should have just smiled and carried on walking.

The girl who fell into me stops. 'Are you like, real British with a proper accent, or one of those really annoying ones?'

'I . . . I should be going.' I step back a little as the girl giggles again.

'Oh, it's a proper one!' She beams at me and puts a hand on her hip. 'Did you just move here?'

I also should have listened to the attitude-filled warning about American girls and British guys my brother gave me before I left. Or learnt how to speak like one.

'Yeah . . . Last week. I really have to go. Sorry girls. Have a good night.' I sidestep.

'Then you must need someone to show you around!'

'I have a map, but thanks.' I wave awkwardly and turn away.

'Well, how about my number in case you change your mind?'

'Really, I'm good.'

'I could take yours!'

The brick wall across the street is looking like a really, really good place to bang my head against right now.

'I don't have one.' I all but run around the corner and the rest of the way to my apartment before I take a breather.

I let myself into the block, see the lift is out of action, and climb the stairs. My apartment is a welcome sight, and I drop onto my sofa, letting the door swing shut by itself.

God. Damn.

I'm no stranger when it comes to attention from girls. I mean, I've had girlfriends in the past and a few one-nighters, but I've never experienced anything quite like that. And all because I'm bloody British.

Am I gonna have that whenever I talk to a girl? 'Cause if that's the case, I really need some lessons on how to speak like an American.

'Hello?' I answer my phone as the screen lights up.

'Darling!' My mother's voice trills down the phone. I slide down the cushions, wishing the sofa would just open up and swallow me.

'Mum,' I reply. 'How are you?'

'I'm fine, Blake. How are you? You haven't called me.'

'I've been busy. You know, settling in and stuff.'

'*And stuff?* What is "stuff"?'

I pause. 'Dance.'

'So you can find time to prance around like a fairy but not to call your mother?'

'I came to New York to dance, Mum. Remember that?'

'Yes, yes, so you say. What I'd like to know is when you're coming home. It's ever so quiet around here.'

'I'm not coming home.'

She says nothing for a minute that seems like an hour. 'I thought you may have had enough by now.'

And there it is: the famous Smith parents' belief in their children. Or maybe they reserve this special brand just for me.

'I've been here a little over a week,' I remind her.

'Well, yes, but you've never really been away from home for that long. Goodness, Blake, you went to your grandparents for a weekend when you were eleven and hated it so much you never went back without us. Although, it was your father's parents, so perhaps I can understand that.'

'Yes, thank you, Mother,' I say dryly. 'In case you fail to notice, I am no longer eleven years old. I'm twenty-one. You know. An *adult*.'

'Then whyever are you talking to me like you're a hormonal teenage girl?'

I close my eyes and take a deep breath. God I love my mother, I really do, but she is the most testing woman on Earth. I admire her for demanding respect at all times, but honestly, if she's gonna piss me off, I'm going to talk to her like I'm a child. Sometimes that's the only way to get her to listen to me.

'Anyway, never mind all that. I'm calling to let you know the good news!'

'The good news? Did Kiera finally give in to your match-making?'

'No.' She sounds slightly put out. 'Although, I believe she's warming up to Dr. Lyle's son, Martin. He's a bit of a sap, but he has a bright future and stands to partner in his father's practice, so he's definitely suitable for her.'

And he's about as interesting as a one hundred meter race being run by a group of slugs.

I make a non-committal sort of noise I hope she'll take as an agreement. Occasionally it's easier to just say nothing.

'So, my news!'

Spit it out, woman.

'My shoes are moving Stateside!'

Oh God no.

'They are?' I ask hesitantly.

'Yes! I have a long weekend of meetings in New York in two

weeks' time, and I wanted to let you know now so you can make sure your schedule is clear. It would be nice to have dinner one night and catch up. You can tell me all about your fair-er, dancing.'

I fall sideways, burying my face in a cushion. 'That's great, Mum. I'm really happy for you. I know you've waited for this.' Okay, so I'm a half-hearted happy for her. At least the half of me that's happy is beyond ecstatic . . . If only because now Dad doesn't have to hear her bitching about American fashion chains and their rejection of her British designs any longer.

'It's been a long time coming. So, about dinner. I land on Thursday morning, so Thursday night would be best for me. I can't be late though, as I have a meeting at eight a.m. on Friday and the jet lag will be a killer as it is.'

'I have dance class on Thursdays.'

'Well, you'll have to miss a class.'

'No can do, Mum. I could be dying and Bianca would expect me to be there, shoes on and ready to perform to a world class standard.'

'Well, when do you leave your class?'

'Seven-thirty.'

'I suppose we can have dinner at eight.' She sighs. 'Really, I can't wait for the day you'll give up on this silly dream of dancing.'

I bite my tongue as she carries on her all-familiar tirade about my choice to dance. As always, Tori doesn't factor into it. And it makes me even more determined to succeed.

And even more pissed that Mum's shoes finally cross the Atlantic mere days after I do.

~

I head into Bianca's studio for an afternoon dance session. There isn't really enough room to practice in my apartment, so I pulled her aside after our last class and asked to use the space this weekend. She readily agreed, telling me she'll be doing paperwork anyway.

The large room is eerily silent without anyone else here. The only time it's been this quiet is on Thursday when I watched Abbi dance to a melody only she could hear. Even then, I was too enthralled by her graceful movements to notice the lack of background noise.

I slip off my joggers and hoodie and swap my socks for ballet shoes. My eyes trawl around the studio, and I can't remember the last time I had this much room to dance alone. A part of me doesn't want to remember. So I don't.

I dance instead.

I throw myself into it with everything I have. All the rising emotion inside me – the uncertainty about moving here, the hesitance of living alone, the fear of failure – comes pouring out through the tips of my fingers and my toes. I dance unconsciously, aware of my feet touching the floor and lifting off but not aware of anything else. My posture, positions, steps . . . I don't know anything about them.

They're just there.

I stop, my breathing heavy. Emotion and ballet has always been a heady mixture for me, both a blessing and a curse. Today, it seems to be the latter, and I blame Mum's phone call. She always brings out the worst in me.

I cross the floor toward my bag, ready to go sooner than I expected, but Bianca's voice stops me.

'I don't see people like you often.'

'I'm not quite sure how I'm meant to take that.' I turn to her, my hand hovering over my hoodie.

She smiles. 'It's a compliment. Usually, the people that dance as well as you do don't need me. They're already at Juilliard. Teaching someone of your skill is a rare treat for me, and this year I have two of you.'

'Abbi.'

Her smile twitches into a smirk. 'Yes. Both of you have a quality about you I can't put my finger on. I've seen hundreds, maybe even thousands of dancers, yet you two are something completely different. It's almost as if you're both meant to dance, alone and together.'

'I'm not sure about that.'

'I am.' She crosses the room, her bare feet silent against the floor. 'Every year I kick off my classes with a *grand pas de deux*. I'm pairing you with Abbi for three reasons. One: you're the only person she's spoken to, and that's important for her. Two: your builds match each other. And three . . .' Bianca looks up, tilting her head to the side. '. . . The romantic ballerina inside me is too curious to see what you two will come up with.'

I frown. 'Why is it so important for her to have spoken to someone?'

'Because it is.'

I remember the shadows in her eyes. The ones that captured my attention from the first second I looked into those baby blues. The ones that echo my sister's.

'She dances for more than just the love of ballet, doesn't she?' I question softly.

Bianca takes some papers from the top of the piano. 'You're asking me questions I cannot answer, Blake. Abbi's reason for dancing is hers and hers alone, and the only person with any right to share that is her.' Her eyes meet mine as she walks back toward her office. 'Perhaps, in time, she'll share it with you herself. I sincerely hope she does.'

She disappears through the doors, leaving me staring after her and hoping for the same thing.

Abbi

I barely have a chance to comprehend the auburn hair flying at me before my best friend's arms wrap around me. Maddie squeezes me tightly, and as I hug her back, breathing in her familiar smell, my eyes begin to burn with tears. I never realize how much I've missed her until I get to see her. It's only been four months, but so much has happened since her last trip home, it feels like so much longer.

'God! Your hair! You!' She squeezes me again. 'You're at home! You're okay.'

I pull back and look at her. 'I'm okay. Of course I'm okay.'

Her green eyes sparkle with unshed tears, and she nods. 'I just . . . I wanted you to get better so bad, and now you are.'

'Well, sort of. I'm getting better. Slowly.'

Maddie finally lets me go and wipes under her eyes. 'I'm gonna grab coffee, okay?'

I nod, and she turns toward the counter in Starbucks. I sit back down at the small table – our table – and wait for her to return. Saturday mornings at Starbucks are always crazy, and it's hard to be here. It's hard to be so exposed to so many different people.

It feels like every pair of eyes that looks my way is scrutinizing me. Every look is a judgment. Every laugh is about me. Every conversation is about the girl in the corner.

And the funny thing is, no one in here knows me. They have no idea who I am or what I've been through. But it doesn't stop me feeling naked.

'Phew.' Maddie drops opposite me and places two coffees and two muffins in front of me. 'Don't tell Braden. He thinks

I eat too many of these things . . .' She waves her blueberry muffin. '. . . So I have to eat them when he's not around. I think I'm gonna scoff down like one hundred this weekend.'

I smile wryly. 'Maddie, under the thumb?'

'Psssh. The only thing about him I'm ever under is his whole body – because he's the one under the thumb the rest of the time. Believe me.'

'I believe you.' And I do – Maddie is the kind of person that could wrap a plank of wood round her finger. 'Where is he, anyway? I thought he was coming with you.'

She sighs. 'He was. His nan died last weekend so he's gone home to see his mom and help her sort some stuff. I told him I'd go, but he practically frog marched me to the freakin' airport and threw me on the plane. Her funeral is next weekend, and I'm going back with him then.'

'I wouldn't have minded if you'd gone with him!'

'I know, but he wasn't having it. He told me to, and I quote, "Go and have a girly weekend and eat those fuckin' muffins you adore so much."' She smiles.

'Hate to say it, Mads, but he has you worked out.' I tilt my coffee toward her.

'Yeah, he does, but I just bribe him and it works.'

'I don't want to know.' I shake my head.

'Anyway, enough about my caveman. I want to know about you. There's only so much we can talk about on the phone, and it's not the same as sitting here with you, so tell me everything. How are you really doing?'

I shrug a shoulder. 'Okay, I guess. Some days are harder than others. I feel pretty good today, but that could change later.'

She chews the inside of her lip. 'Do you still . . .' She pauses. 'I hate asking this. God!'

I stare at her, knowing what she's asking, but wanting her to actually say it. She doesn't. Instead, her hand creeps across the table and wraps around my wrist. Her thumb strokes along the inside of my wrist, and I breathe in sharply.

'Do you?'

I shake my head, taking my hand away. 'It's hard, but I dance instead. That and Mom decided to hide anything with even half a sharp edge. If Dad's to be believed, she even tried to hide the forks.' I smirk at Maddie, and she responds kindly.

'Typical. But I'm glad, Abbi. I'm glad you found something other than that to help. And it seems fitting that the thing that helps you is the one thing you refused to give up when I did.' Maddie's smirk changes to a wide grin.

'Hey, I loved ballet. I still do. It's what keeps me going.'

She nods slowly, and I know where our conversation is about to go. I can feel it descending on us, a heavy storm cloud weighed down with inches upon inches of torrential rain.

'Do you . . . Do you know about Pearce?'

I nod.

'Shit.' She smacks the table. 'How did you find out?'

'Jake. I saw him a few days ago and he told me.'

'Asshole!' She snaps her jaw together. 'I told him to keep his sorry ass out of it. Shit, Abbi. I'm so sorry I didn't tell you what happened. I didn't want to say it over the phone, and then you were leaving that place and I didn't want to push you back. I was gonna tell you this weekend.'

I shrug. 'Hey, it's okay. I had to find out sometime, right? I don't think I care, if I'm honest. I was scared to see him again, so finding out I won't be kind of makes it better. Makes it easier to be home. Last week I was scared I'd run into him every time I turned a corner or walked into a store, but now I'm not. I feel kind of . . . freer. Like I honestly know he can't hurt me anymore. I knew it before, but I really do believe it now.'

Maddie picks at her cupcake and chews, deep in her thoughts. 'I don't know if I care. I mean, okay, obviously I care a bit. He is my brother; an asshole brother, but my brother all the same. I don't want him to be there, but a part of me can't help but think he deserves it. After what he did to you, and then deciding to deal . . . How fucking stupid could he be?' She shakes her hair out. 'He made those choices and now it's costing him fifteen years of his life. After everything Mom taught us, he went and did it all anyway. She'd be so disappointed if she could see him now, and I'm damn glad she can't.'

I lean forward and take her hand. She squeezes my fingers. 'I'm okay,' she says with a sniff.

'Mads, it's okay to be upset he's in prison. He's still your brother, and he wasn't an asshole until he got to high school.'

'The problem is, that's the Pearce I remember. The non-dickhead one.'

'You know what?' I look from my coffee to her. 'I think that's the same problem I had. I think I fell in love with the Pearce that threw water balloons at us, that stole your mom's freshly baked cookies from the cooling rack and threw rocks at the boys that bullied us.' My eyes travel to the window, and my heart clenches with the realization that what I'm saying is completely true. 'I think I fell in love with the idea of the person he could be, not the person he is, and because of that I never truly saw him for what he was. I was wrapped up in a fairy tale, but everyone knows fairy tales aren't real.'

'My brother will always be an asshole, but that doesn't mean fairy tales don't exist. Remember, every fairy tale has a bad guy and a bad patch, but they all have a happy ending too. You had your bad patch, now you just have to wait for your happy ending.'

I smile sadly at her hopeful face. 'I don't believe in happy endings, Maddie. Not anymore. I'm alive. That in itself is enough of a happy ending for me.'

~

'Mom? Mom!'

'Your leotard is in the dryer, your tights are on the back of your chair, and the new can of hairspray you asked for is in the bathroom.'

I blink at my dad, hidden behind his newspaper. 'Well, damn, Dad. When did you get a sex change?'

He drops the paper an inch so I can see his eyes. 'Funny, Abigail. Your mother gave me those instructions before she left for some coffee date with her friends.'

'And you remembered? I'm impressed. Maybe you're not as old as I thought you were.'

The paper falls onto his lap, and he peers at me over the rims of his reading glasses. His lips are twitching, and I don't try to hide the wide grin on my face as I pass into the kitchen.

'She made me repeat it to her near twenty times. I thought I should say it as soon as I heard you, so I wouldn't forget to tell you I had something to tell you,' he calls.

I shut the fridge door and lean against the kitchen doorframe. 'Wait, is it too late to take back that age thing? 'Cause forgetting about forgetting about something is real bad, Dad.'

'This conversation is starting to confuse me. It's far too early on a Sunday morning.'

'It's eleven a.m.'

'Is it?'

'Yup. Not exactly the crack of dawn.' I give his pajama pants a meaningful look.

He glances down at them and back up at me. 'Don't you have a dance class to be getting ready for?'

'Going. Going!' I turn around, then stop and look over my shoulder. 'Maddie will be here soon. She's coming to class with me.'

Dad groans. 'Oh God. I've seen Maddie dance once – it wasn't pretty.'

I laugh. 'She's watching. Something about wanting to see the Hot British Guy.'

'And how would she know there's a British guy that's hot in your class?'

I really wasn't meant to say that out loud.

'Perhaps she bugged the dance studio? Who knows?' I try, smiling sweetly.

'You know, Abbi, I'm pretty sure I should be rolling up my sleeves—'

'After changing out of your pajama pants, preferably.'

'Well, okay. As I was saying, darling, I think I should be rolling up my sleeves and marching to this class with you to check out this hot British guy for myself.'

'That could be kinda embarrassing.' I flinch. 'And totally unnecessary, I might add.'

'But I don't feel the need to. I find myself quite liking the fact you've described a guy as "hot".'

I turn back to him. 'I never said I did that.'

'You didn't deny it.'

'Well, no. But.' I fidget. 'I. Yeah.'

'Like I said, I quite like it.'

'That's not normal, Dad.'

'Perhaps not, but the fact you've described someone that way after what you went through makes me feel like a part of my baby girl is still in there. And the fact you've said it to Maddie, she's going to class with you, and you'll no doubt spend your next ten phone calls running up my phone bill by talking about him, makes me insanely happy.'

'Dad, I'm depressed, not blind. And is that permission to run up the phone bill?'

'What? No. I didn't say you could. I said you would.'

I laugh, cross the room and bend down to hug him. He rubs my back gently, and I press my lips to his cheek. 'Love you, Daddy.'

'And I love you, Princess. Now go and get ready to torment the hot British guy, and I'll send the firecracker up when she gets here.'

He pats my arm and smiles. I leave the living room to the shuffle of his paper, grab my leotard from the dryer in the utility room, and head upstairs to find my tights. Just as Dad said, on the back of my chair in my room.

I change into my ballet clothes and sweep my hair into a slick bun. My eyes are clearer and brighter than I've seen in a long time. There's more color in my cheeks and my hair is shinier. I glance at the scales, wondering whether or not I want to step on them. After all the weight I lost when I was first in St. Morris's, it's been a battle to put it back on, and even though my curves are slowly reappearing, it's still daunting.

I pull off my pants and step on the glass surface before I can think any more into it. The red numbers on the digital screen fluctuate slightly, and I draw my bottom lip between my teeth as I wait for them to stop. Then they do. And I smile. I've avoided the scales for two weeks and it was worth it, because I've gained three pounds.

Those three pounds are everything to me.

Maddie's laughter drifts up the stairs, and I step back into my sweatpants and go down to meet her.

'Oh good. You're ready. Let's go. I want to see Hot British Guy,' she says as soon as my feet hit the bottom stair.

'He has a name, y'know,' I mutter, grabbing my bag.

'Really? You never mentioned it,' she teases me.

'Oh, ha.' I open the door. 'You do realize my Sunday class is three hours long, right?'

'You're kidding.'

'Nope.'

'Then you, Abigail Jenkins, are very damn lucky I enjoy watching you dance.'

I smile at her, and we get into the taxi waiting outside to take us across the bridge to Bianca's studio. The journey is quick, and when we get there, Maddie stops and stares at the small building housing the studio.

'It's . . . different than I expected,' she hedges.

I raise an eyebrow at her. 'What? Did you expect Juilliard?'

'Not exactly. But Juilliard is so . . . pretty. And this is, well, not.'

I back against the door and push it open, a small, knowing smile on my face. 'You haven't seen the inside yet.'

She wordlessly follows me down the small corridor leading to the main studio. I glance back to see her eyes widen and her jaw drop open. I know she's experiencing what I did when I walked into Bianca's studio for the first time – complete and utter disbelief that a studio so professional and perfect could be in such a bland-looking building.

'Damn,' she whispers. 'This is some studio.' Her eyes travel across it, drinking in every inch of the room, before resting on the corner. 'Oh, *hot damn!*'

I follow her gaze and my eyes land on Blake's back. If the messy brown hair combined with the fact he's early isn't a giveaway it's him, it's the way he stands. Strong and tall without a hint of a slouch. His posture is almost regal, and my gaze skirts up and down his body before I realize what I'm doing and pull it away.

'Is that the British guy?' Maddie nudges my arm. 'Wait, it is. You're drooling!'

I snap my head round to look at her. 'I am so not!'

She studies my face for a second and smirks. 'Just a little. God, I don't blame you.'

'You have a boyfriend,' I remind her.

'I can look, Abbi. Especially when *that* is the view.'

I roll my eyes, heading toward the benches where Blake is stood. 'California is corrupting you, Maddie.'

'Eh, maybe a little.' She shrugs a shoulder and follows me.

Blake turns as I put my bag down and grins at me. 'Abbi.'

'Blake.' I return his smile, albeit more hesitantly.

'So,' he leans against the wall, looking at me casually. 'I heard Bianca is pairing us off today so we can choreograph our own dance. Something about her seeing how ready we really are for her class.'

'Where did you hear that?' I grab my water bottle, a bolt of fear shooting through my body.

Pairing. Choreographing. That means out of studio time with someone. One on one endless dancing with a guy.

A level of intimacy I'm not quite ready for.

'I . . . Er . . . She told me,' he admits with a shrug. 'I came here to practice yesterday and she mentioned it then.'

'Oh.' I pause. 'Has she paired us already?'

'No idea.' Blake shrugs and glances over my shoulder at Maddie.

'Oh, Blake, this is Maddie, my best friend. Maddie, Blake.' I introduce them and step to the side to change.

'Are you joining the class?' Blake asks her.

She bursts into laughter. 'God no. I can't dance. I'm just here to watch.'

'The studio would need closing down if Maddie tried to dance,' I mutter, tying the ribbons on my shoes.

'Shut up,' she replies, laughing a little. Grinning at her, I back toward the *barre*. Blake follows, and we take our usual places at the back of the studio.

Bianca strolls into the large room with delicate yet purposeful steps, and stops in front of us, standing in first position. Her clasped hands hover in front of her stomach as her eyes comb across us, and I feel the heat of her stare scrutinizing every single person here.

'*Pas de deux.*' Her words are sharp and short, cutting through the silence that comes with her presence. 'A couple. At Juilliard, not only will you be expected to dance to perfection as an individual, but also as a couple. If you can't do that, you need to go away, learn how to, and then come back. Remember, I'm here to hone your skills, not teach you new ones.

'That said, after watching you for your last two lessons, I've paired you all off with the dancer I think you'll work best with. You have one month to choreograph a *pas de deux*, put it to music and perform it to the highest possible standard in a mini showcase at a small theatre owned by a friend of mine. Friends and family will be invited, so you *must* get it right. So . . .'

I fight to stay focused on Bianca's voice and grip the *barre* tightly. The idea of spending endless hours with someone I don't know, dancing with them, sharing with them the deepest part of me, scares me beyond belief. I knew it would happen eventually. I knew I'd have to do this sooner or later, but I thought it would be later. I never thought I'd be in this position three lessons in.

I can't do it. I'm not ready for this. I'm not ready to bare my soul to anyone.

'Abbi?'

I draw myself from the harsh, doubting voice ringing in my ears and focus on the voice that's speaking my name. I don't want to; I don't want to know who I'm going to have to spend hours upon hours with over the next month.

Green eyes stare back at me when I turn to the voice. Blake.

'Are you all right?'

'I . . . Yeah.' I smile tentatively. 'Just . . . Thinking.'

He watches me for an everlasting second, his eyes never wavering from mine. It's as if he can see something no one else can and he can understand what I can't say. But that's crazy, because everything is inside, locked away, where no one can see or understand it.

I take a deep breath and close my eyes. When I open them again, he's walking backward. But still watching me, this time with an intensity that makes me want to squirm. It makes me want to rub my hands over my arms and hide, and it's a stare that makes me feel as if I'm being stripped bare. As if every time he blinks he peels a layer away. And no matter how much I want to or how hard I try, I can't tear my eyes away from his.

'Are you coming?' he asks.

'Where?'

His lips twitch. 'We have a dance to choreograph.'

Blake

I fiddle with the scrap of paper Abbi wrote her number on last Sunday. I flip it between my fingers repeatedly, my eyes darting to and from my phone.

And I feel like a complete and utter dork.

I know nothing about this girl besides her name and the fact she can dance as well as any seasoned ballerina. I also know she's beautiful – you'd have to be completely blind not to see that – and I am stupidly fucking attracted to her lithe little body. But that's it. I have no idea what she does aside from dance, if she has a boyfriend, or why she gets a shadow behind her eyes when she dances. But I want to.

I spent all day yesterday convincing myself I want to know because we'll be spending a lot of time together over the next month. That we'll work best as a *pas de deux* if we're friends. That to build the element of trust needed between dance partners, we should know each other as more than just dancers. And when I was telling myself that, I was denying the fact it's because the shadows in her eyes are too familiar.

I was denying the fact I want to know Abbi because something about her reminds me of Tori. Something I can't put my finger on; perhaps it's the way she loses herself in dance, or the way she seems so delicate, so fragile. Maybe it's because sometimes her smiles seem a little forced.

Or maybe that's me. Maybe I'm seeing something that isn't there, reading too much into it. She could just be shy. And here I am comparing her to my dead sister.

Maybe it's all in my head and I'm looking for something that reminds me of Tori to hold on to. Maybe it's a combination of both. That would definitely explain why something about Abbi bugs me. Why something about her taps on my shoulder repeatedly until I give in and think about it.

I grab the phone and dial her number before I can think about it anymore and it drives me insane. She answers on the third ring.

'Hello?' her voice is quiet and wary.

'It's Blake.' *God, I'm so eloquent.* My mother would have a fit if she could hear me now.

'Oh!' I hear a shuffle. 'Hi.'

'Hi.' I pause, looking around my apartment. 'I hope you don't mind me phoning you.'

'No, I don't mind you *calling* me.' The hint of laughter in her voice makes me chuckle.

'I'm sorry – I hope you don't mind me *calling* you, then.'

'No. If I minded, I wouldn't have given you my cell number.'

'You know, if you said that to someone in the UK, they'd wonder why you were in prison.'

Her giggles ring down the phone. 'It's not my fault you British people talk strange.'

'Hey! The language is called "English" for a reason, you know. British and English are pretty much the same thing. It's you bloody Americans that have changed the words.'

'Whatever. You freakin' British just think you have some claim to the language because you're from England.'

'I think we'll have to come back to this,' I muse.

'I agree.'

'So, the reason I *called.*'

I almost hear her smile. 'Yes?'

'I know we have class tonight, but I was just wondering if you were free today. You know, before class. I thought we could get to know each other. Or something.' I scratch at the back of my neck as I wait for her reply.

'S-sure. What were you thinking?'

'Uh . . .' I laugh nervously. 'There's something really funny about that, because my plan is kind of half-assed.'

'You don't know anywhere in Brooklyn or New York to go,' she states, amusement lacing her tone. I'm seriously wondering if we'll ever have a conversation where she doesn't laugh at me.

'Yeah . . . That's pretty much it.'

'Right. Well, it depends where you live.'

'Brooklyn.'

'Oh, me too. So, do you know where the Starbucks is downtown?'

'Uhh . . .' I try to remember what I know of downtown from walking to and from the restaurant, but I can't think of a Starbucks.

'Whole Foods?'

'That I do know. Not much of a day out, I gotta say.'

'And there's the famous British humor,' she retorts dryly. I grin. 'If you can make it without getting lost . . .'

'Oi!'

'. . . then meet me there in half an hour, and I'll show you some of Brooklyn. Okay?'

'Sounds good to me. I'll see you then.' I sink back into my sofa, leaning my head back over the top. 'Jesus Christ,' I mutter to myself. I rub my hand down my face.

I only have half an hour, and I might know where Whole Foods is, but I have no idea how to get there by foot. That, and I'm still in my damn pajamas.

~

Abbi is sitting on the wall outside Whole Foods, her legs swinging, with her head bent forward and her brown hair hanging loose around her face. She tucks it behind her ear and looks up as I approach.

'Not bad,' she says, checking her watch. 'Only ten minutes late.'

'Yeah. I cheated,' I admit. 'I got lost after five minutes and called a taxi.'

Her lips pull up on one side. 'I thought you said you knew where Whole Foods was?'

'I did. However, I didn't say I knew how to get here.' I lean against the wall and gaze up at her. 'So, where are you taking me?'

She jumps from the wall, landing gracefully on her toes. She lowers herself onto her heels and swings her head round to look at me. 'Prospect Park. It's one of my favorite places, especially in early summer, so I thought it was as good a place as any to start.'

'I've never heard of it.'

'That's because most people think "Central Park" whenever the words New York and park are put together, even if they mean New York state opposed to city.' She smooths a lock of hair between her finger and thumb. 'Which is a shame, because Prospect Park is beautiful.'

'Lead the way.'

'Are you kidding? It's the other side of Brooklyn. You need to flag us down a cab.' Abbi turns and smirks at me.

No way. 'Do you know how hard it is to get one of those things?'

'It's not hard. You just wave at one and it'll stop.'

'If it's so easy, you do it.'

'If it's so hard, you need the practice.' She grins. 'One is coming down the street now. Try and get it.'

I look down the busy road and spy a canary car coming toward us. When it gets close enough for the driver to see us, I do as Abbi told me to and motion to him. The driver completely ignores me and drives straight past. Abbi tries to hide a small giggle behind her hand. There are little crinkles around her blue eyes that tells me she's smiling, and even the fact it's hidden doesn't stop me from fighting my own.

'Try again,' she urges me.

I do.

And again.

And again.

And again.

'I give up!' I throw my arms up. 'I really do give up. Why you have to wave at these guys is beyond me. In London we just call the taxi service and tell them to come to a certain place and they do. I feel like a right bloody lemon standing here waving at taxis.'

Abbi doesn't try to hide her smile this time. She grabs the lamppost, raises herself onto her tiptoes and waves in the direction of an approaching taxi. The taxi slows as it nears us and pulls up by the curb. I stare at Abbi in shock.

'See?' She smiles. 'Easy.'

'I have no idea how you just did that.' I open the door of the taxi. She climbs in, and I slide in next to her. She directs the driver to Prospect Park, smiling smugly to herself, but doesn't say another word until we arrive. I pay the driver, and we get out, and I get my first look at her favorite place.

The large arch that greets us immediately reminds me of the Arc de Triomphe in Paris. The stone is expertly carved and the statues of horses and men adorning it look regal and very military.

'Soldiers' and Sailors' Arch,' Abbi says softly from behind me. 'My favorite entrance. When I was a kid I used to come here and stare at it for hours. I don't know why, but it just amazed me.'

'I can see why.' My eyes flit from statue to statue, and I barely notice when she walks through the arch to cross the road.

'Are you coming or are you just gonna stand there like a lemon all day?' She crosses the road when there's a break in the traffic, and I jog to catch her up. More monuments and arches are just inside the entrance to the park, all surrounded by lush green bushes and trees as they come into their summer bloom. Already I can see why Abbi is so taken with this place.

'This place looks huge,' I mumble.

'That's because it is.' She runs her hand along the rough bark of the tree. 'I think that's why I like it. It's a great place to disappear in.'

'For someone who lives for the limelight, you really like to hide a lot,' I say without thinking.

Her steps falter for a second. An unsettling cloud lowers over us, and I know I've said the wrong thing.

'Even people who live in a spotlight need to hide once in a while.' Her voice is soft, barely audible over the gentle breeze rustling through the trees surrounding us. 'If you promise you won't try to find me, I'll show you where I hide.' She glances over her shoulder, and through the playful glint in her eyes are the shadows. Ever-present, they pull me in and entrance me as she takes a few skips away from me.

I hold up two fingers. 'I promise. Scouts honor.'

'Were you ever a boy scout?' She stops.

'No. Well, once. I hated the uniform, so I quit.' I shrug. 'Plus my brother loved it. There was no way I was going to spend more time with Jase than I needed to, believe me.'

'Don't you get along?'

'About as well as water and oil,' I reply dryly. 'We're not that bad now. You'd think being the only boys in a family of six kids, we'd be close, but we're not really. He's seventeen, and I won't lie, his "I know everything and I'm always right" teen attitude really pisses me off.'

'Ever thought your "You don't know everything and you're nearly always wrong" adult attitude might annoy him?' Abbi asks with a raised eyebrow as we walk down a seemingly never-ending path through the park.

'Not really.'

'It probably does.'

'How do you know?'

She points to herself. 'I'm eighteen.'

'And to think I left London happy, knowing I wouldn't have to deal with any more teenage girls. Damn it.'

'You're really lucky I'm about as strong as a newborn baby or I'd throw you over this bridge for that comment.'

'Bridge?' I look down and realize we are indeed standing on a bridge. Below us is a mini waterfall surrounded by rocks and boulders. The water falls into a clear pool, and numerous birds I don't know the names of fly around. Some zip off into the trees, and others land on the rocks and stare into the water before taking flight once again.

It's completely silent apart from the water rushing and the birds in the trees singing. I didn't notice how empty the park is until now, or even how beautiful it looks.

And Abbi is completely right. This is the perfect place to hide, to get lost, to disappear. I get the feeling we've barely even scraped the surface of what Prospect Park has to offer. Growing up in London and spending half-term holidays in my paternal grandparents' country house means I'm no stranger to nature or parks, but I can honestly say none of them hold a candle to this place.

I turn to Abbi to tell her this, to thank her for showing me this of all places, but she's not next to me. I spin on the spot, looking for her, but she's nowhere to be seen.

'Abbi?!'

Giggles travel up to my ears, and I lean over the side of the bridge. She's sitting on the boulder in the center of the falls, her shoes in her hand and her feet dangling in the water.

'I told you this is where I come to hide.' There's a teasing lilt to her voice. 'Fallkill Falls. Only one of my hiding places, but by far the best one. The falls are linked to a whole stream of falls and pools and ravines. This one is further away from the main paths so less people come here. It's usually only hardcore nature-lovers, or real-life-lovers looking for five minutes of privacy.'

I fold my arms against the side of the bridge and smirk. 'I bet that's a nice sight to wander onto.'

'It's only happened once, and I'd prefer not to repeat the experience.' She shudders and tucks her hair behind her ear again.

I laugh and swing myself up onto the bridge. I scale the side of it until I can reach a rock with my foot and climb down. Abbi watches me as I pull my shoes off and step into the cool water. She scoots over on the boulder, so I can sit next to her, and tucks some hair behind her ear.

'I can see it being a perfect place for real-life-lovers,' I muse and look at the water rushing past. 'These rocks would make for some interesting positions for sure.'

Abbi gives a quiet snort and glances at me. 'Like what?'

'Uh.' I hadn't thought of that. 'I'm not a walking Karma Sutra, you know.'

'Really?' She raises an eyebrow. 'You're male, right?'

I turn my face toward her, my eyes meeting her bright blue ones. 'I can assure you, Abbi, I'm *all* male.'

She blushes. 'Well most guys I know have the Karma Sutra burned into their brains.'

'That's probably because the guys you know haven't passed puberty.'

'True, but they still know it.'

I grin slowly, putting one of my hands behind her, and lean back. I don't take my eyes from hers, and her tongue runs across her lips when the flush disappears from her cheeks. 'That's because *boys* need the Karma Sutra. They haven't worked out there are more ways to make a woman happy than just using your dick.'

Her eyes widen and her lips part as blood rushes to her cheeks again. She pushes hair away from her face and drops her eyes for a second. Only a second. Before I can say another thing, those baby blues are focused back on mine and holding me trapped.

'I'm guessing you consider yourself more than a boy?'

'I know I'm not a boy. I can probably use my hands better than boys can use their tool.'

She coughs and looks away. 'Point taken.'

I watch her, still smiling. 'I'm guessing you've only ever been with a boy.'

'Who said I've been with anyone?' she asks quietly.

'No one can look the way you do and be a virgin.'

Her lips twitch. 'This conversation is getting real personal, y'know.'

'We're here to get to know each other.' I grin. 'And I maintain my last statement. There's no way you're a virgin.'

'I think I'm taking that as a compliment.'

'Good. It's meant to be. But, uh . . .' I nudge her and she looks at me. 'If you are a virgin . . .'

Her lips twist upward, and she shoves me off the boulder before I can finish my sentence. I laugh as I try to steady myself on the small pebbles underfoot.

'Idiot,' she mutters, smiling.

I take a step but get my footing wrong and fall backward. Pebbles dig into my butt and Abbi doubles over with laughter. Hell no. I put my shoes on the boulder next to me and crawl across the small but strong stream of water toward her. My hands find her bare ankles and tug on them.

'Blake!' she cries, sliding down the rock. I laugh at the shocked look on her face as she falls into the water. It splashes as she lands in front of me. I grin.

'Not so funny now, huh?' I tease.

'I'll give you funny!' She shoves me again and I fall sideways. My hand grabs hers at the last minute and I pull her with me, both of us laughing. She lands half on me and half in the water, and freezes.

Her body and her eyes tell different stories. Her body is frozen and the only part of her that's moving is the rapid rising and falling of her chest. Her hand, pressed against my chest, trembles in something akin to fear. But her eyes aren't wide and scared. They're hooded and full of laughter. They're focused on mine, intense, unrelenting, unwavering. They're beautiful. *She's beautiful.* My hand on her waist twitches, and water rushes past us as we lie here.

Slowly, Abbi pulls herself off me and stands. She grabs her shoes from the boulder and takes tentative steps over to mine as I get up.

'Careful,' she warns softly. 'The pebbles are loose.'

'You don't say,' I counter dryly when she hands me my shoes. 'Thank you.'

'You're welcome.' She steps up onto the rocks and puts her shoes on the bridge. I follow her up, and she pauses just before she climbs over the bridge railing to speak in a quiet voice. 'I'm not, by the way.'

She doesn't look at me.

'Not what?'

'A virgin.'

For some reason, that annoys me.

Abbi

'Mom, it's been a year.'

'I know, darling, but I'm worried.'

'I'm not perfect, but I think I can shave my legs without feeling the need to retrace all my old scars.' My mouth twists, and I feel a sting of annoyance toward her.

'I didn't mean—'

'You know, if you really want to, you can come and watch me do it. Just to make sure.' It comes out snarkier than I intended, but sooner or later she's going to have to start trusting me. 'Whatever it was that made me cut, I've got it under control.' *Almost.* 'I can fight the urges. I'm strong enough now.' *Nearly.*

'I'm just worried about you, Abbi.' She rubs her forehead.

'Oh, for goodness sake, Miranda. Let the girl shave her legs like a normal eighteen year old,' Dad butts in from over his newspaper. 'She's already said you can sit and watch her do it if it makes you feel better.'

I curl my fingers around my glass, dropping my eyes to the table. I wish she would trust me. The mistakes of my past are exactly that – mistakes. I know the pain they caused her and I don't want to do that again.

Mom sighs. Dad puts his paper in his lap, takes off his glasses and levels his gaze on her.

'Miranda, dear, she's not going to get better if you keep wrapping her up in cotton wool. I know you're worried. I am too, but we have to let her have some of her freedom. If Abbi wants to shave her legs instead of using that dreadful smelling cream you buy her, let her. She isn't a child anymore. She knows the consequences of her actions.'

'And *she* is sitting right here,' I mutter, tapping the glass instead of holding it. I breathe out and meet Mom's eyes. 'Dad's right, Mom. I'm not made of china. I'm not going to break at the sight of a razor blade. Honestly, I just want to shave my legs. That's it. I wouldn't ask if I didn't think I was strong enough.'

Mom presses the heels of her hands into her eyes and sighs deeply. It's a pain-filled sigh, and she's probably doing what Dad refers to as 'The Kindergarten Thing'. On my first day of Kindergarten, she bawled for half an hour before leaving me. As I've gotten older, that's changed to agitation – like she wants me to stay her baby forever. Hence Dad naming it.

'Fine. Fine. You can shave your legs, but I'm not showing you where the razors are.'

'*Fine*.' I grit my teeth. This is the best I'm gonna get. It's all she's gonna give, but something is better than nothing.

I press my fingers to the pulse point at my wrist as she leaves the room and remind myself I'm not the only one struggling with my recovery. It must be hard for her to feel so helpless. And, as frustrating as this whole protecting me thing is, if it makes her feel better, I guess I just have to deal with it. I have my way of coping. This is hers, I suppose.

She comes back into the room and hands me a bright pink razor with what looks like a hammer-proof safeguard on. I swallow the sarcastic comment and thank her quietly.

My hands shake as I enter the bathroom. I put the razor on the side of the bath and sit on the closed toilet seat, focusing on the lather I have to work up with the shaving foam. I concentrate on my movements right now instead of the ones I will make.

Tap. Sponge. Legs.

Because no matter how confident I was just two minutes ago, no matter how much bravado I put on for the sake of my parents, I am scared. I'm scared of the urges that build inside me.

It was all I knew for so long. Cutting was my escape, the

way to let the pain out. The pain left with the blood, it trickled out with the sting and washed away. But now I have other ways to deal with the pain.

Other ways I still don't fully understand. Other ways I'm still learning about.

And that uncertainty scares me, because I know how strong the urges can be.

I spray some shaving foam into the palm of my hand and begin to work it into my wet legs, massaging my calves and knees. When my legs are white, I rinse my hands off under the tap and pick up the razor.

My fingers hover over the guard. Am I really ready to do this? Was Mom right? Am I still too 'damaged' to even shave my legs?

Am I really strong enough to keep the demons at bay? To resist making my blood flow?

My fingertips close down on the guard, making my decision for me, and pull it off. I take a deep breath as I rest my foot against the side of the bath and touch the razor to my skin. Sickness balls in my stomach as I lightly drag the razor up my shin, but I'm not sure what the sickness is from.

Fear? The urge? The possibility and knowledge I could let it all out, that I could let it go?

I train my eyes on the blade as if my steady, intense gaze will make it behave. Like the blade is the one to blame for it all. Like I never cracked a razor under my foot and dragged the sharp piece of metal across my skin. Like it was never me at all.

Shave. Rinse. Shave. Rinse. Shave. Rinse.

I go through the motions on my right leg, my eyes harsher than a mother's glare at a child who just scribbled on her newly-painted walls. I swap my legs, using breathing exercises Dr. Hausen taught me before I came home.

Swallow. Shave. Rinse. Deep breath. Shave. Rinse.

The longer I hold the razor in my hand the more uncertain I become of myself. What will I do with it after? Will I throw it in the trash? Will I hand it to Mom to get rid of? Will I just clean it and leave it on the side of the bathtub?

So many questions that demand answers swirl in my brain, blurring my vision and clouding my mind. Each becomes louder and louder until the uncertainty becomes booming shouts pounding between my ears instead of soft whispers in the corners of my mind. My grip tightens around the razor as I try to breathe evenly, try not to let the anxiety overtake me. Anxiety breeds depression. Depression breeds pain. Pain breeds–

A nick on my ankle. A tiny cut, one that is barely visible to the eye. This I know without looking. I can feel the sting, the red hot burn of my blood mixing with the air.

Pain breeds blood.

My grip tightens again, and I grab the towel rail with my free hand. I shake, feeling a tiny trail of blood trickle down from my ankle and along the curve of my foot.

The smallest cuts always bleed the most.

I remember the first time I made myself bleed. The night flashes before my eyes, and I finally remember why I did it. It's the one question I haven't been able to answer. The why. Why did I cut myself? What made me do it? The searing question that constantly surrounds me and my favored coping mechanism.

The coping mechanism that started with a nick on the ankle.

We had argued relentlessly. For hours, it seemed. A constant back and forth, the way it always was when it came to him needing to get his fix. I wanted him to stop this time. I promised him I would help – whatever he needed. He said all he needed was the drug and that I could get him that.

I refused. I wasn't his servant – I was his girlfriend and I was determined to help him. I knew this wasn't Pearce deep down. I knew the real Pearce and I knew he was buried under all the pain and addiction somewhere. I knew the real Pearce was broken and mourning the loss of his mother.

He didn't agree. He reached his boiling point. I should have known by then to leave – to run as fast as I damn well could and get as far away from him as possible. I knew in his comedown, his craving stage, he was the most volatile. I knew all that mattered to him was the drug – whichever it was that day – and getting more.

But I never did run. I still held onto the memory of his calmest comedown, the one where he cried on my lap for hours. The one where he cried himself to sleep. I always waited for that comedown to happen again, but it never did.

He wasn't always violent. That night, he was. He'd slammed me into the wall as he'd left his apartment and sprained my wrist. Mom and Dad had been away on a business meeting in Boston, so when I arrived home, I was free to cry. Free to let it all out without question.

I had cried under a hot shower, letting my tears blend with the water, and grabbed my razor to shave my legs. It was there, the hot water beating on my back as I bent over, my foot on the side of the bath, my leg covered in shaving foam, that I cut my ankle.

It bled immediately. The bright red blood joined with the white of the foam that had dripped onto my foot, the pink mixture hitting the water. More blood fell, and I watched, transfixed. I watched until my brain registered the sting. The sting that was stronger than the one inside. The sweet sting of release.

I didn't think as I smacked the razor against the tiles, cracking the plastic. My nimble fingers pulled it apart, letting the plastic drop to the ground.

The blade was cool between my fingers. Wet, but cool. I ran my finger along the sharp edge, staring at the still bleeding cut on my ankle. My back pressed against the tiles, I slowly slid down to the floor. My foot still rested on the side of the bath.

The blade moved toward it, my hand acting of its own accord. It touched my skin, lightly at first, then stronger. My hand shook, and I bit my lip to stop the whimper as it broke my skin. A tiny dot of blood bubbled up on my foot. My eyes moved from the blade to the blood. My teeth released my lip, and my hand moved.

The blade sliced smoothly along my foot. The sting, the burn. It was all I knew. All I could focus on. The bright red, the scarlet blood mixing with the clearness of the water. Mixing perfect with pain. Tainting it. Destroying it.
The same way Pearce was destroying me.

I can't breathe. My chest is too tight, the lump in my throat too big. My teeth are clamped too firmly around my tongue, hoping the small pain there will override the urges.

The frantic shake of my hands leads me to almost drop the razor, but the tightness of my grip means the handle is firmly in place. I remember it, that moment I realized for the first time that it was freeing to bleed. There was no limit. I could cut once, twice, three times, keep bleeding for minutes, and the physical pain would take over the emotional. It would wipe it out.

More blood trickles down my foot and lands on the white tiled floor. It taints the floor the same way it tainted the shower water that first time.

A tiny speck, a burst of painful color on something so calm and pure.

Do it. Just one. No one needs to know. Just once. Let the pain flow.

I squeeze my eyes shut, my whole body tense. My fingers are wrapped so hard around the handle of the razor I'm sure it's about to shatter, but it doesn't. It stays whole in my hand.

One little cut. Let out all the pain. Let it go.

I shake my head. At nothing. At no one. Because I know, or a part of me does, at least, that the voices aren't real. The voices are me. As crazy as it sounds, it's all me. I'm contradicting myself at every turn. Every voice. Every whisper. Every shout.

It's all me. It always has been.

And I can fight it.

I can drop the razor, wipe off my legs and walk. I can.

But I don't.

I stay, in limbo. Shaking, panicking, crying. Tears roll down my cheeks with the force of the fight inside.

There's no way to describe the fight. No words to convey the suffocating darkness that pounds down from every angle. No words to explain the tiny speck of light that can pull you out.

And I have to remember, the light. The light is where I want to be. The light is the aim. It's always the aim.

But what is the light?

I drop my chin to my chest as I feel the darkness pounding me. I know what the light is. I know, but I can't remember. I hold the razor away from my body, fighting in the face of a coming defeat. I can feel it. I can feel the urge taking me over, the sting still present on my ankle and getting stronger with every passing second.

And Juilliard.

Juilliard. Ballet.

The dream. The aim. The light.

Juilliard is my light.

And I grab at it. I grab at the light inside my mind and drop the razor into the bathtub. I open my eyes, snatch the sponge and wipe my legs, not caring that one of them is half done. The tears have slowed, and I wrench myself upwards, refusing to look at the razor. If I look, I'll break.

If I break . . .

I stumble into my bedroom and toward my iPod. I stab at the buttons, almost blindly, whispering Juilliard out loud. Tchaikovsky's *Swan Lake* fills my room as my back falls against the door I don't remember shutting. The soothing music flows through me, and in my mind I envision myself as the Swan Princess. I envision every step, every move.

My breathing slows, and I sit. Listening. Imagining.

Until the sudden ringing of my alarm breaks the silence. I look at my clock. It reads five-thirty in the afternoon.

Five-thirty means ballet.

It means the dream. The light.

And, I realize as I get up and grab my ballet clothes, fingering the leotard, it means I fought the urge.

I beat the blood.

~

I stand in *arabesque en pointe* in front of Blake. He wraps an arm around my waist just below my ribs, and his other goes around my leg above my knee. Slowly, he tilts me downward, bending one of his knees, and I bend my standing leg into a parallel *passé*. My core muscles are tight, my back arched, and my gaze is drawn upwards to meet his.

He smiles, and I return it. He holds me there for a minute, his hands warm on my body, his eyes never wavering from mine, before he easily lifts me upright and back onto *pointe*.

'Lifting you is like lifting a feather,' he comments. 'It's hard to believe you have enough muscle in your tiny body to hold yourself in that position for that long so easily.'

I lower my feet back into first position, my smile still playing on my lips. 'Surprise.'

'Indeed. Shall we try the first few steps? See if it works?'

I nod. 'Sure.'

Blake steps up to my side and places a hand on my stomach. The fingers of his other hand slide across my back and curl around my waist, raising with me as I move back *en pointe*. I try to hide the tensing of my body at his touch, try to hide the irrational sliver of fear snaking through my body.

Slowly, he begins to walk around me, moving me to the music, performing our opening *promenade*. As we spin, I move my arms into third position and extend my right foot into the *attitude* position. My eyes are forward, away from Blake, but I know his steps are precise and at exact intervals. I also know he's doing it as easily as he breathes. We're the same in that dancing is almost unconscious for us both. It just happens.

We move into the rest of our *entrée*, dancing together as if we've done so our whole lives. The familiar feeling of letting go comes over me, and I close my eyes, losing myself in our movements both seperately and together. Now, Blake's touch is no longer threatening. It doesn't scare me, not when the moves are all I can feel.

The moment ends too soon, and I come crashing back down to reality. My ankle throbs, as if to remind me what life really is, and my chest tightens. I take a long, deep breath and try to remember that I'm safe. That this is ballet. That Blake won't hurt me – that he can't hurt me here. That no one can.

But it doesn't work. The panic rises in my chest, a tiny ball of it swelling and pulsing until it consumes my core, twisting and turning in my stomach. My deep breaths become short and sharp, my eyes burn with tears and my hands shake uncontrollably. Blood pounds through my body, strengthening the throb at my ankle, rushing to every part of my body scarred by my past.

Each scar burns. Each breath is harsh. Each blink drops a tear.

'Abbi.' Hands frame my face. Soft, delicate hands. 'Abbi. Come back, honey. Breathe . . . No, no. Slowly. In . . . One, two, three . . . And back out. That's it. And again. In . . . Two, three . . . Out . . . In . . . One, two, three.'

Bianca's voice cuts through the fog swirling in my mind. Her hands against my cheeks ground me and slowly pull me out of myself, bringing me back to right now. Stopping me falling further into my past.

I look at her through blurry eyes. She smiles and places my fingers on my wrist.

'Feel. Remember,' she whispers. 'You're still alive – you're still here.'

I do. I slip my fingers inside my sleeve and press them to my pulse point harshly. My pulse thuds, lightning fast, and I count five beats of my heart for every breath I take, reducing the beats until both have settled to normal again. Bianca hands me a tissue, and I dab under my eyes, realizing we're sitting in her office.

'Bad day?' She strokes my hair from my face.

I nod. 'Really bad. I thought maybe tonight would help, but for the first time, I was wrong.'

'What started it?'

'I . . . I don't know,' I answer softly, looking out of the small window behind her desk. 'I haven't had an attack in weeks. I usually notice when they're coming and I can fight them, but this one just hit me. It came on so suddenly I didn't even realize until it was too late.'

Bianca nods slowly. 'Call Dr. Hausen and speak to her about it, Abbi. I know you don't want to, but you need to figure out why it happened and why you couldn't stop it.'

'I know.' I pull my gaze back to her. 'Can I leave early? Please?'

She takes my hand. 'Of course you can.'

I call Dad and ask him to come and get me when she leaves the room. Time seems to drag as I wait for his message that he's outside. When it comes, I grab my things Bianca brought in for me and leave the studio. Dad asks me no questions as I silently climb in the back seat. I bring my knees to my chest, hug them tight and look out of the car window as he pulls away from the red-brick building.

I can't remember the last time I felt as out of control as I did today.

Blake

'Fuck it!' I drop the spoon for the fifth time tonight.

'You wash your damn hands with butter before you got here or what, kid?' Joe hollers.

'Might as well have,' I grumble, bending to pick it up. I throw it in the sink and take a clean one from the rack. My pan on the hob starts to bubble frantically, and I rush over to the cooker to find the rice I was cooking boiling over.

'*Shiiiiit*,' I hiss, turning the gas off and taking the handle of the pan. I empty it into a colander in the sink. There's half an inch of rice stuck to the bottom. My body deflates and I bang my head against the fridge.

Hard.

Joe puts a hand on my shoulder. 'Look, Blake, I don't know what's going on with you tonight, but perhaps it's best if you leave early. We're quiet for a Friday and you'd be taking off in an hour anyway.'

'No.' I shake my head, grabbing a scouring pad to clean out the pan. 'I'm good, Chef. Really. I'll finish out my shift.'

'Son.' He squeezes my shoulder. 'Go home. No good you being here and beating yourself up every time you make a mistake. Get yourself a good night's sleep and come in here tomorrow for your lunch shift, alright?'

I sigh, drop the scourer, and nod. 'Got it.'

He pats my back a few times and disappears back into the main kitchen area, yelling at Matt. I pull off my chef clothes and shove them in my bag, leaving the stifling building in record time.

There's a chill in the evening air when I step outside, and

I breathe in deeply and gratefully. My steps are slow and lazy as I make my way home, my head somewhere up in the clouds. The waning light doesn't bother me as I trundle through Brooklyn's streets. I notice nothing and nobody around me.

All I can think of is a pair of blue eyes, wide and frantic. All I can focus on is the fear and confusion that glazed them over, clouding them until they were barely recognizable. All I care about is that she's okay.

My craziness is made worse because she wasn't in class yesterday. Because Bianca just shook her head with a hint of sadness when I asked where she was. Because somewhere in the back of my mind, I recognize the fear that shone in her eyes. I recognize the panic, the painful tears that dripped from her eyes, the heartbreaking shaking of her body as I carried her from the studio to Bianca's office.

And the sobs. I recognize the body-wracking sobs because I listened to my sister cry them for months.

Every minute we spend together, I see more and more of Tori in Abbi. But I also see something Tori never had – a spark. It's a spark that holds an honest to God dream.

Yesterday though . . . There was no spark. Every bit of light in Abbi's body went out. She was a different person – there was no fun glint in her eye, no amused smirk, and no sarcastic comments. The shadows that hide in the depths of her eyes took her over completely.

The way Tori's used to.

I have no idea why Abbi broke down; all I know is that I want to know. I want to know why she fell apart, why someone who's so silently strong had a moment of such crippling weakness. And I want to make it better. Something about her is so endearing I can't help but be pulled in by her – I can't help but want to want her.

I want to hold her waist as she gets lost in the dance. I want to spin her round en *pointe* until she doesn't know which way is up anymore. I want to lift her above my head and dance her across the stage so gracefully she believes she's flying.

I want to take the tears and the pain and change them into a smile and happiness.

Maybe that's why, when I enter my apartment, I change into a polo top and jeans and call her number without a bloody clue what I'm gonna say to her.

'Hey,' I say softly when she answers.

'Hi.'

'You weren't in class yesterday . . . I wanted to make sure you were okay.'

'I . . .' She pauses, and I swallow as I wait for her reply. 'I know it's getting late, but I thought of another place to show you in Brooklyn if you want to see.'

I don't miss that she's avoiding my question, but something in me hopes she'll talk more if we're face to face.

'I think I can deal with that. As long as we don't meet at Whole Foods again.'

'No . . . No Whole Foods. Promise.' If I didn't know better I'd swear she was smiling a little.

'Where to then?'

'Brooklyn Promenade.'

~

I climb from the taxi and get my first look at the promenade. Directly across the East River is the lower Manhattan skyline on backdrop of the setting sun. I stop for a second, staring dumbly at the golden hues of the sunset crawling across the sky, only broken by towering skyscrapers. Brooklyn Bridge stands to my right, stretching across the river, and I can't help but wonder if I'm looking at one of the most amazing things this side of the Atlantic.

I draw my eyes away and look to the actual promenade. Benches stretch along the length of it, backed by trees and dimly lit lampposts every few feet. Couples, families and groups of friends stroll up and down the promenade, some sit on the benches. They're all laughing and joking, and I rush past behind the benches searching for Abbi.

I find her a good few feet away from the majority of people here. She's sitting on the back of one of the benches with her elbows on her knees. Her hair is swept to one side and tucked behind her ear, giving me a perfect view of her profile as she gazes out at the city.

'It's beautiful, isn't it?' she asks, turning her face toward me.

'Yeah,' I reply, not taking my eyes from her. 'Yeah. It is.'

She stares at me for a beat before looking away again.

'This doesn't look like somewhere you'd hide.' I climb up onto the bench next to her, perching on the back the same way she is.

'Sometimes the best hiding place is in plain sight.' Peering sideways at me, she smooths her hair back around her neck when a breeze sends it flying. 'How many people do you think you walk past every day that are hiding from something?'

'Point taken.' I nod.

'I come here to remember that life goes on. It's always so busy; the promenade is always full of people, cars are always racing over Brooklyn Bridge, and New York is always alive. Sometimes your world just stops, you know? And that's when I need to remember it's still turning.'

I don't reply, instead watch the sun drop down even further. Gradually, one by one, the buildings of Manhattan begin to light up. The sunset is washed out by the brightness of the buildings reflecting both in the water and against the sky. Shades of orange, pink, purple and blue fill the sky behind the city as the artificial lights mix with the natural one, creating something I'm sure you can't see anywhere else in the world.

I don't reply, even as the colorful sky is taken over by the inky blackness of the night sky. There are no stars here, their light drowned out by the city.

'You asked me if I'm okay,' Abbi says, breaking my reverie.

'I don't know how to answer that. Sometimes I am, sometimes I'm not. Sometimes I don't even know myself.'

I wait for her to continue, watching her as she fiddles with a lock of her hair.

'I was diagnosed with depression a year ago. It's not something I usually tell people, but after Tuesday, I feel like you have a right to know.'

'You don't have to tell me anything.'

'No, I do. You deserve to know this much, at least.' She takes a deep breath, finally looking at me properly. Her blue eyes are wide and earnest, completely clear of everything but a tiny dot of fear. Fear of what, I don't know. I just know I see that fear.

'I don't know what happened on Tuesday. The panic attacks . . . They kind of come along with my depression, and there's always something that starts them. Usually I can feel when one's coming and stop it, I can fight it, but I couldn't on Tuesday. I haven't had one for weeks now, and I have no idea what caused the last one. I guess I was lucky it happened when I was in a place where there was someone who knew how to calm me down.'

I scratch my nose, remembering how swiftly Bianca moved to her side. 'Bianca was with you in seconds, and asked me to carry you into her office. No one really noticed – and she didn't want you in full view of everyone.'

'Thank you,' she whispers. 'For getting me out of the studio.'

'It's okay. Really.' We both smile at each other. 'Can I ask you something?'

'Go ahead. I can't promise I'll answer, though.'

'Warn a guy next time, can ya? You scared the shit out of me. I've been wondering if I'm really that bloody bad at dancing.' I wink at her, and she laughs quietly.

'That's it. It must be your dancing. Why didn't I think of it before?' She shakes her head. 'I'm gonna have to talk to Bianca and get her to find me a new partner.'

I half-smirk, happy to see a light back in her eyes. 'Shut up,' I mutter.

Her lips twitch with a suppressed grin. 'I really want some ice cream. Let's get some.'

'You realize it's almost nine p.m., don't you?' I raise my eyebrows at her.

Abbi shrugs, jumping up from the bench. 'It's never too late for ice cream. Especially not from Holly's place.'

'Of course,' I mumble as I get up. 'An ice cream parlor open at nine o'clock. Bloody Americans.'

'I heard that, freakin' British,' Abbi replies, her cheeks twitching with the fight of a smile. 'It's perfectly normal for an ice cream shop to be open at this time. At least, it is if you're Holly's. I actually have no idea about any other places.'

I shake my head, completely amused, and follow her away from the promenade, leaving behind the bright skyline. She runs her hand along the bushes as we walk, and I wonder if that's one of her little quirks. She did it with almost every bush and tree we passed in Prospect Park, too.

I watch her as she picks off a leaf and tears it up, sprinkling the ripped pieces on the pavement as we walk.

'What did that leaf ever do to you?' I ask, drawing level with her.

She glances in my direction. 'It was in my way.'

'And the pavement deserved being covered in the leaf?'

'The pavement?' She smiles.

I rub my hand down my face. 'The pavement. What we're walking on. You know – the paved thing?'

'Oh. You mean the sidewalk.'

I stare at her. 'Why the hell do you call it a sidewalk?'

'Because it's at the sides of the road and you walk on it?' Abbi snorts, stopping outside a building with a sign lit up announcing it as Holly's Ice Cream Parlor. 'I have no idea. I didn't call it that. I told you before, it's not my fault if you Brits don't talk properly.'

'I'm not getting into this again.' I push open the glass door of the building and let her pass through. 'Not when I'm still trying to understand why anyone would eat ice cream at this time of night.'

'You don't have to understand it. You just have to do it. Ice cream tastes best at this time of night.'

'Okay. I'll take your word for it.' I look at all the names on the boards hanging behind the counter, then at the freezers in front of me. And drop my jaw. I've never seen so many types of bloody ice cream in my life, and I have no idea what any of the dishes on the board are called.

'You've never been to an ice cream shop before, have you?' Abbi asks me in a voice that says she thinks I'm completely hopeless.

Honestly, I'm a little inclined to believe her on the hopeless thing. London has been holding out on me, clearly.

'Never in my life.'

'I thought I heard your voice.' A young woman, no older than thirty, comes bustling out from behind a beaded curtain, and beams at Abbi. An apron is tied around her waist, and she wipes her hands on it, her brown eyes flitting between the two of us. 'Oh dear,' she mutters, her eyes settling on Abbi. 'He's a newbie, isn't he?'

Abbi nods. 'Yep.'

'I thought so. He looks as lost as a penguin in the desert, that one. What shall we give him, Abbi?'

'I was thinking the chocolate sundae. The double one. With extra brownies.' She pauses, then nods. 'Yep. That one.'

The woman – who I'm guessing is Holly – grins. 'I agree It's always a good startin' place. And you'll have the Rainbow Splash?'

'You bet.' Abbi turns to me, smiling.

'I'd love the chocolate sundae, thanks.' I try for annoyed, but completely fail.

'See? I knew you would.' She dances across the parlor and sits on one of the high stools at a small round table, spinning to face me. 'Everyone loves chocolate sundaes.'

I follow her over and sit opposite her. 'So why didn't you get the chocolate one?'

Holly sets two glasses full of ice cream in front of us. One is layered with vanilla and chocolate ice cream, chocolate brownies, chocolate sauce and topped with a bit of cream and colorful sprinkles. The other is a mix of what looks like every color ice cream Holly has in the freezers, layered with strawberry and toffee sauce and topped with biscuit pieces, chocolate chips, and a whole pot of sprinkles.

'That was quick,' I say.

'I've been doing this since I was fifteen,' Holly replies. 'No one in this city can whip up an ice cream faster than I can.'

'Or better,' Abbi interjects, licking her spoon.

Holly winks. 'Enjoy.' She turns and strolls to the back of the shop.

'And to answer your question . . .' Abbi's feet kick mine under the table. 'If I ordered the chocolate sundae, I wouldn't get to do this.'

She leans forward and sticks her spoon in my dish, taking a mound of ice cream and brownie. She closes her mouth around my ice cream before I can say anything, crinkles forming around her eyes.

'Just as well you didn't, then,' I reply, twirling my spoon between my fingers. 'Because that's a great idea.' I dip my spoon into her ice cream but come away with a pile of sprinkles and barely a slither of ice cream.

Abbi laughs loudly, clapping her hand over her mouth to stifle it. I run my tongue across my teeth, staring hopelessly at my spoon, and try not to smile at the sound of her laughter. For all the sadness she has locked away in her body, she has the lightest, happiest laugh I've ever heard, and it's almost impossible to not want to laugh along with her.

I look at her, and her eyes are closed as her giggles peter out. She opens her eyes, showing me their brilliantly blue hue. I stab my spoon childishly into my ice cream, take a big scoop, and shove it into my mouth.

And I completely and utterly underestimated how fucking cold this ice cream is.

My eyes widen as I swallow the lump of frozen cream.

Abbi purses her lips and her shoulders shake yet again with laughter.

'You seem to have a habit of making a bit of a twat of yourself,' she observes.

I wipe some cream from the corner of my mouth. 'I think you bring it out in me.'

'Is that a good thing?'

I tilt my head to the side and watch her lick her spoon clean. 'As long as you don't do it when we dance.'

She smiles. 'I think I can manage that.'

'By the way . . .' I point my spoon at her. '. . . You have ice cream all around your mouth.'

She wipes at her lips with her fingers and looks at them, then at me. 'No I don't.' She narrows her eyes.

I grin and stick my spoon in her ice cream again. This time I get a spoonful of ice cream, and I poke my tongue out at Abbi. She half-smirks, staring at me. My eyes flit between her and the spoon, and I slowly move it in her direction. She opens her mouth and closes her lips around the spoon, sweeping the ice cream from it.

'The stealing was utterly pointless,' I say, observing the smeared spoon.

'Oh. Hang on.' She reaches forward and snatches it. She beams at me, and her tongue flicks out. It licks across my spoon, removing every last trace of ice cream, and I can't focus on anything but that pink tongue sliding back behind even pinker lips. She puts the spoon back into my hand. 'Missed a bit.'

My fingers close around it. 'Uh huh.'

Abbi

I finger the material of the red knee-length dress, holding onto the long lace sleeve. My eyes comb over the boat neckline and the lace body, down to the black belt at the waist and the plain skater style skirt. I want this dress – I want it badly. But the sleeves get me.

For so long I haven't worn anything other than long, solid sleeves that hide the scars that cover the underside of my arms. The white lines stay hidden, my secret from the world. And the problem with the sleeves on this dress is it has holes. Tiny holes, not big enough to see the blemishes marring my pale skin, but they're still holes.

'Try it on,' Mom urges from behind me. 'It's a lovely dress, Abbi. Very you. Very *new* you. That color will look lovely with your hair.'

'I don't know,' I reply, still staring at the sleeve in my hand. 'I don't really have anywhere to wear it. There's not much point in buying something that will just sit in my closet forever.'

Mom rifles through the racks behind me. 'If there's one thing I've learned in my too many years of life, it's that a woman always needs a secret weapon. Sometimes it's a little black dress, but there's nothing like a good red number to knock a man off his feet and keep him on his ass.'

'Why would I want to keep any man on his ass?'

'So he can see your shoes, darling.'

'No man will ever care about my shoes, Mom.'

'He doesn't *need* to care about your shoes. It'll just make his life easier if he can see what's going to be walking all over him for the entirety of your relationship.'

My lips curve upwards. 'Then the red number isn't necessary,' I say almost sadly, the smile dropping from my lips as I drop the sleeve. 'I can't see myself having a relationship any time soon. If ever.'

I shrug a shoulder, and Mom grabs my arm.

'Abigail Jenkins,' she begins, turning me round to her. 'One complete and utter bastard does not represent the male race. They might all be a bit stupid sometimes, but Pearce Stevens is most definitely in the minority. One day, you'll meet someone that will be worth all the effort that comes with having a true, life-changing relationship. It might not be today, it might not be next year, but you will. And when you find him, I expect you to wear this dress with a pair of killer heels and knock him on his ass so hard he can't sit on anything except for a rubber ring for the next week.'

'Mom . . .' I roll my eyes.

'No.' She cups my chin, bringing my eyes to hers. 'You, baby girl, are stronger than even you know. I can see it in your eyes right now. One day you'll find a man who will love you the way you deserve to be loved, and he will treat you like the princess you spent your childhood claiming you were. This dress may be sat in your closet for however long, but you buy it, and when you meet him you damn well wear it.'

I sigh and stare again at the dress. Mom's right – I don't even have to wear it yet. Besides, by the time I'm ready to wear it, my scars might not bother me so much. They might not control me the way they do right now. When I wear it, everything won't be so raw. Maybe the feelings and the memories will be as smooth as the skin that's healed.

'Okay,' I acquiesce. 'I'll get it.'

Mom smiles and grabs my size from the rail, whisking it off to the counter to pay before I can blink. She returns a few minutes later with a triumphant smile, handing me the bag.

'Thank you,' I say softly.

'It's not the first time I've bought you a dress.' She laughs. 'But you're welcome.'

'For the dress, and for *making* me have it.'

Mom wraps an arm around my shoulders as we leave the store. 'Just make sure you save it for the right guy. And you let me buy you the shoes.'

'You bet.' I laugh. 'Hey, Mom?'

'Mm?'

I curl into her side the way I used to as a child. 'Thank you. For being there and never giving up even when I did. I don't . . .' I look down. 'I don't know if I'd cope if I didn't have you.'

'Oh, honey.' She squeezes me. 'You don't need to thank me for anything. You're my baby, and I'm always going to be there. You should never give up on something you believe in, and I believe in you. So, thank *you* for not giving up even though you think you did.'

She's right. I didn't give up, not really. Not in my heart. If I'd given up in my heart I'd still be in my room at St. Morris's.

My cell buzzes in my jacket pocket, and I pull it out to see I have two messages. One from Maddie asking me about Hot British Guy, and one from said Hot British Guy asking what I'm doing.

Just shopping with Mom. Going home now, I reply.

Work sucked. I'm at the studio. Want to practice?

I'm in NYC already but I don't have my stuff. It'll take an hour to get it and back.

Damn it.

'Hey, Mom?' I grip my phone tightly.

'Yes?'

'I was wondering . . . You know Bianca has us doing a *grand pas de deux*?'

'Hmm.'

'My dance partner just text me. He wants to practice, but I don't have any of my ballet stuff with me. I was wondering . . . If . . . maybe . . . we could get him from the studio? And we could practice in the garage?' I look down as she unlocks the car.

'This is Hot British Guy, right?'

'I . . .' I look up to her smiling face. 'Dad is such a teenage girl sometimes.'

Mom laughs. 'I agree with you completely, Abbi. Tell him we'll be there in ten minutes.' She winks and gets in the car. I take a deep breath, wondering if I'll regret this, and tell Blake to wait outside.

~

'This is the hot British guy?' Dad asks after I introduce him to Blake.

'Dad!' I half-yell, my cheeks flaming. 'Oh my God,' I mutter. Blake turns to me with a raised eyebrow.

'I . . . Go back to your paper, Dad. Geez.' I glance at Blake. 'Follow me.' I lead him through the kitchen and into the garage-come-studio to the sound of Dad's raucous laughter. 'I'll be back in a minute.'

I run up the stairs, change, and come back down as I'm tying my hair into a bun. Dad's still laughing to himself in the front room, and I poke my head round the door and point at him threateningly.

'You!'

He just laughs louder.

'Don't encourage him, darling.' Mom pats my shoulder. 'I'm sure he'll calm down soon.'

'He's a bloody nightmare,' I mutter.

'She's . . . even . . . talking like one,' Dad wheezes out through his laughter.

I screw my face up and flick my spare hairband at him. It hits his paper and falls to the floor. Mom rolls her eyes, sighs, and announces she's going to work in the office. Dad winks at me, and I smile.

'Hey, Dad?'

'What?'

'Thank you.'

'You do realize I just embarrassed you, don't you?' He frowns at me.

'Yeah. But I kinda liked it. It's the thing a parent of a normal person would do, you know? You've never treated me like glass like Mom does sometimes.'

'Normal is overrated. Now, go and dance with your hot British boy.'

'Blake,' I call over my shoulder. 'His name is Blake.'

'Eh, same thing.'

I shake my head and push the door open. Blake is leaning against the *barre*, his arms folded across his chest, he smirks at me as soon as I shut the door.

'Hot British Guy, huh?'

'I so did not say that,' I lie, turning away. 'It was Maddie.'

'I'm starting to think she had an ulterior motive for coming to that dance class.'

'Do you watch a lot of movies or something? 'Cause you're so wrong.'

'Mhmm.'

He's standing right behind me, just a whisper of space between us. I swallow the bubble that rises in my throat and try to relax. His body moves to the side of me, and he places his hands on my stomach and waist. I move *en pointe,* knowing dance is the only way I'll be able to combat the uncertainty and anxiousness rising in my mind.

I focus on the dance instead of the feel of his hands against my body with only a thin piece of material separating his palms and my bare skin. I focus on the positioning of my legs and arms instead of the warmth of his breath across my ear and neck. And I focus on the next step instead of the subtle change of fear to something almost unrecognizable to me. Something that makes me want to run away and stay. Something that makes me want to push him away and pull him closer.

But I can't. I can feel the heat from his hands curving around me and the way his breath flutters across my skin. I can hear the heaviness of his breathing, and I know his heart is beating as fast as mine. Mine isn't from the dance. It's never from the dance when he's around. It's always something more, something that tugs at me relentlessly. It tugs me toward him and keeps me in place.

It's something that scares me, but it thrills me at the same time. Spine-tingling, stomach-fluttering, lip-parting thrills.

We move through the steps of our *entrée* with ease, and I feel him begin to slow as we come to the end of it.

'Just dance,' I whisper, not ready to stop the freeing feeling flowing through me. I'm not ready for him to let go . . . Not yet. I want this feeling to last. 'Just dance.'

He does. He guides me through step after step, spin after turn, *plié* after lift. We cover every inch of the garage floor space, kicking up spots of dust from the spots I don't use.

Blake's hands leave me for a second, and my body breaks away from his. *En pointe*, I *pirouette*, again and again and again, never losing balance, never getting dizzy. I spin on the tips of my toes, dropping for a split second before I rise back up. I glance up as I spin, and Blake's stood watching me. His legs parted, his arms out, and after one final spin, I take his cue.

I *grand pas de chat* toward him, my legs extended as I fly through the air as if I'm weightless. But I don't hit the floor. My hands fall on his shoulders, and his hands grip my waist to keep me suspended in the air above him. His hold on me is steady, not even a tremble in his arms.

I open my eyes. Our foreheads are almost touching, our gazes fixed on the other. My breathing is hard and fast, matching his breath for breath, but I'm not even sure if it's from the dance or from . . . now.

I don't know if the adrenaline rushing through my body is from the thrill of the jump or if the pounding of my heart is from the endless *pirouettes*. In this moment, with nothing between us except a sliver of air, I don't know what I'm feeling.

I want to believe the goosepimples on the back of my neck are from the ease of us dancing together. I want to believe the tightness in my chest is from being short of breath.

And I want to believe I want Blake to put me down and let me go. I want to believe it so, so badly. But I don't, at all. Because I can't believe something that isn't true.

Right now, with his eyes so intensely focused on me, I don't want him to let go at all.

Slowly, after I don't know how long, he lowers me. My toes touch the ground, and I come off *pointe*, falling into first position before completely relaxing. His hands fall from my waist, and mine from his shoulders. I take a deep breath and step back, dropping my eyes to the ground.

'You know, I don't think we're going to need the full time Bianca gave us,' he says after a moment of silence. 'Once we have the *adagio* perfect, that is.'

'I think you could be right.' I glance up at him. 'Bianca really does know how to pair her dancers off, huh?'

Something flares in his eyes. Something I don't understand. Something I both want to and don't want to understand.

Something I wish I hadn't seen.

'Yeah. Yeah, she does.'

~

'What if I feel things I don't want to?'

'Do you mean your urges? The flashbacks?'

'No.' I run my thumb across my bottom lip. 'Things that aren't really . . . bad. Not that kind of bad, anyway.'

Dr. Hausen sits forward, peering at me over her glasses. 'You'll have to elaborate, Abbi. I'm not following.'

'What if . . . What if I was feeling things an eighteen-year-old-girl should be feeling? About . . . a guy.'

Her mouth quirks up. 'Is this a hypothetical question?'

I stop rubbing my lip, my eyes answering her question silently.

'You're scared.'

I nod.

'Why?'

'Because he hurt me,' I say matter-of-factly, sinking my hands into my hair and winding it round my fingers. 'I gave him every part of me I dared, and Pearce took it and he destroyed it. He tore it up into a million unfixable pieces and then he destroyed even those pieces!'

'But this guy . . .'

'Blake.'

'Blake isn't like Pearce, correct?'

I think of his green eyes, his messy brown hair, and his silent confidence. The warmth of his hands, the surety of his step, and the connection we have as dancers.

'No. They're like the poles, completely opposite.'

'So why are you afraid?'

'I thought I could help Pearce and I got it wrong. I was wrong about everything about him. What if I could be wrong this time? What if I embrace the possible feelings I'm starting to feel and I'm wrong? Pearce nearly killed me. If Maddie hadn't turned up and called an ambulance, I'm pretty sure I would be dead now. In fact, I know I would be. I've seen the files. I know that if I hadn't have passed out from the pain and I'd kept cutting I would have died faster. What if that happens again?'

'Do you want it to happen again? Do you want to go back to that day?'

'No,' I say automatically, honestly, and drop my hands to my lap. 'Not at all. That's why I'm so scared.'

'Do you think Blake would hurt you?'

'I didn't think Pearce would hurt me.'

Dr. Hausen tuts, leaning back in her chair and crossing her legs. 'I didn't ask you that. Forget Pearce. You know he can't hurt you anymore. I asked you if you think *Blake* would hurt you.'

'No. I don't think he would hurt me.'

'In that case . . .'

I look at her, finally, and she's looking intently at me.

'Sometimes you have to take a risk. Anything you decide is going to go one of two ways; you'll either get it wrong and move on, or you'll get it right and live in that moment. Both of those outcomes will change your life. Both of them will alter the way you think, and both of them will affect decisions you make for the rest of your life, but that doesn't mean they should make your future decisions for you.

'Your past doesn't control your future, Abbi. In fact, your past doesn't have to dictate anything about your life if you don't want it to. Right now, you're letting your past make your decisions for you. You're letting it hold you back. You can't compare a tiger to a leopard – they might be the same species, but they look and act differently.'

'So I shouldn't compare Blake to Pearce just because they're both males.'

'Precisely. I'm not saying you should throw yourself head first into a relationship with Blake . . .'

'You're saying *I* should make the choice about how I feel and act, instead of letting my past do it for me.'

'Correct.'

'But what if I don't want to feel anything for him?'

'Then that's your choice. But think very carefully before you make a decision. After all, you never know when something beautiful might happen.'

Blake

I should have kissed her.

I should have lowered her to the ground sooner, brushed that stray lock of hair from her face, and bloody well kissed her

But something stopped me. Something in her eyes – a wariness, a hesitance – it hit me full force in the gut and it made me stop.

There's more to her depression than she said. It doesn't take a genius to work it out – she's hiding in plain sight, keeping a part of her buried under the weight of her sadness.

Just like Tori.

But is she? Is she like Tori? No one believed her. I was the only one that ever listened to her, that ever believed there was truly something wrong with her. Mum brushed it off as teenage attention seeking, while Dad claimed it was merely her hormones and she'd get over it soon. Aren't sixteen-year-old girls extra dramatic, after all? According to my parents, yes, they are.

But not to me. I was the one who crept into her room at night when she cried and held her as tightly as my twelve-year-old body could. I was the one who came away with mascara-stained t-shirts and wet jumpers.

Even Kiera, a year younger than Tori, never believed her. She believed Mum, believed Tori just got the overdramatic gene. Allie, Laura and Jase were all too young to understand. Hell, they were too young to even notice. I'm pretty sure I would have been had I not spent every spare second with her.

But I still never understood completely. I never truly got how deep her pain ran, how stinging each rejection from our parents was, how much every word from the bullies that tormented her cut her. Every word cut into her spirit deeper than the blades she took to her skin. They took more out of her than every drop of blood she spilled.

I don't get it even now. I don't understand why she never said anything – to me, to anyone. But I hate it; I hate that she suffered alone, silently, and that she died the same way. I hate the fact I was too late.

Every single fucking time.

I was always one step behind. Always one minute too late. And always one dream ahead.

I'm determined not to be that person with Abbi. I'm determined not to be one step behind her. I don't even want to be one step in front. I've known her for three weeks, short enough that I still remember the first time I saw her in the studio. The only place I want to be stepping is right alongside her.

In time with her.

On the studio floor.

On the stage.

On her damn American sidewalk.

Dance steps or normal steps – I don't care. If she cries, I don't want to let go when she's done. If she tries to run, I want to chase her and catch her. And if she tries to let go, I want to make her hold on.

~

'I feel like all I ever do when I'm not at work is be with you,' I tease, opening the door.

'That's because you keep calling me,' Abbi replies, stepping into my apartment and looking around. 'I was considering having a date with my pajamas and the movie, *Ghost*, but then you said you were cooking. I couldn't resist. It's Chinese night at my parents' and I'm really not a Chinese food person.'

'Really?' I shut the door. 'How can you not like Chinese?'

She shrugs. 'I just don't, so it was a no brainer. Greasy take-out food, or home cooked goodness. At least I hope it's good or I've just wasted my time coming here.'

I smirk. 'I'm a chef, so I'd like to think it's good.'

'Really? And to think I can barely make toast.'

'Good job it's me cooking. Can't have you choreographing on a stomach filled with burnt toast now, can we?'

'Hey.' She frowns at me. 'Okay, you have a point.'

I laugh. 'Take a seat . . . Well, anywhere. You can sit in the front room and shout at me, or in the kitchen and talk to me.'

'Let's go for talking,' she says, perching on a chair at the kitchen table.

I throw her a smile over my shoulder and grab a knife from the block on the counter. I set it on the side and put the chicken and potatoes in the oven dish.

'What are you making?'

'A summer chicken dish.'

'It's not *quite* summer yet. It's a bit slow this year.'

'Eh, it's close enough. Besides, it won't matter when you taste this.'

'Cocky,' Abbi accuses playfully.

'No, confident.' I grin at the garlic I'm crushing. 'My childhood nanny used to cook this, and I made her write it down when I was ten so I'd be able to make it one day. I was the really annoying kid that was always under her feet when she was in the kitchen, and she agreed on the terms if I left her alone. She didn't say how long I had to leave her alone for, so I was back "helping" her the next day.'

'You had a nanny? Wow.'

'It's not that great. Honestly, I'd rather my Dad played football with us more than once a year.'

'Where in London does your family live?'

'Chelsea.' I put the dish in the oven, check the temperature, and lean against the counter. 'My dad is a lawyer with the family firm, and my mum has her own shoe label. Both of them work stupid hours, so they had no choice but to hire a nanny. It means none of us ever wanted for anything except them.'

'Really? You never saw them?' Abbi leans her elbows on the table and props her chin on her hands.

I shake my head. 'Not really. Especially once Dad realized I had no intention of following in both his and Granddad's footsteps by becoming a lawyer. He was pretty pissed off when I decided to become a chef. His parents are old fashioned, and I think Granddad engrained in him that only women should be in a kitchen.'

Abbi snorts in disbelief. 'And then you moved here. To dance.'

A sly smile graces my lips. 'That went down about as well as an uncontrolled demolition. I started dancing when I was four, and both my parents put it down to me simply copying my eldest sister, so they left me to it. Needless to say, they weren't happy when I was still dancing at twelve while my eight-year-old brother was banging in the goals for a local kids' football team.'

'Foot – oh, soccer. Never mind.' Abbi smiles. 'Did they help you move here?'

Now it's my turn to snort. 'No. They didn't help – at all. I walked straight into an apprenticeship when I left school and saved almost every penny since. I paid for it all myself. I've spoken to my mum once since I landed, my brother twice, and I haven't spoken to my father and sisters at all.'

'Wow. I couldn't imagine not speaking to my parents for that long.'

I shrug, turning to the chopping board and grabbing a courgette. 'It's just how it is. My family isn't exactly tight-knit. In fact, the only reason I spoke to my mum was because she's coming here next week to close a deal to do with her shoes.'

'Well, that's good. You'll spend some time together, right?'

'If one meal the night she arrives counts as spending time together. Apparently that's the only time she can "fit me in" – and even then she wasn't happy I wouldn't miss dance to see her.'

Abbi's silent as I finish preparing dinner, and I can feel her eyes on my back. I spin round to face her.

'I guess it's true what they say,' she says softly. 'Money really doesn't buy you happiness.'

'I'm not gonna lie. It made me happy as a kid – I mean, who wouldn't want the coolest trainers and the newest toys? Then I grew up and those things stopped making me happy. They were just that – things. I realized while money could buy me everything I needed, it wouldn't get me anything I wanted because I just wanted real happiness. The things that give you real happiness are priceless.'

Her eyes linger on mine for a long second.

'So . . .' I break the silence. 'This won't be ready for a while. Do you want to start on the dance while I clear up?'

'I can help—'

'No, you're a guest. I'll do this.'

'Okay. In the front room?'

'Comfy sofa or wooden chair. Your choice.'

'Yeah . . . The sofa works great.' She smiles and heads toward the front room. She pauses by my bookcase and touches a finger to a frame there. 'She's pretty. Who is it?'

'My sister, Tori.'

'I thought you had five brothers and sisters? Why is there just a picture of her?' She sighs. 'I'm sorry. That was kinda nosey, huh?'

I glance over at her and smile sadly. 'There's a picture of me and the others on the windowsill, but I was closest to Tori.'

'Was?' She goes silent for a long moment, and her lips part when she realizes what I mean. 'Oh. You mean . . .'

'She died nine years ago.' I put the chopping board down on the counter and look out of the kitchen window. Footsteps sound as Abbi crosses the kitchen floor, and her hand touches my lower back softly, her head resting against my arm.

'I'm sorry. I shouldn't have asked,' she says quietly.

I shake my head. 'You didn't know. I don't talk about her much. It's hard.'

She nods. 'I get that. Kinda. I remember when Maddie's mom was killed – she couldn't talk about it for months. Even

I struggled for a few weeks. I know it's not the same, but yeah. For what it's worth, I think Tori would be proud of you.'

I don't tell her how much her words mean to me. To tell her that would be to tell her everything about my family and my sister. And that day. I'd have to relive that day.

Instead, I nod, then turn my head and rest it atop hers for a few seconds. She doesn't freeze or tense up at that simple touch like she has so many times before without realizing it. Her face turns into my arm and her arm rubs a slow circle on my back. Then she takes a deep breath, and sits on the sofa, away from me.

I want to turn around. I want to turn around, take her in my arms and breathe her in while I let the pain of remembering my sister leave me. But that would be too much for her. So even though it kills me a little to leave her there on the other side of the room, alone, I do. I go back to clearing the dirty dishes, and leave her to the choreographing.

~

'Tori, why are you bleeding?' I'd only walked into her room because Mum was getting annoyed that she wasn't ready for dinner. 'Do you need a bandage?'

My sister tore some tissues out of the box on her bedside table and put them on the cut on her arm. 'No, Blake. I don't – it was an accident.' She pointed to the newspaper clippings all over her floor. 'I'm doing my coursework for art and dropped the scissors. I sharpened the blades earlier, and they cut my arm.'

'Oh. Does it hurt?' I tried to peer round at her arm, but she grabbed some more tissues and pulled her sleeve over it.

'No. No, it doesn't hurt. At all.'

'Good. Mum wants you to come down for dinner.'

'I'll just be a minute, okay?' She smiled.

''Kay, Tori.' I smiled back at her and turned around.

'Uh, Blake?'

'Yeah?' I glanced over my shoulder.

'Don't . . . Er, don't tell Mum about my arm, alright? You know how clumsy I am. She'll just worry and give me Laura's toddler scissors or something.'

'I won't. Just like when you cut your leg at hockey last week, right?'

'Right,' Tori replied in a sad voice, her green eyes wide as they found mine. 'Just like last week.'

Abbi

'I didn't know you could drive.'

I glance over at Blake, amused. 'You sound shocked.'

'I am. A little.' He looks out the window. 'And I still have no bloody idea where you're taking me or why I agreed to come.'

'Just . . . It'll be worth it. I promise.'

'Let me guess – it's one of your favorite places.'

I grin, changing gear. 'How did you know?'

Out of the corner of my eye, and I can just make out his raised eyebrows and smirking mouth.

'Abbi,' he says. '*Everywhere* you've shown me is your favorite place. The park, the promenade, Holly's . . . Now wherever the hell we're going is, too.'

'So I have a lot of favorite places. Shoot me.' I shrug a shoulder. 'You'll love it here. I promise.'

'You've been right about every other place so far, so I guess I should trust you. But did we really have to go after dance?'

'You work almost every night. This is a place you have to see at night. It adds to the magic.'

'Can you tell me where we're going now?'

'You sound like a child.' I laugh. 'Okay, okay. We're going to Coney Island.'

'Helpful, Abbi. Really helpful.' Blake groans. 'Where and what is Coney Island?'

'Well, it's an island of sorts.'

'You took your smart-arse pills today.'

I giggle. 'Say that again.'

He frowns at me. 'Say what?'

'"Arse".'

I stop at some lights and look at him. He's smiling, his striking green eyes alight with silent laughter.

'Why?'

'Just say it.'

'Arse.'

I giggle again.

'Why is that so funny?'

I shrug as I pull away and turn the corner that leads to the parking lot. 'It's just the way you say it. I think it's your accent – it's that proper British one. A *Downton Abbey* accent.'

A heart-stopping, breathtaking, giggle-inducing British accent.

'I think I'm supposed to be flattered by that.'

'Aren't you?'

'I'm undecided.' He laughs, and we both climb from the car. The sea breeze crawls across the beach to where we're standing, and I zip my sweatshirt up even though it's June and summer is finally taking over from spring.

Where in Brooklyn I'm constantly surrounded by the past, Coney Island is one of the few places untainted by any memories of Pearce. Here, I'm totally free from everything to do with him. I can just be me – the me I want to be.

Maybe that's why I brought Blake here. Perhaps subconsciously, I wanted to take him to a place that has no association with Pearce to work out how I feel emotionally. Because I feel something physically.

I feel butterflies in my stomach when he looks at me, and shivers tickle their way across my skin when he touches me. Every time he laughs I have to fight the urge to laugh with him.

But my emotions are so confused. So frail. So volatile.

And I'm not sure if anyone can handle the rollercoaster that is my fight with depression.

'Where are you taking me?' Blake's voice pulls me from my rapidly darkening thoughts, and I focus on crossing the street to the amusement parks. I look in the direction of the Wonder Wheel standing tall.

'Really? You're telling me you can't see the giant damn wheel over there?' I ask him in disbelief.

'Of course I can bloody see it. That wheel is huge.'

'Well then. We're going there.'

'You brought me to a fair?'

'Of sorts. It's more of an amusement park, really. Plus, the beach is great for a relaxing walk. Sometimes I need a break even from dancing.'

Blake nods slowly. 'So you're telling me you wanted to walk on the beach and dragged me along for the ride?'

'Something like that.' I grin up at him.

'How do you know I didn't have other plans?'

'Because you agreed to come.' I pause as I put my hands in my sweater pockets. 'And you don't know anyone else in Brooklyn.'

We walk into Deno's Park and he nudges me with his elbow. 'Shut up. Are we going on that wheel or what?'

~

'You could have warned me the damn thing wasn't stationary,' Blake grumbles, shuddering.

I laugh. 'It's a wheel. Why the hell would it be still?'

'I meant the carts, Abbi! Damn thing nearly threw me out!'

'Don't be such a wimp,' I tease. 'I'm a girl and I took it better than you did!'

'And I bet you've done it a thousand times. In England, those things have stationary carts. The way they *should* be.'

I turn and walk backwards, smiling at him in the waning light. He runs his fingers through his already messy hair, ruffling it even more, and smiles lopsidedly at me.

'What?'

'If you keep moaning, I think I'll just run back to my car and leave you here.'

He raises his eyebrows. 'You think if you ran from me I couldn't catch you?'

I shrug carelessly, backing into the crowd. 'Why don't you try it?'

His eyes flare, and my heart thumps as I tear my gaze from his and push my way through the people around me. A small giggle bubbles inside my chest, and I clamp my hand over my mouth to stop it escaping. I look over my shoulder but I can't see him anywhere, so I cheat, skipping out of the park and onto the boardwalk.

My feet hit the wood, my footsteps barely distinguishable from those around me. Children storm up and down the boardwalk, laughing and shouting as they chase each other, running circles around their parents. I sidestep to avoid two small boys screaming at each other as their father pretends to be a monster.

I'm momentarily distracted by the memory of Maddie's father doing the same thing to her and me as our pigtails flew wildly behind us. We nearly always went onto the beach to try and outrun him but it failed every time, ending with us both rolling around in the sand. But that was the fun part – all of us knew how it would end, and although her dad pretended to be mad, he always laughed just as hard as we did. And he still chased us the next time we came.

My lips curve upwards, warmth spreading through my body. For once a happy memory – one that defined a huge part of my childhood. One that will stay with me forever.

'I told you I'd catch you.'

I jump and scream, pressing a hand to my chest. Blake's hands are hot on my arms, even through the material of my sweater, and he laughs loudly as I let all the air whoosh from my lungs.

'You ass!' I breathe out, shoving his chest. 'I can't believe you just did that.'

'What? Scared you or caught you?' He grins, and his eyes hold a playful challenge.

'Both,' I reply, putting my hands on my hips and staring up at him.

His grin widens, a hint of a small, sassy boy sneaking through. 'You shouldn't try to run, Abbi.'

'And why's that?'

He steps forward, his toes almost touching mine. I take in a deep breath, my eyes fixed to him as the contradictory sparks of serious and teasing flash through his green eyes and captivate me.

'You can't run from someone who really wants to catch you. That's why.'

I close my eyes for a split second, and in that time, it seems like the evening sky gives way to the night one. I could swear it wasn't this dark five minutes ago, but maybe I'm wrong. Maybe I've been standing here with my eyes on Blake's for longer than I thought.

'Then the cotton candy inside the amusement park should be really, really scared right about now,' I whisper.

His lips twitch on one side. 'Maybe it's not just the cotton candy that should be worried.'

My chest tightens, a mixture of fear and apprehension restricting my ability to breathe. Anticipation sneaks its way in, winding itself around the stronger feelings of fear and beating it down. I feel it taking over, tingling through my whole body, even down to my toes. My lips part of their own accord, making my shallow breaths feel scratchy as my mouth and throat go dry.

Blake's eyes flick to my lips, and I can see the indecision flitting across his features in the mar of his brow, the twitch of his mouth, the slight clench of his jaw.

Do it. Don't. Do it. Don't. Do it. Don't.

My feelings battle inside me, clashing over and over until I'm uncertain whether I want to end it and either grab him or run from him or stay here. Just stay here – his body closer to mine than I thought I'd ever allow and his eyes searing into me every place they look.

Slowly, he reaches a hand up and tucks my wayward hair behind my ear. 'Let's go scare some cotton candy.'

He steps back and turns toward the amusement park, walking in the direction of it before I can respond. I stare after him for a few beats as my body relaxes, a tinge of disappointment nudging at the back of my mind.

I welcome that nudge. I welcome it because it tells me what I wanted to know. It tells me there's something there for Blake that's more than physical, more than pure attraction. It tells me he's slowly chipping away at the walls I've so carefully constructed.

More than that, it reminds me of what it's like to feel something other than pain, guilt, and self-loathing.

I quickly slip my fingers beneath the wrist of my sweater and hold onto my pulse point for a second. My strong, racing pulse.

For the first time in over a year, I don't just feel alive.

I feel like I'm *living*.

I run after Blake, catching him as he's leaving the park again. He's holding cotton candy on a stick, and when he recognizes me, he holds it out to me.

'Where's yours?' I take the stick. 'Thank you.'

'I don't like candy floss that much.'

'Candy floss.'

'No. We are not going there again. Absolutely not.' He shakes his head, and we walk straight across the boardwalk to the beach.

'Go on. Please. Just once.' I look up at him through my eyelashes and pick some cotton candy off the stick, putting it in my mouth and letting it fizz on my tongue.

'Bloody hell,' he mutters. 'Fine. Candy floss. Happy?'

I smile sassily at him. 'Very. I love the way you talk.'

'Love it, or find it funny?'

'A bit of both, actually.' I pick some more of the pink sugar off. 'But in the best kind of way.'

'Then you won't mind if I do this.' He reaches over and takes a chunk of my cotton candy, shoving it in his mouth with a grin.

'Hey! I thought you didn't like it!'

'I said I didn't like it much. Not that I didn't like it at all.' He leans over again and takes some more. I swat at him as he laughs, and he bats back at me. Our arms tangle, and my hand ends up hooked around his elbow.

My fingers flex against his tightened bicep, and instead of pulling my hand away, I curve it round his arm. He steps closer, our sides brushing together, and I wait for the tensing of my back, the flood of fear. Whatever I'm expecting doesn't come. I feel nothing but comfort being so close to him.

I take the stick of my cotton candy in my other hand, the one wrapped around his arm, and glare up at Blake as he takes a third piece.

'For someone that doesn't like this stuff much, you're really pushing it.'

'I have to have the taste for it. Apparently I have that taste tonight.'

I roll my eyes but the smile on my lips gives me away. His own smile warms me, and when he takes yet another piece of it, I get ready to yell at him. Instead of taking it to his mouth, he puts it to mine. I stick out my tongue, and he puts the pink fluff on it. It melts straight away.

Blake turns his head out to sea as we walk slowly across the sand. The breeze blows through my hair, and I sigh silently. My arm tightens around his again, and he pulls me into his body more. I rest my head against his bicep, still picking at the cotton candy, and wonder what has really changed in the last three weeks.

I don't need to ask though. Not really.

Something so simple has changed. Something so trivial, yet so important to me. Something I never thought I'd do again. Something, three weeks ago, I would have laughed at.

Something called trust.

Because, a voice in the back of my mind whispers, I trust Blake.

Heart and soul.

~

I stare blankly at my ceiling. The whiteness of it is so clean. So *clinical*. And it does nothing but remind me of the starkness of my room in St. Morris's and the starkness I tried so hard to leave behind when I returned home.

My fingers twitch and my eyelids close and open rhythmically. They're the only parts of my body that are moving. The rest of me is deathly still, and I can feel myself remembering why I hate white so much.

White is a blank canvas. Anything can be drawn onto it and anything can be projected, meaning anything can be seen. Anything at all – like a shadow puppet, or a crazy piece of art.

Or a memory.

A memory can form and instead of it playing behind your eyes, you could watch it on the plain surface in front of you. Instead of it staying locked up inside where it should be, it could break free, a movie playing only for you.

My hands, linked together by my fingers and resting on my stomach, tense. My eyes burn and my head pounds as a memory pulls itself up from the depths of my mind. I'm sinking, falling deeper and deeper into the past, flattening under the suffocating weight of it.

And everything stops.

I can't feel my heart beating. I can't feel the rise and fall of my chest as I breathe frantically, gasping and choking as I take in too much air too quickly. I can't feel my legs despite my best efforts to move them, and my arms feel like lead weights against my body. I'm paralyzed, stuck in a day long past, facing a person I trusted and loved. Facing the person that betrayed me and abused me in the worst ways. Facing the person that drained the will to live from my body day by day.

It's like I'm straight back there. It's as real as the day it happened.

I'm shaking just as hard as I was then; I'm just as scared as I was. I'm still cowering under the cold blue-green eyes that pinned me in place, and I can still feel the throbbing of my ankle as I fell backwards. I can hear my voice as I pleaded with him to stop, to calm down, to just take a step back and breathe for a minute. I can hear my crying over his deathly calm voice, the one that was more threatening than any amount of yelling he could do.

And the worst, I can feel his skin against mine. I can feel the tightening of his fingers as he grabbed my wrists and pinned them against the bed, the heaviness of his body as he pushed me into the mattress, the soreness of his thumb digging into my jaw as he held my face level with his.

I can hear his raspy whisper as he quietly threatened me, and smell the lingering essence of beer and vodka on his breath as it swept across my face.

I can hear, see, feel.

Everything.

All of it.

Just as clearly as when it really happened. It's there, playing in front of me, around me, on me.

Real.

I know it's not. A tiny part of my mind is screaming at me that it's not real, it's not really happening, it's all in my head, but my logic can't override my fear. I can't break free from the hold this Pearce has over me.

I can't rid myself of the pain or the feeling of dirt across my skin. I can't stop the sobs that are wracking my body or the floods of tears I know are falling from my eyes. And the shouts. I can't stop the shouts, because I want it to stop. More than anything. I just want it to stop. I need it to stop. I can't make it stop, though, because I'm not in control.

I can do nothing but ride it out. I can do nothing but lie here, watching the memory play out in my mind and on my ceiling. I can't fight it, I can't focus on anything other than this. It's the last memory I have of him. The worst one. The one that crushed whatever spirit I had left. It's the one that tipped me over the edge.

And it stops.

He's gone. The touch of his hands, the smell of alcohol, the blackness as I held my eyes tightly shut, it's all gone.

And in its place is the warm embrace of my mom, rocking me gently and whispering in my ear with a shaky, tear-filled voice that everything will be okay.

Blake

If emotions were visible, Abbi's would look the way the sky does when there's a huge storm brewing. They'd look like the clouds do at the point of indecision, when they're not quite sure whether or not they want to let loose and pelt you with everything they have. Her frustration each time she fucks up a step is like a bolt of lightning; fast, startling, and deadly. Her determination is the thunder, rolling overhead, peaking and dropping every so often.

And the storm is visible in her eyes. In her eyes, I can see the heavy clouds, full of rain, the way I imagine her eyes are full of held-back tears. The shadows there are darker than usual, and they just keep darkening, taking her over.

She *pirouettes* out of time and stops at the *barre*, smacking it with her hands. She grips it tightly, bending forward and hanging her head so her chin touches her chest. She looks so helpless standing there, her back heaving with the deep breaths she's taking to calm herself.

I recognize it. I recognize it all.

This is her having a bad day, one of the days when the depression claws at her and doesn't let up. When it won't let her breathe or even think for herself.

I watched Tori act the same – the uneven steps, the uneasy leaps and turns, the overwhelming anger at something you should be able to but can't control. And then I held her while she cried it all out.

I won't watch Abbi cry it out. I can't watch her do that.

I cross the empty studio floor, the rest of the class long gone, and stop just behind her. Her knuckles are white from her strong grip on the *barre*, and I uncurl her fingers from it. She flinches like my touch is burning her, and I take a deep breath in, reminding myself she's not really here. Whatever is driving her right now, it's not completely her.

Depression is a crazy thing. It can take the most headstrong, rational person and turn them into a quivering, blubbering mess of heartbreak over seemingly nothing at all.

Abbi's head is still hanging and her eyes are focused on the floor. I pull her into the center of the room silently, the only sounds the swishing of our shoes against the floor. I stand to her side, wrap an arm around her back, and cup her chin with my other hand. I raise it up slowly so her eyes are facing the corner of the room, and take my hand away to rest it on her stomach.

Seconds pass until she moves *en pointe* shakily, and I give her a minute to gain her balance before I walk around her. My eyes never leave her, flickering up and down her profile, from the furrow in her brow to the downturn of her lips. I guide her round, feeling the movement of her stomach as she breathes in and out again.

She drops from *pointe*, and shoves my arms away. She tears her bun out and lets her hair fall loose as she storms across the room. Her hands fall back on the *barre* and she steps back so she's leaning right forward.

'Abbi—'

She shakes her head. Her silence is worse than any word she could say or any sound she could make. Abbi turns to face me, her hair falling naturally around her face and her eyes filling with the tears I know she's been holding in. Her lips quiver as she swallows, and I've never seen anyone look quite as vulnerable as she does right now.

'I can't do it,' she says so quietly I can barely hear it. 'It's not working. I can't dance today. I'm just one big mess.'

I look at her dead on, my stomach twisting at the absolute pain in her eyes. She's no mess. Her emotions might be, but she isn't. 'Then you're one hell of a beautiful mess.'

She shakes her head again. It's like the few sentences she just said are all she can manage. She looks like every ounce of fight is draining slowly from her body. Today, she looks an awful lot like giving up.

Her hands rub her face, her thumbs swiping under her eyes. I want to say something – anything – but I can't find the words. Hell, I don't even think I *have* the bloody words. She drops to sit on her ankles, resting her forehead against her knees, and links her fingers. Her arms stretch out in front of her making her sleeves rise up, exposing her bare skin.

My heart stops.

If we'd been anywhere else I wouldn't have noticed. If it had been any other day, I wouldn't have even looked.

The harsh studio lights bear down on her, highlighting the thin white lines that crisscross on her wrists. The lines that speak louder than words, cry harsher than any sob and hold more pain than any other injury.

But I can't look away. I can't tear my gaze from them, even as I'm transported back to my sister's room.

I see the very same lines on Tori's arms, some white, some pink, some still red. The bumps, the bruises, the accidental cuts – the second I saw her arms it all made sense to me. But it was still too late. I was still too late.

I shake the memory away. Abbi's looking at me, her eyes wide. She realizes my gaze is falling to her wrists and stands quicker than I've ever seen her move, yanking her sleeves over her hands. Her feet pound against the floor as she runs toward her bag.

No. Not this time.

I race to her and stop in front of her. She crashes into me, and I grab her shoulders to stop her from going anywhere. Tears spill from her eyes and she fights me, turning her shoulders and wriggling as she tries to get away from me. Her head shakes, and mine does too, both of us stuck in limbo until one of us gives in.

But I won't give in.

I won't let her go.

It's not a want anymore. It's not an interest, a concern for her. It's a need. I need to know what would cause her to do that to herself.

I need to know what it is that's so bad it would make her take something to her beautiful skin and break it that way.

'Let me go,' she begs. 'Please, Blake.'

I shake my head. 'No. Not until you talk to me.'

She tries harder to throw me off her. 'There's nothing to talk about!'

'That's bullshit, and you know it.'

'It doesn't matter. It doesn't matter anymore. None of them matter a single damn bit!'

'It matters to me.'

She stops moving. Her eyes crash into mine as she snaps her head up, and her lips purse. 'Well it shouldn't. It doesn't matter to me anymore.'

'Then why are you hiding them?'

'Because I hate them!' She finally knocks my hands off and turns, walking a few paces before stopping. 'I hate them and everything they are. Everything they mean. Everything they remind me of. *I hate them.*'

Her voice is thick with tears both falling and unshed and her shoulders rise and fall with each heavy breath she takes. Standing in the middle of this huge studio, she looks tiny. And with her shoulders falling forward, her head hanging and her arms tucked around her, she looks completely and utterly broken.

She looks exactly how my heart feels.

Silence lingers between us. No words are spoken, and I'm waiting for her to say something. Anything. Even if she just tells me to piss off, that'll do, even if it's not what I want.

'They remind me of how things were,' she whispers, her voice barely there yet seems to echo off the walls. 'They're everything my life was. Everything I don't want it to be again. They're hideous. They're the ugliest thing I've ever seen, and

I can't believe I ever thought what caused them was beautiful. They taint my skin in the worst way, and I'm ashamed of them. If I knew I'd be stuck with them for the rest of my life I would never have done it or I would have cut even deeper.' Her voice trails off at the end.

My stomach rolls. 'Don't say that. Ever.'

'It's true.'

I press my chest against her shuddering back, pull her into me, and rest my cheek against the side of her head. My hands take her arm and I ease the material of her leotard up to her elbows. She breathes in sharply and squeezes her eyes shut when I touch my thumb to her wrist.

The scars stretch up the inside of her arm, crossing each other and disappearing under her sleeve. I can barely believe what I'm looking at – each one of them is perfectly healed, some of them barely visible to my eyes. I know we see different things when we look at her arms.

'How many?' I whisper, my voice thick. 'How many are there?'

'I don't know. Hundreds, maybe. Everywhere. They're everywhere.'

And I wonder how I missed it. Her body is always covered. Where the other girls wear no tights and short-sleeved leotards, Abbi is always wrapped under opaque tights or leggings and long sleeves. Even out of class, she's always hidden.

I brush my thumb up her arm, running it over the light bumps. 'Why? Why did you do it?'

'Because it made the pain stop.' She breathes, brushing her thumb along her skin after mine. 'No matter how much it hurt, it always made it stop.'

'I don't understand.'

She laughs sadly, tears still streaming down her cheeks. 'You don't have to understand. It's better if you don't.' She curls her fingers around her sleeve and pulls it down, covering her arm back up. My hands drop from her and she steps away.

'What if I want to understand?'

Tired eyes look back at me. 'Then you're stuck wanting, because I'll never tell. Not you.'

I frown. 'Why?'

'Because . . .' she says in the softest tone I've ever heard her use. 'You're much too perfect to be tarred by the mess that is my imperfect life. You're much too perfect to know anything about the things that haunt me. I would never forgive myself if I destroyed you the way I'm so destroyed.'

'You're not destroyed, and I'm far from perfect.' I take her chin in my hand, making her look at me, and rub my thumb across her cheek. It wipes away a tear only for another to replace it. And another. And another. 'I'm nowhere near close to perfect, and even if I was, it wouldn't make me want to know everything about you any less than I do right now. It wouldn't stop me wanting to look into your eyes and put that spark I'm pretty fond of back in there. You might think you're imperfect, and you might be right, but there's nothing more perfect than imperfection. If I cared about true perfection I'd be stuck chasing something that doesn't exist for the next forever.'

Abbi shakes, her eyes closing.

'Everything you see as a flaw – your scars, your demons, your darkness – that's what makes you so damn beautiful. The only flaw is that you can't see it. But I can. I see it every single time I look at you, and I won't stop bugging the crap out of you until you can look in the mirror and see it for yourself.'

She half-laughs, half-sobs, and her legs buckle. I catch her and pull her to me. My hand slides to the back of her head as we sink to the floor. Her hands grip my leotard, her face pressed into my chest, and I hold her shaking body against mine tighter than I've ever held anyone or anything before.

~

I twirl the empty beer bottle between my hands repeatedly. Tori's face stares back at me from the bookcase, her green eyes illuminated by the sunshine in the background and her brown waves framing her cheeks. Her smile is wide and it's a genuine one. A rare occurrence, something that could come and go faster than a shooting star. Sometimes I was afraid I would miss it if I blinked too slowly.

Now I have a permanent smile. A constant reminder of the girl that was buried deep inside, fighting a battle only she truly knew.

The only problem with that picture is it feels almost empty. It's been almost ten years since she died, and every day that picture has lost a little of its light. The warmth has slowly left it, more so since I left London and arrived here in Brooklyn.

As much as I love Tori, a part of me resents her. A part of me hates her for leaving me to do this alone – what we should have been doing together. A part of me can't forgive her for the choices she made, and I don't know if I'll ever be able to. It still hurts as much as it did the day she died. I don't think it'll ever hurt any less.

My phone rings from the kitchen side, but I make no move to answer it. And it rings. And it rings. And it rings. Then stops, before starting up again. I leave it to go to voicemail for a second time, still teasing the neck of my bottle, and clench my teeth when it rings for a third time. Only one person would call me this persistently.

My mother.

I lope across the kitchen and snatch up the simultaneously ringing and vibrating device. 'Mum.'

'Whatever took you so long?'

'Hello to you too,' I reply sarcastically, leaving the bottle by the sink.

'Attitude, Blake,' she chastises me. 'I was only calling to arrange our dinner on Thursday.'

'And it couldn't wait until tomorrow? It's midnight.'

'Not here it isn't.' She sniffs. 'Besides, you are awake.'

'Fine.'

'Have you found anywhere for us to eat? Not that place you work at. You know I'm particular about my seafood.'

And the rest of your life.

'Actually, I thought I'd cook,' I reply.

'I thought you had dance class.'

'I do. But that doesn't mean I can't still cook, Mum.'

'It would be much easier if we just went out somewhere.'

I grit my teeth. 'I have another guest. Someone I want you to meet.' *If she agrees.*

'Oh?' Her voice goes up an octave, and I can tell I've finally got her attention. 'A girl?'

'Yes.'

Mum is silent as she thinks it over just like she thinks over every single detail of her life. Have dinner in a fancy restaurant or let your son cook and meet someone important to him – it shouldn't be a hard choice. She should go for the second option without even needing to think it over, but I don't expect her to. I expect her to push for the restaurant.

'Okay,' she agrees, albeit reluctantly. 'Call me when you finish your class and you're home. I'll come when you're ready. I suppose one night of your cooking won't kill me.'

'Gee, thanks, Mum.'

'You're welcome. Now go to bed. I'll see you on Thursday. Goodbye, Blake.' She hangs up before I can respond. I scowl at the phone and slam it on the side, wondering if I've just made a very, very bad decision.

Abbi

Dr. Hausen looks at me expectantly, her eyes soft behind her glasses. As usual, her hair is pinned back from her face, but instead of her usual suit, today she's wearing jeans and a sweater. Her clipboard is nowhere in sight, her hands clutching a steaming mug of coffee.

At least there's no damn clicky pen.

Today isn't our usual meet. Today she's supposed to spend the day running group workshops with the guys here at St. Morris' instead of her one on one appointments, but she's here with me instead. She's taken an hour of her time away from them to sort out the mess flying around my head.

'So, tell me more,' she finally says. 'You weren't exactly descriptive in your phone call.'

I take a deep breath in and push my sleeves up. I lay my hands palm up on my legs, exposing the scars for her to see. It's unnecessary; she knows exactly what they are and what they look like, but the words are caught in my throat. The only way I can tell her is by showing her.

'Tell me,' she repeats. 'You don't have to hide here, Abbi, you know that. This is a safe place for you. Dig deep inside and find the words to tell me.'

'Blake . . .' I swallow. 'He saw them.'

'How?'

The words that were stuck just seconds ago come flowing out. I tell her about the flashback, how real the memory of the night Pearce almost raped me was, and I tell her how it made me feel. I describe to her how I know I should have stayed in bed, but instead went to class and messed almost everything up. And then I say how nothing makes sense to me anymore, because Blake shouldn't have reacted the way he did.

'How should he have reacted? In your mind,' Dr. Hausen prompts. 'What's the "right" way for him to react to your scars?'

'He should have grabbed his stuff and got away from me. He should have been horrified by them the way I am, and he shouldn't even think about coming near me again.'

'What did he do?'

I look at the floor, my eyes tracing the boxed pattern on the rug beneath us. 'He held me. He held me and wouldn't let me go. Even when I pushed him away, he held me again and again and he didn't let go of me. He let me cry into his chest, and he didn't promise it would be okay. He didn't make me promises no one can keep.'

'What did he say?'

'He just promised he would be there. That's it. I cried harder than I have in so long, and he just promised he'd be there until it didn't hurt anymore, but that's impossible. He can't be there until it stops because it'll never stop hurting.'

'How do you know that?'

'I just do. I know he won't be there all the time, but a part of me wants to believe it.' I look at her. 'Is that silly? That after the last few weeks of not wanting to believe him, I suddenly do. It sounds silly to me.'

'You said last time you trust him to an extent. Have you thought that maybe your switch in feelings is you starting to trust in *yourself* and *your* ability to make decisions? After all, if you trust him, there's no reason not to believe what he says, and if you believe it, there's no reason not to want to.'

I chew on my bottom lip for a second, peeling a bit of skin off with my teeth. 'I guess that makes sense.'

'Tell me how you felt when Blake saw your scars. That moment you realized it wasn't your secret anymore.'

Fear.

Nothing but pure fear.

It was the fear of explaining. Of him knowing everything,

really everything, and learning that my depression runs deeper than the scars themselves. It was the fear of him learning everything Pearce did to me, how he abused and defiled me, and of him walking away. I was scared he'd walk right out of the studio and I'd lose the only person I trust other than Maddie. And then there was – and still is – the fear for me.

That's the strongest fear I have where Blake Smith is concerned. The fear that he might just break my heart if he walked away.

'That's why he can't know,' I explain. 'It's selfish and imma-ture, but every time I see him I feel like I'm losing a little part of myself into him. It's like he has a hold on my heart and each time we dance, laugh, play, he tugs it a little closer to the palm of his heart. Nothing scares me more than the thought he might just take it with him.'

'He didn't run at the sight of your scars. They're the physical embodiment of your depression, the way your feelings mani-fested themselves, and he didn't go. What makes you think he'd leave you behind if he knew about what you've suffered?'

My eyes go to the window, and loud laughter creeps in through the open window. They're all down in the yard waiting for Dr. Hausen to finish here with me, and for a moment, I want to go and join them. I want to lock myself away from the world and settle into the routine that structured my life for a year. Here where it's safe and there's no reason for me to feel anything for anyone.

'Abbi?'

'Pearce tried his damned hardest to go the whole way. If it wasn't for Jake walking in as he was about to rip off my pants, he would have. But that doesn't mean I feel any less dirty or any less ashamed. I still feel dirty from it and what happened afterward. I feel damaged by it, almost. If Blake knew what he'd almost done . . .' I trail off and shake my head.

'If Blake knew . . .'

'You know what? It doesn't matter. Blake won't find out. No one will.'

Dr. Hausen puts her mug of coffee on the table next to her and leans forward, sliding her glasses from her face. 'You can't always keep things a secret, no matter how buried you think they are.'

'But I can try. I can always try.'

~

The rain is comforting. It beats steadily against my window, breaking the silence that's resting heavily in my room. The droplets run down the glass, racing each other to the bottom. The calming effect it has on me is more important than ever today.

The last few days have been a never-ending chain of emotion. The flashbacks have been so strong I've found myself checking the mirror to see if there's a bruise somewhere on my body or if it's in my head. I can feel myself falling into the darkness again, spiraling downward without any control.

But I know we all have a darkness inside us.

For some people it's obvious, a heavy cloud hanging over them wherever they go. For others, like me, it's a silent whisper, like a gentle spring breeze. It's always there, swirling around me and sinking into my skin as I try desperately to fight the pull. There are many ways to describe depression, and I've heard them all. I've thought them all at some point.

A demon. A black hole. An empty abyss. A clawing hold.

They're all right yet they're all so wrong. Everyone has their own experiences of it, their own way of fighting, their own way of coping. I've finally worked out what depression is to me, and I know in my heart that's the only reason I haven't desperately searched the house for something with a sharp edge.

For me, depression is the ever-present sinking feeling weighing my heart down. It's the constant downturn of my lips and the dullness of my eyes. It's the heavy sigh I breathe when I realize there's yet another day to get through. And it's the tiny breath of air in my ear that reminds me it's so easy to end it all.

Emma Hart

But for every inch of darkness inside, there's a centimeter of light.

It's the light that keeps me going. It's the promise of tomorrow in the setting sun and the certainty of next week on the calendar. It's the lifelong dream of the little girl inside that refuses to give up. It's the 'what if' that counters every dark thought.

The light is the single star surrounded by a sea of darkness. It's the spot you're drawn to, each and every time. The spot you can't let go.

There are so many spots of light in my life – my parents, ballet, Maddie . . . Blake. The problem is I only have two hands, meaning every time I hold onto one of them, another floats away until I grab it back again. A vicious circle that will just keep turning.

But I know this. Which means I can fight it. I can push against the pull, smile through the tears and shine a light in the dark. And, one day, I can fight it and I can win. One day I'll control the depression, not the other way around, and I hold onto that thought each and every day.

I glance to the clock and realize I have to leave to meet Blake. I'd love nothing more than to stay here in bed, in the silence of my house, and avoid him. Since I have to see him for dance, avoidance isn't an option, so I have to pull on some big girl panties and face him.

The sky has cleared when I get downstairs so I leave my coat behind. I splash through the puddles like a child as I head toward Starbucks. My feet are twitching with the need to dance – but not alone. Despite what's happening in my head, my heart and my body are crying out for the closeness and security dancing with Blake brings me.

'If I didn't know better, I'd say you were about to walk right past me.'

I turn in the direction of his voice and smile. 'Good job you know better, isn't it?'

His lips curve upwards, and I cross the street. He's leaning against the wall, his hands in the pockets of his jeans and his eyes intent on me from beneath his hair.

'You could really do with a haircut,' I say, noticing the way it's curling over his ears.

'Hi, Abbi. I'm great, thanks, hope you are too. Oh, no, I haven't done much today. Just work. What's that? Oh, same old, same old. Joe shouting, Matt moaning and crazy people ordering more seafood than is healthy. And yes, you are correct, I do need a haircut.'

'You know, I can see you really annoying me doing that.'

He pushes off the wall, grinning. 'So my shining manners haven't annoyed you yet?'

'*Yet.*' I laugh. 'There's still plenty of time.'

'Then I should probably tell you you're having dinner at mine on Thursday before you are annoyed at me.'

I look at him. 'I am, am I?'

'I think I was supposed to ask instead of tell you.'

'I think that's usually how it goes, yeah.'

'Well, see.' He shifts uncomfortably, looking more like a sheepish teen than a grown man. 'Mum is here this weekend, and I'd rather cook my own food than go for a meal in New York with her.'

'And where do I come into this?'

He shifts again, and I stifle my smile.

'I kinda, sorta, maybe told her I'd cook because I wanted her to meet you,' he mumbles.

I raise an eyebrow when he stops outside Prospect Park. 'Why did you do that?'

'Because I was hoping it wouldn't mean I'd have to put on a damn shirt and remember my posh-boy manners in some bloody overpriced restaurant.'

'And it worked.' I purse my lips. 'By the way, I'm impressed you knew how to get here from Starbucks.'

'Yeah, I used Google map, but whatever.'

I laugh. 'So you need me to come and have dinner at your place and meet your mom on Thursday after dance.'

'My mum.'

'Huh?' I glance over my shoulder at him as I pass the many memorials guarding the opening of the park.

'My mum,' he repeats, his lips tugging into an amused smile. 'Not my "mom".'

'Seriously? There's a one letter difference. Same thing. Freakin' British.'

'Bloody Americans.' He laughs, making me smile. 'But yeah. Basically. Please?'

'What do I get out of this?' I tease.

'You get to . . . er . . . Well, I'd say meet my mum, but that's not always pleasant. She's kind of . . . particular about people. She's also probably a little pissed she spent three years trying to marry me off to various daughters of her friends' and I'm still single.'

'You're making this sound so appealing I can barely contain my excitement.'

'I'm not convincing you, am I?' He sighs. 'I guess I'll have to learn how to iron a damn shirt and shine my shoes. And to think, I was going to make lasagna.'

I pause and turn to look at him. His lips are turned downwards, and his shoulders are up by his ears like he's paused mid-shrug. If he thinks he's fooling me, he obviously thinks I'm stupid, because I can see the glint of laughter in his eyes.

'Oh, alright.' I sigh the words out heavily, playing along. 'I'll come over. Can't have you *ironing* now, can we?' I roll my eyes.

Blake grins, and we start walking again. 'Ironing is the cruelest kind of torture.'

'You're so male it's unreal.'

'And to think it was only a couple of weeks ago you were checking if I was all male.'

Ass. 'I'm still debating it, actually. I think it's the eyelashes – you have girly eyelashes. They make you pretty.'

'Pretty? Flippin' pretty?' He shakes his head. 'You could seriously damage that manhood calling me pretty.'

I smile. 'But you are pretty. Like a little poodle puppy with a bow on its head.'

'You did not just compare me to a poodle, Abbi.'

I cover my mouth and nibble on my thumbnail. 'It's fair,' I argue. 'You just sprung a Meet The Parents on me.'

'Yeah.' He scratches behind his neck. 'You know, you don't have to. I suppose I could survive the posh-boy torture for one night.'

'No. I said I would, so I will.'

'It was the pout mixed with puppy dog eyes, wasn't it? That's why you agreed.' he says. 'I knew that would work.'

'Pfft. You do good puppy dog eyes, pretty little poodle, but no. I just really love lasagna.' I shrug, and he nudges me with his elbow. I shove him back, fighting my laughter, and he reaches for me. His arm curls around my shoulders, pulling me close to him, and I wrap my arms around my stomach. His thumb rubs across the material of my sweater on the top of my arm, relaxing me.

I remind myself I'm in a place safe from the past. That I'm in a place where only the present is important. The past and even the future are irrelevant. Only the here and now matters, and the here and now is a touch so casual and comforting that means so much. And there isn't a part of me that wants to pull away from Blake.

We walk in silence for a while, only birdsong and the rushing of the ravine breaking the peace, until we come to one of the rustic shelters that stand on the edge of the lake. The wooden buildings gaze out over the water, and I can clearly see Duck Island from here even though night is starting to fall.

'We always seem to be somewhere when it's getting dark,' I comment absently, stepping from Blake's hold and walking to the edge of the shelter. I look over the water, a few lone ducks still swimming along.

I see him shrug as he steps up beside me. He rests his elbows on the ledge and leans forward, his bicep brushing my arm.

'Hiding in plain sight,' he says simply.

I blink harshly, suddenly glad for the darkening of the sky. Something I said so casually, like it meant nothing, and he's remembered it. He's remembered it and somehow he's applied it to everything we've done so far. He's letting me hide right where he can see me.

He seems to understand so much about me – about how I feel, how to deal with the crazy breakdowns that can happen any second. He doesn't blink at them and nothing seems to faze him. It's unnerving and reassuring at the same time.

'It's my favorite time of day,' I admit, twiddling my fingers. 'Right now, when day is giving way to night. It's the point I can drop the fake smile and stop pretending like everything is perfect. There are so many shadows and dark places I can barely recognize my own amongst them, and it's a relief.'

'You can't pretend all the time.' He turns his face toward mine, and his eyes are so serious I have to fight not to look back at him. 'Anyone who smiles the way you do can't have a fake one all the time. Either that, or you're an even better actress than you are a dancer and I don't see how that's possible.'

'Maybe not all the time,' I say slowly and quietly. 'I don't always need to pretend. Sometimes it really is okay.'

'Like when you dance.'

I tilt my head toward him, my eyes meeting his through my hair, and I whisper, 'Like when I'm with you.'

Rain begins to fall again, splashing into the lake and bouncing off the roof of the shelter. Blake smiles softly and reaches his hand out, pushing my hair from my face. He tucks it behind my ear and his thumb brushes my cheek.

'Then I feel obligated to make sure you don't have to pretend everything is okay tonight. I feel like it should really be okay.' He straightens and walks backwards. 'Come and dance.'

'What?'

He steps out into the rain, his eyes on me, and holds his arms out. The rain is steadily getting heavier, soaking him. His t-shirt clings to his body, showing every inch of muscle on his body, and I can't help but look. My eyes can't help but trace the light indents separating each pack of muscle on his stomach and they can't help but comb over his chest and broad shoulders.

I know how solid those packs of muscle are. I've cried into them. I've clung to those shoulders. I've been held by those arms. Each time he's been there, never expecting anything more than what I've given him. *And I haven't exactly given him much.*

Guys like him shouldn't exist in real life. I wasn't lying when I told him he's too perfect for me to destroy. He is. His looks, his dancing, the way he's always there . . . I never expected to meet anyone after Pearce and I definitely didn't expect to meet anyone like Blake.

Someone pinch me. I have to be dreaming.

'Come dance,' he repeats, spinning suddenly.

'You're insane.' I shake my head. 'I'll get soaked.'

Blake grins. 'Isn't that the point of dancing in the rain?'

'It's getting crazy out there. I'm getting wet even standing here because of the damn windows!' I move into the center of the shelter. 'Freakin' hell.'

'So what's the problem? Come on.' He holds a hand out, his long fingers begging me to grasp them. I look from his hand to his eyes, his twitching lips, his wet hair dripping down his face.

'I . . . No.'

'Trust me.' He's not asking me. 'Trust me, Abbi. Just two minutes. That's all you have to do. Just take my hand and dance in the rain with me for two short minutes.'

'Why are you so determined to get me out there? If you want to dance, we can do that here.'

He steps back under the shelter and takes my hovering hand. He's wet but heat radiates off him and wraps around me. Our faces are inches apart as I look up at him and he down at me.

'Because I see the way you lose yourself when you dance and I want you to lose yourself like that with *me*. I want you to get lost in me. It's selfish but I don't care.'

I breathe in sharply and try to ignore the way his grip on my hand tightens. 'I don't . . . I don't know if I can let myself,' I whisper.

'Sure you can. You just admitted you don't have to pretend with me. And you don't.' Blake takes my other hand and slowly pulls me forward. 'All you have to do is close your eyes. I promise you, you won't get lost alone.'

'Close my eyes?'

'Yep.'

I take a deep breath in, hardly believing a walk in the park has turned into something so insane. So scarily thrilling.

I close my eyes.

'Now what?'

'Now, you feel,' he answers, pulling me forward. The first drops of rain hit my head and face, cold against my skin.

'Feel what?'

'Everything.' More rain. 'Feel the rain on your skin. Feel the touch of my skin against yours. Feel the wet ground slipping and sliding beneath your feet. And dance with me like your life depends on it.'

The rain is cold as it beats down against us from all directions. My hair is already sticking to my face, and I can feel my clothes clinging to every part of my body.

One of Blake's hands leaves mine and settles on my waist, pulling our bodies closer. I rest my hand on his shoulder, and he spins us round. He spins us and spins us and spins us until I no longer know which way is up. Until our bodies are held together by bunches of wet material, and I'm sure mud is halfway up my jeans from all our stepping and splashing in the small puddles forming around us.

His hands are hot against me. His whole body is a raging inferno, contrasting the iciness of the rain against my back. He spins us again, completely in control, and a small laugh leaves me as the ridiculousness of what we're doing sinks in. My head tilts back, and I laugh again, feeling the drops hit my face. I imagine how we must look to someone walking past; dancing on the muddy grass in the pouring rain, laughing like we don't have a care in the world.

But we do. We both have cares, we both have secrets we keep from the other. Dance is our freedom to lose ourselves.

I open my eyes for the first time since he told me to close them and raise my head back up. His green ones stare back at me, unguarded and raw. In them I see a myriad of emotions: uncertainty, pain, happiness, and shadows that are close to mirroring my own. Shadows I've never noticed before, never had any idea about.

We stop moving, and I swallow. He raises our clasped hands to the side of my head and scrapes my wet hair from my face.

'Trust me,' he says softly, his words barely audible over the steady beat of nature's music.

My eyes close at the soft sweep of his lips over mine. My back goes rigid, but as his fingers stroke across it and our mouths meet for a second time, it relaxes. I relax into him completely, losing myself the way he wants me to.

I'm losing myself in a way I never thought I would again.

I'm losing myself in the steadiness of his hand on my back, his chest pressing against me, his lips caressing mine.

I'm losing myself in him.

Blake's face hovers in front of mine as he draws back, and neither of us speak for a second.

'What was that?' I whisper, breaking the silence, too afraid to talk louder in case it breaks this moment.

Because this is the defining moment. It's the one that's been building between us – the one that would make me or break me. The one in which the lines between friends and more blur, warping into something that can and will change everything.

He laughs lowly and lets my hand go. His fingers run through my hair as he stares into my eyes. 'That was me keeping my promise. I got lost right along with you.'

I let my hands slide across his shoulders and clasp behind his neck. 'Do you get lost often?'

'Only when I'm with you,' he whispers.

I feel light, lighter than I have in a long time. Like I can truly breathe and I'm not being suffocated by the weight of my feelings. I have to grab this moment while I can, because I know if this is the only moment I ever feel this way, if tomorrow I go back to being drowned by the darkness, I'll regret it if I don't. If I don't take a risk right now I'll forever hate myself for it.

So I raise myself onto my tiptoes and press my lips to Blake's. My body flattens against his, and he tightens his grip on me, kissing me softly and slowly.

A fire sparks in my stomach, the flames flickering and growing with every pound of my heart against my chest. A fire I don't think anything or anyone could put out.

And I let the flames flicker, I let my heart pound, and I let the rain fall down onto me. I let the world pass me by, and I lose myself wholly in Blake.

Blake

Abbi perches on the edge of my sofa, fidgeting with my TV remote. She's staring blankly at the screen but not really watching it. I dry my hands on a tea towel and join her on the sofa, putting my arm along the back of the cushions.

'Don't be scared,' I tease her. 'I promise Mum won't eat you.'

She punches my knee gently, leaning back and resting her head against my arm. 'I'm not scared.'

'Liar.' I twist a lock of her hair around my finger.

'Maybe a little,' she gives in. 'I just . . . I don't know.'

'I didn't exactly paint a great picture of her before. We don't have the greatest relationship, I admit, but she's not all bad.' There's a knock at the door, causing me to take a deep breath. 'And she's here.'

Abbi swallows and sits up straighter, tucking her hair behind her ear. I pause for a second before getting up to answer the door. I open it to the woman I grew up with.

Her blonde hair is perfectly coiffed, not a grey hair in sight, and her eyes are as vivid as ever, framed delicately by mascara. Powder creases in the light wrinkles covering her face, and the smile on her face could almost – almost – be described as genuine.

'Blake!' Mum holds her arms out and wraps them around me a little stiffly.

'Mum.' I try to inject some excitement into my voice but it falls flat. Luckily, she doesn't notice.

'You look well.' She steps into the apartment, and her eyes flick around the front room, lingering for a second on Abbi.

'So do you. Mum . . .' I turn, and Abbi is standing in front of the sofa, her hands clasped in front of her. 'This is Abbi. Abbi, this is my mum, Cara.'

Mum shakes Abbi's hand and they exchange pleasantries. Abbi looks nervous but puts on a wide smile anyway. It only just occurs to me that I might have forced her into this. Tori hated being around people, especially people she didn't know, and I've never seen Abbi talk to anyone at ballet other than me or Bianca.

Well, shit. Now I feel like a class jerk.

'Er, Mum, can I get you a glass of wine? Dinner won't be long. It's just cooking now.'

'That would be lovely.' She sits herself on the sofa with the elegance given to her by her staunch middle-class upbringing, the one she pressed heavily onto me as a child . . . Yet I still throw myself back on the sofa the way I did when I was three.

'Abbi?' I glance her way as I open the fridge and pull out Mum's favorite Pinot Grigio.

'Hm?' She looks a little more relaxed.

'Wine?'

'Oh. Um, sure.'

I pour three glasses and carry them into the front room. I take a seat next to Abbi, resisting the urge to throw myself down. The fact I still have a rebellious streak at twenty-one amuses me somewhat.

'So, Blake,' Mum begins. 'Tell me about your job.'

'At the restaurant?' I raise my eyebrows.

'Do you have another job I don't know about?'

'No.'

'Then yes, that's the one I'd like to know about.'

Deep breath, Blake. 'There's not much to tell, really. It's not bad hours, it pays well, and it's fairly close to here. It gets rather busy on a weekend, as these places do, but nothing too hard to handle. My boss is a good guy to work with, and I've already got better on the seafood side of things.'

'Wonderful.' Mum smiles. 'I'm glad it's going well for you, darling. Mind you, I didn't think it could be worse than that dreadful job you had in London. I will never understand why you took it in the first place, not when Yvette Mayfair offered you a job in her restaurant.'

'Yvette was paying me less an hour than the other place. It was worth it for a year to get the last of the money I needed to live here.'

Mum sniffs. 'Yes, well. Like I said, this job sounds like a much better alternative for you and your skills.'

'I agree.' I look at the clock. 'I have to check on dinner. I'll be right back.'

I put my glass on the table and all but run into the kitchen. I feel a momentary twinge of guilt for leaving Abbi alone with her, but my God, five minutes in her presence and I'm already regretting agreeing to have dinner with her.

The lasagna is done and I plate up. After calling Abbi and Mum into the kitchen, breaking what I imagine was a slightly awkward silence, I take the opportunity to ask Mum about everyone back home.

'Your father is working too many hours, as usual,' she replies with a heavy sigh. 'I keep telling him to give that junior of his the simple work – you know, phone calls and filing and the like – but he refuses. Insists the boy is merely a helping hand until Jason goes to university in September and comes to do work experience with him.'

I frown. 'I thought Jase was going up in the United academy? He's one of their best players!'

'Yes, well, that's still an option. He hasn't quite made his choice yet, but obviously university is the better option for him. Your father is working on it.'

I bite my tongue to stop myself snapping at her. 'Mum, Jase's wanted to play for that team since he was old enough to kick a ball. He has a chance now, a real chance. Surely you can't take that away from him?'

'I'm doing nothing of the sort.' She sniffs again and sips her wine. 'He needs to understand he has options. Not everyone has to go off and chase a crazy dream.'

Abbi's foot touches mine gently under the table, and I take a deep breath, smiling falsely.

'Of course. He should explore his options.' The ones he wants to. Not the ones forced onto him by overbearing parents.

'So, Abbi.' Mum turns to her. 'What do you do besides dance?'

'Oh. Nothing right now,' Abbi replies quietly. 'Dance takes up most of my time.'

'Blake has told me what a wonderful dancer you are. The way he speaks, I'm surprised you're not already in Juilliard.'

'I wasn't well when the last auditions came round, so I've had to wait it out. I'm still recovering now, but hopefully I'll make the next ones.'

'You will.' I smile at her, and she returns it.

'Such a shame,' Mum muses, the sympathy in her voice real. 'Lovely you're recovering, though. If you don't mind my asking, were you terribly ill?'

I freeze.

'Well.' Abbi puts her fork down on her plate and looks up. 'I guess that depends on how you view "terribly ill". I wouldn't say so, not anymore, but then I guess depression is only as bad as you let it be.'

Heavy silence falls over the table, and I catch the tremble of Mum's hand.

'You poor thing,' Mum responds, her voice as steady as ever. 'What a dreadful thing to deal with for someone so young.'

Like you don't know.

'Yeah, well, it's like I said. It's only as bad as you let it be. Thankfully, I have some control over it now, and dancing helps. Oh, and Blake. He's very supportive.'

'I'm sure he is.' Mum looks up at me, her eyes getting colder by the second. I raise an eyebrow questioningly, playing dumb. She glances toward the watch on her wrist, setting her cutlery down. 'Is that the time?'

'It's only eight-thirty,' I say casually.

'Yes, well, I'm afraid my jet-lag is catching up, and I have an early meeting tomorrow, so I'm going to have to call it a night. I'm ever so sorry.'

Liar.

'Oh, that's a shame.' Apparently, I lie as well as she does . . .

'You understand, don't you, Blake?'

'Of course, Mum. Do you need me to phone for a taxi?'

'You're quite alright.' She stands, smoothing out her skirt. 'I hired a chauffeur for my stay. I considered a car, but everyone knows you simply don't drive in New York.'

I stand and follow her into the front room where she grabs her bag. 'Well, it was lovely to see you. Even if it was only a short visit,' I try.

'And you, darling. You look well. Anyway, I must get back to the hotel and get to bed.' She pauses by the front door. 'I'll phone you before I leave.'

I smile, leaning in and pecking her cheek. 'Great. Have a safe journey across the bridge.'

'Have a nice evening.' She shuts the door behind her, and I breathe a sigh of relief, leaning against it.

I shake my head. Flippin' heck. That just went from bad to worse to downright hellish.

'That went well,' Abbi says dryly, echoing my thoughts. 'Like a train crash.'

'I was waiting for the unicorns and rainbows to burst through the door,' I reply.

'I don't think she likes me much.'

'I wouldn't worry too much. She doesn't particularly like me either.' I shrug, and she giggles. 'What's so funny?'

'This is totally off topic,' she begins. 'But when you talk to her you speak differently. You got all posh-sounding the second she walked through the door. I thought I'd stepped into Buckingham Palace or something.'

I groan. 'Really? I thought I'd left that hoity-toity shit at Gatwick airport.'

She props her chin on her hand, smiling. 'I kind of liked it.'

'Really?' I tilt my head to the side and sit back down. 'How much did you like it?'

'*Downton Abbey* liked it.'

'Which means . . .?'

'I watch that show religiously just for the accents. So, really, really liked it.'

'How much is really, really liked it?'

'I think it speaks for itself, Blake.'

She stares at me with wide, amused eyes, and the curve of her pink lips is too tempting. I press my mouth to hers, then brush my lips across hers softly.

'Liked it that much?' I murmur, my face close to hers. She nods, and I lean in again, placing my hand at the side of her head. My fingers tangle gently in her hair, my thumb brushes across her cheek, and she moves closer. She clasps her hand around my arm, holding onto me, and I urge her into deepening the kiss. She does, and as I flick my tongue across her lips, I can taste the lingering flavor of the wine we've been drinking. Her grip on my arm tightens, and I pull back reluctantly.

I might not know the reasons behind her pain, but I'll be damned if I'll push her into something she's not comfortable with.

'You're so in tune with me it's scary,' she whispers.

'I'm not sure about that,' I reply. 'But if talking like a right posh bastard gets me a kiss like that, I'm gonna do it more bloody often.'

She laughs quietly, opening her eyes to mine. Her eyelashes tickle her skin when she blinks, and the vividness of her eyes has me almost drowning in them. Looking at her like this, this close to her, Mum's visit is barely even a memory.

Something about Abbi Jenkins has a hold on me I couldn't break if I wanted to. She's got me so strongly that I almost forget everything else exists when we're together, and each touch we share dulls the pain of the past as she drives me to look toward the future.

And I don't think she knows just how much she amazes me.

Abbi

My hand hovers over the studio door uncertainly. One phone call from Bianca is all it's taken to drag me down here, yet I don't even know why I'm here. It's not a class day, and I can't think of anything she could say in person she couldn't tell me over the phone.

I curl my fingers around the handle and pull it open. The faint sounds of the piano drift back to me, and I realize Fridays are one of the days she teaches her younger class. Now I'm even more confused why I'm here. Still, I walk down the hall and peek through the door.

Two rows of little girls dressed in baby pink, lilac or pale blue leotards face the front, all doing *demi-plies* perfectly in time with the music. My lips curve into a smile. They all look adorable.

Bianca notices me and says something to the girls. They all nod, never breaking their dancing. She walks toward me, tall and regal, and joins me in the hall.

'I'm glad you came down,' she says.

'I'm a little confused why you needed me here.'

'It's simple.' Bianca smiles. 'A friend runs a ballet studio on the other side of the city for teens, and she's putting on a production at the end of August of *Swan Lake*. The group of children she was using for the animals are no longer able to be a part of it, and as the show is a sell-out, she refuses to cancel it. She contacted me last night and asked if my girls would like to take the place of the animals. It means a lot of hard work for them, but I know they can do it.'

'And where do I come into this?' I look from the tiny dancers to Bianca.

'I can't keep my eyes on every single girl as they learn the steps. Their time to learn their parts is limited, so I need help.'

'You . . . You want me to help?'

'I can't think of anyone better for it.' She touches my arm. 'I'm not asking this as a favor, Abbi, I'm hiring you to help me. I'll pay you, and who knows, if everything works well, I may have need of an assistant permanently.'

I swallow, pressing my fingers to the window. 'I don't know if I can do it. I mean, I don't know if I'm ready to do something like that.'

'I called Dr. Hausen this morning,' Bianca admits quietly. 'I asked her for her opinion, and she believes it'll be good for you. She and I both agree that having a job will focus your mind on something other than the way you've been feeling lately—'

'You noticed.'

'And there's no better job for you than doing this – the very thing you love. I adore letting myself go and dancing, but my favorite part of everything is watching the delight on one of these girls' faces when they finally get that step they've been stuck on for ages. And –' She taps my shoulder, making me look at her. 'There's nothing better than seeing someone find herself and start to live again.'

'I guess you're right. It would be good for me, and ballet does make me feel alive. Really alive.'

'Having an incredibly handsome partner with a British accent goes a long way, too.' Bianca winks at me playfully. I blush. 'I knew it!'

'I have no idea what you're talking about,' I lie, my lips twitching. 'Blake and I are friends. Very good friends.'

'Abbi, honey, I've seen the way he looks at you. There's no friendship in that look.' She pats my shoulder, leaning into the door, ready to open it. 'But as much as I'd love to go all gossip girl on you and grill you, that's not my business. I also have a class to teach, and perhaps an assistant to introduce?'

I drop my small smile, take a deep breath in, and gaze at

the girls. They're still dancing, all in perfect sync. It wouldn't be hard to teach them. I know *Swan Lake's* dances like I know mine and Blake's *pas de deux*. Besides, if Dr. Hausen thinks it's a good idea . . . Maybe it's time to step outside of my comfort zone again.

'Okay. I'll do it.'

Bianca beams and opens the door. She claps her hands three times, and the girls all stop, moving into first position. I hover by the door, my stomach rolling as nerves kick in. I clasp my hands in front of my stomach to hide their gentle shake.

'Girls, I have someone to introduce to you.' Bianca gestures to me. 'This is Abbi, and she's my new assistant. She'll be helping me in your classes for the next few months.'

I walk toward Bianca slowly, feeling twelve pairs of inquisitive eyes on me. 'Hi, everyone.' I wave slightly.

'You're all wondering why I have an assistant. Right?' Bianca looks out at the nodding heads. 'Well, at the end of the summer, instead of doing our usual production here for your parents you'll be part of a larger one on stage. A friend of mine is putting on *Swan Lake*, and she needs some animals. I told her I have twelve little animals in my lower class that would be perfect for her.'

Gasps and squeals radiate through the group, and I can't help but smile at the looks on their little faces. They're completely shocked but wearing the biggest smiles known to man, and the excitement shining from their wide eyes is testament to how much they want to do this.

'It's going to mean a lot of hard work from you, girls, and perhaps some Saturday sessions, too. That's why I have Abbi; she's kindly agreed to help me teach you your dances. She's one of the best dancers in my higher group, so in ten years' time when she's jetting around the world as a famous ballerina, I expect you all to brag about how she taught you to dance in your first on-stage ballet.' Bianca winks at me again. 'Now, I'm going to be *really* naughty, so sssh. I'm going to get a glass of water and leave you with Abbi to get to know each other for ten minutes.'

All the girls immediately crowd around me, excitedly bouncing. I get the feeling their excitement is more from the news they'll be doing their first dance in a real theatre, but I feel wanted nonetheless. And it feels kind of . . . nice.

'You really gotta stop throwing me these curveballs,' I mutter as Bianca passes me.

'I have no idea what you mean.' She leaves the studio, followed by her uncle, and I'm suddenly alone with twelve very chatty seven and eight year olds.

'How about we all sit down?' I suggest, looking out at a sea of faces. 'Then we can all chat easier. Okay?'

Choruses of 'yeah' and 'okay' come to me, and I sit cross-legged on the studio floor. They all copy me, sitting with their backs perfectly straight.

'How about we introduce ourselves first? Our name, age, and a little something about us. I'll start.' I shift slightly. 'I'm Abbi, I'm eighteen, and I'm training with Bianca to get into Juilliard.'

As we travel around the group, I learn names I've already forgotten and the strangest facts about them. Kids really don't have a brain-to-mouth filter, and I have to stifle my giggles more than once.

'Okay, now that I know you all, do you have any questions for me?'

Rosie, a small girl with brown hair puts her hand up. 'Have you ever danced *Swan Lake*?'

I nod. 'Lots. It's my favorite ballet.'

'How many characters have you been?'

'Quite a few. I was Odette when I was sixteen for our Christmas production.'

'I thought everyone danced *The Nutcracker* at Christmas?' Bailey, a blonde girl, pipes up.

'Sometimes, sometimes not,' I answer. 'I did that when I was a bit older than you.'

'I bet you played Clara.'

I don't know who said that, but I gasp in pretend shock. 'How did you know?'

'You look like a Clara,' the same voice says matter-of-factly.

'Have you ever been on a really big theatre stage?' Another voice.

'Yep. Lots of times.'

'What's it like?'

I smile, remembering the feeling of being free on the stage in the darkness, save for one spotlight on you. 'It's the best thing ever. It's really fun, and not nearly as scary as you think it'll be. You'll see.'

'What if we're too scared to try?' A small voice asks me. I look in the direction of it, and it belongs to a red-haired girl hiding behind her hand whose name I don't remember.

'I don't believe any of you are too scared to try. I bet you'd all be awesome on stage.'

'But there's so many people.'

'It's dark,' I counter. 'You can't see them, and you forget all about them when you dance. I promise. And, don't tell Bianca I said this . . .' I gesture for them all to lean in, and they do. 'But if you're really, really, *really* scared, just imagine all of the audience in their underwear with bunny rabbit ears on their head.'

All the girls burst into laughter, giggling uncontrollably. I grin at them all, knowing I've made the right decision to help Bianca with them.

If twelve happy, excited faces can't brighten my day three times a week, then there's no way I should be out of St. Morris'.

~

The house is eerily quiet with Mom and Dad away on a business trip. It's the first they've taken since I came home, and the freedom is wonderful. There are no worried eyes glancing at me if I'm still in my pajamas at midday or intent stares whenever I go near the cutlery draw.

If I stood a chance at not burning my toast, I'd really enjoy buttering it.

I'm a little scared. The knowledge of what I could do is tormenting me. The weight of my pain from the last few days – although peppered with everything that's good – is slowly getting too much to bear. Now I'm alone, it feels heavier than ever. So I do what I should do and pick up the phone to call Dr. Hausen before Blake arrives to practice.

'To what do I owe the pleasure?' Dr. Hausen answers.

'I'm home alone this weekend and I'm scared,' I blurt out.

'What—'

'I'm scared I won't be strong enough to fight the urges if I have a bad night. The last time I was home alone was the night that was almost my last. What do I do if I feel like that again? Maddie isn't here this time.'

'Abbi . . . Abbi,' she says softly. 'I need you to breathe for me. Like we practiced before. Slowly.'

She's right. I need to calm down. I need to breathe. I close my eyes with the phone still against my ear and breathe slowly to Dr. Hausen's counting. It takes a few minutes, but eventually my breathing goes back to normal.

'Good. That's good. How are you now?'

'I'm okay. It was just . . . a moment.'

'We're all allowed a moment every now and then, Abbi. They make it better – they allow you to let it all out.'

I nod, like I'm reassuring myself. 'Right. Moments are okay. I know that.'

'You do know that, and that's why I'm certain you'll be fine this weekend. You know how to stop the panic attacks and you know how to battle the urges. The only difference is that this time, you must do it for yourself, and not your parents. That's all.'

'For myself,' I mutter. 'Okay. Myself.' I sigh heavily.

'I'm on call this weekend. If you need me, you know where I am. You can call or you could even come to St. Morris' if you need the company.'

I promised myself the day I left I'd never go back unless it was for our sessions, but it sounds almost appealing right now.

I can't deny I'm tempted, but I draw on that inner strength everyone is so certain I have and politely refuse.

'Blake will be here tonight to practice, and I can always go and see Bianca in the studio if I need to. I think I'm just panicking for no reason. I'm sure I'll be fine.' I'm not sure who I'm trying to convince.

'You know where I am if you need anything.' The line clicks off, and I put my cell down.

Deathly silence wraps around me, allowing whispers to nudge at my mind. Allowing twitches to take my fingers. Allowing my teeth to bite down on the inside of my cheek.

I grab the remote and turn on the television to drown it out. Despite what I said to Dr. Hausen only a moment ago, I'm not sure I will be okay. My eyes flick to the clock above the fireplace to see how much longer I have to be alone. Blake should be here any second, so I sit on my hands and blow out my cheeks. But the whispers are still there.

They're always there.

In the back of my mind, they start off almost completely silently, getting louder and louder every minute you ignore them until they're screaming at you. Until their shouts and yells take over everything else, until the urges they support are the only things you can focus on.

I focus on the *Gilmore Girls*, listening to their voices instead of the anxiety building in my body. Goddammit, where is Blake? I rock forward slightly and push my whole body weight into my hands to stop myself. My eyes travel to the window where I can see the sun illuminate the low-lying clouds as it begins its descent.

Descent. Rib to hip. Knee to Ankle. Ankle to toe.

I screw my eyes shut, shaking my head.

Descent. Eyes to feet. Fist to cheek. Cheek to floor.

And I can feel it pulling me under. A memory of my own creation, born of my own anxiety. I can feel the tug in my mind and the shake of my body as faint music replaces the television and Pearce's hands replace mine.

★

'Pearce,' I'd begged him. 'Please, let's just go. You know Owen won't ever give you what he owes you, not when you still owe his brother money.'

'It's not even his real fucking brother, Abbi. You know that. Owen's just a spineless little dick who hides behind him.'

'It doesn't matter what Owen is. You know he won't pay up!'

He grabbed my arm and slammed my back against the brick wall. Pain seared through me, but I bit my lip and hid my grimace.

'Gary isn't here this weekend. Five minutes inside Owen's house with him, and the asshole will cough up the cash.'

'You don't know that,' I whispered.

'You're not stupid, Abbi. You know I'll get my money.' His eyes burned into me, anger sparking deep in them. 'Don't you? You know I'll get it.'

I said nothing. He pushed me further into the wall.

'Don't you?!'

'Yes,' I replied quietly, turning my face away from him. 'I know you will.'

'Good.' He released me without another word and stormed down the street toward Owen's house. I followed him slowly, letting my feet drag against the floor. My arm throbbed where he grabbed me, and I was certain there was a scrape on my back from the rough brickwork of the wall. I put a hand to my arm and flinched.

And I hoped to God there wasn't a hand print there. I could explain away a bruise if anyone saw it, but there was no explaining a hand print.

Loud knocks at the door pull me from my past, and my arm burns. I look down and see my hand wrapped around it in the same place Pearce bruised me. A hand print never came, but that wasn't the worst injury that night. The worst one was the cut across my leg from the glass he threw.

I say worst, but it was both the worst and the best. It had stung me and numbed me at the same time. It had made it easier to take the verbal abuse he'd inevitably thrown at me like it was my fault Gary had cancelled his weekend away and given Pearce a black eye for his troubles.

'Abbi!' Blake yells over his knocks, reminding me he's there.

I lower my hand from my arm and walk toward the front door. The whispers are there still, stronger, begging me to do the very thing I promised myself I wouldn't. I stretch my fingers out, even digging my nails into my palms too tempting. Even the sting from that would be bad. Too much. Too tempting.

I open the door and look up at Blake. His hand pauses in mid-air and his eyes flit over my face, taking me in.

'What . . .' he says softly. 'Oh, Abbi.'

I look at him, not saying a thing as he steps inside and shuts the door behind him. His hands frame my face, and he wipes away the tears falling down my face. I drop my eyes, hiding them although he'll never know the reason I'm crying and shaking.

'Talk to me,' he whispers, pulling me into him. I shake my head against him, my arms hanging limply by my sides. His touch quiets the whispers but it's not enough. They're still there.

'I think I need to be alone tonight.' I pry myself from his hands and wander into my kitchen.

'Hell no. You're not getting rid of me that bloody easily.' His footsteps echo as he follows me.

I cross my arms and look out the window, my back to him. 'I think I need to be alone,' I repeat.

'I'm not even thinking about leaving until you tell me what's wrong.'

'I'm fine.'

'Yeah, if you can call crying and shaking like fuck "fine"!'

I flinch at the volume of his voice. 'I don't want to talk about it.'

'Abbi.'

'I said I don't want to talk about it.'

'I do. I want to know what's got you so upset. What's hurting you so much?'

'I said . . .' I grit my teeth. 'No!'

'Goddammit, Abs!' he shouts. 'Don't push me away like this! Let me help you!'

'I don't need help!' The words are a blatant lie, but my next are the truth. 'This depression . . . it's destroying me even more than before. Slowly, it's tearing me apart inside. I fight it every day. God, I fight it! Every day it's a fight to get up, to get dressed, to leave the house. Every single day I'm haunted by things that have been and it's hard. It's so damn hard, but I have to keep fighting. I have to do it alone. No one can help me – only I can do that. Only I can make it all better, but I don't even know if I *can,* so Mom, Dad, Dr. Hausen, Bianca, even you . . . You can't make it better. You can't make it go away.

'You can't save me, Blake. Do you get that? *You. Can't. Save. Me.*' I turn around, dropping my arms to my sides, and meet his emotion-filled green eyes. 'I've tried to believe it. I want to believe it, but I'm not a princess, Juilliard isn't a fairy tale castle, and you aren't a prince riding in on a white horse to slay the dragon. Some things in life aren't worth saving, and some aren't able to be saved. I'm pretty sure I can't *be* saved.'

'You're wrong. You can be saved if you'd just let me help you!'

Impulsively I grab a glass from the side and smash it on the floor. Anger, helplessness, frustration, pain; they all heighten inside me to almost an uncontrollable level. But Blake doesn't even flinch. His eyes don't even fall to the glass. They never leave mine.

'Can you save that, Blake?' I gesture to the glass, my chest heaving with every breath I'm suddenly struggling to take. 'Can you?!'

'You can't compare yourself to a broken glass; that's different.'

'No, it's not. Not at all. You see those pieces on the floor? There are hundreds of thousands of shards, and no matter how hard you try you will never be able to get them all and put them back together. Even if you do, it won't be perfectly. There will always, always be a part missing from it. There will always be one piece that you won't be able to keep hold of.

'*I* am that glass! I'm shattered, torn, broken. I'm irreparable.' I walk backwards into the wall, my whole body tight. My trembling hands flatten against the wall, and I keep eye contact with him. 'It doesn't matter how hard you try. I'll never be whole again. I'll never be the princess climbing onto the back of your horse. I will never, ever be the same person I was before.'

He steps forward, and when he speaks, there's desperation tinging his tone. 'You're not the person you used to be because that was never the person you were meant to be. I want to help you, Abs. I wish you'd let me help you!'

'I don't want your help!' I scream, pushing myself into the wall and hanging my head. 'I don't want your help. I want you to leave. I want to be alone.'

The sharp, cooling slice of a blade drifting across skin. The slow, stinging parting of flesh. The warm, relieving trickling of blood. Red against white.

'So you can search your house top to bottom for something sharp enough to cut yourself with?' His words are shorter and sharper than I've ever heard him use, the venom in them chilling me.

My breath catches and my head snaps back up. Our gazes collide. He looks nothing like the Blake I know. His eyes are cold, every sparkle and shine gone from them as they burn into me, slicing into me harder than any blade ever could. I try to curl my fingers into my palms, craving the feeling of my nails digging into them. A brief respite.

'Is that it?' he says in the same biting tone.

Nails. Palm. Sting.

'No,' I answer, but my voice is weak and unconvincing even to me.

'Open your hands,' he orders. I shake my head, bringing my fisted hands to my stomach. 'Open your hands!'

'No!'

His feet thud against the wooden floor as he storms over to me. His hands close around my fists, his fingers prying between mine.

'No!' I cry again, feeling the heat of tears fall over my eyes as he succeeds in dragging my nails away.

'I won't let you do this to yourself.' He grinds his teeth, holding my hands tightly.

'You don't understand!' I sob, my throat closing up as panic takes me over. 'You don't get it. I need something. I haven't for so long, but I can't do it anymore. I need it. I can't keep remembering. It hurts too much. Let me go. Please.'

I shake my arms and kick out at him, desperately trying to get him to let me go. My body thrashes as he pushes his against mine, trapping me against the wall, and I scream, feeling Pearce press against me instead of Blake.

I'm hurled back in time yet again.

Pearce. Music. Alcohol. Drugs. His hand. My face.

'Sssshh.'

I'm rocking. And screaming. Screaming loudly, a scream that breaks even my heart. I can't breathe. Panic. Weight on my body. I need to get it off. Get him off. Get him away.

'Get off. Please. Let me . . . Go. Now. Please,' I sob out. 'Don't hurt me. Please.' I stretch my legs out, and my face is buried in a shoulder.

'I have you.' British accent. Blake. 'You are safe, Abbi. I promise you.'

I'm shaking. Hard. I want him to let me go and hold me at the same time. 'No. Never safe.'

'Yes,' he whispers in my ear, his arms tightening slightly around me. My fingers are curled into his shirt, holding him as tight as he's holding me. 'I promise you, you will always be safe around me.'

I swallow, closing my eyes, and try to regain control of my breathing just like Dr. Hausen taught me. Deep breaths, count to three. In, out. In, out.

'I will never be safe,' I whisper hoarsely. 'There's nothing outside that can hurt me any more than what is inside. You don't understand that.'

'Oh, I understand.' He breathes out shakily. 'I understand that better than you think.'

'You don't. You won't ever get it.'

He releases me, his hands moving to either side of my face. My eyes open. Our faces are perfectly aligned. I'm still grasping his shirt, and he wipes his thumbs under my eyes.

'You know Tori died. What you don't know is I watched her slice deeper and deeper every day until she finally hit gold.' His voice quivers. 'And I didn't do a *single fucking thing* to stop her, because everyone made me believe it was for attention. I've lived with that guilt for ten years. I'll be damned if I'm gonna sit here and watch you do the same thing.'

More tears stream from my eyes at the raw pain in his voice, and I remember and I know. I know because I was so close. So, so close. I was minutes away from nothing, then Maddie found me.

'Saving me won't bring her back,' I croak. 'It won't make it easier and it won't make it go away. Don't save me to make up for not saving her. I'm not a project.'

'I never said you were.' His voice drops to a bare whisper and he puts one of his hands into my hair, his fingers threading through it. 'I'm not trying to save you because I couldn't save her. I'm trying to save you because I don't think I could cope if I lost you too.'

Tears brim in his eyes, and I've never seen him look so vulnerable. I imagine how we must look right now, crouched on my kitchen floor, both of us shaking. Both of us crying. Both of us broken, yet holding onto each other like that's all that can fix us.

'I won't watch you do it too. You are so, so much stronger than that. You are so much stronger than she was, Abs.' He moves his thumb under my eye to wipe away the wetness there. 'You are everything I wish my sister was and so much more, and it's that so much more that means you can push me away all you like because I won't go. That darkness you have inside, the one that pulls you under, I swear I won't let you fall into it. I won't let you fall anywhere unless it's my arms you're falling into.'

I shake my head because I can't. I won't. I don't want to fall anywhere. At all. Because falling means hitting the bottom, and hitting the bottom means pain. Hurt. Anguish.

And I have enough of that.

'I'm not strong, Blake. Not really. I still feel everything and I still think the bad things. I still want to give in. Depression . . . it's like drowning, like being pulled to the bottom of the ocean, except everyone around you is swimming and breathing on the surface. It's like being in a crowd of people where you're screaming and no one can hear you. It's everything nightmares are made of.'

'Then let me be the one to teach you swim again,' he whispers, moving his face to mine. 'Let me hear you and let me be the one to remind you how to live.'

A shudder wracks my body, and I feel the tightening of my chest that always precedes the suffocation of the darkness. I release his shirt and wrap my arms around his neck, burying my face into his skin. Blake's arms go round my body in one smooth movement, holding me tightly against him, and he moves us so his back is against the wall and I'm sitting on him.

I still feel it. I want to feel the sting. I want the sharpness of the blade against my flesh. I want the release it gives me. Until Blake presses his lips to my temple and my heart thuds once. Loudly. Reminding me I'm still alive.

And all there is, is Blake. The feel of his arms around mine. My skin against his. His breath against my ear. The tightness of his hold, so tight it rivals the tightness of the hold my depression has on me.

The sudden clarifying reminder that pain doesn't have to equal feeling. I can live without hurting. I can live without the sting.

My fingers thread into his hair, and he bends his face into mine even though it's still pressed against his neck. He cups my chin and nudges my face upwards. Our eyes meet, and the tears that were brimming in his not long ago have spilled down his cheeks.

'You don't need it. I promise. You're more than that. Don't let it all destroy the person I know,' he whispers and his lip quivers. 'Let me help you, Abbi. Not because of my sister or anything else. Let me help you because I need to.'

'I can't replace her.'

'I know. I don't want you to replace her. I want you to be you. I don't want another sister. I want you. That's it. I don't want us to be skirting around the topic of us anymore. I want you and all your shattered pieces, if you think you can handle all my broken bits.'

'I don't know.'

'Try. Because I won't stop trying.'

I have no doubt. He hasn't stopped trying since our first dance together, and his eyes promise me what his words do. So no matter how much it scares me, no matter how much I want to hide, I give him what he deserves. What, in my heart, I truly want.

'I'll try.'

Because amidst all the chaos and heartbreak holding us together, he is my light in the dark.

Blake

She feels so small in my arms.

Her body is quivering and her chest is still heaving. My top is soaked from her tears, but I don't care. The only thing I care about is the words she just said. Two tiny words that mean so much.

Two tiny words that have the immense power to change everything.

I tangle my fingers in her hair, breathe in, and tighten my hold on her. I don't want to say what I'm about to. I don't even want to think about it, but I have to. I need her to understand that I know. I *know* the pain she carries even if I don't get it.

I need her to understand I can hold onto her broken heart the way she needs me to.

'Tori and I were inseparable. We danced together almost every day whether we had class or not, and when I was eight, we had our dream. We promised each other that when we were old enough, we'd leave London, fly to New York, and go to Juilliard. I always thought she'd go first since she was four years older than me, but she insisted she'd wait for me. She said she'd work and save all her money to get us here, then even if it all fell apart for her, she'd stay and watch me take the college by storm.' I swallow, feeling the same sting I always do. 'She was my best friend as well as my sister, and it drove my parents batty. They hated I was closer to her than my brother – my only brother. My father dreamt of weekend football matches watching his boys play so he could boast to his friends. My relationship with Tori destroyed it. I was never going to be the dirty, ruffed-up boy my father desired me to be on a football pitch. In my mother's words, I was always going to be "the fairy on a stage".'

'Blake,' Abbi whispers, clenching my top tighter.

'We spent hours making our plans. Where we'd live, where we'd work, what we'd see. Tori said more than once we'd be like live-in tourists. I couldn't wait. I wanted nothing more than to achieve my dream with my favorite person. But it would never happen.

'If I knew then what I know now, I would have tried harder to make her talk to me. If I knew I'd lose her just four years later, I would have never left her side. And I definitely wouldn't have listened to my parents denying the very existence of depression. To them it was taboo, not something to be discussed, and there was no way on Earth their perfect baby girl was suffering from it. There was no way she was being bullied at the top-notch private girls' school they sent her to. In their eyes, Tori was doing nothing but seeking attention.

'I hid everything for her. The late night crying sessions were blown off as the time of the month, or a sad film or television show. Even a sad chapter in her favorite book. Every cut or mark on her body was passed off as an injury from dance, hockey, anything. She had an excuse for every single one, and I never questioned it. I was only twelve. I didn't have any reason to believe she would lie to me. Even when she asked me not to tell Mum about it, I didn't ask why. I wasn't blind – where I was the black sheep of the family, Tori was the eldest and the golden girl. But they never cared enough to listen.'

'Blake—'

'I found her.' I pause for a moment, choking back the tears building in me as the memory plays in my mind. 'I found her in her room, curled into a ball on her blood-stained bed. She'd sliced her arms to pieces, but that was nothing compared to the gash on her thigh. She knew what she was doing – the coroner's report later showed she'd severed right through her main artery. Every time I think about her that's what I see. I see her surrounded by her soft toys, each of them a reminder of the girl she used to be. I see her art coursework scattered across her bedroom floor and the knife she'd used to make the cuts. And the worst thing, the thing that haunts me the most is I see her holding her ballet shoes to her chest.

'She knew what would happen. It was never a cry for help, not for Tori. It was always the real deal. And the worst thing about it all is she never should have been alone that afternoon. Jase had a football game, a final of a local competition, and Dad insisted we all went. Tori got to stay behind because she was studying for her exams, but I was forced into going. And I did. I went, and that's what I found when I came home. My last memory of my big sister was always supposed to be of us dancing together at Juilliard, but instead it's of her dead body.'

Abbi's arms slide around me, and she pulls me closer to her. Her fingers splay across my back, like she's trying to wrap every part of me up.

'And no one dares to speak about her. Just me. I'm the only one who remembers she even existed. And it fucking kills me.' I close my eyes as the tears I've fought this whole time spill out and down my cheeks. They roll down silently, nothing like the tears that fell the day I found Tori. I can hear it in my head; my shouts for help, my inconsolable sobbing, the scrambles of my parents, my mother's cries, Kiera's shushing and shuffling of the other kids. Yet over it all I hear one long scream filled with more pain than I ever thought one person could feel. My scream. The one that belonged to the bond I'd had with Tori, the bond that had shattered the second my eyes fell on her broken, still body.

Abbi's arms tighten around me. 'I'm sorry.'

'Don't be sorry. You didn't make that choice, did you? She did. No one can apologize for her mistakes.'

'No, I didn't, but I almost did.' Her whispers are muffled, and I'm certain I wouldn't have heard her if it wasn't my shoulder she was snuggled into.

'What?'

She takes a deep breath and pulls back. Her fingers slip under her sleeves, and she rolls them up to her elbows, doing the same with her sweatpants to her knees. Finally, she pulls her top up, exposing her stomach, and drops her head.

I comb my eyes over her bare skin. Almost every inch is covered with white lines, long and short, deep and shallow, and I can't stop myself from reaching for her. My fingers run over her arms, her legs, her stomach, feeling every bump across her skin.

'Almost,' she whispers, stilling my hands against her stomach. 'I get why Tori did it. I understand. Sometimes it gets too much. Sometimes—' She breathes in heavily. 'Sometimes just once isn't enough. It's addictive. The release you get, however short, it's like a drug. Once you've done it once, you keep doing it, over and over. Tori knew what she was doing, and I did too. I didn't want to hurt anymore, I didn't want to keep getting hurt, but it was too late for me to get out that way, so I took the easy way. The coward's way. I just wanted a life where I'd be happy, where I wouldn't be controlled by him. I didn't want a life where I wondered when the next argument or fight would be, and I was in too deep to get out. I was too broken and too weak to even fight with him anymore. I didn't want that for myself.

'If Maddie hadn't found me, I wouldn't be here now. I tried what Tori did – hit the main arteries and just bled. Unlike Tori, I misjudged it. When I woke up, they told me I was half an inch away from it. If I'd hit it I wouldn't have been around for Maddie to save. It would have been too late for me.'

Him. Argument. Fight.

'Who is "him"?' My arms are tense. The thought that someone, anyone, could have hurt her so badly she wanted to take her own life sparks a fury in me I didn't know I had.

She curls her fingers around mine. '*He* doesn't matter. He can't hurt me anymore. Only I can do that now.'

'You can, but you won't.' I tug her clothes down, covering the marks, and look her in the eyes. 'If it hurts I want to know.'

'It's not a pain you can take away.'

'No, but it's a pain I can ride out with you. I can be there and hold you whenever you need it. You don't have to do this alone anymore, Abbi.'

'I've never been alone,' she whispers. 'When I left the hospital I didn't come home. They sent me to a mental institution. I came home six weeks ago.'

Shit.

I tug her into my body, needing to do nothing but just hold her.

'They sent me there so I couldn't try again. So I couldn't get that half an inch over.'

'Would you have? If you'd come straight home?'

'I don't know. Maybe.' She shrugs, laying her head against me. 'Last year feels like a lifetime away, but even then I remember thinking I didn't get it right for a reason. If I was truly meant to go, if it was meant to work, I would have hit the artery dead on, or Maddie wouldn't have found me. That half an inch saved my life.'

I bend my head forward, letting my lips press against the top of her head. 'I'm really, really glad you missed.'

Abbi curves her arms around me, tucking her legs under her. She turns her face into my chest. 'Me too.'

~

Pain shoots through my neck as I try to move, and cramp takes my calf hostage.

'Bastard,' I mutter, rubbing both my neck and my leg at the same time. This is why no one should sleep on a sofa – especially not if it's only two seats and you're over six foot tall. It's like trying to get a blow-up bed back to the size it was when it first came out the box.

A royal pain in the arse.

I roll over on Abbi's sofa, rubbing my eyes. When I open them, I find her sitting cross-legged on the floor with a book open in her lap. Her hair is flowing over her shoulders, and for the first time since I met her, she's wearing something other than long sleeves. Her tank top and yoga pants show her scars clearly even in the low morning light.

I ease myself up onto my elbow. 'Good reading?'

Abbi pushes her hair back from her face as she tilts her face up to me. 'Depends on your definition of "good" at six in the morning.'

'Okay.' I rub a hand down my face. 'There is nothing that could even be considered good at six a.m.'

She smiles slightly. 'It's my diary. From St. Morris's . . . The mental institution.'

'Ah.' I push myself to a sitting position. 'I can't imagine that's light morning reading.'

A small laugh leaves her. 'Not exactly.' She closes the book and runs her finger across the cover. 'I haven't looked at it since I left. I shoved it in a drawer when I got home and left it there. I didn't want to look at it. I thought it was the most stupid and pointless thing ever – writing in a diary wasn't going to help me get better. Dr. Hausen – my psychiatrist – made me do it. She said even if I just wrote one line a day about how I was feeling, it would help me.'

'Did it help?'

'No.' She laughs sadly. 'I felt like an idiot every single night because it didn't help me in the slightest, but it wasn't supposed to help me. Not then. I didn't realize it until I started reading this morning.'

'Call me stupid, but I'm really not following.'

Abbi brings her eyes to mine. 'It was never to help me get better. Dr. Hausen made me write in it in the hopes I'd look back on it one day and realize how far I'd come.'

'Have you?'

'Look for yourself.' She tosses me the book and it lands in my lap.

I pick up the red, hard-backed book and glance at her. 'Are you sure? I looked in my sister's diary once, and she chased me with my brother's baseball bat when she caught me.'

Abbi's lips twitch into a smile. 'I'm sure. You've already seen me at my worst and there's nothing in that book I won't eventually tell you.'

'Well, okay.' I open it to the first page and start to read, flicking through the pages.

April 6th
I don't know why I have to write in this. It won't help. I can't use words to describe 'how I feel' every day. I don't even feel anything. I'm just numb. Numb to everything.

April 12th
The last pages here are blank. Why? Because I still feel nothing. How can you write when you have no feelings?

April 18th
Mom and Dad keep coming. Maddie keeps coming. Pearce hasn't come. I don't know why it bothers me. Maybe it doesn't. I don't know.

I just want everyone to leave me alone. I wish Maddie had never found me.

April 22nd
Maddie is going. To California. Our crazy dream from our childhood. She's doing it, and I'm stuck in here. I feel. Finally. I feel angry. Angry because I should be going with her. At least Dr. Hausen will be glad to hear I can finally feel something.

April 30th
Group therapy. It's crap. None of them know what I go through, what I remember. None of them are like me. They're

all crazy – screaming crazy. I'm not. I'm just quiet, happy to
be left alone. I wish they would leave me alone.

'You didn't exactly get on board with the everyday thing,
huh?' I smirk.

'No . . . I got better toward the end, but at first I wasn't
interested. I wasn't interested in much of anything, to be honest.
I was too wrapped up in a world of pain and haunted by
memories. They were still too fresh . . . Too real to think about
anything else.' She waves at the book. 'Read as much as you
want.'

I don't miss the way her voice dips, lowering until it's almost
a whisper, or the way she picks at the skin around her nails. I
look at the open diary in my hands and shut it, dropping it on
the floor next to me.

'I don't need to read it.'

Abbi's head snaps up.

'As much as I want to know, you'll tell me when you're ready.
I won't push you into it.'

She looks at me earnestly for a moment before getting up
and climbing onto the sofa next to me. I put my arm out,
and she snuggles into my side, laying her head against my
chest.

'Thank you,' she whispers. 'For not judging me because of
the scars.'

'I would never judge you for marks of your strength.'

'We see them very differently.'

I take her hand in mine, linking our fingers together, and
stroke my thumb across the back of her hand. 'One day I hope
you'll look in the mirror and see what I see.'

'I'll be happy if one day I can look in the mirror and not
see a broken girl,' she says sadly and tilts her head back to
look at me. 'What if it's too much, Blake? What if everything
in my past and yours is too much? What if you see Tori whenever you look at me, or if what I'm dealing with is too close
to what she did? What if . . .' She swallows. 'What if we both

have so much pain inside of us we end up breaking each other's hearts?'

'Hey.' I lean my head back on the sofa, taking her with me, and squeeze her. 'That's a lot of what ifs right there, Abs. You don't know any of that will happen, and if it does, then we'll have to cross that bridge when we get to it. There's no point in dwelling on things that might be, 'cause they could just as easily *not* be. Besides, you can't break something that's already broken. If we both just stay a little broken, we should be just fine.'

She smiles through the hesitance in her eyes, and it's one that lights up her whole face. 'I guess that's one way to look at it.'

I smile back at her, releasing her hand and trailing mine up her arm to cup the back of her head. 'No,' I mutter, pulling her into me. 'It's the only way to look at it.'

I bring her lips to mine and kiss her gently. She curls her fingers into the blanket wrinkled at my waist, and sighs into my mouth.

'By all accounts, I should be running away from any guy that tries to touch me,' Abbi muses. 'But I don't feel like I need to. I'm not scared of us at all.'

'Were you ever scared of us?'

'Of a relationship. Not of you. I don't think I've ever felt like I needed to be scared of you.'

'Well, that's reassuring.' I laugh.

'Oh, shush.' She laughs with me.

I brush some hair from her face and think about the second time we met. 'I guess I was right after all.'

'What?'

'My supposed pick-up line.'

'Oh, god.'

'Oi.' I run my thumb across her bottom lip. 'You don't argue with fate.'

She closes her eyes for a second and runs a finger along her thigh, tracing the place I'd imagine her scar is. When she opens her eyes, she looks directly into mine, emotion shining through in them.

'No. I guess you definitely don't.'

~

Two days without my mother has been bliss. When this morning rolled around, I almost thought she wouldn't call – for the first time ever, I hoped she wouldn't call. Listening to her talk about Dad trying to push Jase into working with him although she knows it isn't what he wants to do made me realize how stifling my life in London was. I never really got that until I tasted freedom. Hopefully, Jase will get the same chance.

For now, though, my freedom is on hold as Mum did call. And demanded I get my ass round to her hotel room right now.

Okay. So she didn't quite say it like that, but she may as well have. The disappointment in her tone was enough of an indicator of how fun this conversation is going to be.

I knock on her hotel room door, shoving my hands in my pockets while I wait for her to answer. She does after a few minutes, a glass of white wine in hand.

'I'm glad you could find the time to come here,' Mum says, walking into her room.

'You honestly made it sound like I didn't have much of a choice.' I nudge the door shut behind me. 'What's wrong?'

'I don't want you to take this the wrong way, Blake, but I think you should come home.'

I stare at her, unmoving, for a long moment before I speak. 'I'm sorry, I don't think I heard you correctly.'

Mum sighs, putting her glass on the side. 'I think it would be better if you came home and moved back in with us. I spoke to Yvette this morning – she said there's a job open for you if you want it.'

'No way.' I shake my head, folding my arms across my chest. 'I *live* here, Mum. You never cared where I lived before – why does it matter so much now?'

'That isn't true,' she protests. 'You know I'm busy with work. I didn't think you'd stay here as long as you have, I'll be honest, son. I thought you'd be back in a couple of weeks.'

'You do realize I'm an adult, therefore perfectly capable of taking care of myself?'

'Yes, yes, I know you are.' She sighs heavily and rubs her temples, like this conversation is wearing her down already. 'I just don't know if New York is right for you.'

It clicks.

'This is about Abbi, isn't it?'

Mum says nothing, busying herself with packing her suit-case.

'Isn't it?' I raise my voice. She hesitates long enough for me to catch it. 'Unreal. Even for you, Mum, this is bloody unreal.'

'She's not exactly who I pictured my son ending up with. Then again, I didn't expect him to be a dancer either.'

'I get it – I do. I'm the disappointment and all that, but I don't get what Abbi has to do with this.'

'She's not good enough for you.'

'What?' I half-yell, half-laugh. 'What the hell makes you think that? Doesn't she have enough money? Enough connections in your social circle?'

'It's not that at all.'

'Then what is it?!'

'She's . . .' Mum slams her suitcase shut, turning and facing me. 'She's *ill*, Blake. It's not fair for you to take on that burden. You know what happens with people like her—'

'"People like her?"' I shake my head slowly, throwing my arms up. 'Exactly what does that mean?'

'You know what it means.'

'So because my sister killed herself, and Abbi has depression it means she will too? God, Mum. Talk about tarring people with the same brush.'

Mum breathes in sharply. 'This is not about your sister.'

'It never is, is it?'

'Blake.'

'No, Mum. It is about Tori, otherwise you wouldn't have a problem with a girl you've met *once*. You know nothing about Abbi yet you feel like you can judge her just because she has depression. Why? Because she doesn't hide it? Because she accepts the fact she has it? What is it that bothers you, really?'

'I find it very hard to believe you have any interest in this girl other than trying to save her because none of us saved Tori,' she spits.

'And she starts again,' I mutter, rubbing my hands down my face. 'It's not because of Tori. Maybe that's what drew me to her in the first place, but when I look at Abbi all I see is Abbi. Not Tori, not the past. I see Abbi and the goddamn future. Do you understand that, Mum? I don't see the weakness Tori had, or the way she gave up. I see a girl who accepts the shit she's been thrown and gets the hell on with it – I see someone with a dream and a fight for life Tori never had. Abbi wants to live, and I want to help her do that. For her. No one else.'

Mum is quiet for a long second. 'You came here for Tori.'

'Wrong. I came here for me. I won't leave because of the promise I made her, but I came here for me.'

'You are making a *mistake*, Blake.'

'I think I'm old enough to decide that for myself,' I reply coldly. 'I'm sorry I wasn't interested enough in law to work with Dad, or attracted enough to the stuck-up girls you shoved in my face for years. I'm sorry I never played football like Jase does, but mostly I'm sorry you and Dad have never been able to accept me for who I am. And I'm not coming home. I'm making a life here in New York for myself. I have a job, a place to live, a route to my dream, and despite what you say, I have a girl I'd move heaven and earth for if I had to. If me being happy is disappointing to you, then that's your problem, Mum.' I glance at my watch. 'Now, if you'll excuse me, I have to go. I have a job to get to.'

I ignore her shocked calls, shouting my name, and disappear down the hall to the lift. The doors shut in front of me, and I breathe out, relaxing my shoulders.

Good God.

I should have done that bloody years ago.

Abbi

I run my fingers down the seam of the short-sleeved leotard I haven't worn for two years. I have no idea if it'll even fit me now.

I breathe deeply and step out of my clothes, ready to pull it on. Even if I only ever wear it at home when I dance in the garage, it's something, and it's more than I would have done before.

I catch my reflection in the mirror as I straighten, the leotard still in my hand. I close my eyes. My number one rule is not to get changed in front of the mirror, not to see the marks that cover my body, but this time it feels different. I feel like I can open my eyes and look at them for the first time ever.

So I do.

My eyes crawl across my slender frame, toned from dancing, and they take in every spot, blemish and scar marring my skin. I look at every one, examining them like I can remember when each one happened. The last ones are the easiest to see – they're whiter, thicker, and more raised than the others.

Each one has a story to tell, each one a scene in a horrifying chapter of my life I can't delete.

I scrutinize them all from my arms to my legs. And finally, I accept them for what they are.

Battle scars.

No matter how unsightly they are or how ashamed of them I am, no matter how I might try to hide them or forget about their existence, that's the bottom line. That's the basic truth I will never be able to escape from.

They're my battle scars, earned over a time when I was honestly fighting for my life. They're the things that remind me that even in the face of true pain, I was able to stay strong and keep fighting. I was able to face each day head on, albeit with fears and worries, but I still did it.

And that's all my depression is now. Another battle scar. A silent one that will never be shown, a scar just for me, but a scar all the same. And just like the others, this too will fade.

Depression: the name given to being strong enough to face the outside world despite the crumbling inside.

I put my legs into the leotard and pull it up my body. It rolls up my stomach, and my arms go in, tugging it all the way up. And it fits. It fits just as snugly as it did two years ago, and the black lycra against my pale skin is more striking than I remember. I step backwards slowly, my eyes on my reflection, and stop. My hair flows over one shoulder, and if it wasn't for the darkened color of it, I'd almost think I was looking at the Abbi I was before.

But I'm not, and I never will again. I'm looking at me, the new me, the me I was supposed to be all along. The broken, damaged me that is somehow still holding onto life.

Somehow.

There is no somehow, I realize as I touch my finger to my cheek. I'm not holding onto life itself – merely the smaller things that make it up.

My parents. Maddie. Dance. Juilliard. *Blake.*

I don't have to hold onto all of them, only a little part. As long as I'm holding onto a small part of them, then I have a hold on life. I just need to remember what makes life worth living, and that's the center of it. They are the things my world revolves around, even if Blake did sneak his way in smoother than a ninja could.

If I can keep a hold on them, I can keep a hold on life. And faced with the honesty of my scars, I know I can.

Because I'm strong.

I'm not a shadow of the person I was.

She is a shadow of me.

~

Blake's hands are warm on my waist as he lifts me from my *plié* and onto his shoulder. My arms are in fifth position, raised and curved above my head, and my back is poker straight. There's nothing comfortable about this position – I think sitting on hot coals would be more comfortable, to be completely honest, but it's vital to our dance.

I take a deep breath as I feel Blake's body shift, and he drops me into a fish dive. His fingers curve around my thigh and he holds me steady as we spin, my body stretched out. He lowers me gradually, spinning at an almost glacial pace, and I move into *arabesque*, one leg out behind me. I bring it down and straighten my body up, Blake's hands moving to my stomach and my hand to *promenade*. I count his turns, and on five, he releases me, leaving me to *fouette* until I drill my way through the floor.

I still, finishing the *adage* section of our dance, and turn my eyes to him. It's the first time I've truly watched him dance. The first time I've truly let myself watch him, and I'm spellbound. My eyes follow his every move, fluid and precise as he dances across the floor. Every step, arm position, turn, leap, every single thing about his dance is beautiful. It's a struggle to stay standing as I watch him. All I want to do is sink to the floor and stare at him dancing the way a child stares at the television.

And he doesn't even know. He's so lost in his moves, so focused on what he's doing, I'd bet anything he can't feel my gaze searing into him and burning holes in his back.

He stops, his variation over, and his eyes slowly open. A smirk graces his lips when he sees me staring at him, and I drop my eyes to the floor.

At least I'm still standing and not on my ass.

I step into my dance with the ease of someone that's done these steps their whole life. In reality, I made them up last night. I walked into the garage after Blake went to work, dressed in my short leotard, and let myself go completely. And this dance, filled with *bourreés*, *coupés*, and one of my favorite steps, an *échappe sauté,* is a dance from the heart. It tells a story from despair to fleeting moments of true happiness, starting off slowly and building in speed until the *coda* section of our dance, when Blake comes back into it.

This dance is easy. True. Real. Free.

This dance is everything I feel when I dance.

Everything I want to be.

Blake's hand clasping mine and pulling me to him signals the start of the *coda,* and I don't bat an eyelid as we dance alongside each other. It's only been mere weeks we've danced together but it feels so much longer. I know, after this weekend, what we have is so much more than just a *pas de deux.* What we have away from the studio strengthens what we have inside.

He knows my every move and adjusts to it without thinking, even when I make a split second decision and change out a step for something else. He doesn't stop, he doesn't say a word, and he doesn't get annoyed. He simply changes direction, falling in with me.

And when his hands rest on my waist again, strong and determined, I push off as he lifts. The explosive motion results in a perfect *grande jeté,* my legs completely straight in their split as Blake lifts me through the air. I feel weightless, like I'm flying, and my drop back down is easy. My feet touch the ground and my knees bend. Blake's hands travel from my waist down my arms to my hands and I push up *en pointe,* arching my back and dropping my head behind me. My arms are stretched to the sides, and the only thing stopping me falling backward is Blake's grip on my fingers.

His lips touch mine, a barely there brush, and he flicks me back up. *That wasn't in the original dance.*

I spin away from him, pause a moment, then turn back. His arms are stretched toward me, his eyes intent on mine, and I spring to him. Like that time in the garage, my hands hit his shoulders, his hands grip my waist, and he propels me into the air above him. Our faces are so close I can feel his breath across my lips, and I smile. My legs split sideways, and I hold them for a long beat, then wrap them around Blake's waist.

He laughs quietly, splaying his fingers round my back. I smile, dropping my face down to his, and wrap my arms around his neck.

'This isn't part of the dance,' he whispers, still laughing.

I shake my head, smiling, and touch my lips to his.

Three weeks ago, I couldn't take the closeness of dancing with him. It scared me. It was too much to deal with. Three weeks ago, I ran out of class because everything felt wrong.

Now, with my body wrapped around his, and him holding me for all it's worth, everything feels right.

~

'You didn't tell me you were changing the dance.'

'You didn't tell me *you* were.'

Blake turns, grinning. 'For the record, I like the new ending.'

I roll my eyes. 'Of course you do.'

'What?' He puts a large plastic bowl filled with popcorn on his coffee table and drops himself backward onto the sofa. 'What do you expect from a guy?'

'Honestly, I don't know.' A sad tinge works its way into my voice.

He leans his head back and looks at me. 'I want to ask why that sounds like an honest answer instead of a sarcastic one.'

'It sounds like it because it is.' I smile sadly and pick some lint off my jeans. 'I really don't know what to expect. He . . . Pearce . . . He gave a new meaning to the words "Always expect the unexpected". He took everything I expected and made me think I was wrong.'

'I'm not gonna like this, am I?' Blake mutters, taking my hand and threading his fingers through mine.

'Probably not,' I admit. 'But . . . I want you to know . . . If any of what I'm about to say makes you feel any differently, I won't be offended if—'

He cups my chin and raises my face so we're eye-to-eye. 'Abbi, there is nothing you could say to me that would make me feel any differently. Whatever's happened to you in the past is just that. In the past. None of that will make a blind bit of difference to how I feel about you right now.'

I nod, silence falling as I try to gather my words. With Dr. Hausen it was easier. My brain had blocked out most of the memories, locking them away and letting them out gradually. Now they're all out. They're ready to haunt me the second I let them.

If I let them.

'I guess I should start at the beginning and tell you Pearce is Maddie's brother. Yep.' I hold my hand up to stop him talking. 'The Maddie you met. Their mom was killed in a drive-by shooting a few years ago. She wasn't the target – she was just an innocent bystander caught in the wrong place at the wrong time. Maddie was there when it happened, and her death all but tore her family apart. Her dad isn't the guy he was, and Pearce did what most grieving people did; he looked for an outlet for his emotions, a way to ease his pain. In high school it was easy enough, so he started staying out at weekends and partying. Alcohol soon turned to drugs, and casual usage became a full-blown addiction. By mine and Maddie's senior year, he was hooked on heroin, but it wasn't so bad there was no Pearce left in him. Or so we thought, and for some goddamn stupid reason, he and I ended up in a relationship.

'I thought I could help him. I loved their mom almost as much as they did – her death killed me, too – but I was wrong. I didn't know it then. I wouldn't know it for a while. Our relationship started as any other did, until he started talking me into going to parties with him. Maddie came too, and it wasn't until then we realized Pearce needed heroin to survive. He was one hundred percent addicted, needing an almost constant high, and if he didn't get that high, he would turn.

'On his comedown or his craving stages, he was volatile. He was almost evil, possessed with nothing but the need for more of the drug. God forbid you got in his way during those times. If you did, it didn't end well for you. He had a barrage of verbal abuse he'd throw at you, and he knew how to throw a good punch.' I close my eyes and whisper, 'And he didn't care who you were. His friend, a stranger . . . His girlfriend.'

Blake's hand tightens around mine.

'As his girlfriend, I got the worst end of the deal. He was paranoid from using the drugs and he was obsessed with the idea his friends were trying to take me from him. I don't know why it bothered him – he didn't really want me himself. I was more an accessory for him, something to look pretty on his arm. Something to hide the reality of what he was.

'Anyway, the paranoia meant I was barely allowed to leave his side at a party. The few times I was, Maddie had to be there, and then she was lecturing me about leaving him, so I ended up just staying with him. Which meant I was there for every stage of his addiction. His craving, his high, and his comedown. I took the brunt of it all. Verbal and physical. He didn't care who I was in that state. All he wanted was the drug, and it's like he thought I was the one keeping him from it. I was, at first, then I learnt it was pointless because he was going to get it anyway. But I still thought I could save him. I always thought I could save him from himself.'

I breathe in deeply, and open my eyes to stop the images playing in quick succession behind them. I need to stop the box of memories opening and flooding into me, taking me under, drowning me in pain. I need to pause it, let the words come as I want them to, not as the past does.

'He's the reason you cut, isn't he?' Blake asks me softly, yet angrily.

I nod. 'The pain from cutting took away the pain from him. When I cut, I couldn't feel the bruises from the punches or the kicks. I couldn't feel the pain inside from the person I trusted, the person I was sure I loved, breaking me into two. I lived in fear constantly. I had to double check what I was wearing, the way I'd done my hair, how I was acting, who I was talking to, the plans I was making. All of it had to be Pearce-approved. I wasn't allowed to look attractive for other guys or spend my weekends with the girls like I used to.

'Maddie kept trying to get through to me. She'd accepted Pearce for what he was – hopelessly addicted to heroin without an escape in sight. I didn't want to accept that, so I didn't. Or maybe I was too scared to accept it. I think that's probably right, considering how much I feared him. Eventually, she gave up because she couldn't get through to me. I was blinded by the Pearce I remembered and a faint childish hope that Pearce would one day come back. He never did and he never would.'

I open my eyes, and Blake holds my hand even tighter. His jaw is clenched shut and his eyes are hard.

'I put up with it for so long. All the abuse . . . The kicks, the punches, the shoves . . . I hid it every time, relishing the winter when I could wear thick sweaters to cover the bruises on my arms – from slipping on the ice. No one knew, no one except Maddie, but even then she couldn't prove it. I'd never admit it. I was stuck in a loop; go out, get hit, come home, cut. It repeated itself several times a week until I finally broke. Until he finally broke me.

'His friends were all assholes, but I'll always silently thank Jake for walking in when he did. If he didn't walk in with the heroin that would calm Pearce, I have no doubt he would have taken it further than he ever did. His temperament, that day, had changed from physically violent to . . . something worse. You know, I can't even say the words. It's been a year, and he never actually did it, but I still can't say them.

'That's when I decided. I knew I'd never been that scared in my life before. I couldn't cry, I couldn't scream, I could barely even talk. My parents were out of town on a work trip, so I gathered all the razors I could find and snapped them under my foot to take the blades out. I was scared they'd get blunt and I wouldn't be able to move to get another, that I'd be stuck in some sort of crazy limbo between life and death until I was found. Then I ran a bath, stripped to my underwear, and climbed in.'

The water had been hot, red hot, but I'd barely felt it as I sank my body into the tub. All I felt was the ice-cold metal already slicing into my palm where I was gripping it so tightly, and the sweet release of my blood breaking through my skin. I opened my hand, looked at the blades, and set them, all except one, on the side of the bath.

'It was freeing, knowing what I was doing. In my mind there was no way it wouldn't work. There was no way anyone could know or that anyone would find me. I was spurred on by the thought I wouldn't be in pain anymore.'

'Weren't you scared?'

'There's no reason to be scared of death if you're already living in hell.'

The blade slid across my skin easily, and a part of me reveled in the splitting of my skin and the spilling of my blood. I took the metal from my skin and touched it to a different place, leisurely moving it across my stomach. I watched in awe as my blood mixed with the bath water, swirling and swilling around me.

A part of me knew this was wrong, knew what I was feeling wasn't right, but I couldn't stop. I had to make the pain stop, because that was all I could feel. I was numb physically, exhausted mentally, and drained emotionally.

I just wanted to breathe again.

Blake's arms go around me, and his chest heaves. He buries his face in my hair, and I squeeze my eyes shut as I remember. I remember the sting, the only thing I felt at all, and I remember counting the minutes and cuts, keeping them in time with the other. One cut per minute. One fresh bleed every sixty seconds.

★

Tears wracked my body, great heaving sobs, and I jabbed the tiny blade into my skin over and over. I wasn't even cutting anymore, I was shredding. I was shredding and mauling my skin like it would make me bleed faster. I sliced my way up my leg to my thigh, where I paused, trying to determine where my artery was. Where I could cut to end it in minutes.

'Then I got desperate. I wasn't bleeding fast enough. I needed to bleed more, faster, harder, deeper. I needed it over, and I needed it over right that second.'

I had only a rough idea. I took a punt. I pushed the razor blade into my skin harder than I ever had and tore it up my leg. Blood spilled out of the gash, flooding the water with a brilliant, vivid red, and I sobbed harder and harder. I sobbed for everything I was leaving behind and the pain that would be caused.

But my pain was greater than any that would be caused by my death. No one could possibly hurt more than I was.

'That's the last thing I remember,' I whisper, turning my face so my ear is over Blake's heart. The steady thumping calms me. 'I passed out from blood loss. I don't know how long I was there before Maddie found me, but she did. I hate myself for that, you know? I hate that out of all the people in the world that could find me that way, it was my best friend. She'd already watched her mom die in front of her, and I'd left the very real possibility she was going to watch her best friend die, too.'

'But you didn't,' Blake says hoarsely.

I shake my head. 'No. I didn't. She called an ambulance, and they saved me. They told me later about the cut on my thigh, but apparently I'd done enough of a job I would have been dead within the hour if Maddie didn't come.'

'What if she didn't?'

'Then I would have haunted her late ass for the rest of her life.' I laugh a little. 'I used to wish she didn't come, but now I'm glad she did. She really did save my life.'

Blake breathes in heavily. 'And goddamn it, Abbi, I'm glad she did.'

'Me too.'

'But her brother or not, I think I might just fucking kill him if I ever see him.'

A smile twitches at my lips. 'You'll be waiting a while. He's in jail.'

'For what he did to you?'

'No. For drugs. Fifteen years. I never went to the police – there was no point. I was too ill to stand in court and I didn't even know he'd been arrested until I came home. He's getting what he deserves. His life is on hold and mine is going on. It's a long, hard slog sometimes, but I'm living. He's just alive.'

Blake strokes my hair gently, his fingers threading through the strands, and I feel him press a kiss to the top of my head.

'Bloody right you're living,' he says. 'And, I promise you, I'll show you exactly what you should expect from a guy.'

'Which is what?'

'Everything you could ever want and need. But that rule only applies to you, because we all have to get what we deserve, and you deserve the world and more.'

I wrap my arms around his waist and bury my face in his neck. 'I already have it.'

Blake

The week leading up to our performance is filled with a heady mixture of work, endless dancing sessions, and watching Abbi fight with herself over the choice she's made about us. I see it every time we dance – the things that haunt her are all too real now she's finally let herself talk to me about it. They're so real even I can see them, and they hang over her like the weighty cloud they are.

I've lost count of how many times I've told her we'll slow down and take a step back. I've also lost count of how many times she's told me to shut up.

Today is the first time I've seen her excited. She's practically bouncing on the balls of her feet with a childish smile on her face as we wait outside her house for Maddie, her boyfriend, and her dad.

'So Maddie and Braden met because of a game, right?' I frown.

'Yeah. Both of their friends challenged them to make the other fall in love with them within a month. Kind of coincidental, I know, but hey.'

'I'm guessing they both succeeded.'

'God, you're clever today.' She grins at me.

I smirk, tugging on a lock of her hair. 'Don't start with me, Jenkins.'

'Or what, Smith?'

'Or this.' I pull her against me and hold her tightly.

'I don't see the problem.' She relaxes into my hold.

'I guess that kind of backfired, right?'

'Yep.' She laughs. 'Okay, um, something you should know about Braden.'

'This doesn't sound good.'

'No, it's not bad. He's just . . . Well, he's kind of obnoxious if I'm honest. He's the guy you love to hate.'

'Fuckin' hell, my reputation precedes me again,' a guy's voice says from behind Abbi.

'Dollar,' Maddie's voice demands. 'Now.'

'Mads . . .'

'No. One dollar, Braden.'

Braden sighs, digging into his pocket, and looks at Abbi. 'You heard this crap, Abbi? She's making me pay every time I swear. My girlfriend and my mother are conspiring against me.'

'So she should,' Abbi replies. 'You swear too much.'

'Thank you.' Maddie takes the dollar from Braden's hand and tucks it into her own pocket. 'Don't worry, it's going to a good cause.'

'Sure as hell isn't,' Braden mutters.

'Hey, if you stop swearing now, you won't have to take me to dinner at all.'

Abbi snorts. 'You're making him take you to dinner with the money you're taking for him swearing?'

Maddie beams. 'Yep. I debated a pair of shoes first, but thought he should see *some* of it. Although, the shoe thing is totally plausible. The amount he swears, it'd only take a couple of months to save up for some Jimmy Choos or something.'

'You're not buying fu—' Braden pauses. 'Fudging shoes with the money you take off me for swearing.'

She narrows her eyes, flicking her hair over her shoulder. 'I'm debating charging you fifty cents for an almost swear.'

I smile into the back of Abbi's head, understanding why Maddie is Abbi's best friend. The girl is bloody brilliant.

'Don't make me threaten you, Stevens,' Braden threatens.

'Honey . . .' Maddie places her hands on his chest and gazes up at him. 'There's nothing you could threaten me with that wouldn't hurt you more. Sweet of you to try, though.' She pats him and winks at me. 'Hi, Blake. Meet my caveman, Braden Caveman, this is Blake.'

'Alright, mate,' I say, and we shake hands briefly.

'I will be soon. Abbi, tell me your dad has beer in that house.'

'Of course he does. It's the fourth of July. What do you take him for?' Abbi scoffs.

'I told you.' Maddie pokes his arm. 'Now you and Blake can go inside and find her dad and do guy stuff.'

'Tryin' to get rid of me, Angel?' Braden looks at her.

'Me? Never.' Maddie turns to me. 'Between you and me, I am. He's done nothing but talk about how this is the first Independence Day he's spent not on the beach, the poor baby.'

'I swear, Maddie . . .'

'Yes, Braden, you do. You swear a freakin' lot. We all know.'

He takes a deep breath but there's a smile tugging at the corners of his mouth. 'You know what? I'm gonna go get that beer.' He looks at me. 'Comin'?'

Go and get a beer, or stay with what looks like Double Trouble. No brainer. 'Yep, I'm coming.'

We all walk into the house, Abbi and Maddie heading toward the stairs and us to the garden.

Maddie pauses. 'Braden?'

'Yes, Angel?' He turns around, a smile on his face.

She twists her lips into an amused smirk. 'Be nice.'

'I'm always nice.' He grins.

~

Abbi was right. The guy is obnoxious, but you can't help but like him. He's honest and has no issues with saying what's on his mind when it's on his mind. Quite like Maddie, so I'm not surprised they have constant banter and entertain everyone around them.

And, since beer loosens people's tongues, she's already added seven dollars to her collection.

'I carry one dollar bills around for that reason,' he grumbles, handing over the ninth. 'She better pick a damn expensive restaurant, I tell you that.'

'She's a girl. She'll have no problems there,' I reply.

'Ha! True that.' He leans back on the chair. 'Better the restaurant than the shoes. She has enough, and half of them are in my freakin' bedroom.'

I smirk. 'So you guys are at college in California, right?'

'Yeah. I grew up there.'

'Why didn't you stay down there for this weekend?'

'Almost did. I would have if it wasn't for Maddie. Fourth of July was her mom's favorite holiday when she was alive. It didn't feel right asking her to stay with my parents when I knew she really wanted to be here. Besides, she misses Abbi like fuckin' crazy when she's at college.'

'Abbi's the same about her.' I look over at them giggling like two kids.

'They're joined at the damn hip when they're together. I remember the first time I came home with Maddie and she introduced us. Abbi was a total different person, but the second those girls got talking she turned into the girl she is right now. I'm pretty sure she hated me at first, if I'm honest.' He pauses. 'In fact, I'm not entirely sure she likes me that much now.'

We both laugh.

'She does.' I watch her as she tucks her hair behind her ear, exposing the side of her face to me. 'She's comfortable with you, at least. I can tell.'

I can feel Braden's eyes on me, as if he's deciding whether or not to say something. The silence lasts only a minute.

'She's told you.'

Not a question.

I nod.

'Everything?'

'In as few words as she could.'

'Shit the bed.' He exhales and turns to look at the girls. 'She trusts you.'

'I know.'

'Nah, man. I mean she really fuckin' trusts you. She could barely tell herself about what she'd been through three months ago, and now she's told you everything. That's important for her, y'know? When I first met her she was a shadow of the person she is now, and she was adamant all she cared about was Juilliard. No guys. She wasn't interested in relationships at all, and who can blame her? That asshole Pearce fucked her over good, and if I'd known it all when the shit turned up in Berkeley I would have ripped his goddamn head off.' Braden takes a deep breath. 'Abbi swore she'd never tell anyone what she'd been through; she was certain the only people that would ever know would be Maddie, Dr. Hausen, and me. She trusts me because Maddie does. But now you know, and *she* told you.

'I tell you what, dude. She's told you, and that means she trusts you more than just the normal way. She's trusting you with her heart and is giving you the power to destroy it. After the way Pearce destroyed her, I can hardly fucking believe it, yet at the same time, it's totally believable.'

'That last statement makes no sense at all.'

'I can't believe it 'cause of how certain she was before, but I can believe it 'cause the whole time we've talked, you ain't taken your eyes off her.'

With that sentence, I know he gets it. He gets it better than anyone could.

'Would you take your eyes off if you had a girl like her?'

'You've seen my girl, right?' Braden laughs. 'I've had my ass kicked in English more times than I fuckin' remember because she's distracted me. Ever since we met, it was always her. I'd put a bet on it was the same for you.'

'Pretty much.'

The girls cross the garden toward us as Abbi's dad comes out of the house, fireworks in his arms. Maddie's dad follows him out, having showed up an hour or so earlier, carrying just a lighter and whistling. Abbi's mum rolls her eyes at them.

'I wonder when you two will grow up,' she muses.

'Never,' Maddie's dad declares. 'Growing up is far too boring.'

'And if we grew up, we wouldn't have an excuse for the antics we get up to on our fishing weekends!' Abbi's dad puts in.

'I don't want to know,' her mum mutters to herself.

'By the way, mate.' I nudge Braden as Maddie and Abbi approach us. 'You owe Maddie nine dollars.'

'Fuck.' He pauses. 'Make that ten.'

'Hey.' I glance at him. 'I won't tell if you don't.'

He turns his face toward me, a smug smile gracing his lips. 'Know what, man? I think I like you.'

Maddie stops in front of us and combs her eyes over me before looking at Braden. 'You didn't get your club out, then?'

'For the love of God, Maddie.'

She perches on his knee and pinches his cheek. 'You're so easy to wind up.'

'She's right,' Abbi agrees. 'So, how much do you owe her?'

'Nothing,' he lies.

'Really?' Maddie and Abbi say in unison, looking at me with raised eyebrows.

'Bloody hell, that was creepy,' I mutter. 'Really. He didn't swear once.'

Braden grins, wrapping his arms around Maddie's waist and kissing her cheek. 'Looks like we're stuck with McDonald's, Mads.'

A loud bang interrupts whatever she was about to reply with, making us all jump. Abbi trips over her feet and falls onto my lap. I laugh, both at her and the look on her dad's face.

'S'alright,' he calls and waves us all off. 'Lit the damn thing by accident.'

Maddie's dad grins, flicking the lighter in his hand.

'Dad!' Maddie yells. 'Stop being a child!'

'Again with the growing up.' Abbi's mum sighs, looking at me. 'You'll get used to these two, Blake.'

'No he won't,' Abbi argues. 'I'm still not used to it and I've lived with it for my whole life.'

'Watch it, Princess,' her dad calls. 'I still buy your birthday presents!'

'I get to dance on my birthday this year,' she shouts back. 'That's the best present.'

Birthday?

'Wait, when's your birthday?' I curl my arm around her waist and poke her side.

'. . . Sunday.'

'Performance day?'

'. . . Yes.'

'Why didn't you tell me?'

'Because Abbi hates birthdays,' Maddie replies for her. 'For someone who dreams of being in the spotlight, she sure hates the limelight.'

'I'm pretty sure I've said that before,' I think out loud.

'Damn, you really didn't know?' Braden asks in awe.

'No idea, mate.'

He shakes his head. 'Shoulda told him, Abbi. You know guys need six months' notice to get birthdays and shi-*eeeeeeet* right.' He glances at Maddie who narrows her eyes. 'I said sheet, I said sheet!'

'Mmm.'

Abbi smiles. 'I hate birthdays. I don't like the fuss.'

'How am I supposed to find you something for your birthday in a day?'

'Fireworks!' Both Abbi and Maddie's dad's yell excitedly.

'That's where they get it,' Braden mutters.

'I don't need anything for my birthday,' Abbi protests, tucking her fingers around mine. 'I get to dance on my birthday. There's nothing that can top that.'

'Oh damn,' Braden says in the same mutter. 'Now she's done it.'

'Done what?' Abbi looks around.

'You've said nothing can beat dancing on your birthday. That shit is a challenge.' He digs into his pocket and hands Maddie a dollar before she's even opened her mouth. 'Now he's gonna have to find something to top it.'

'No, he doesn't!'

'I do,' I say. 'In one bloody day.'

Maddie smiles slyly. 'It's a good job I'm here. Blake, what are you doing tomorrow?'

'Apparently, shopping for a present for Abbi.'

'No shopping needed. I know exactly what you can get her.'

Abbi

My hand hovers over Dr. Hausen's door. I know it's not too late to change my mind, turn around, and go. She doesn't know I'm here, and that's both a blessing and a curse. A blessing because it means there's no expectations. A curse because it means I don't have to go in there.

But I do. I know in my heart I do.

So I knock on her door with three short, sharp taps.

'Come in,' she calls.

Slowly, I push the door open and step inside the office I know so well. From the motivational quotes framed on the walls to the comfy red armchairs and the mahogany furniture. It's all comforting.

'Abbi,' she says, surprise in her voice. 'I wasn't expecting to see you today.'

'I wasn't expecting to come here,' I admit. 'But I need to talk to you . . . Ask you something.'

She tilts her head to the side, lowering her glasses. 'On or off your record?'

'On.'

'Take a seat.'

Questions are coming off her in waves as she gets my file and sits opposite me. She opens it, grabs her favorite clicky pen, and settles back in her chair.

'What do you need to ask?'

'You said my recovery would be at my pace, and within reason, I had control of it.'

'I did.'

I swallow. 'Okay. Well, I want to change something.'

Dr. Hausen sits up straight. 'What would you like to change?'

'My medication.'

She pauses. 'Alright. You've got my attention.'

I cross my legs and look directly at her. 'I don't think I need the highest dose anymore. I think – no, I know, I'm coping better than I was before. I still get the nightmares and flashbacks, but I can deal with them now. I don't feel as if I rely on the pills anymore. They're like a safety net for me and my emotions now instead.'

'And you don't think that safety net is a good thing?' She scrawls something on her pad.

'No, it is. But I don't think I need one as big. I'd like to think I could maybe catch myself before I needed that net.' I look down and pick at a tiny hole in my leggings. 'I mean, you said I was stronger than most people in here, right? You said I was the one that could fight it and get better. How can I fight it if there's a wall of cotton wool around me? As long as the pills are there, keeping my crazy in check, I won't be able to fight it. They'll always cushion the fall.'

'You realize leaving them behind is a gradual process, don't you? It's not something that happens overnight. In your case, it may take a year before you're fully weaned from them.'

'I know that. I'm not saying I'm necessarily ready to give them up entirely. Actually, that's quite a scary thought. I just think I'm ready to step back a little. Take back some of the control you believe I have.'

'I believe you have?'

'And me. I've come this far, haven't I? I must have some control over my feelings and my depression. I'm still alive. I have to believe I can control whatever's inside.'

Dr. Hausen is quiet for a long minute. I look up, and there's a small smile on her face.

'You know your mind better than anyone else. I can look at you and make a medical evaluation, but only you can make a true one. If you believe you're ready to lower your dosage, then I'm happy to put you down to the next one and see how you go. You know you can change back up anytime, don't you?'

I nod.

'And our weekly sessions will remain that way for now. It's even more important now. Even if all we do is have a coffee and chat about the weather.'

I nod again. 'I understand. I just . . . I really feel like I'm ready.'

'I'll get that arranged for tomorrow. I can call when they're ready for you to pick up.'

'I'll get Dad to come by when he finishes work tomorrow night.'

'That'll work. Was that all?'

'Yep.' I get up and walk toward the door with a slight bounce in my step. 'Thank you.' I open it.

'Abbi?'

I look over my shoulder. 'Yes?'

Dr. Hausen looks at me, her pen spinning between her fingers. 'I have to ask . . . What's changed?'

I smile slowly and genuinely. 'I stopped existing and started living.'

~

I fall into Blake's arms in the wings after our dance. My feet lift off the floor as he spins me, my face buried in his neck. I can't fight the smile on my face – it's been too long since I stepped foot on a real stage and danced below the bright lights without a care in the world. It's been a long, long time since I felt that at home.

That alone is the best birthday present anyone could have given me.

Blake squeezes me tightly, pressing his lips to the side of my head. 'I hope your mum recorded that like she said she would.'

'Why?'

'Because I want to send it to my mum to piss her off,' he mumbles into my hair. I laugh, pulling back.

'Mature, Blake. Real mature.'

'Oh well.' He shrugs, looking down at me with those green eyes of his. Green eyes that suddenly have a mischievous twinkle in them. 'Are you ready?'

'Ready for what?' I narrow my eyes.

'To get out of here. We have a place to go.'

'We do?'

He nods and puts his hand against my cheek. 'I still owe you a birthday present.'

'Blake.'

'No, Abs. I've got you something, but you can absolutely blame Maddie if you hate it because she organized it all. However, if you love it, you should know it was all my idea.'

I grin. 'Okay. I'm not gonna win here. Where is my present?'

'It's an hour and a half away.'

'That's . . . quite a way.'

'But it'll be worth it.' He takes my hand and leads me to the back of the theatre to the dressing rooms. 'Meet me at the back door in ten minutes. Oh, and give me your car keys.'

'What?' I squeak. 'Why the hell do you need my keys?'

'I don't, and neither do you. I'm going to give them to your mum.'

'Why?'

'Just hand them over.'

'Okay, hang on.' I run into my dressing room, grab my keys from my purse, and smack them into his hand. 'I'm starting to get worried about this present, you know.'

'Don't be,' he says as he backs away from me. 'Ten minutes.'

I take a deep breath and nod, then shut the door. My brain is whirring with thoughts of what he could have planned, but none of them seem realistic.

And here was me thinking I'd got to nine p.m. without a big fuss. I should be so lucky.

I change from my ballet clothes into my normal ones and

pack all my things away. A quick glance around the dressing room reveals I have everything, so I run down the stairs to the back door. Blake's waiting there, two bags in hand – his ballet bag, and another one.

'What's that?' I point to the bag. 'Hey, is that mine?'

He smirks. 'Come on.'

My eyes narrow as I follow him out toward a silver Ford. 'You don't have a car,' I state.

'Correct. I hired this.'

'You *hired* a car? What are you? A car employer?'

'Uh . . . Do you say rented? 'Cause this is a hire car to me.'

'Yep. We say rented.' I smirk. He's so cute. 'Freakin' British'.

Blake's fingers brush mine as he takes my dance bag from me, his lips curved on one side. 'Bloody Americans,' he whispers, his eyes boring into mine. He takes the bag and throws it in the trunk, slamming the top down. 'Are you getting in?' he asks, walking to the passenger side.

I swallow my smile, fighting my complete and utter amusement, and cross my arms over my chest. 'I'd love to, but I don't have the keys.'

'You don't need the keys. I'm driving.'

'Not from the passenger side you're not.'

He looks down, pausing for a moment, and drops his forehead onto the roof of the car. I giggle into my hands.

'Goddamn it. You're all backwards over here!' he cries, walking round the front of the car.

I climb in the passenger side and turn my face toward him. 'Just, for God sake, don't forget we drive on the *other* side of the road to you guys, too.'

'Why did I ever think this was a good idea?'

I grin. 'I told you not to worry.'

He grunts and starts the car up. He eyes the space where a gear stick would be. 'Now I'm really glad Maddie made me go for an automatic. I don't think I could use a gear stick with my right hand.'

'All our rentals are automatic.'

He looks at me. 'You know how confusing you guys are, right?'

'Yep. Are you sure you can drive this and get us wherever the hell we're going in one piece?'

'I'm sure. Now, do me a favor and go to sleep or something.'

I put my belt on and settle back in my chair as he backs out of the parking lot. 'When I've made sure you're on the right side of the road.'

'Or the wrong side,' he mutters. 'Depends how you look at it.'

I cover my smile with my hand. 'You know where we're going, right?'

He nods. 'Google maps. Works every time. Go to sleep, Abbi.'

~

The soft brush of Blake's lips across mine wakes me. I smile, stretching out in my seat.

'Are we here?' I flop my head to the side and look at him through sleepy eyes.

He leans over and brushes some hair from my face. 'Yes, we're here.'

'Um . . . Where is here?'

'We're in the Poconos Mountains,' Blake says quietly and opens my door for me.

'We're not even in New York *state?*' My eyebrows shoot up.

'No. But before you say anything else, I want you to do one thing.'

If it's possible, my eyebrows go even higher.

'Look up.'

I do. I tilt my head back, and in the darkness, the complete and utter consuming darkness that surrounds us, the night sky is bright with lights of its own creation. The stars are brighter and bigger than I've ever seen them, hundreds of thousands of lights breaking through the darkness.

'Oh,' I breathe out, spinning around. They're everywhere,

twinkling even through the leaves of the tallest trees. 'They're beautiful . . . But why here?'

Blake takes my hands in his. 'You can hide in plain sight here. It's a giant, never-ending Prospect Park. And the stars? Well . . . The stars, the things you never see in Brooklyn, they're the things everyone never sees about you. And more importantly, they're the tiny specks of light you hold on to inside, just outside. The sky is your depression and the stars are the things that keep you going when you feel the darkness closing in on you. I wanted to give you a visual, something you can keep forever and look at whenever it gets hard.'

He drops my hands and reaches into the back seat of the car.

'What are you . . .' I stop talking when I see the camera in his hands. 'Something I can keep forever,' I repeat in quiet awe. My tear-filled eyes meet his as he places it in my shaky hand.

'And look at whenever it gets hard. That's my present for you.'

'Hope.' The tears creep out of the corners of my eyes. 'You're giving me hope.'

Blake wipes away the wetness falling down my cheeks. 'I'm giving you another reason to live.'

I turn my cheek into his palm and close my hand over his. 'You gave me that the day you walked into Bianca's studio. I just didn't know it then.'

Blake

'You have to remember,' Tori had said, 'to relax. Let yourself fall into the dance, Blake. No, no. Your shoulders are too tight!'

She batted my hands away and walked behind me. She smacked me between my shoulder blades. Hard.

'Ouch! What did you do that for?' I awkwardly tried to reach for the spot.

'Have your shoulders relaxed?'

I rolled them. 'Yes.'

'Then I did it to relax your shoulders,' she huffed. 'You won't be able to do it right if you're tensed up. It'll be like dancing with a plank of wood!'

'I don't even have to know this yet!'

'But I do, Blake. I have to get this routine right or I won't be able to dance in the Christmas production. Please help me. Please,' she whined, dragging the last word out. Her green eyes blinked at me innocently, and I sighed helplessly.

Of course I would help her. I would learn dance steps four years above my level because she needed me to. She knew I'd do anything for her.

'Fine,' I grumbled in the way only an eleven year old could. 'But you owe me, Tori. Again.'

'I know, I know.' She kissed the top of my head. 'You're the best.'

'Just don't slap me again.'

'I won't. I promise – but you have to relax, okay?'

'I get it!'

'No, really, Blake. You can't dance if you're tense, not ballet.'

'Your keeping on is making me tense,' I said pointedly, folding my arms across my chest.

Tori just smiled. 'Only because you're not listening to me!'

'Al-right!' I moaned. 'I'm listening.'

She ruffled my hair. 'You have to dance the way you fall in love; effortlessly, unrelentingly, and with everything you have.'

'I'm never going to fall in love,' I protested. 'Girls are annoying.'

'You say that now, but one day you will.'

'No, I won't. Ever.'

'Everyone falls in love, little brother. At some point in your life, you'll fall in love with someone and when you do, you'll be unable to distinguish the feelings between dance and love. And if you're really lucky, she'll be the dance you fall in love with.'

My eyes snap open. I can still hear her voice ringing in my ears and echoing around the small log cabin. That dream was real, all too real, even after all these years.

Ten years have passed since that conversation and I've been waiting since then to prove her right or wrong. I threw myself into dance the way she said – I gave it my all and then some. I planned for the future and I dreamed bigger than anyone I know. I never stopped or gave up on dancing no matter what was thrown my way. Even through my parents' disappointment, I never pushed it to the side. I kept on fighting to dance although it seemed impossible at times.

It seems silly now to look back and think those words came from a fifteen-year-old girl. What did Tori know about love? She was still a child, whose only true happiness came from the same place mine did – holding onto a *barre*.

But she was right. She was so, completely right.

Love and dance are one and the same. They're easy, like breathing, and if it's for you then it's natural. There's no second thoughts, no doubts. You don't think it's not for you, not even for a second. In fact you know. You just *know* it's all you're ever going to need.

Abbi shifts slightly in her sleep, and I hold her closer to me. She tucks her head under my chin, snuggling in.

Abbi is it. She's my dance. I fell in love with her the way

Tori always said I would, and it was so effortless I didn't even notice. It's grown slowly, building and transforming each time she's smiled at me or laughed with me. It means I can't walk away, no matter what she tells me, because of the sheer, unrelenting force of it inside. It keeps me tied to her and everything she'd rather hide. It keeps me living, because she's filled a part of me that's been missing for a long time.

She can never replace my sister. I'm not stupid enough to think that, but just because she can't replace her doesn't mean she can't stand alongside her in my heart, and it doesn't mean I love Tori any less for loving Abbi.

I can love them both the same in entirely different ways, all the while thanking the shit out of whoever is in the sky that Abbi didn't follow in Tori's footsteps.

~

'You have to be freaking kidding me,' Abbi deadpans, staring at the canoe.

'Would it be funny if I said no?'

'No. No, it wouldn't be. There is no way in hell *that* . . .' She looks at me and points accusingly at the canoe. '. . . Is funny. In any way. At all.'

'I guess you don't really feel up to going in it then, huh?'

'Do I look like a girl who goes canoeing? Honestly?'

I say nothing, trying to control the twitching of my lips. She picks up the bright orange life jacket.

'And this. I'm not wearing it. I'm not going on that boat. I hate boats.'

'There's nothing wrong with boats.'

'If it's not on dry land, there damn well is something wrong with it.' She folds her arms across her chest defiantly.

'Well, you do have two options, actually,' I say slowly.

'And they are?'

'You put this on . . .' I take the jacket from her. '. . . And get in the boat . . .'

'Nuh-uh.'

'Or you put the jacket on and get in the water. Either way, you're putting the jacket on.'

Her mouth drops open. 'You dare throw me in that water, Blake Smith, and I swear to God . . .'

I grin. 'What?'

She pauses. 'I don't know. I haven't come up with anything yet.'

I laugh and touch her face. 'Abbi, please. Just put the jacket on and get in the boat. I promise it'll be okay.'

She narrows her eyes. 'Hmmm.'

'*Please,*' I beg. 'Don't make me do the pouting and puppy-dog-eyes thing again. You know you have no chance then.'

'Why is it so important that I get on the damn boat?'

'It just is. It's part of your birthday surprise, okay?'

She softens a little. 'Blake, you've already given me enough.'

'No, I haven't.' I put her arms in the jacket and do it up at the front. My hands hover over the zip as I look down at her. 'When I think about what you give me every single day, I have a lot of things to make up for.'

I spin her around and nudge her toward the boat. I grab my own jacket and put it on while steadying the boat for her. She steps in and sits down tentatively, looking completely out of her comfort zone.

'I cannot believe I'm doing this,' she mutters. 'I really can't.'

'You don't have to believe it. You just have to do it.' I push the oar into the water and move us off into the center of the river.

Abbi's silent for a moment. 'So, where are we going?'

'Oh, just down the river a ways.'

'That's a vague answer.'

'Yes . . .'

'Blake,' she says sternly. 'Do you even know where we're going?'

'Of course I know where we're going. I always know where we're going.'

'Oh no . . .'

'I just don't necessarily know exactly how to get there.'

She hits the boat. 'Blake!'

'What? Don't blame me.' I glance over my shoulder into her narrowed yet slightly amused eyes. 'Blame Google. They're the ones who haven't developed maps that work in the mountains.'

'You . . . I don't even know what to say.' I catch her shaking her head. 'We're in a boat on a river in the middle of the Poconos, and we could end up anywhere. I feel so reassured right now.'

'As long as we don't end up in the Atlantic, I figure we're okay.'

Abbi sighs heavily. 'So you say. So you say.'

~

I smile smugly at the look on her face.

'You did this?'

I nod. 'I told you it would be okay, didn't I?'

'Okay? *Okay?*' Abbi stares at me like I'm insane. 'Blake, you've organized a goddamn picnic in the middle of the Poconos, shadowed by the mountains and overlooking the most incredible lake I've ever seen, just for my birthday. And you say it's "okay"?'

'What would you say it is?'

'I don't think I know,' she whispers, her eyes filling with softness. 'But I do know it's the most amazing thing anyone has ever done for me.'

She wraps her arms around my neck, squeezing me. I slide my arms around her waist, smiling.

'In that case, this whole getaway thing was totally my idea. Maddie had no say in it at all.'

She laughs into my shoulder. 'Nice try.'

I shrug, leading her to the blanket and sitting her down. 'The getaway was Maddie's idea. The Poconos was mine. Like I said last night, it reminded me of a giant Prospect Park.'

Abbi looks around, taking in the varying shades of green on the trees and bushes, the wild flowers dotted around the bottom of them, and the crystal clear blue of the lake. 'It is exactly like that.' She touches the blanket. 'I think I have a new favorite place.'

'I'm not coming here every time you need to hide,' I mutter playfully.

Her lips curve into a gentle smile. 'You won't need to. I think I'll just hide under my covers from now on. It doesn't matter where I go, my past will still find me. I can't fight against it, I just have to go with it. That's the only way I'll ever beat this. Acceptance is key to moving on.'

I shake my head slowly, just looking at her – from the curve of her eyebrows to the pink of her cheeks and the tiny curl in her hair to the slight upturn of her nose.

'What?'

'Ever think that the really bad shit always happens to the best people?' I think out loud. 'The people that always deserve it the least get hit with the biggest piles of crap.'

'I guess,' she replies slowly. 'But I'd like to think the best people get hit with the bad stuff because they can handle it. What doesn't kill you can only make you stronger and all that. I think I'm stronger for all my bad stuff. At least, I should be since it didn't kill me. No one knows why stuff happens, good or bad, but there's always a reason.'

I think about that for a moment. 'I guess you're right.'

'Well, if I hadn't been through what I have, then we wouldn't have met, would we?'

'I suppose not.' I smile. 'Good things have to fall apart sometimes, if only to make way for the even better things to fall together.'

'Exactly. And as corny as it is, I think I'll choose to believe I had to deal with all Pearce's crap so I could be here today.' She looks at me and smiles softly, her eyes wide. 'I know it hasn't been easy to be around me sometimes, and that might not change any time soon, but I'm really glad you stuck it out.'

'Yeah, well, you are a bit of a pain in the arse.'

She raises an eyebrow, amused.

'I mean, you're a total nuisance, and I can never get anything done when you're around because you just distract me, but—'

She grabs the collar of my top and pulls my face toward hers, covering my mouth with hers. I blink, taken aback for a second, before I sink my fingers into her hair and follow her lead. Her teeth graze across my bottom lip, tugging on it gently, and it's not the only part of my body it's tugging.

I move forward and push into her until she lies back. One of my hands supports me as we lower and the other is wrapped around her, holding our bodies together. My body covers hers and my knee slips between hers. She runs her tongue along my lip and *fucking hell. This is driving me insane.* Her fingers entwine in my hair, holding me to her, and I kiss her with everything I have. I take the kiss deeper until everything else has disappeared. Everything except her soft but strong body lying beneath mine, her tongue stroking mine, and her fingers wrapped in my hair.

'*But,*' I whisper against her lips, kissing her once more. 'I can't imagine not sticking it out with you. I'd be crazy if I didn't. In fact, I think I might be a little crazy anyway.'

She giggles, my forehead resting against hers. 'Then we can be a little crazy together.'

I smile widely, a small laugh escaping me. 'Always.'

Abbi

My eyes follow Blake as he moves around the kitchen with ease. The muscles on his back move as he chops and peels, and his biceps flex as he searches through the cupboards. I swing my legs from my perch on the table and laugh as he tugs a bowl from a low cupboard and almost falls backward.

He shoots me a look, smirking, and stands. Ingredients for whatever he's cooking are all laid out on the table next to me, and I clasp my hands in my lap. He's wearing a black shirt, and the open bag of flour is just too tempting . . .

'God. That was traumatic.'

'You got a bowl from the cupboard.'

'And?' He steps up to me. 'I should have known it would have been in the place I'd look.'

'Then you should have looked there first, shouldn't you?'

'You're hilarious.' He smirks. I grin.

'It's one of my better qualities. I thought you'd know that by now.' I poke his arm.

He weighs out some flour and sieves it into the bowl. 'Oh, I do. I just try to ignore your so-called humor.'

'It's because you're British,' I say matter-of-factly. 'Everyone knows Brits have an odd sense of humor.'

'I do not.'

'You do. And you all talk about the weather too much.'

Blake opens his mouth to argue but swiftly shuts it again, nodding. 'I'll give you that. Although it is a great conversation starter.'

'Better than your lame pick-up lines?'

His green eyes flick to me. 'Nothing beats my lame chat-up lines, and you know it.'

'Debatable.'

'Oi. It worked, didn't it?' He raises his eyebrows and touches his finger to my nose. His flour-covered finger.

'Did you just get flour on my nose?'

'Um. No.' He cracks an egg into the bowl.

I wipe at my nose and white powder falls into my lap. Without hesitating, I shove my hand in the flour bag and throw a handful at him. It settles on his hair, his face and his black shirt. A small childish part of me giggles in glee.

Blake stops and turns his head toward me slowly. I smile sheepishly.

'I didn't mean to get that much?' It comes out as a question instead of a statement, and Blake catches his tongue between his teeth. His eyes twinkle mischievously, his smile filling with sass. My own eyes widen.

'Oh no. No. No. No!' I jump from the table and run around it straight into a cloud of flour. I cough and sputter, glaring at him. 'That was not fair!'

'Neither was what you did. Now we're even.' That spark is still in his eye.

'I don't believe you.'

'You're right not to.' He throws another handful of flour at me, and I shriek, shaking my head like it'll clear it from my hair.

'Oh, that's it!' I grab the bag from the table and shake it in his direction. He steps back, laughing, and we do a funny kind of dance around the kitchen table. I laugh with him, taking in the way he looks with the flour clinging to him, and wonder how I look. Probably just as dumb as he does.

'Even,' Blake repeats, holding his hands up. 'Let's call it quits.'

'Fine,' I say after a moment. 'But the flour goes in the cupboard.'

'Deal.'

I put the flour away, but when I turn around Blake's hands frame my face, wet and sticky. I shriek.

'What the hell!'

'Egg.'

My mouth drops open and I stare at him in disbelief. 'You sneaky jerk!'

The cheek-aching smile on his face makes him look five years younger, and I have to fight my own smile. I dip my hands into the bowl, getting them covered in both egg and flour. The thick, gloopy mixture sticks to my fingers, and I run at Blake.

'Shit!' He laughs harder. 'Abbi. Abbi!'

I smear my hands down his face and scream. His white hands frame my face, his fingers sinking into my hair. I grab his arms, feeling like I'm going to fall backward, and close my eyes at the firm press of his lips to mine.

I half-gasp at the intensity of the kiss, feeling it right down to my toes. They curl against the wooden floor, lifting me up slightly, and my fingers dig into Blake's arms. He's never kissed me this way – hell, I've never been kissed this way by anyone, and as his tongue flicks across my bottom lip and he sucks it lightly between his, warmth pools in the pit of my stomach. I ache in a way I haven't for so long, an ache stronger and heavier than I thought it would be when I felt it again.

His hand threads into my hair, and I lean against him. His lips moving over mine both enthrall me and scare me, making me want to hold him tighter and run at the same time as the ache in me just intensifies.

Blake's arm slides down and around my waist, holding me in place and making my decision for me. I let my hands travel up his arms to his neck, and hold onto him for dear life. I hold onto him like I'm drowning and he's the only thing that can keep me afloat and save me.

And I may just be drowning – only this time, I'm not drowning under the pressure of my depression.

This time, I'm falling into my feelings for him, letting them

consume me and take me under. I'm drowning in the possi-
bilities of tomorrow, the maybes of us. I'm breathing fresher
air than I have in months, dreaming of a future that holds more
than just dance.

Because I'm in love with him.

And I feel it. I feel it with every part of me, but I'm not
scared, and I'm not even surprised. I think I always knew. I
always knew my heart was in his hands, so I go with it. I ignore
the screaming in the back of my head and let my heart and
my body do the talking.

I know the exact moment the screaming stops and my wants
overtake my fears because one of the binds tying the depression
to me snaps. Usually it's a slow fray of a rope coming apart,
but this was a clean cut, a swift slicing of the steel rods holding
the darkness in place.

My back melds against the wall, and I tangle my fingers in
his hair, wetness sliding down my cheeks. With each tear that
slides from my closed eyes another bit of weight lifts.

'Abbi,' he whispers, pulling away and moving his hand from
the back of my head. He cups my cheek and wipes the tears
away, leaning his forehead against mine. 'Don't cry. Please don't
cry. We don't have to—'

'I'm not crying for that,' I half-laugh, half-hiccup. 'I'm not
crying because I'm remembering or because it hurts. I'm crying
because I'm letting go of that hurt, at least a little. And now
I'm crying because I don't want you to stop.'

Blake breathes out slowly, his hot breath fanning across my
lips. 'I mean it, Abs. We don't have to do anything you're not
ready for. I'll go and put that bloody chick-flick on and start
the pastry again and—'

I yank his head back so he's looking me in the eyes. So he
knows I mean what I'm about to say.

'Blake Smith, if you let me go and walk away from me right
now to make fucking pastry, I will never speak to you again.
Ever.'

He blinks at me. 'I'm not sure I've ever heard you swear.'

'Do me a favor.'

'I'm kind of debating not making the pastry again, if you're wondering.'

'You talk too much,' I mutter. 'For five minutes, can you just shut the hell up and kiss me again?'

His fingers cup the back of my neck, pulling me away from the wall and toward him. 'Since you asked so nicely . . .'

He takes my mouth with his again, this time harder, more needing, and I open for him when his tongue flicks against my lips. His hand moves down and curves around my ass cheeks, pulling my pelvis against his. An inch of doubt from the darkness flashes in the back of my mind when I feel him hard against my thigh, but I bat it away forcefully.

My head has controlled this too long. My head is what holds me back. Tonight my heart has taken the reins. I'm not thinking. I'm just feeling.

He kicks the bedroom door open and walks me backward into the room. My legs buckle when they hit the bed, and Blake puts an arm out to slowly lower us back. His body settles on top of mine, lean and muscular. I let go of his hair and slide my hands down his back to the hem of his shirt. I curl my fingers around the material, pulling it up, and he pauses.

'Shut. Up,' I mumble against his mouth before he can say a word. His whole body shakes as he laughs silently, and I feel the smile on his lips.

'I think I like this side of you,' he whispers, kissing along my jaw.

I pull the shirt up his body and over his head, my hands falling back onto hot, smooth skin. His lips travel down my neck, dropping open-mouthed kisses against my still-floury skin, and I breathe in. I breathe *him* in. And it's not enough.

It hits me too fast. Hits me that I more than just want tonight with Blake. I need it. I need every single bit of him he has to give me. And the only reason I have is that I just do.

It's startling and scary. It's a hard and fast realization, something I can't even comprehend, but I need this. I need him the way I love him – so completely and utterly it'll consume me if I don't give in to it.

His hands take my shirt from my body with the same ease he kisses me with. His fingers unbutton my jeans as deftly as he makes his way across my stomach with his mouth. His eyes comb up and down my body and drink in every inch of me with the same heat that's pounding through my blood right now.

His body falling back to mine has the same force as my leg hooking around his. His tongue is as probing as mine. Everything about us is in tandem, from our movements to our breathing to our silent pleas to each other.

I hook my fingers inside his jeans and tug them down, along with his boxer shorts. His hands hold my waist as his tongue flicks along the curve of my chest, dipping in and out of the cup of my bra. Goosebumps erupt across my skin, a contrast to the heat of his breath snaking across my skin. His fingers unclip my bra and move downwards, probing my skin until they reach the hem of my panties.

Blake's tongue circles my breasts, his fingers hook inside the material at my hips, then his mouth moves to my ear.

'If at any point you want to stop, just say the word, and I'll stop. I mean it. Any second.'

I nod, turning my face into his and brushing our lips together. I lift my legs as he slides my underwear down them, exposing every part of me to him. Exposing every pounding pulse point. Every throbbing vein. Every begging body part.

Every scar.

He reaches under the pillow and pulls out a small square foil. He tears the packet open and rolls the condom onto himself. I wrap my legs around his waist, gripping his hair tightly, and look into his eyes.

I want to see green eyes as he slips inside of me. Nothing but clear, honest, green eyes.

Pain sears through me for a few seconds as he pushes inside of me. I fight against the cry that wants to leave me and the arch of my back. He stops when he's fully inside, resting his body down onto mine.

Blake takes my hand with his and brings it to his face. My wrist touches his lips, and he kisses his way up my arm. He drops my arm and does the same to the other, pressing his mouth to my scarred wrist and arm.

And he looks me in the eyes, slowly pulling out of me and easing himself back in. I open my legs a little further, the discomfort disappearing, and stare into a sea of green. Transfixed on him, I barely hear his words as I begin to fully take him.

'You're beautiful, Abbi, and so are the scars. Every. Single. One.'

And I believe him.

Epilogue
Abbi

One Year Later

I tap my fingers against the table, staring at the envelope in front of me. It's big, and the Juilliard logo on the address label taunts me.

This envelope holds my future. It's the beginning or the end of everything I've worked so hard for over the last twelve months. It's the result of the very thing that started my healing so long ago, and the thing that has kept me going ever since.

It's the thing that led me to Blake.

And he already knows. He knows he'll be at Juilliard next semester, because unlike me, he's not scared of what's inside the envelope. He tore his open the second I walked through the door.

That was two hours ago.

'Abbi,' he says softly. 'Babe, you've been sitting there for ages. Just open it.'

'I tore the flap,' I protest lamely.

'Tearing the flap isn't going to give you the answer you want.'

'The letter might not, either.'

'You don't know unless you open it.'

I purse my lips. 'I don't want to know.'

He sits opposite me and pushes the letter closer to me.

'I'm scared,' I admit, staring at the Juilliard logo.

'I know. But the only thing worse than them saying "no" is

not knowing. The longer you leave it the harder it's going to get to open it.'

'Do it for me?' I glance up at him.

'I already know what the letter says. It doesn't take a genius to work out.'

'But if it doesn't say yes . . . If there's no Juilliard for me . . . It'll all have been for nothing.' My voice trails off.

'No, it won't have been. And I know you. You'll just go storming back into Bianca's studio, work your pretty little ass off and go back next year to kick them in the teeth with the way you dance.'

My lips twitch. 'You said ass. Not arse.'

Blake smirks. 'Bloody Americans rubbing off on me.'

I roll my eyes. And sigh. 'Okay.' I smack my hand down on top of the envelope. 'I'll do it.'

I slide the envelope along the table and turn it over, exposing the tiny rip in the corner of the flap. Blake looks at it then up at me.

'You call that a rip?'

'Shut up,' I mutter, slipping my finger under it. I run it along the length of the envelope, slide my hand inside, grab the piece of paper and shut my eyes as I pull it out.

'Cheater!' Blake exclaims.

'Just . . . a minute.' I take a deep breath. 'Can you see what it says?'

'I'm not saying. You'll have to open your eyes.'

'I don't want you to tell me. I just want to know if you can.'

'I'm nodding or shaking my head.'

'God! You're such a kid.'

He laughs. 'So are you.'

'Okay.' I take another deep breath and hold the letter tighter, reminding myself it's not the end of the world if it's a no. Like Blake said, there's always another dance and another year to try.

But I want it. I want it so, so badly I can't bear it.

This dream has allowed me to take hold of my past and beat

it down, putting it where it belongs in a box only I have the key to. This dream has allowed me to live and love again, and it never occurred to me until this morning it might not come true this year. I was so focused on getting to Juilliard, I never thought they might say no. I never wanted to think about what would happen if they said no.

I'm stronger now, I remind myself. I control the depression, it doesn't control me. I faced my demons head on, and while I'll never be *normal*, I'll always be me, scars and all. And that's enough.

So. I have to take whatever is in this letter and accept it the way I accepted the past.

A third deep breath, and my fist clenches on the table. And I open my eyes.

Dear Abbi,

Congratulations! It gives me great pleasure to inform you that the Juilliard Dance Division and the Committee on Admissions have granted you admission to the Bachelor of Fine Arts program at The Juilliard School for the 2011-2012 academic year.

I look at Blake, tears in my eyes. I cover my mouth with my hand and whisper, 'I did it.'

He smiles slowly, his green eyes alight. 'You did it.'

I did it.

WORTH THE RISK

Chapter One – Roxy

It's been six months.

Twenty-six weeks. One hundred and eighty-two days. Two hundred and sixty-two thousand, nine hundred and seventy-four minutes. Or perhaps the most accurate: fifteen million, five hundred and fifty-two thousand seconds.

At least that's how it feels. It feels like a short slice of forever since I last saw my brother, but I remember the moment he died like yesterday. It's so clear, like I'm watching a movie play out in my mind. I remember the glare of headlights. The screech of the tires as the car swerved. My own ear-piercing scream as I watched it smash head on into a tree.

And the guilt. The guilt of not forcing him to get into Selena's car instead of Stu's. That's almost as bad as the memory itself – knowing I could have prevented it if I hadn't let it go as easily as I always did.

Six months and it still hurts as much as it did then. I miss him as fiercely as I have every day since he died, and I know without a doubt whoever said time is a healer is a great big fucking liar. Nothing has healed; *I* haven't healed. I've been broken, my heart ripped to pieces, alone in my grief and unable to explain to anyone how I feel.

So I don't. I don't explain, I don't even try to, and I don't feel. I block it out, knowing it exists but choosing not to acknowledge it.

If I didn't, I'd lose whatever will is keeping me alive. I didn't just lose my brother that night. I lost a part of my very soul.

The vodka burns my throat as it goes down. It settles into

a warm pool in my belly, and I savor that feeling for a moment. It'll be gone as quickly as it came, a fleeting spark of happiness. I eye the bottle, wondering if I can get away with another one before Selena finds me.

And she will. She'll know exactly where I've disappeared to . . . To the place where she can't keep her eyes on me.

'How many have you had?' Selena's voice travels over the music booming through the house. Shit.

I sigh. 'Two.'

'Bullshit, Roxy.' My best friend steps in front of me, her hands on her hips. 'How. Many?'

'Four,' I lie for the second time. 'I promise.'

She scrutinizes me with her brown eyes, flicking them from my face to the bottle behind me. 'Hmm. Okay.'

'Don't you trust me, Leney?' I smirk.

Her eyebrow shoots up. 'About as much as I trust my sister with my make-up bag.'

'Ouch.' I put a hand to my chest. 'That hurts.'

Selena snorts. 'Spare me your dramatics, Roxy. You know I trust you with everything but the crap you keep putting in your body.'

'It's just vodka.'

'And the rest.'

'I have no idea what you're talking about.'

'If you think I didn't see you sneaking off with Layla, you're wrong.'

'Please.' I brush my hair from my face and turn to pour a drink. 'I didn't do anything.'

'Look at me,' Selena demands.

'Are you fucking kidding me?' I slam the bottle down over the music.

'If you didn't take anything, you'll turn your ass around and look at me.'

Fuck me. 'Fine.' I turn my face to her and look her in the eyes. 'See? I didn't take anything.' Tonight. Yet.

'Alright. I believe you. This time.' She sighs and takes the glass I offer her. 'I just worry about you—'

'Yeah, yeah, I've heard it all.' I take a drink. 'You're worried about my drinking, suspected drug use and relationships. My mom already gave me the grilling. *Again.*'

'Okay, as your best friend – you can hardly call what you have relationships.'

'No, you can.' My eyes scan the heaving room. 'However short, they have all the ingredients. Attraction, want, and a mutual understanding of what's expected. In this case, it's nothing goes past one night. Hey – if they're lucky, they might even get my name.'

Selena shakes her head, and I laugh.

'What? I might push the limits, but I'm always careful. I make sure I can get home safely if I've been drinking and I always use protection.'

'You're a damn idiot, girl.'

'Probably. But at least I'm a sensible one.' I grin.

She runs her finger around the top of her glass. 'Do you think he'd want to see you like this? Doing this to yourself?'

I freeze, every part of my body going cold. 'I'm not doing anything to myself, and I'm sure as shit not talking about him tonight, Leney.'

I down the rest of my glass, the vodka stronger than the Red Bull, and push off from the table. My eyes fix on a broad-shouldered guy in the middle of the crowd, his short, light hair spiked up, and I move toward him, emotion rushing through my body.

Shit, Selena knows better than to mention my brother.

Someone grabs my hand, stopping me and spinning me round. I press up against a hard chest and look up.

'Olly.' My hand rests on his chest. 'Can I help you?'

He looks down at my chest and back up. 'Several ways.'

I slide my hand up to his face, running my thumb along his jaw. He tilts his head down, his lips brushing across the pad of my thumb.

'Oh, sorry. You must have missed the rhetorical part of that question.' I smile sweetly, stepping back and breaking our contact. 'Maybe some other time.'

'You're a tease, Roxy Hughes.'

'Me? Never.' I glance over my shoulder and wink at him. I've barely taken five steps when I'm pulled into another chest. A very, very hard chest. My eyes flick upwards into a pair of bright blue ones I don't recognize. *Oh.* That sure doesn't happen often in Verity Point.

'Well, hello.' The words escape me.

'Hello,' he replies, his eyes skimming me appreciatively. 'I've had the shittest night ever, so do me a favor and tell me you're here alone.'

Okay, Mr. Terrible-Pick-Up line, usually you'd get your ass kicked, but I'll be damned if I'm gonna walk away from someone this damn hot.

I run my eyes over his brown hair, his sharp features, his broad shoulders and toned biceps. 'I was here alone.' I flick my hair over my shoulder and rest a hand on his waist. 'Now I'm here with you. How does that sound?'

His lips curve to one side as his arm slides around my back, pulling me into him. 'That sounds real good to me.'

The crowd suddenly closes in on us, my senior class a mass of grinding bodies. The mixture of probably too many shots, the pounding music, and the muscular body against mine becomes heady, and I let myself go.

My body moves with the guy's. His hand trails down my back to the curve of my ass and cups it. My pelvis pushes into his, and as we move I feel him steadily get harder. And bigger. *Holy shit.* His growing erection pushes into my hip, and I resist the urge to lick my lips and leave the party already.

Damn, two out of three for one night won't be bad. God knows Selena is on my case tonight, so it looks like whoever this guy is will have to be my drug of choice.

Just, for the love of God, let this guy know what he's doing in bed. Please.

He dips his head towards mine, touching his lips to mine. They're warm and probing, and he wastes no time slipping his tongue across the seam of my lips. My hand curls around his neck, pulling him closer, and I open for him. Our tongues meet in an easy dance, stroking and searching the other's mouth. I feel the familiar clenching and warming of my nether regions as I imagine what else he could do with that tongue. I push my hips into him without realizing.

His lips leave mine and travel along my jaw to my ear. 'What's your name?'

I laugh. 'You don't really need my name, do you?'

'Good answer.' He smiles against my hair, running a hand along my side and down to my thigh. His finger creeps under the hem of my skirt, tickling my bare skin. 'In that case, I have a room at the B'n'B around the corner.'

'As long as we sneak in round the back,' I reply. 'My aunt owns that place.' And wouldn't that be a story for the next family dinner?

'A girl who takes a risk,' he murmurs, looking at me. 'I like that.'

I look up at him through my lashes. 'That's not all you'll like.'

He grins like the cat who's just got the cream and we step into the hall. 'Let's get out of here.'

'Give me two minutes.'

I find Selena in the kitchen and tap her shoulder. 'Hey, I'm leaving.'

'What . . .' Her eyes glance over my shoulder. '*Oh*. Okay, I guess. But text me later, promise?'

I roll my eyes. 'Jesus, Leney. Okay, I promise to text you and tell you I'm not gagged and bound in a river somewhere.'

'You're a bitch, Roxy.' She shakes her head. 'Who is he?'

I walk backwards, my lips quirking. 'I have no fucking idea.'

~

Careful not to wake whatever his name is, I ignore the pounding in my head and sneak out. In hindsight, maybe half a bottle of Jack with . . . whatever his name was . . . wasn't the best idea. Actually, no *maybe* about it. It definitely wasn't the best idea. Not when I know Mom is gonna give me another talk when I get home. The same talk my aunt would have given me if I hadn't left the B'n'B in the middle of the night.

Verity Point is dead. At eight in the morning, everyone is still in bed. If it wasn't a Saturday, I would be too. I'd be snuggled under my covers, either escaping in dreams or trapped by nightmares.

My feet drag, feeling as heavy as my head, as the big iron cast gate to the graveyard comes into view. I hesitate with every step I take. It's pointless and unnecessary. My feet and I both know we'll pass through the gate, follow the path, and sit in front of Cam's grave like we do every Saturday morning. Like we have every Saturday since his funeral.

And we do. I slip through the gate and take the path that leads to where he lies. The branches of the trees lining the gravelly walk reach out over me, shading me from the rising summer sun and the heat it brings. The short walk is as full of heartache as always, and I still wonder if one day Cam will appear from behind the trees and tell me it was all a joke.

I hope he will. I hope the same way I once hoped he'd stop treating me like a little kid. I hope with everything I have, with all that I am. I hope one day I'll wake up and it'll all be a terrible dream. But I know it won't happen . . . The same way he never stopped treating me like the six year old he wished I still was. I swallow and look up as I enter his section of the graveyard.

And stop, because for the first time, I'm not alone here.

Kyle.

Of course he'd be here – I knew he was coming home yesterday, and that he would make Cam his first stop, first thing. He's crouched in front of the headstone, his face in his hands and his brown hair flopping over his fingers. I can almost taste the pain coming off of him, and it wraps around me, making me hurt even more. Me? I can deal with the pain of losing Cam, but I can't deal with seeing Kyle suffer that same pain.

I wasn't the only person to lose a part of myself that night. My heart climbs into my throat, skipping almost painfully. And it's wrong. So, so wrong, but it's an automatic reaction to him. It's the same reaction he's elicited from me for the last four years – not that it matters, or even that anyone knows. I'm just Cam's kid sister, and I always have been. I always will be, and I've accepted that. I just wish that acceptance would drown out the ever-present feelings I have for him, the ones that are roaring up even now. This time, though, the spikes of attraction are mixed with a hint of anger.

Anger because he wasn't here then. He wasn't there when Cam was dying in the hospital and he wasn't here when he was being lowered into that goddamn hole.

He was the only person that could have made it easier to deal with losing my brother . . . But he wasn't here. I needed him, and he was at the other end of the coast.

'Roxy.'

I blink, fighting back the burn in my eyes. 'You weren't here,' I say softly, a hint of accusation in my tone.

Kyle stands and runs a hand through his brown hair. 'I know. I wish . . . I just . . .' He looks back at the gravestone for a second and sighs. 'How are you?' His eyes rise to mine.

'I hope you don't exactly expect me to answer that.' I walk toward the grave and stop next to him, staring at the darkened inscription on the gray marble.

Cameron John Hughes.

His name is all I can look at. I don't need to look at the dates or the eulogy saying how amazing he is. I know that already, and the date of his death is burned into my mind. *January 10th.*

'Rox . . .'

I shake my head. 'Don't. Don't give me your sympathy, Kyle. It's six months too late.'

'I'd just gone back. I didn't have the money for another flight.'

'We would have paid for you. Mom and Dad would have got you the ticket. You know that.' I drop to the ground and cross my legs.

'They'd just lost their son. I wasn't about to ask them to do that for me.' He sits down next to me and hooks his arms around his legs. The same way Cam used to sit.

I look at the grass. 'I would have driven to get you. I would have driven through the night if that's what it took.'

'Roxy, you can barely drive to Portland without breaking a sweat.'

'I would have driven there for Cam,' I say quietly. 'He would have wanted you there.'

Kyle lets out a long breath, dropping his head. 'Shit, I know. I shoulda been there. I bet he's haunting me now and cursing my ass for not being here for you.'

I laugh sadly. 'You didn't need to be here for me.' *I wanted you to be.* 'You needed to be here for you. I know you'll never forgive yourself.' I pick at the grass, snapping off blades and letting them drop back to the ground. Causing death in a place full of it.

'I'll never forgive myself for not convincing him to come to Berkeley with me. If he had, it never would have happened.'

'I'll never forgive myself for letting him get in that car with Stu. We all knew he'd had a few to drink. If he'd got in with me and Selena, it never would have happened.'

'Jesus, Rox! It ain't your fault. Cam was as stubborn as a goddamn mule. He never did anything unless his royal ass wanted to.'

I look at him properly for the first time. There are slight shadows under his brown eyes and there's a sadness lingering in them I've never seen. Other than that he's the same Kyle I've always known. His skin is tanned from living in California, and his body is just as lean as it's always been.

'Then how could it possibly be your fault?' I question.

His eyes meet mine fully, and his lips twitch up at one side. 'Touché, Roxanne. Touché.'

'Don't call me Roxanne.' I elbow him. 'You know I hate it.'

'I know. That's why I do it.' He laughs quietly. 'You know what worries me about Cam being gone?'

'Who'll cause trouble with you now?'

'Partly . . . But mostly it's who'll keep your ass in check.'

'My ass doesn't need keeping anywhere, thank you very much.'

'No, it does. It needs keeping in your pants.'

My eyes trace Cam's name. 'I believe the location of my ass is none of your business.'

He snorts. 'It is if I'm the one keeping it in check.'

That sounds way more appealing than it should.

'Cam didn't keep *my* ass in check. He made sure everyone else kept *theirs* in it.'

'Then I'll do the same,' Kyle says nonchalantly.

I shake my head, a bitter laugh in my throat, and get up. 'You're not my brother, Kyle. I only have one of those.' I kiss my fingers and press them to the top of the gravestone, letting my hand fall away slowly before turning away.

'No, but I promised him I'd look after you if anything happened to him.'

I pause. 'I don't need looking after. I'm not a kid anymore.'

He laughs. 'I know that, Rox. *Believe* me, girl, I know you're not a kid. I'll argue your other point, though.'

'There is no argument.' I turn back to him, my arms folded across my chest.

'That's not what I've heard.' His eyes pierce mine. 'There's quite a few people who think you need an awful lot of looking after.'

'Unreal. This place is fucking unreal. You've been back, what? Twelve hours? And people are already talking about me.' I let that bitter laugh leave as my head shakes yet again. 'I'll say it again; I don't need looking after, regardless of what people may think. You weren't here for me when I needed you,

Kyle, whatever your reason for that is, so there's no need for you to be here for me when I don't need you!'

'No one's talking about you.' He gets up and walks toward me, stopping half a foot away. 'It might surprise you that while I was at college and you were here transforming yourself into the resident bad girl, I was talking to your parents every weekend.' His eyes flick over my body. 'You tell me I wasn't there for you, but I was there for your mom when you weren't.'

'Don't you dare.'

'What? Tell you the truth?' He raises his eyebrows. 'No one else does, do they?'

I say nothing.

'I didn't think so. You might think I wasn't there for you, Rox, but I was. Every day. I didn't have to be here to care.' His voice softens and he tucks my hair behind my ear. 'You just never looked for it.'

My arms drop, and I swallow, my chest tightening. A lump rises in my throat, and I fight against the tears burning my eyes. 'That doesn't matter.' I step back and point at the ground. 'You weren't *here*. You weren't in the place that mattered when it mattered!'

'Go home.' Kyle looks at me steadily. 'Go home and sleep off that killer hangover, and I'll see you later when you've calmed down.'

I spin on my heel, my fists clenching at my sides. 'Remember, you're not my brother!' I throw back at him.

'I know. But I'm the closest damn thing you have.'

That's the problem. And it always will be.

I don't know what I'm more angry about – whether it's the fact he's come back and said all that shit, or because he still sees me as Cam's kid sister. A part of me, a tiny part of me hoped he'd come back and I'd be more than that. That he'd look at me in a way different to the brotherly way he always has.

A stupid, stupid goddamn part of me that needs shooting.

I swipe hot, angry tears from my eyes and turn into the

woods. Kyle might be back for the summer but that doesn't give him the right to act all protective of me. It doesn't give him the right to do anything at all.

Fuck him.

Chapter Two – Kyle

She isn't the girl I left here at the beginning of the year.

No. Roxy Hughes has definitely changed. Gone is the sweet, soft-spoken girl I knew. She's been replaced with someone completely different. Someone alien.

I didn't believe what everyone had been telling me until this morning. I didn't believe my little Roxy could be so careless and devil-may-care, but she is. It's not hard for me to imagine her getting wasted every weekend and doing God knows what with God knows who.

Shit. What the fuck happened to her? Of all the ways she could have dealt with Cam dying, she's chosen this? Ruining herself?

I shake my head in my hands, and my eyes fall on the framed image hanging above the fireplace. It's of me, Cam, and Roxy from a year ago, taken right after our last football game of high school. Cam and I are both grinning from the win, our helmets tucked under our arms, and Roxy's sandwiched between us. Her black hair is over one shoulder, and her blue eyes are as bright as the smile gracing her lips.

A heavy sense of loneliness hits me in the gut. I've barely been home a day, but I can feel it. I can feel the gaping hole left by Cam's absence. It's like Verity Point has lost a part of the town – and it has. It's lost the life and soul of the party, the joker, the class clown. That was Cam; the guy who could make everyone laugh without even trying. But I've lost more than that. I've lost my best friend, my partner-in-crime, and my brother.

Chopping my fucking leg off would have been less painful

than being home and knowing he's not here. Knowing he won't ever be here again.

The front door opens, and I still stare at the picture.

'Alright, son?' Dad asks, walking into the front room.

'It isn't the same, is it?' I don't turn around. 'Without him here. I can feel it.'

He sighs and throws his jacket on the chair before sitting down next to me. He leans forward, his elbows on his knees, and clasps his hands. Scamp, our terrier, bounds over to me and wags his tail against my leg. I scratch the top of his head absently.

'Nope. Hasn't been since the moment he died. It's too quiet around here. It was bad enough when you left – we only had one half of the dynamic duo we'd all come to secretly love, no matter how many tricks you played on us.'

I smile.

'You leaving for college left a gap here . . . But Cam? Cam's death has left a damn canyon. There isn't a person in this town that doesn't miss him.'

'I don't need you tell me that, Dad. Everyone loved Cam. He was the golden boy.'

Dad nods. 'Roxy's taken it the hardest.'

'Yeah . . . I saw her earlier.' I rub my face.

'Sounds fun,' he replies dryly.

'About as fun as finals. She pretty much let me have it at one point. I guess everyone's been treating her like a princess, right?'

'You guess right.' Dad settles back on the sofa. 'No one wanted to tell her no at first. Everyone thought her acting out was her way of coping, but it just got worse. By the time Ray and Myra realized how bad she was, it was too late. I spoke to him last week about her, and he's lost for what to do. She won't listen to them.'

'You know she won't. Roxy was the sweetest damn girl ever, but that doesn't change how headstrong she's always been. Tell her she's wrong, and she'll do all she can to prove she's right.

Tell her no, and sure as hell she'll go and do it.' I pause. 'What about Selena? She must have tried.'

'Every weekend, Ray said. At this point, Selena goes along with her just to make sure she gets home safely. Or so she says. If you believe the rumors, Roxy usually takes a detour on her way home, if you get my meaning.'

My jaw clenches, my teeth grinding together. That riles me and brings out every protective instinct in my body. The thought of Roxy sleeping with random guys after getting herself wasted . . .

'Let me guess, there's a party tonight?' I look at my dad.

'Even if there wasn't, I don't doubt Roxy would find one.'

I stand up, pulling my cell from my pocket and scrolling down to Si's name. My closest friend aside from Cam. I fire off a message asking if he knows where Roxy will be tonight. Dad's sympathy-filled eyes meet mine when I look up.

'I know you always promised Cam . . .' he starts.

'I owe him this much, Dad. I wasn't here six months ago but I am now, so I can try and sort the shit she's getting herself in.' My cell buzzes and I glance at the screen. Si's reply. I scan the message, getting the place of the party.

'Alright. If anyone can knock some sense into her, it's you.'

'I'll try, at least.'

And I don't exactly want to watch her destroy herself, either.

~

Miami's football program has done Si good. Since I saw him at Christmas, he's put on another half a stone of pure muscle. He was easily our top linebacker – hell, he was probably the best guy on our damn team at school.

'Never thought I'd see Selena having a party,' I mutter.

Si snorts as we walk in. 'Three guesses who convinced her.'

I don't need three. I wish I did though. 'She's really that bad?'

'You'll see for yourself tonight.' Si shoulders his way through a group of girls toward the fridge. He pulls out two beers, hands me one, and leans against the side.

'Great,' I say dryly, leaning next to him. I look out over the large kitchen, my eyes scanning heads for the raven black hair I know so well. 'How many fucking people are here?'

'Too many. Thanks in part to—'

'Roxy,' I finish for him.

'Out of town party a month or so ago. Selena told me she hooked up with one of the guys there and apparently has herself a small fan club. They're here tonight.'

'Hence why you're here.'

'Like I'm gonna leave my cousin with a bunch of guys I don't know. I'm pissed she went out of Verity to party as it is.' Si swigs from the bottle and eyes me. 'You really think I'd be here if it wasn't for that? Selena is the sensible one out of those two.'

'Mmm.' A flash of black hair catches my eye from the corner of the kitchen. My muscles tense at the way she flicks her hair flirtatiously over her shoulder. The smile on Roxy's face isn't one I've seen before. It's almost predatory, focused on some guy in front of her I don't know. She puts a hand on her hip and runs her fingers in small circles over her chest.

Her very on display chest.

The red shirt she's wearing leaves little to the imagination, clinging to her body so tightly the buttons across her breasts are almost popping open. Her faded blue jeans, tucked into Uggs, are so tight they're practically embedded into her skin. She looks comfortable and casual . . . And sexy. Very fucking sexy.

I shift uncomfortably as the thought crosses my mind. I've never thought of Roxy that way before. Sure, I've always known she was beautiful, maybe even been attracted to her a few times, but I've never devoured her body with my eyes the way I am right now.

Her laugh travels to my ears over the music, and I bring the beer bottle to my mouth to hide the tightening of my jaw.

'Who's that jerk?' Si nudges me, nodding in the direction of Roxy.

'Your guess is as good as mine.'

'You look pissed.'

'I don't like the way he's looking at her, that's all.'

'He looks like he wants to do more than talk to her.'

'Si.'

'Well. He does.' Si laughs. 'Want me to take him outside?'

I laugh with him. 'Nah. I'll just keep an eye on him – and her – and make sure he keeps his hands to himself.'

'Tom Parks, twenty-two, lives in Portland. Visiting a sick aunt who lives on the other side of the falls.' Selena stops in front of us and holds out two beers.

'How do you know that?' Si raises an eyebrow at her.

'Roxy may not give a crap about the names of the guys she fucks, but I always find out.' She tilts her glass in Roxy's direction. 'I can't stop her doing what she wants to, but I can try to keep her safe.'

'He's a jerk,' I say, looking at her. 'Does he know she's only just eighteen?'

'Of course he does. Everyone here knows Roxy.' A bitter laugh leaves her. 'He knows and he doesn't care. He likes younger girls if you believe what you hear.'

'Shit, Leney. Rumors are crap and you know it,' Si scoffs.

'Hey, every rumor has a bit of truth to it. Where did it come from otherwise?' She jabs his chest.

'She's got a point,' I acquiesce, watching Roxy lead Tom into the front room. 'And *he's* got a shock comin' to him.'

'She'll kill you, Kyle. She's real pissed at you still.'

'So she told me this morning.' I pop the cap of the beer and glance at her. 'Do I look like I give a shit if she's annoyed at me or not?'

Selena smirks. 'Not really.'

'There we go then.' I head toward the front room. 'If you'll excuse me, I've got a wayward little ass to keep out of trouble.'

The volume of the music increases as I pass through the

people milling around, stopping every now and then to greet and chat to the people I've grown up with. One thing is noticeable: Cam's name is never mentioned. The subject of him isn't even touched upon, and it annoys me even though I know it's not because he's been forgotten. I can still talk about him.

Roxy is easy to find when I step into Selena's huge front room. She's in the middle of the room, running her hands through her hair and moving her body in time with the music. And the way she moves it . . .

My eyes aren't the only ones on her. Every guy in the room is looking at her, eating her alive. They're all wishing they were the lucky bastard with his hands on her hips, his front against her back, his smug smirk in her hair.

I just wish I could punch him.

I sit in the corner of the room, making casual conversation with people I haven't seen since Christmas. I keep my gaze on and around Roxy, never letting her leave my sight. My fist clenches with every drink she has, and by midnight I've lost count.

I'm half pissed at her and half impressed at the amount her little body can hold.

She stumbles a little and waves Tom off after catching her. She passes, not seeing me, and heads in the direction of the kitchen with him hot on her heels. Fuck this. I get up and follow them, catching sight of Roxy just as she steps outside. Selena catches my eye as I walk past and sighs dejectedly.

Yeah, I'm feeling that myself.

It's cold outside, but I don't notice. I just notice Roxy's shaking head and Tom getting closer to her than he should be in her state. She holds her hands up, and he grabs them, his fingers flexing around her wrists.

'Get off me.' She tries to shake him off.

'You just need to calm down,' he replies, and she winces.

Hell fucking no.

I storm across the garden and hit him with a glare made

from stone. My hands cover his and I unpeel his fingers from her one by one. Roxy lowers her arms.

'Watch who you're putting your fucking hands on.' My voice is hard. A warning.

Because anyone who hurts Roxy gets hurt back.

I put my arm around her shoulders and tuck her into my side. She looks up at me with one eyebrow raised. 'I've been looking for you all night.'

'Who the fuck is this?' Tom's eyes jump from Roxy to me.

'I'm her boyfriend,' I reply before Roxy can. She tenses, and I look down at her. 'You win. You proved you could pull someone else before me, but I think it's time we got going.'

I spin us away from Tom before he says another word and lead her round the side of the house, digging my keys from my pocket. Roxy pulls away from me.

'What the hell was that, Kyle?'

'Get in the car.' I unlock it and open the passenger door.

'Fuck no,' she spits. 'You've been drinking.'

I level my gaze on her. 'I had two bottles over three hours ago – I'm as sober as they come. Now get your ass in my fucking car before I put it in there.'

She glares at me, and I pat the door. Slowly, she sits in the seat, and I slam the door on her. I watch her as she rubs her wrists one after the other.

'Did he hurt you?'

'What was all that about?' she repeats.

'Did he hurt you?!' I smack the steering wheel and level my gaze on her.

'I'm fine,' she mutters.

'Right. And to answer your question, I have no idea what you're talking about.'

'That! In the yard!' She turns in her seat. 'My fucking *boyfriend*?'

I hide the twitch of my lips. 'It was all I could come up with.'

'Fuck!' She puts her hand on her forehead. 'Why did you do that?'

'Roxy, you're absolutely wasted. There was no way I was letting you go home with that jerk.'

'I'm old enough to decide that for myself.'

'But not clear headed enough. Besides, you didn't exactly look like you were welcoming his advances.' I shoot her a meaningful look.

She pauses, sucking her bottom lip into her mouth and nibbling on it. 'I just needed a few minutes.'

'Mhmm. And if I didn't come out when I did?'

She says nothing.

'Good job I decided to come over tonight, isn't it?'

'I told you earlier. I don't need you.'

I pull into her drive, parking behind her mom's car, and turn to her. 'Obviously, you do.'

'You're a fucking ass, Kyle.' She shoves the door open. I get to her before she walks away and stand in front of her.

'True, but I'm a fucking ass who probably stopped yours getting raped tonight.'

Roxy freezes. 'That wouldn't have happened.' Uncertainty filters through her words, a tiny waver I know well.

'How do you know?'

Nothing.

'It isn't worth the risk, is it? Like I said, lucky for you, I was there.'

She lifts her head until her blue eyes collide with mine. 'And now you can say you fulfilled your promise to Cam. Now you can leave me to it.'

'So you can do the same thing next weekend?'

'That's nothing to do with you.'

'Wrong. It's everything to do with me.'

'How is it?'

'Because I care.'

'Well, don't.' She snatches her arm from my grip and opens her front door. 'Go back to California, Kyle. I don't want you to care.'

The door shuts behind her, and I stare at it for a second.

What the hell happened to her? Everything she's been tonight
– from her actions to her words, even her facial expressions –
they really are nothing like the person I remember. It's as if
she's been taken over by something or someone else.

And I hate it.

I sigh, turning from the house. 'Goodnight, Roxy.'

Chapter Three – Roxy

The morning after is always a complete bitch. The hangover, the empty, sick feeling in your stomach, and the blurring of your memories. My brain has blocked out random chunks of last night after around ten p.m., and all I can really remember is dancing with Tom then leaving with Kyle. I have no idea about the rest of the night, or why my wrists are aching.

'Roxy! Get up!' Mom yells up the stairs.

'I am!' I call back, rolling out of bed.

'I need to open the café, and we're going to be late!'

'Alright! Give me five minutes.' I rub my face as I grab my jeans from the back of my chair. I throw on a shirt and slip my arms into a sweater. I rush through make-up and hair in two minutes, and practically fall down the stairs.

Mom looks me up and down when I pull my boots on. 'At least you look presentable.'

'So glad you approve,' I mutter dryly.

She sighs. 'Roxy . . .'

'Let's go, Mom.' I open the front door. 'Don't want to be late, remember?'

I hear her sigh again as I walk to her car. She can sigh all she likes – she told me to hurry so I'm not stopping for a heart-to-heart in the damn hallway. I just want to get to the café, do my shift, and then call Selena to find out what I did – or didn't – do last night.

We pull up to R & C's, the café Mom's owned for the last twelve years. She named it R & C's after me and Cam – she said we were her pride and joy and so was the café, so it made sense to name it after us. The inside is even decorated in our favorite colors – blue and purple. At least they were when she freshened it up five years ago.

I walk across the royal blue tiled floor to the counter and look over the café. The white walls are covered in photos of the Columbia Gorge and Mt. Hood through the seasons. They start in spring to the left of the counter and spread round the café, finishing in winter to the right of the counter. The images hang between the small menu boards with the specials on, their alternative blue and purple frames bright against the walls. The tables are half covered with table covers, alternating like the frames and the menus that sit on them. If there's a blue cover, there's a purple menu.

Mom really went all out on her design. She put as much love into opening the café as she did raising us, and it's all that's kept her going the last few months.

Mom flips the sign on the door to 'Open', and I start up the coffee machine. Sundays at the café are easy; old Mr. Yeo will be in for his coffee and waffles in fifteen minutes, followed by the Stevens sisters for their weekly cake treat ten minutes later, then Louisa, my cousin, will be in to drink us out of coffee as she writes another chapter or so on her next book. Always the same people at the same time.

Just how I like it. It gives me something to concentrate on, and if I'm doing that, I'm not thinking about the photo of Cam right in front of me on the counter. If I'm not thinking about him, I can almost pretend I'm not hurting.

Just like Mom does.

Two weeks to grieve, to hurt, then she was back at it – throwing herself into work. She insisted the café had to be opened, that life had to go on. Our lives didn't stop just because Cam's did. The truth of it plagues me and taunts me every day, and I'll never know how it's so damn easy for her to walk on in here each morning, put a smile on her face, and pretend everything is fan-freaking-tastic.

I don't know how she does it. I never will.

I tie my apron around my waist and tuck a pad and pen

into one of the pockets as the doors open. Mr. Yeo walks in, ten minutes early, and I know instantly today is going to go horribly.

Mr. Yeo is never early.

'Good mornin', young Roxanne,' he says in his usual chipper tone.

I smile despite his use of my full name. 'Good morning, Mr. Yeo. Your usual?'

'Of course, girl. When have I ever had anything else?' He chuckles, sitting at his table by the window. He rests his cane against the wall behind him and settles down.

'Mom.' I poke my head into the kitchen. 'Mr. Yeo's here.'

'He's early.' She looks at me, surprised.

'Yep.' I sigh and grab a mug for his coffee. As I prepare his drink, my foot taps against the floor in a quiet beat to the radio Mom insists on having on in the background. I carry the mug across the café and set it in front of Mr. Yeo. He gets his paper out and lays it on the table.

'How are you, my dear?' he asks.

'I'm okay, thanks. How's my favorite customer?'

'Favorite customer? There's favoritism?' Isla Stevens cries as she walks through the door. 'Well I never, Roxy. I thought I'd be your favorite!'

'No, that would be me,' her twin sister, Marie, pitches in, patting her graying hair. I laugh and lead them to the counter.

'Now, ladies, no need to fight. How about we make you my favorite female customers?'

'Hmph. I suppose we can share that,' Isla mutters.

'Goodness me, Isla. We've shared a womb, clothes, a house, and you're fussing over a favorite customer title.' Marie shakes her head and leans toward me. 'She always was the fussy one.'

'You forgot boyfriends,' Isla adds. 'I believe we shared a few of those back in the day.'

I raise my eyebrows and move to the cake section. 'I'm not sure I want to listen to any more of this conversation.'

The twins laugh. 'Oh, dear,' Isla giggles. 'Not like *that*.'

'Like that? I didn't say anything.' I plate up the two slices of carrot cake.

'No, but you were thinking it. After all . . .'

'. . . We know what you young'uns are like these days,' Marie finishes her sister's sentence. 'All that trashy television.'

'Which you enjoy.'

'Shush, Isla. Don't tell everyone.'

I smile. Isla rolls her eyes. 'Dear, Marie. Anyway, Roxy.'

I look up from the register and freeze when I see the glint in her eyes. 'Um, yes?'

'We've heard something.' Marie taps the counter.

'That happens when you have ears,' I respond, tapping mine. She looks at her sister. 'She thinks she's funny.'

'They all do,' Isla replies.

I grin.

Marie looks back to me. 'We've heard a bit of gossip. About you, dear.'

Well, isn't that a surprise.

'Enlighten me,' I say.

Isla leans forward, pressing her chest against the counter. 'We heard,' she whispers, 'that that hunk of a boy, Kyle, is your boyfriend.'

The twins look at me expectantly, both with excitement shimmering behind their hazel eyes.

I snort loudly and slap my hand over my mouth. 'Uh, ladies, there's a reason things are called *gossip*. It's because they're not true.'

Their faces drop. 'Oh, damn,' Isla mutters. 'Those would have been some pretty babies.'

'Right you are, Isla. Very pretty. And Cam would have approved.'

'The only male Cam ever approved of me dating was a Hollywood star – and even then he had to be on screen,' I remind them.

'Well, it's still a shame,' Marie murmurs, taking her plate.

'We could do with a bit of juice around here these days. Nothing exciting ever happens anymore.'

'I agree . . .' Isla nods as they both walk over to their table. I look at them hopelessly, shaking my head. The kitchen bell rings for food and I walk in to get Mr. Yeo's waffles.

'I'm sure I just heard the twins,' Mom says, wiping the side down.

'You did. Being their usual crazy selves.' I grab the plate. 'Gossiping.'

She laughs. 'You wouldn't think they were in their fifties. More like their fif*teens*, if there were such a thing.'

'I think there is. It's reserved just for them.' I leave the kitchen and give Mr. Yeo his breakfast.

I'm wiping the counter down when the door opens again. I swear, if this is Louisa early, too . . .

'You look like crap,' Selena announces.

'Gee, thanks. You look amazing yourself.'

She sits at the counter. 'I'll have a lemonade with a dose of what the freaking hell was wrong with you last night?'

I purse my lips, grabbing a glass and filling it with ice. 'I have no idea what you're on about.'

'Of course you don't.' She sighs as I put the glass in front of her and lean on the counter.

'Really, I don't. I can't remember much.'

Her lips twist up on one side. 'You mean you don't remember Kyle claiming he was your boyfriend? Oh, this is awesome.'

'He did what?' I glance over her shoulder at the Stevens sisters. 'You know what? My morning suddenly makes sense.'

'He pretended to be your boyfriend to get you away from that Tom guy you were hanging with.'

'Why the hell did he do that?'

'You were too drunk, and Tom was too grabby.' Selena shrugs. 'He pretty much dragged you from my house.'

'Asshole!'

'Yep, you mentioned that a few times to him last night apparently. He called me when he'd taken you home.'

'I can't believe he did that,' I grumble. 'He's not my damn keeper!'

'You need one,' my cousin's voice says from the doorway. I look up as she strolls toward me.

'Oh, don't you start as well.' I stand and grab a mug for her first coffee.

'I'm just sayin', Rox.' Louisa holds her hands up, her laptop bag slung over her shoulder. 'You think you're good, but you're not.'

I catch her eye, and my heart sinks when I catch her meaning.

'Please tell me the reason you were at the B'n'B on Friday night wasn't what I think it is.'

'Shut up,' I hiss under my breath, glancing at a suspiciously silent Isla and Marie. I put Louisa's coffee in front of her. 'I'm not talking about that here.'

'That's a yes.' My cousin sighs. 'God, Rox. You really have to—'

'Give it a damn rest,' I snap. 'I'm not a child.'

'You know he wouldn't have wanted you to act this way,' Selena says softly.

'She's right,' Louisa says. 'Cam would have gone crazy seeing you behave this way.'

'Then he shouldn't have got in the car knowing Stu was absolutely fucking steaming, should he? He should have got in with us.'

'You know that isn't fair,' Lou says with an edge to her voice.

'No, what isn't fair is that he died. What isn't fair is that I'm just trying to cope and I can't even grieve for him without everyone going on at me.' I snatch up my cloth.

'You're not grieving, Roxy.'

'Everyone grieves in different ways. This is mine, okay?' I stare at her and point at her laptop bag. 'Are you gonna work on that book? It won't write and publish itself, you know.'

Louisa chews the inside of her cheek, and sighs. 'Fine. I get it.' She turns and sits at the table nearest to the counter.

I resume my cleaning of the counter unnecessarily and feel Selena's eyes on me. I turn to face her.

'What?'

She sips her lemonade. 'She's right, you know.'

I scoff, turning to the coffee machine. 'Oh cry me a fucking river, why don't you?'

'Just saying.'

'Well don't.'

~

It's not a problem if I know I'm doing it.

This is what I'm telling myself; it's what I have to tell myself. I have to believe I don't have a problem and my coping mechanism hasn't developed into more than just that. It hasn't. It can't have. The drink, the sex, the . . . *occasional* drug use . . . is a habit, not an addiction. I can live without it.

Maybe . . .

His room hasn't been touched. I know because I'm the only one that ever opens the door. I'm the only one brave enough to step into the place that was his sanctuary and filled with everything that made Cam, Cam.

It still smells like him. His half-empty *Davidoff* sits on his desk, the underlying musky smell still lingering in the air as if it was only sprayed recently. The bed is still perfectly made, and there's still a weeks' worth of clean clothes piled on his chair. He never put them away – instead waiting until Mom gave in and did it or he could bribe me to.

I sit on his bed and lean back against the wall. My legs bend upward and I wrap my arms around my knees. Every part of me aches with missing him. It's a feeling that runs deeper than anything I've ever known, so deep I feel it right to my bones. Being in his room only makes it worse, but it's all I have left of him. The memories aren't enough yet.

I need to be in his room surrounded by him. By his smell, by the clothes I sneak out when Mom isn't around, returning them only once they no longer hold his scent. I still call his cell to hear his voice on the answer phone. I still check his Facebook every day for a stupid status update or a picture of a cat with some silly caption.

Of course they never come. And it hurts – every time I look at the date of his last post, a grumpy cat picture, my stomach sinks a little more, twisting painfully with every millimeter it drops. The same feeling hits when I look at the sneakers he'll never wear again or think of the pink shirt he bought for my graduation to piss me off.

The shirt he'll never wear. The graduation he never got to attend.

I reach to the side and smooth my hand across the comforter. The navy fleece blanket gives way to the lighter blue sheet beneath it, both smelling of his *Davidoff* and fresh laundry. It amazes me that his room still smells like him. It's almost as if he can't let go either, even though he has no hold on his life.

I hope it never leaves. I hope his things still smell like my big brother, my idol, as long as I'm here. I know I taint it every time I walk in here but I can't help it. It's a catch-22 . . . I either preserve the thing that reminds me of him the most by staying away, making the preservation irrelevant, or I keep removing a little of it by coming in when I get lonely.

The smell will fade eventually, this I know, and that's what keeps me coming in here. Either way, the musky yet fresh fragrance will disappear, so I might as well make the most of it while I can. Besides, I adore the smell, even if I did taunt him about it constantly when he was alive.

'You'll choke her,' I'd warned him, leaning against the doorframe.

'Oh, ha ha. And you're the expert on dating, I suppose.'

'I'm not allowed to date, Cameron. Remember?'

He chuckled and sprayed again.

I wrinkled my nose. 'Kay, seriously. She'll be drowning in that stuff.'

'If I have my way, she'll be drowning in Eau De Cam.' My brother winked.

I gagged. 'You smell like a cheap whore.'

Another chuckle accompanied the kiss to my forehead. 'How do you know I'm not?'

I scoot off the bed and open one of his drawers. His sweaters are lined up, all folded neatly, and I grab one from the top of a pile. I pull it over my head and look in his mirror. The hoodie swamps me, but I don't care. I hunch my shoulders and bury my nose in the collar, smiling when I smell *Davidoff*. He must have worn this before he died and put it back in his drawer.

Little shit. I always knew he could put his own damn washing away.

The house is still silent since Dad helps Mom at the café on Tuesdays. I curl my fingers around my cell as I go downstairs, my thumb rubbing over the unlock key.

I could call Layla now. I could get her to meet me, give me what I want, and then it wouldn't hurt anymore. I wouldn't feel so lost without Cam because I'd be lost somewhere else.

Somewhere else . . .

A knock sounds at the door as I put my hand on the handle.

'Kyle,' his name leaves my mouth in an exclamation of surprise. What's he doing here? Didn't he get it before? I don't need him.

Or rather, I don't want to need him.

'Roxy. I wasn't sure if you were here.' He scratches the side of his nose, looking down at me with his soft brown eyes. 'Can I come in?'

I step to the side. 'You don't need to ask. You never have before.'

'Yeah, well. It doesn't feel the same without him here.' His eyes focus on Cam's sweater, and I wrap my arms around my body. 'You wear that better than he ever did.'

I snort, shutting the door behind him. 'Right. I look like I'm wearing a tent.'

Kyle shrugs, wandering into the front room and looking around. He doesn't say anything for a moment, his eyes flitting from picture to picture. Me. Cam. Cam and Kyle. Cam and I. All three of us. 'I wanted to talk to you.'

'I don't want to hear it.' I storm into the kitchen.

'That's nice. You don't even know what I want to talk about.'

'Probably the same old bullshit everyone else does.'

'Or maybe it's not anything to do with you. It might surprise you to learn not everything is about you, Roxanne Hughes. As much as you apparently think otherwise,' he finishes.

My mouth drops open, and I turn to him. He leans against the doorframe connecting the kitchen and the front room, his hands in his pockets and his hair sweeping casually over his forehead.

'Wow, I don't remember you being this much of a dickhead when you left here last summer,' I snap, disguising the sting of his words.

'And I don't remember you being this much of a bitch, so I guess we're on a level playing field here.'

I cock my thumb in the direction of the door. 'You know the way out.'

Kyle doesn't move. His head tilts to the side and his eyes study me. 'You're cute.'

'Excuse me?'

'I said you're cute.'

'I heard what you said.' I snap my jaw up. 'By "excuse me", I meant what the fuck?'

'I know.' The bastard grins. He fucking *grins*.

'Something funny?'

'You really, really don't want me to answer that.'

I stare at him stonily, trying to ignore the flipping of my stomach. The way he smiles . . . I've seen him do it thousands of times and it never gets old. It's playful and endearing and annoying at the same time.

'I wish I could wipe that smile off your face,' I lie.

'Really? Because I wish someone would put one on yours.'

'There'd be more of a chance if you didn't come over here and talk to me like shit.'

Kyle laughs. 'Right. I guess you've already forgotten who started with the sass?'

I open my mouth and pause. Oh yeah. That was me . . .

'Exactly.' He pushes off from the doorframe and crosses the kitchen, his stride strong and determined. I keep my eyes on him as he moves closer to me and leans his hip against the counter. 'You know, just because I want to talk to you doesn't mean it's about you.'

'That's the only reason most people do these days.'

'And whose fault is that?' One of his eyebrows goes up. 'I got home four days ago and even I can see you need a damn good talking to.'

'Hey—'

'But that's not what I'm talking about.'

I narrow my eyes, putting my hands in the front pocket of Cam's hoodie. 'What, then?'

'Cam.'

I shake my head.

'Yes.'

'No.' I move away from him. 'I can't—'

'You might not need me, but maybe I need you for this.'

His words stop me in my tracks. 'Why? You could talk to Si, or Ben, or even Lewis. Why me?'

'Because.' He pauses and exhales a loud, pained breath. 'Because no one knew Cam the way we did, Rox. No one could possibly imagine how much it fucking hurts to be here without him. Except you.'

I squeeze my eyes shut and open the front door. 'I'm sorry,' I whisper. 'I can't help you.'

'Jesus, Roxy.' Kyle's feet thud against the laminate floor, and the air shifts when he stops in front of me. He takes a lock of my hair between his fingers, twirling it 'You take stubborn to a whole new level. I need to talk about him, okay? I need to remember him with someone who loved him even more than I did. Without him here . . . I feel lost. Completely fucking lost.'

I open my eyes. His face is right in front of mine, his eyes on mine, and I swallow. My heart picks up pace from both his closeness and the raw pain in his voice I feel right through me.

'I'm not ready to talk about him.'

'It's been six months.'

'And?' I knock his hand from my hair. 'I know. But that doesn't mean I want to talk about him, Kyle. You have to understand that.'

He smiles sadly. 'And that's your problem.'

'I don't have a problem.'

'Oh, you have several.' His laugh is as hopeless as his smile is sad. 'You're just too busy hiding behind all the shit you do to yourself to realize it.'

'You said you didn't want to talk about that.'

'I said I didn't want to. Not that I wouldn't.'

'Asshole.'

'So you keep saying.' He backs away from the house, dangling his keys from his hand. 'I won't give up on it, Roxy.'

'On what?' I frown.

'On getting you to talk about him. You need it as much as I do. Difference is I can admit it.'

'Kyle—'

'Iz comes back in a few days. She wanted me to tell you.' He gets into his car with the mention of his sister, salutes me, and reverses. I stare after him as he drives down the street. My cell feels heavy in my pocket, and I pull it out. My thumb swipes across the screen to Layla's number and hovers over the call button.

A fat tear rolls down my cheek, and I tap it. That conversation pushed me over the edge and tore open my already gaping wound. My body stings with the reality of it – I'm not the same person I was before and neither is Kyle. We've both grown up and been changed by the loss of the person that held us anywhere near each other.

I redial Layla's number and accept the truth.

The day I lost Cam, I lost Kyle too.

Chapter Four – Kyle

'What are you doing here?' Roxy asks as I walk through the café's front door.

'Your customer service could use some work,' I reply, sitting on a stool at the counter.

'I'm sorry.' She smiles sweetly. 'Can I get you anything?'

'Coffee.'

'In a mug or over your head?'

'Over yours, if possible.'

She purses her lips and turns to the machine. Her ponytail swishes over her shoulder, exposing the curve of her neck. I narrow my eyes at her.

'You should probably take your hair down.' My jaw snaps shut.

'What? Is having it up too promiscuous?' she barks.

'No, but the small hickey you clearly haven't noticed on the back of your neck is.'

A quiet slap rings out as she puts her hand over her neck. 'Are you kidding?' She turns back to me slowly.

If my eyes are as hard as my clenched jaw, she shouldn't even have to ask. 'Do I fucking look like I am? Cover that shit up, Rox.'

'I can't have my hair down.'

'Bullshit. Selena wears hers down all the time when she's working.' I nod to her hair. 'Take it down.'

'Fuck you,' she replies.

I jump from the stool and move round the corner of the counter. I pull the hairband out in one swift movement, and her hair drops and falls around her shoulders.

'Kyle!' She spins and stares at me, her eyes wide. 'Give me that!' She makes a swipe for the band.

'No.'

'Yes!'

I grin and shove it down the front of my pants. 'Want it now?'

She stops. 'You're not a child. Don't be so stupid.'

My elbows rest on the counter and I lean toward her. 'And you're not a whore. So don't be stupid.'

'Again, nothing to do with you.'

'It is if someone's trying to eat your neck every time you drop your pants.'

'Ouch. Say it like it is, why don't you?'

'Someone has to.'

'What is it?' She leans on the counter too, her face level with mine, and her lips curve up. 'Is no one asking you to drop your pants?'

I move closer to her, tilting my head to one side slightly. 'Rox, if someone had me dropping my pants, you'd hear about it across town.'

'Likely because they'd be screaming at you to leave them alone.'

'Wrong. You'd hear it because they'd be screaming for more, and don't you doubt it.'

She swallows and straightens. 'Someone just needs to give you a good punch, y'know that?'

'Someone needs to give you several.' I laugh.

'You're so funny,' she bites out. 'Don't you have anything better to be doing?'

I sit back on the stool. 'Not really. I'm still waiting for my coffee, by the way.'

She clicks her tongue, sighs, and turns to the machine again. Her dark hair falls down her back, a kink halfway down where she had it tied up. My eyes go down, further again, and I look over her body.

Even in her work clothes you can see every one of her curves, from her waist to her hips and her ass to her thighs. And I should not be looking at her this way, but God fucking damn.

I can't help the stir in me at the sight of her. I'd have to be blind not to be attracted to her, and every time she opens that mouth of hers and tears into me it gets harder not to shut her up with my own.

'Here.' She puts a mug in front of me.

'Thank you.' I take the mug and smile at her. She freezes for a second, her blue eyes on mine.

'How do you do that?'

'Do what?'

'That.' She waves her arms. 'Be a prize dickhead one minute, then charming as hell the next?'

'It's a skill. I was born with it, Rox.'

'Yeah? How's that skill working out for you?'

'Wanna find out?' I raise my eyebrows as the door opens and Mia, a girl we went to school with, walks in.

'With her? Really?' Roxy hisses.

'Get ready for a lesson in seduction.' I wink and turn to Mia. 'Well, hey, Mia. How are you?'

She stops next to me and tosses her brown hair over her shoulder. 'I'm good, Kyle. How are you?'

'Better for seeing you.' I run my eyes over her body appreciatively. She's not a patch on Roxy, but she's attractive enough. 'Looks like Florida has been treating you well. It is Florida, right?'

'Yeah.' She leans against the counter, smiling. 'Hey, Roxy, can I get two coffees to go?'

'Sure,' Roxy answers tightly.

I smile slowly and sexily at Mia. She blinks once and takes a deep breath. I lean toward her.

'Hey, what are you doing tomorrow night?' I ask her. 'How about . . .' I glance at her chest. 'Catching up?'

She runs her tongue along the inside of her bottom lip. 'Nothing I can't cancel. Catching up sounds great.'

'Why don't you meet me here about seven?'

'Perfect.' She takes the two cups from the counter and throws down a fiver. 'I'll see you tomorrow, Kyle.'

'You sure will.' I give her that grin again, and she smiles like a little girl as she turns and bounds out of the café. She looks back before she disappears around the corner and gives me a small wave.

I look at Roxy. She's glaring at the door, her blue eyes hard and unforgiving.

'And that, Roxy, is how my charm is working for me.'

'You don't even like her,' she throws at me. 'You only did that to make a point.'

'And?' I raise an eyebrow, stand, and drop my own five-dollar bill on top of Mia's. 'Like you said, no one else round here is trying to get into my pants. See ya.'

She stares after me as I walk out of the café. Her eyes burn into me until I disappear from her view, and even then I can feel her gaze on me.

So she's right. I only asked Mia out to make a point – whatever point that was. Except it kinda backfired.

Now I'm stuck with a date I'm not interested in. And a hairband down my pants.

Fucking hell.

~

'Help me,' I say into my phone.

'What have you done this time?' My sister sighs.

'I'd love to say nothing, but I can't.' I pause. 'How do I get out of a date?'

Iz laughs. 'Aren't most guys trying to *get* dates, not get out of them?'

'Whatever. I'm not most guys. Just tell me.'

'I don't know, Ky, sorry. I've never got out of a date before. Funnily enough I only agree to ones I want.' Amusement laces every one of her words. 'In fact, why are you even trying to get out of a date?'

'Yeah, that doesn't matter,' I say quickly. 'What's the kindest way to let a girl down?'

She says nothing.

'Hello? Iz?'

'I'm not sure whether to bug you to tell me why or tell you there's no kind way to let a girl down.' She grunts. 'And I'm trying to pack. Closing this stupid . . . fucking . . . suitcase . . . is . . . impossible!' Her last words sound like she's saying them through clenched teeth, and I imagine her sitting on a suitcase, holding her phone to her ear with one hand and the other fighting a zip.

I chuckle. 'Maybe you stop buying so many clothes.'

'Maybe you should shut . . . Ah, shit. The zip broke.'

'How can you even afford so many clothes?'

'It's called a job. You should try it sometime.' She injects ten tons of sarcasm into her words, then mutters, 'Stupid suitcase.'

'God, you're funny,' I say. 'So you can't help me then?'

'Nope. Sorry.'

'Good to know I've just wasted the last ten minutes of my life.' I hear another grunt down the phone. 'I'll leave you to packing up your mall-sized wardrobe.'

'Wait! You're still picking me up from the airport, right?'

'Yes, Iz. I gotta go. Don't break anymore suitcases.'

'Asshat!' she calls as I hang up.

I sigh and lie back on my bed. What use it is having a sister – who is single and actively dating other guys – if she can't help you with the best way to let a girl down?

The only choice I have is to make other plans. Then I can call Mia and tell her I have to do something really important. Believable? Yes. Kind? Well, sort of. As kind as I think I'm going to get. I could lie about other plans – but that would make me a dick.

Just like planning a date to piss Roxy off does . . .

Right. Well, I have to think of some shitty excuse soon, since it's almost four, and if I don't call her soon I'll have to go out with her.

The doorbell rings as I ponder that last thought. Fuck. Maybe I can help Dad with something and hope she isn't the kind of girl who asks so many questions she might as well have the size of my dick too.

Who am I kidding? She's a girl.

I make my way downstairs and open the door to—

'Roxy.'

'Can we talk?' She looks up at me and continues before I can answer. 'Fabulous.'

I raise my eyebrows as she sneaks past me into the front room. 'Of course we can, Roxy. Come on in and have a seat.'

Her eyes shoot daggers at me. 'Why are you so determined to treat me like a child?'

'We're here again? Really?' I shut the door and walk toward her. 'One, I'm not treating you like a child, and two, I'm making sure you don't get in any serious trouble.'

'Right,' she draws the word out. 'Like Cam would?'

'Yep.' Mostly . . .

'Except with a lot less brother and a lot more petty.'

Chapter Five – Roxy

Kyle stops a foot away from me. 'You what?'

'You heard what I said.' I put my hands on my hips and stare at him. 'Getting a date with Mia to prove an unnecessary point to me? Nice one.'

'Who said it was to prove a point to you?'

'Well it definitely isn't because you like her. You never spoke to her in school.'

'How do you know that?'

I raise an eyebrow. 'She was in half your classes, and I walked past her with Lucy one time. She was complaining about how you're "so hot" but you'd barely said a word to her since you were in fifth grade. Then, another time, she was practically peeing her panties because you'd said "thank you" when she lent you a pen.'

He grins and shoves his hands in his pockets. 'Really?'

'Ugh! You are so "that" guy!' I throw myself onto the sofa.

'That happened though, yeah?'

I grab a cushion and chuck it in his direction. 'You're only going out with her because you wanted to show your charm off, and I get it. Point made.'

Kyle sits next to me and pushes the cushion into my face. I smack at his arm and hug the cushion.

'Say it,' he says through a grin.

'What?'

'Say, "Kyle has epic powers of seduction and could charm the panties off a nun."'

My lips twitch. 'Are you for real?'

'Say it.' He mock frowns. 'And I'll cancel the date with Mia.'

Damn him. 'I don't give a shit if you go on a date with Bimbo Barbie.'

'Ooh, touchy. I don't believe you, by the way.'

I don't believe me either.

'Whatever.'

He slides across the sofa and runs a finger along my arm. A shudder goes through me at the tickling sensation and I shake him off.

'Go away,' I mutter. 'I'm not saying it.'

A grin spreads across his face, that one that gives me jelly-knees, and before I can do anything he grabs my sides. I shriek as his fingers move against me, tickling me. I fall backward, half-laughing and beg him to stop.

'Kyle, Kyle . . . Kyle!' I yell through my giggles as I slide right down the sofa.

'Say it,' he demands through his own laughter.

A little yapping bark rings out through the room and I get a face-full of terrier.

'Scamp!' I cry, turning my face into the pillow. 'Get off, you stupid dog!'

'Hey, don't talk about my dude that way.' Kyle tickles me again, and Scamp yaps a few more times. He jumps off me when I scream and kick my legs at Kyle.

'Stop,' I beg, my stomach hurting. It's tense from laughing and being tickled, and I need to catch my breath.

'Say it,' Kyle repeats again.

'You sound like a broken record,' I mumble and turn my face toward him. And realize he's lying on top of me, his hands at my sides, and his face just inches from mine. The tension in my stomach spreads through my body and changes into something more than just laughter tension. It becomes thicker and stronger, zinging between and wrapping around us both.

I can feel all of his weight on me. I can feel each muscle and the rise and fall of his chest against my side. His breath is warm across my neck, and my skin prickles every time he takes a breath.

'Say it,' he whispers again. 'Say I'm a seduction god and I'll get off you.'

The temptation not to say anything is almost too much, but my brain is smarter than my body, and my mouth forms the words.

'I, Roxy Hughes, accept and understand that Kyle Daniels is a god of epic seduction, capable of charming the iron-clad panties off a whole nunnery.' They roll off my tongue, and he grins again, his eyes creasing at the corners. They sparkle, full of mischief and happiness, and they taunt me. They taunt me and make me want more. So much more.

For the record, my own panties might be kind of charmed right now.

He reaches into his pocket and pulls out his cell. His fingers move across the keys quickly before he puts it back into his pocket. 'Done. "Date" cancelled.'

'You cancelled it by text? You jerk.' My lips twitch and I'm all too aware of the fact he hasn't got off me yet.

'Easier to ignore when she asks me everything but the size of my dick.' He winks.

'Typical guy.' I roll my eyes and push at his chest. 'Get off me, idiot.'

'I see you're back to the bitch-talk.' He sits up slowly, his eyes focused on mine.

'Yep. It's the only way to deal with guys who text girls to cancel on them.' I struggle to keep my smile to myself as I stand, pausing to scratch Scamp behind the ears.

'Where are you going?'

'Uh, home?' I raise an eyebrow. 'Mission accomplished here.'

As in, I got you to cancel your date with Bimbo Barbie while not looking like a jealous asshole in the process.

'Uh, no you're not.' Kyle grabs my hand, and tugs me back onto the sofa. I fall back, my legs landing on his lap. He puts his hands on them, holding me in place.

'Why not?' My lips twist.

'You made me cancel my date. Now you have to entertain me for the rest of the day.'

I could take that thought so many ways.

I have to remember this is Kyle. This isn't some guy at a party. This won't ever go past flirting . . . Hell, it probably isn't even flirting – just joking about – regardless of what my tingly spine and jelly knees say.

'Entertain you how?'

Scamp jumps onto my lap and curls into a ball. I smile and scratch the back of his head.

'Stupid dog thinks he's still a puppy,' Kyle mutters.

'I thought you said not to call him stupid.'

'He's my dog, I can call him what I want.'

I dig my heels into his thigh and he grabs my foot. I grin. 'Don't be mean to Scampy.' The dog in question looks up at me and I bend my face to him. 'Meanie, isn't he. Yes he is,' I coo, rubbing his ears, and Scamp pants.

'He has such a crush on you it's disturbing,' Kyle pats his back.

'He has good taste,' I mutter. *Unlike someone.*

'Mmph,' he grumbles in return.

'Do you remember when you got Scamp?' I ask quietly.

A small laugh leaves Kyle. 'How could I forget? He was like six months or something, wasn't he?'

'And had an intense attraction to me.'

'Not you. Your leg.' He pats my shin.

'Cam, I want a puppy too!' I had looked up from Scamp with wide eyes.

'Rox, we can't get a puppy. The cat would kill it.'

'The cat's gonna die soon. I don't care.' I put the puppy down. 'I want a dog.'

'Why are you asking me? I don't decide.'

'So you can convince your mom, obviously.' Kyle rolled his eyes.

'Exactly.' I pouted. 'Please, Cam!'

My brother sighed and tilted his head back to the sky. 'Fourteen years old and still getting her way like she did when she was five. God sake, Roxy. I'll ask Mom when we get home, alright?'

'Yay!' I clapped my hands and froze when I felt something on my leg. Scamp was against my leg, his front paws wrapped around it, humping for all he was worth. 'Oh my God! What's he doing?!' I shrieked, shaking my leg to get him off.

'Don't . . .' Kyle shouted through laughter. 'Move,' he tried again.

I looked at Cam. He was leaning against the wall and his hand held his stomach as he roared with laughter.

'Get him off! Cam! Get him off!'

Neither of them could move for laughing, and Scamp only got off when I shoved him off myself.

'Cam?' I said when they'd calmed down.

'Yeah, Roxy?'

'I don't want a dog anymore.'

That was the moment. Even though I hated them both, that was the moment my fourteen-year-old heart developed a crush on the guy sitting next to me. Maybe it was the smile. Maybe it was look in his eyes when he glanced at me. Maybe it was the laughter.

Or maybe it was a combination of all those things that set hyperactive butterflies off in my stomach.

'You know, you should have got him off me.'

Kyle sighs happily. 'I know, Rox. But it was so fucking funny. The look on your face . . .' He smirks. 'You looked absolutely horrified.'

'Of course I did. My first experience to do with anything sexual belonged to my leg and your dog.'

'Hear that, boy?' he tugs on the dog's ear. 'You were right in there. Maybe you should have asked first though.'

'Right. Because I would have agreed to that.' I roll my eyes. 'I hope he knows I haven't forgiven him yet.'

Scamp lifts his head, sniffs at me, and jumps down. I raise my eyebrows when he stalks into the kitchen.

'Touchy,' I mutter.

'Spends too much time with Iz when she's home,' Kyle offers.

We smile at each other, and I drop my eyes to my lap.

'I should go now.'

'Why? Have a hot date?' He raises his eyebrows.

'Oh yeah,' I reply dryly. 'Because dating is what I do.'

'Ooh, touchy touchy.'

'Fuck you.' Amusement sneaks into my words, and I shove his arm. 'No, I'm sure you have better things to do than spend your night with me.'

'You seem to have forgotten you cancelled my date.'

'Fake date.'

'Whatever. I don't have anything to do. So get your ass into my kitchen, make me some popcorn, and watch a movie with me.'

Like we used to do when Cam was alive. It was their thing from about age seven – Friday nights at my house were movie nights. Of course, the movies evolved from *Pokemon* to *Rocky* and *Die Hard*, but it was their routine.

Until I crashed it. I only did it to annoy them, but it was fun. So I started crashing every weekend until it became the norm. And I always, always made the popcorn.

I swallow as Kyle pulls me up and pushes me toward the kitchen. I pause by the doorframe and look at him over my shoulder.

'I don't . . .' I take a deep breath. He needs this more than I don't, and if it'll make him happy, I'll swallow back the lump in my throat and do it. I'm not the person I was, but I still feel the same way she did. I'd still do anything to put a smile on his face. 'Okay. What are we watching?'

A slow grin breaks out on his face. '*Oceans Eleven*. Obviously.'

George Clooney and Brad Pitt.

The two people I can't say no to.

Damn him.

Chapter Six – Kyle

I throw the football at the wall, catching it each time it bounces back. With each thud I think a different word, any word, in an attempt to get a certain raven-haired beauty off my mind.

It doesn't work. Every word is about her; stubborn, ignorant, lost, guilty, Roxy, Roxy, Roxy.

We've argued every time I've seen her since I got back. She riles me – the way she talks and acts, and I'm not even sure it's because of my promise to Cam. The thought that it's because I want to protect her for me, and that I'm a little jealous of the guys she gives so much of her attention to, keeps growing. It's as if I can't help but fight with her, and I've never felt so unsettled about anything before.

She's Cam's fucking sister. I should be looking at her and thinking about how to take her mind off it, not pissing her off and wondering how her lips would feel against mine. I shouldn't be wondering if they're as soft as they look or if they'll taste as sweet as I know she really is deep down.

Like I was yesterday.

I don't get why she turned up at my front door demanding I cancel with Mia. There's only a few times I've seen her that pissed off – granted most have been since I got back – but that was different. There was a fire in her that set everything inside me alight.

Being so close to her – without her being mad at me – only fueled the insanity inside. My hands on her body. Her laughter in my ear. Our lips close to each others. If she was any other girl, if she deserved anything less than my complete and utter respect, I would have closed every inch of fucking torturous space between our bodies.

'You're going?' I hear Ben ask as he rounds the corner to my yard.

'Of course I am. Selena knows,' Si replies.

'Going where?' I grab the ball and look at them.

'Portland.' Ben holds his hands up.

'Why the hell are you going to Portland?' I throw the ball at Ben. Like I need to ask.

'Because there's some stupid damn party there tonight, and Roxy and Selena are going. Why the fuck else?' He grits his teeth and grabs the ball from Ben. He throws it hard at the ground.

My muscles tighten. 'Have fun with that, man.'

'I will. You're coming with me.'

'Am I fuck!'

'I can't keep Roxy's crazy ass under control, Kyle, you know that,' Si grumbles. 'Only you can do that.'

'I'm not going to Portland. Shit, every time I go near her we end up fighting. I'm not gonna give her another reason to kick my ass tonight. Besides . . .' I lean against the wall. ' . . . She's determined she isn't doing anything wrong, so she isn't gonna listen anyway.'

Ben laughs. 'You just don't want to see her go off with some other guy.'

'Course I fucking don't. I don't feel like knocking a guy out because he crossed the line with her.' *Because he'd be crossing a line I can't.* 'Are they staying there?'

'Not a damn chance. I'm driving them there and I'm driving them the hell back.' Si smirks. 'They're on a curfew.'

Both Ben and I burst out laughing.

'Are you serious?' Ben sputters.

'What do you take me for? Of course I'm fucking serious!' Si chucks the ball at his chest, and he grabs it. 'I'm not hanging around in the city for too long – I don't fancy getting my butt busted by the cops for being at a party underage. They wanna be there for nine, but they don't know they'll be leaving at eleven.'

'Let me get this straight,' I say through my half-smile. 'You're driving an hour each way for a two-hour party?'

'Yep.' He catches the ball back from Ben. 'Roxy doesn't need any more bad influences or dickhead boys from the city giving her ideas. If I have to pull your boyfriend trick tonight then I will.'

I grunt. 'Just keep those asshole city boys away from her.'

'Just go and do it yourself,' Ben puts in. 'Save Si the job.'

'If I'm there tonight I won't be able to get up at six a.m. tomorrow to drag her ass out.'

Now it's Si's turn to laugh. 'You're gonna get Roxy up at six in the morning? You're having a laugh, man.'

'Glad you find it funny, jackass, but I will. Trust me.'

~

'I have no idea why you're standing on my doorstep at six-thirty in the fucking morning.'

I lean against the doorframe, a smirk quirking my lips to one side. 'Well aren't you just the little ray of sunshine on a cloudy day?'

Roxy looks at me flatly. 'I'd prefer to be the bolt of lightning that strikes your ass for waking me up so early.'

'Oh you're going to be so much fun today.' I laugh.

'Who said I'm doing anything with you today?' She sniffs. 'One, the time. Hello, it's the middle of the freakin' night! And two, I could be working.'

'But you're not.'

'You don't know that.'

I grin. 'I do. I stopped by the café yesterday and asked your mom.'

'I could be busy.'

'But you're not,' I say again. 'C'mon, Rox. Stop being goddamn awkward and go and get dressed.'

'Awkward?' She flings the door open wide and stalks into the house. I follow her in. 'You turn up here at a time that's practically illegal and you're calling *me* awkward?' She huffs loudly, much to my amusement, and stomps upstairs.

'Well, damn. And here I was thinking you were eighteen years old not eighteen *months!*'

'Get lost, Kyle!'

I stare after her for a moment and try to decide whether I want to shake my head and sigh or laugh. I go with laughing and make my way into the kitchen. Ray's sitting at the large oak table in the center of the room, sipping a cup of coffee. A smile graces his lips. I shrug when his eyes meet mine and slip in next to him.

'It's too easy,' I mutter.

He nods in agreement. 'It is when you're brave enough to take her shit.'

I half-snort. 'I've never taken her shit, despite her best efforts, and I'm not gonna start now just 'cause she's having a tough time. The rest of us are too. I'm not treating her like a princess unless she starts acting like one instead of the entitled brat crap she's been pulling.'

'Boy, am I glad you're back.' Ray chuckles sadly. 'No one's done that since Cam died. I guess we got a bit soft on her.'

'Hey.' I lean over the table and bat his paper. 'No one blames you for the way she's acting, alright? She makes her own choices and controls her actions, not you or Myra. She knows exactly what she's doing.'

He smiles, but the sadness in his pale blue eyes only deepens. The pain and guilt coming from him is almost palpable, as is the acceptance. Like he's given up on changing Roxy. Like he's given everything he has to give, meaning there's nothing left. Like he's ready to break under the weight of the past six months.

'Oh I know that, son, but it doesn't stop me wondering if I should have done more. I should have protected her from the very path she's heading down. Cam would have hated this.'

Silence hangs between us for a moment with the truth of his words, the only sound the ticking of the clock and Roxy's footsteps shuffling about upstairs. A door slams, taking the weight from the air.

'That's what you've got me for,' I say softly. 'Selena – although she's tried – has no backbone when it comes to Roxy; she's too soft for Roxy's strong and determined ways, and everyone else is just too happy to go along with what she wants. That's the problem with her senior class, they're all like little sheep waiting for someone to follow and right now that person is Roxy.'

'Are you done talking about me like I'm not here?' The girl in question appears in the doorway, her hair pulled back from her face in a ponytail. She tucks her hands inside the sleeves of her oversized sweater and folds her arms across her chest.

'Are you done with the stick up your ass or you wanna keep it there a bit longer?' I shoot back.

She narrows her eyes. 'I'll keep it there, thanks. Never know when I might need it as a weapon.' She turns on her heel and yanks open the front door.

I wink at Ray, scrambling up to follow her out. She's leaning forward on the car, head resting on her arms. I can't keep my eyes from looking at the way her jeans hug her body, curving around her butt just right.

'I'm just wondering; are you too busy thinking about what my brother would want if he was still alive that you're over-looking the fact you're staring at my ass?' Roxy straightens and turns, pinning me with her sparkling eyes. 'Isn't that a damn fine contradiction?'

I walk toward her, smirking. My hand finds the door handle behind her, and I pull the door open, pushing her toward me. She catches herself before she falls right into me, and a spark flares deep in her eyes. She's close enough that I can smell the flowery perfume she wears and see the dot of mascara on her eyelid she didn't wipe off. She's close enough that I can almost feel her against me.

Almost.

I bend my head forward an inch, bringing my face close to hers. Her lips part slightly and her eyes stay on mine.

'Perhaps you should wear looser clothing if you don't want people to stare at your ass,' I whisper before backing off.

'I never said I didn't want people to stare at my ass.' Her gaze follows me as I walk round the car and open my door. 'Maybe I like it when people do.'

I raise an eyebrow at her over the car. 'Then what the hell are you complaining about?'

I sit down, leaving her mouth opening and closing as she tries to find a comeback. She doesn't. She gets into the car silently, refusing to make eye contact, and my lips twitch. I wait for the click of her seatbelt before pulling away from the house.

She was right. I do contradict myself at every turn. I'm all for protecting her for Cam's sake when I'm at home or with the guys, but the second I see her, I'm protecting her for me.

I want to believe it's because she's like a sister to me, but I'm not that stupid. Maybe she was before, but she isn't now. It's been too long and she's changed too much for me to think of her that way.

'Everyone looks at her and sees a quiet kid that's always top of the class. They don't see what we do, and the bottom line is no one in this shitty little town is good enough for her. Hell, no one in this damn country is good enough for my sister, you know that. The only person that even comes close to being good enough is you.'

'That's 'cause I'm your best friend.'

'No it isn't. Well, maybe. Yeah. But even if you weren't, it doesn't take a genius to figure out you're nothing like all these pricks. If she ever has to be with anyone, I hope to shit it's you, man.'

Cam's words from last year ring out clearly in my mind. He really did believe it – he held Roxy on a pedestal so high you needed a fucking airplane to reach her. But that's just how it was; he loved and protected her more than anyone else could ever be capable of. I really am the only person he ever did and

ever would trust anywhere near her. And there's a big part of
me that wants to take advantage of that trust.

'Where are you dragging me?' Roxy finally asks.

'Where do you think?' I glance at her.

She shrugs. 'If I knew I wouldn't have asked, would I?'

'You know,' I start. 'You might as well drop that shit, Rox.'

'What shit?'

'The attitude. You aren't fooling me.'

'I'm not trying to fool anyone.' She shifts in her seat, looking
at her hands in her lap.

My fingers tap against the steering wheel in time with the
song on the radio. 'Right.' I draw the word out, letting her know
I don't believe her at all.

'I'm not!' she protests.

I turn down the dirt track I know she'll recognize and ignore
her. Even her protests aren't fooling me. The fir tree with a
section of bark missing comes into view, and I pull up beside
it.

'The gorge,' Roxy says softly. 'I haven't been here in ages.'

I undo my belt and shift in my seat so I'm facing her, and
she slowly turns her face to mine.

'You aren't fooling me, Roxy. The snarky comments, the
bitching . . .'

'I'm not—'

'You don't need to pretend around me and you damn well
know it. I know you too well to believe you don't give a shit
about anything other than getting yourself fucked up every
weekend. Speak to everyone else like they're shit on your shoe,
pretend to them you don't care and you're okay, but don't
fucking well do it to me.'

Her eyes meet mine, and in them I see the Roxy I know.
The soft-spoken, gentle girl hiding behind the don't-give-a-crap
girl. It lasts a moment before they return to their new normal.

'What's the matter?' She half-smiles. 'Don't you like the new
Roxy?'

Ha! Don't I like the new her. What a bullshit question. There's no way I can tell her there's nothing sexier than a girl who isn't afraid to twist your balls with her words. In fact, I take it back. That's the second sexiest.

There's nothing sexier than a girl who knows she's sexy.

And Roxy Hughes knows it. She knows the effect she has on guys and how easily she can twist them around her finger . . . And she can hold your balls in a vice-like grip with her words.

Which pretty much means she could give Mila Kunis a run for her money in the sexy stakes.

Chapter Seven – Roxy

He's looking at me like he could eat me and he doesn't even know it.

The flaring heat in his eyes answers my question although he doesn't. It also sends an identical heat down my spine, tingling and tickling me in places it shouldn't. I have no right to feel like this even though I've spent years dreaming of me looking at me this way.

Only in those dreams we weren't in a car by the Columbia Gorge and he wasn't chewing my ass out for being such a fucking bitch.

'Regardless of what I think about her . . .' Kyle clears his throat and turns in the direction of the gorge. '. . . I don't think *you* like the new Roxy as much as everyone thinks you do.'

I scoff at him disbelievingly and follow his steps. Leaves, twigs, and branches crunch under my feet as we push through the forest that covers almost every inch of land around the powerful water. Pine cones litter the ground, and I kick one out of the way.

What does Kyle really know anyway? He's only been back a few days. He knows nothing.

The sound of water rushing reaches my ears, the current making it crash against the rocks that stand in its way. Out here it's peaceful. There are no rumors, no backhand comments and snide looks. There's no judgment apart from my own.

'Where are you going?' I call when Kyle deviates from the usual path. He glances over his shoulder, his usually soft brown eyes looking almost black under the trees shading from the early morning sun.

'Trust me,' is all he says.

I pause as he disappears into the thicker trees I've always avoided. It's darker there, and the climb is steeper, but everyone knows there's nothing but trees in that direction. My eyes flick around me, and I realize I only have two options – I walk into the dark, overgrown trees with Kyle or I carry on to our usual place in the dark – but on my own. Mhmm . . .

Leaves and bits of fir tree kick up as I run after him. I wasn't wrong – the rising sun means there's next to no light amongst these trees, and I stop after a minute because I can't find him. He's disappeared into nowhere. Maybe I shouldn't have stopped –

'Boo,' his voice whispers into my ear.

'Holy—' I yell, jumping backward. My heart pounds in my chest as quickly as adrenaline rushes through my veins. Kyle laughs loudly, putting his hand on my back, and I hold my trembling hands to my stomach to still them. The warmth of his hand seeps through my sweater and spreads outward. I shiver, and I'm glad for the guise of him scaring me.

'I really hate you.' I turn my face toward his.

'Nah, you don't. You hate my tricks.'

I purse my lips. 'And you know it.' I shake his hand off my back and step forward. 'Where are you taking me?'

A hint of sadness creeps into his amused smile and his lips drop a fraction. 'Me and Cam were joking around out here one night and stumbled onto this section of the gorge by mistake. In fact, I don't even know if it is a part of it. It's . . . Well. I'll let you see it for yourself.'

'This isn't another one of your tricks, is it?'

He shakes his head as he walks away from me. 'No. I'm not taking you to a small cliff to push you into a pool of water, I promise.'

There's a teasing lilt to his voice, and it makes me bend over and grab a pine cone. I throw it in the direction of his head but miss, sending it sailing over his shoulder instead.

'Yeah, there was absolutely no reason to do that, you know?'

Kyle shrugs. 'We were fourteen. Besides, it was Cam's idea.'

'Oh, I see. Blame my fear of water on my brother. Are you forgetting you're the prick that pushed me?'

'It's been five years, and you still blame me. That's why I had to push you. Cam didn't want the blame,' he grumbles.

'Mmph,' I grunt noncommittally. 'I'll make you pay for it one day.'

He mutters something under his breath, and I frown at his back. Knowing Kyle it was probably something along the lines of he's already paying for it, but the chicken shit could at least say it loud enough for me to hear.

I stumble on a rock and fall sideways into a bigger one. 'Jesus,' I mutter, putting my hands against the rough surface to steady myself.

'Of course,' Kyle throws over his shoulder, 'it doesn't matter whether I push you or not if you can't keep yourself upright.'

'Remind me why I'm here again?' I tilt my head to the side.

Kyle turns and grins. The kind of grin that would hurt his cheeks if he held it long enough, and lights up his eyes with the mischief I know he's hiding. It's also the kind of grin that has the power to turn my legs to jelly . . . And it has.

I think I'll stay sitting down for now.

'You're here because you know I wouldn't leave until you agreed to it.'

'Huh. True.'

He walks toward me and holds his hands out. 'C'mon, clumsy. You aren't getting anywhere sitting on your ass.'

'But I'm tired,' I whine, letting him drag me after him.

He rolls his eyes. 'Then you should go to bed earlier instead of partying in Portland.'

'Fucking Si.'

Kyle responds by dropping my hands and turning onto something that resembles the start of a dirt path. I glance at my boots then at the loose mud, thinking I'd rather be anywhere other than . . . wherever the hell we are. I'm pretty sure we've gone way past the gorge.

And it doesn't matter anymore.

'This is the place you found?' My voice sounds tiny as I look around me.

'Yep.'

The fir trees have thinned out in this tiny area, thickening again as they reach up toward the cloud-tipped mountains. Large rocks and boulders break up the thick grass and wild plants growing on either side of the stream raging along in front of me. The water breaks every now and then, making a detour around the smaller rocks that have naturally fallen away from the mountains and made their way down here. Along the side of the stream tiny trees stretch up bare of leaves or really any life, their gnarled branches curving around each other.

'Where are we?'

Kyle steps up next to me, his arm brushing mine, and shrugs. 'No idea. We really did just find it on a hike one day. If you walk up the mountain another five minutes you can see the gorge. Takes you close to Cape Horn.'

'Huh.' I lean against a boulder and lower my eyes to the water rushing past. 'It's beautiful here.'

'Yep. It's pretty much perfect.' He rests next to me. 'I wanted to show you something important to him – probably the only thing about him you didn't know.'

I turn my face toward him and sweep my hair to one side. 'You didn't have to. This was yours to hold on to.'

'And I wanted to give a piece of it to you. I thought you'd maybe need a place to come away from prying eyes sometimes.' His gaze meets mine when he tilts his head. 'And because I think you need something to hold on to a lot more than I do.'

I swallow, needing to look away but not wanting to. He's right and he knows it. Damn him, he's so right. 'Thank you.'

'You don't need to thank me,' he says softly.

The moment lingers between us, our eyes fixed on each other, my fingers itching to reach out to him.

'Let's walk up.' I need to break this between us. I can't keep imagining things that aren't here. 'I want to see the gorge.'

'I thought you were tired.' Kyle follows me as I walk past him.

'I was. I guess I woke up.' I shrug and shoot a small smile over my shoulder.

'Of course you have,' he mumbles. I give him the bird over my shoulder, much to his amusement.

The walk up the side of the mountain isn't too tough – this is one of the smaller ones and it's not too far up – but it's slippery. It's wet on the ground from all the springs that start high up and snake their way down, twisting and turning. I hop over a small one in my path and almost slip on a bit of mud.

'Okay?' Kyle asks, steadying me with his hands on my waist.

'Um. Yeah.' Um. *No.*

I'm anything but okay when his hands are on me and his voice is in my ear.

'Let me go first. Follow me, alright?'

I nod as he steps around me and starts walking.

'On second thought . . .' He reaches back and links his fingers through mine with a wink. 'Easier to pull you up if you fall.'

Too late . . .

I follow him silently, trying not to focus on the warmth of his hand around mine. Goddammit, brain! Think about the view. It's a nice view.

My eyes flick to Kyle and his butt.

Yep. Definitely a nice view.

I put my hand to my forehead. I need help.

We stop. My gaze falls to the Columbia Gorge – every beautiful, peaceful part of it. The river snakes through the hills and mountains, and everywhere is lined with wild flowers and pine trees. Birds fly overhead, darting through the trees and over the water, some dipping close enough to almost touch the water. At least that's how it looks from up here.

A sigh leaves me. I'd almost forgotten this existed. This perfect place has been a part of our lives for so long, and when one thing was torn away, this nearly was too.

'We spent our childhoods up here,' Kyle says with a sad tone. 'All of us – running through the trees . . .'

'Playing hide and seek. And tag. You guys always pretended it was kiss chase.'

Kyle shrugs a little. 'You, Iz and Selena never moved so fast. It was a great excuse for being home late for dinner – you guys had run off and we needed to find you first.'

'I'd say that was good of you, but we got in so much trouble after the fifth time. It took Mom like a year to believe me when I tried telling her the truth. You always got us in shit.'

He smiles. 'We're big brothers. It's our job.'

'Yeah.' My own smile drops from my face. 'Except there's a vacancy for mine now.'

Kyle turns to me, whispering my name, and I shake my head.

'It's okay,' I lie to myself as much as him.

It's not okay and he knows it. He's the only person I'll ever show it to . . . Even when I don't want to.

'No, it's not okay,' he says quietly.

'Thank you for bringing me up here.'

'Nice change.'

I lean into his arm, our hands still clasped, and my lips give a sad twitch. 'I mean it.'

'Never said you didn't.' He turns his head so his chin rests on top of mine. 'And you're welcome.'

~

Kyle eyes me over the bright blue table and it's disconcerting. Everything in me is urging me to squirm and shift in my seat, but I fight them and remain perfectly still, eyeing him with the same intensity. He smirks, and I raise an eyebrow.

The low hum of noise from the café becomes non-existent when he looks at me so intensely I can't breathe, just like he is now.

'What?' He leans back in his chair.

'Says the one who's been staring at me for the last five minutes without saying a word.'

'I was . . . thinking.'

'I hope you didn't hurt yourself too much.'

'Oh, ha ha ha,' he mutters dryly. 'Think that up all by yourself, did you?'

'As a matter of fact, I did.' I grin.

His lips twitch as he fights his own. 'Did you ever decide where you're going to college? You were stuck between UCLA with Selena, and Miami with Iz last I heard.'

Yep. I'm not having this conversation.

'Um. Yeah. I picked.' I pick at my thumbnail. 'Why don't you tell me about Berkeley?'

His brown eyes scrutinize me. 'College is college. Wake up, go to class, come home, go to bed, repeat. Which did you pick?'

'Uh.'

'Roxy.'

'Shit,' I mumble. 'Neither, okay? None of them.'

'None?'

'None. I'm not going to college.' There.

Kyle rests his elbows on the table and leans toward me. 'Why not?'

I shrug. 'I just . . . didn't want to go this year.'

'So, what . . . You're gonna stay in Verity Point for however long and work here in your mom's café?'

'So what if I am? Is that a crime?' I bristle, sitting up straighter. 'Not everyone wants to go to college, you know.'

Except I do. I do want to go.

'Hey!' Kyle holds his hands up. 'I was only asking. Calm down, Rox.'

I take a deep breath but narrow my eyes at him. 'Yes. I'm going to stay in Verity Point and work here in Mom's café.'

'And next year?'

I hesitate, then shrug again. 'I'll decide when the time comes, I guess.'

He nods slowly, his eyes flitting around the half-full café. 'Are you staying here because of Cam?'

'What are you, Dr. Phil?' I snort. 'It doesn't matter why I'm staying. I just am.'

'Wow. Your attitude really does stink sometimes,' Kyle comments as Selena brings over our dinner. She laughs quietly, turning back to the counter.

'What?' I call after her.

She half-smiles. 'He has a point.'

I look back to Kyle and the smug smile on his face. 'I'm not getting into this again. One unnecessary attitude chat is enough for today.'

Chapter Eight – Kyle

Long, slender fingers curve around my bedroom door and push it open slowly. I fight the twitch on my lips and close my eyes, pretending to be asleep, and count the soft steps on my carpet. One, two, three, four . . .

'Rah!' I yell, sitting up. My sister screams, jumping backward into my closet, and I laugh loudly.

'You asshole!' Iz cries, her hand against her chest.

'You should know better than to creep into my bedroom when you think I'm asleep.'

'What the hell was that scream?' Mom asks, rushing into my room. 'Oh, Isabel! You're home!'

'Five minutes and you're already trying to kill each other,' Dad mutters, following behind Mom.

'I tried sneaking into his room,' Iz sighs.

Dad snorts. 'You should know better than to sneak into his room, sweetheart.'

'That's what I said.' I sit up in bed. 'She's nearly twenty. You'd think she would have learnt she can't surprise me by now.'

'Alright, brat.' Iz grabs a notebook from my desk and throws it at me. 'You win, as usual.'

'Was your flight early?' Mom rushes over to her and hugs her.

'Yep. Why else do you think I'm in Kyle's room and not on the phone demanding he picks me up from the airport?' She grins.

'Alright, what is this? Family meeting in my room?' I look around.

Iz grins again and moves toward my bed. 'Yep. How about a family hug?'

'Yeah . . . You don't wanna do that,' I warn, holding my blanket around my waist tightly. I'm pretty certain she doesn't want to see what is under my boxers.

'Right,' she demands. 'Get up and get dressed. You can take me for breakfast.'

'I really haven't missed your bossy ass,' I mutter as she follows our parents out of the room, but she hears and grins at me over her shoulder. 'Shut the door!' I yell after her.

She laughs as she skips down the hallway, turning and flashing me that grin again at the top of the stairs. Damn, you'd think Iz was five, not nearly twenty. My feet tangle in my covers as I get up, still holding the sheet round my waist, and push my door shut. Fucking sisters.

I pull on some clothes and head downstairs. The hallway is crowded with Iz's bags, and I'm pretty sure she's bought at least one more in the last six months. My eyebrow raises as I look at her questioningly, pointing a finger toward the suitcases.

'Shut up,' she grumbles, grabbing her jacket from the back of the sofa and opening the front door.

I smirk and slide my feet into my sneakers. I catch up with her halfway down the front path. She's flicking her hair over her shoulders so I poke her.

'You're not in Miami anymore, Iz. No fancy surfers here to impress.'

'Oh, ha ha. You're such a dick. It was stuck in my jacket.' She shoves me back. 'I guess we're headed to Myra's?'

'Even though it's not called Myra's, yeah.' I stuff my hands in my pockets and shrug. 'I can't afford anything else. I'm a student.'

'So am I!'

'You have a job.'

'And you should get one.'

'Oh yeah. I forgot about all the spare time I have at college.'

Iz frowns at me. 'You don't do anything besides college. I have college and I'm on the cheer team *and* I can still find time to work and party. Maybe being in a fraternity is frazzling your brain.'

'My brain is not—'

'Let me guess. You spend all your time drinking beer and eyeing up girls.'

'Hey . . .' I pause. 'Maybe sometimes.'

Definitely since I've been home. Except girls is just girl.

'There we go then.'

The café is filled with the older generation of Verity Point grabbing their morning coffees, and Myra runs back and forth behind the counter, putting both normal and take-out mugs in front of the customers. My sister and I make our way to a table in the corner until the queue has thinned, and she goes to order.

'No Roxy?' Iz looks around when she sits down.

I shrug one shoulder. 'Can you see her?'

She hits me with the menu. 'Alright, smartass. I just wanted to see her. Believe it or not, I've missed her cute little butt.'

Resisting the urge to laugh is harder than I thought. 'There's pretty much nothing cute left about Roxy.'

'I don't believe it. I mean, I've been told the same things you were before we got back, about how she was coping, but I just . . . I don't know, Ky. I can't see it.'

'Yeah, well. I have seen it.'

I tell her about the night at Selena's and the way Roxy was with Tom.

'Well, shit,' Iz mutters and looks up, smiling at Myra with our breakfast in her hands. 'Thanks, Myra. How are you?'

'Same as every day, Iz. It's good to have you both back in town.' Myra puts the plates in front of us and squeezes her shoulder, turning back to the counter.

Iz watches her go. 'I feel kinda shit that we've let them all deal with this alone. She looks so sad.'

'At least they had each other,' I mutter under my breath.

'Kyle,' she half-hisses. 'I guess you're right, but we made the decision to go away to school.'

'Hey, Si's in Miami with you.'

'Oh wow. Excuse me while I recount all the times I cried on his shoulder.' She holds up a finger and pretends to think. 'Oh that's right. A big fat freaking none.'

'Whatever.' I shove some pancake in my mouth. 'We're back now. Maybe you can try to talk some sense into Roxy. We just end up arguing every time I try – it's like trying to explain algebra to a one year old. Which, incidentally, would probably be fucking easier.'

Iz snorts. 'If she's really as bad as you say she is, then what she needs is a guy to tame her.'

I snort in return.

'No, I'm being serious. Ana – she's on the cheer team – was like Roxy for our freshmen and half of our sophomore year. Swear to God, Ky, she put the "ut" in slut. She got close to one of the junior guys on the football team and now she's a changed girl. They've been together four months and they're sickeningly cute.'

'I dunno. Maybe it's just a phase.'

She leans in. 'You're not her parent making excuses for her,' she whispers, pointing her fork at me threateningly. 'You and I both know if it was just a short-term solution she would have given it up by now. She isn't stupid. She just needs to let herself grieve for Cam, because it doesn't sound like she has.'

'Ask her and she'll tell you her partying, for a nice word, is her way of grieving.'

Iz shakes her head. 'No, it's her way of coping with his death. She's coping, but she's not accepting or grieving. She needs to accept he's never coming back before she can grieve for him.'

I blink at my sister for a moment. 'Well. At least we know your college degree isn't being wasted, Ms. Psychologist.'

'Go and fuck yourself, Kyle.'

I just grin. I'm actually glad she's back – as annoying as she is, I love her, and I think we're gonna need her brains for sorting out Roxy. Even if her major doesn't help, she has a girl's brain and that accounts for something.

I'm male. To me, females are an enigma who mean what they say but say the opposite of what they mean.

'You're late!' Myra hisses across the near-empty cafe.

'I'm sorry!' Roxy hisses back. 'I fell back to sleep.'

'Well that's fabulous, Roxanne.'

'Hey! Dad knew I had to be here. He didn't wake me up.'

'Don't blame your father because you couldn't get your lazy behind out of bed, my girl.'

'Whatever. I'm here now.'

Iz raises an eyebrow at me, and I nod. Say hello to the new Roxy.

'Don't bother, Roxanne. I've already dealt with the rush by myself, and I can't say I'm particularly in the mood for you this morning now.' Myra turns and storms into the kitchen.

Iz turns, resting her arm on the back of the chair, and looks at Roxy. 'Well, aren't you a joy to be around?'

'Iz?' Roxy's head snaps up and the grin that breaks out on her face makes my lips twitch. 'You're back!'

'Of course I am. I mean, who wouldn't leave Florida in the summer for this poky little town in the middle of nowhere?' My sister rolls her eyes and wraps her arms around Roxy.

'You love it here really.' Roxy sweeps her hair to one side. 'Did you just get back this morning?'

'Yep. And that reminds me . . .' Iz turns to me, a hand on her hip. 'Why didn't you answer your cell last night?'

'I saw your post on Facebook. You know, the one where you told everyone you'd caught an earlier flight and couldn't, and I quote, "wait to call your brat of a brother to come and pick you up at three a.m.", and put my phone on silent.' I tilt my coffee cup toward her, smiling smugly.

'Bastard. I really should watch what I write on there.' She shakes her head and looks at Roxy. 'What are you doing today?'

She shrugs. 'Selena said something about the guys playing football later.' Her blue eyes flick to me, and I nod.

''Bout lunchtime.'

'Well, we'll go and we can catch up while they're all busy,' Iz declares, sitting Roxy down on the chair between us. 'Now help me eat this double portion of pancakes your mom always seems to give me.'

Roxy grabs a fork. 'She thinks you need fattening up.'

I laugh.

'I'm a cheerleader. I'm supposed to be slim.' She replies and eyes the plate warily. 'But these are really good, so who knows, I could be the first fat cheerleader in our team.' Her phone buzzes as she stabs at the pancakes.

Roxy laughs, and it's one of the most genuine laughs I've heard from her since I got back. I smile, looking down at my plate, and when I glance back up she's watching me. Her lips twitch, and she drops her eyes.

I wish she didn't drop them.

There was a spark in them I've really missed seeing.

~

This feels wrong.

It's one thing to throw a ball around in my yard with Si and Ben, but this is something completely different. This is a whole game. Without Cam.

A team without a quarterback.

And none of us want to take that position. So we don't. We skirt around it in both mini-teams, and the whole thing is a complete shambles because everyone knows you can't play football without fucking quarterbacks. But we can't play it without the main joker and prankster either. I could do it – I could play the jokes we used to but it isn't right. I can't do that without him; I don't want to do it without him. We were always a team. CamandKyle. KyleandCam. It's just how it was with everything.

I really do feel like I'm missing a part of me.

I put my hands on my knees, bending at the waist, and shake my head. 'It's no good, guys. We can't play without a quarterback. We all know that.'

'It ain't right to play him.' Mark shrugs. 'All through school we played together, for fuck sake. I can't step into that position any easier than you guys can.'

'He's right,' Ben agrees slowly. 'We're just gonna have to get over it. We can't play seriously anymore.'

I sigh and drop to the ground, the other guys doing the same. Si throws the ball over our heads, and it lands on the grass.

'So what do we do now?' he asks. 'No football. No really fun way to pass this stupidly long summer.'

'We just fuck around.' I shrug. 'Get the girls out here or something.'

Si snorts. 'Right – Iz is usually cheering the game, not playing it, and Roxy and Selena wouldn't want to mess their hair up or break a nail or some shit.'

'Do it for them. Then they have nothing to worry about.'

'Hey, where's Roxy?' Ben looks over at the girls, and my eyes follow his. Selena is staring into the distance and Iz is lying on her stomach, her face in her arms.

'No idea,' I answer, getting up and heading in their direction. I nudge Iz with my foot. 'Where's—'

'She ran off five minutes ago with her phone attached to her ear,' comes her muffled reply. 'She said she had to go somewhere, but really she can't stand watching you guys play football.'

'Ran off,' Selena scoffs and turns her face to me. 'She's gone to meet Layla.'

'Layla?' Iz and I question in unison.

'She's only been here a few months. She caused too much trouble at her last school so her parents packed her off to live with her aunt for her senior year next year – that's Judy, you know, at the florist?' We nod, and she continues, 'Layla is how Roxy fuels her occasional drug use, and she has a cousin in Portland who gets her alcohol whenever she wants it.'

'Shit, Selena. Why didn't you tell me?' Iz pushes herself up.

'Fuck telling you.' I look from my sister to Selena. 'Why the hell didn't you get me?'

'Because no one can stop her,' she says dryly, a hint of sadness creeping in. 'I've tried so many times. When she really misses Cam, like really, she goes to Layla. It's how she forgets he's gone. She drinks herself into next week.'

'What do you mean no one can stop her?' Iz demands.

'Exactly what I said. No one can stop her when she's got her mind set on it. Believe me, I've tried.'

My jaw clenches. 'Where will she be?'

'At Judy's house, but you can't—'

'Just you fucking watch me.' I spin on my heel and run around Si's house.

Like hell will I let her put that crap into her body. I'm not naïve enough to believe she won't find a way to do it without me finding out, but this time she's not. This time she needs to deal with how she feels and not run from it. This time I'm going to make her deal with it even if I have to sit on her until she talks.

Verity Point is so damn small it only takes me two minutes to catch up to Roxy outside Judy's house on the edge of the woods.

'Kyle?' she looks up at me, surprise all over her face.

'Have you been in there?' I nod toward the house.

'I have no idea what you're on about.' She shifts uncomfortably.

'Don't bullshit me, Roxanne.'

Her eyes narrow at my use of her full name. 'Don't—'

'Have you been in the goddamn house?!'

She says nothing, instead turns and stalks into the woods. I rub my hand across my eyes and follow her.

'Roxy.'

'Fuck off, Kyle.'

'Is that a yes?'

'It's a mind your own fucking business!'

I grab her arm and swing her round so she faces me. '*You* are my damn business. You always have been. You're more my business than you realize.'

Her blue eyes widen ever so slightly, and questions shine in them as she looks up at me. I hold her gaze without faltering, wanting her to understand something I don't even understand myself, and tighten my grip on her arm.

'Did you go in?' I ask her again, my voice softer this time.

Roxy breathes in deeply, holding it for a second, and slips her hand into her jacket pocket. I release her arm as she pulls out a small vodka bottle. I hold out my hand. She pauses, closing her eyes as she puts it in my palm. I curl my fingers around her hand, letting them brush across hers as I take it from her. My fingers unscrew the cap and tip the bottle upside down.

The vodka splashes onto the ground, and when she opens her eyes, I rub it into the mud with my foot. I hand her the empty bottle when her eyes meet mine.

'You enjoyed that, didn't you?' she asks, snatching it with venom in her tone.

'Not entirely. Did I enjoy emptying that crap onto the floor? Yep. Did I enjoy taking it from *you*? No. I fucking hated it,' I tell her honestly.

'Right. And I'm supposed to believe that.'

'I hated taking it from you because I know it makes it easier for you. It's just the wrong thing you're using – I think of you using that and I wonder what the hell Cam would think of you. His beloved baby sister using alcohol to forget and get herself in any number of fucked up situations.'

'You always have to bring him up, don't you? Maybe I don't use it for that. Maybe I use it because I like it.'

'I call bullshit on that and every other excuse you have for it. You only "like" it because it lets you forget.'

'And I think I'm allowed to forget, don't you?' She raises her eyebrows and walks further into the trees.

'Yep. Shit, Rox, you were there when he crashed—'

'And the rest.' She stops in front of a large tree, the bottle dropping from her grip. She presses her hands against the trunk, tilting her head down and to the side. 'And the goddamn, nightmare-inducing rest that haunts me every fucking time I close my eyes.'

Her voice is tiny yet it holds so much power and heartbreak. I feel each crack spreading in her heart with each word, and it makes my own ache. It makes every part of my body ache for her, for what she's feeling and the urge to soothe it. My feet ache to walk to her the way my arms ache to hold her close.

'Talk to me,' I say into the gentle breeze rustling the leaves above us. 'Don't use alcohol to forget, Rox. Use me to remember.'

'What good will that do?'

I give into the ache in my legs and crunch twigs under my feet as I walk to her. I stop just behind her and push her hair from her face.

'I don't know, but at least you won't be hurting alone anymore.'

Her eyes are fixed on one spot on the ground, and I'm almost glad I can't see them. 'It wasn't just the crash. It was everything. Everything about the night, I saw it all. Selena called the ambulance, and I stayed by the crushed car watching my brother die and begging him not to leave me. I watched them revive him at the scene and bundle him into the ambulance. Then in the hospital I watched them try and fail to bring him back to life for a second time. The whole time I was begging him not to leave me, not to die. I bargained and I bartered with an invisible entity to save him, to not let him go. And I was alone the whole time. He died before Mom and Dad got to the hospital. His last moments were mine. Just mine. That night was so much more than watching the crash. Do you get that now? It was so much fucking more! I watched my brother die – *die!* – right in front of me, and there wasn't a single freaking thing I could do about it!'

Tears stream from her eyes and streak mascara down her cheeks. I wrap my arm around her shoulders and pull her into me, holding her tightly against my chest. Her silent tears turn into body-shaking sobs as she grips my shirt at my back and her knees give way.

As I thread my hand into her hair and turn her face into my neck, it feels as if everything stops. Nature stills as she cries for what I'm guessing is the first real time since he died. The noises of heartbreak are the only sounds around us. The only thing I know is her trembling body tucked into my arms and the tears soaking into my shirt, the cries from her mouth and the tightness of her fingers as they hold onto me.

And I understand why she does what she does. She holds so much pain, so much guilt and so much anguish in her little body it's a wonder she hasn't broken by now. But there's nothing I can do.

Nothing except hold her. So that's what I do.

I hold her to me and sit down with my back against the tree she was just leaning against. Her knees go either side of my hips and she nestles into me, never letting go as the tears keep falling. I bury my face in her hair, feeling my own tears in the back of my eyes for the loss of the person we both loved.

Because I did. I loved Cam as more than just my friend. I loved him as my brother, my go-to guy, my partner in crime. If guys could have guy soul mates, he was mine. I know my own pain and I feel it every day. I feel it everywhere, but what I feel is nothing compared to what Roxy feels.

And this is what she needs. She needs to remember and cry and hold onto someone who'll never let her hurt without hurting too.

She releases my shirt and wraps her arms around my neck, hiding her face in the crook between my neck and shoulder. My own arm goes tighter around her waist and pulls her closer to me.

The closer she is to me and the longer I hold her, the longer I hold her trembling, sobbing body to me, the more a part of me begins to accept the fact there's so much more than just Cam between us.

Chapter Nine – Roxy

'He's driving too fast.' I'd looked at Selena, worry snaking its way through my body. I knew Stu had drunk more than the legal limit – that's why I'd tried getting Cam in with us.

'Call Cam. Get him to tell Stu to slow down,' she replied, pressing down on the accelerator to keep Stu's Honda in sight.

The repetitive ring buzzed in my ear as I called my brother. My teeth dug into my lip, peeling the top layer of skin away.

'What?'

'He's going too fast, Cam. He's too drunk to be driving like that. Get him to slow down.' I tried to keep my apprehension and nerves tucked away, but there was no fooling him. There never was.

'Rox.' Cam laughed. 'Don't worry. Stu isn't that drunk. He's in total control. Chill out, yeah?'

'Cam, I . . .'

The glare of the headlights cut through the night sharply. Stu's car swerved on the tight country road as he tried to avoid the oncoming car. The line went dead and at the same time a scream left my body and Selena slammed on her brakes. The blue Honda's tires screeched against the uneven surface, skidding and spinning as Stu did his best to regain control of his car. The other car with his too-bright headlights went sideways into the bushes, the engine cutting.

I watched in horror as Stu's car slid head on into a tree. The front of the car crushed against the broad, sturdy trunk, and steam billowed out from under the hood on impact.

'Cam! Caaaaaaaam!' My scream broke the momentary

silence. I fell out of Selena's car in my rush to get to him, to my brother, to make sure he was safe. Fuck the car. I just needed to know he was okay.

I yanked open the passenger side door. Cam was leaning forward, blood pouring from a cut on his head. His airbag hadn't expelled, and he had grazes and cuts all over his face. One of his hands was pressed tightly against his stomach with his fingers curled into his shirt.

'Cam? Oh, God. Cam, Cam. Can you hear me?' I touched his face frantically, slapping his cheeks and pinching his nose as tears streamed down my face. 'Wake up, Cam. Tell me to shut up. For God sake, wake up!'

He didn't. He sat silently, his chest twitching erratically in place of a rhythmic rise and fall. Nothing else mattered in that moment. I just needed to know he was okay, that he was alive. That Stu's stupid, drunk driving hadn't seriously hurt the most important person in my life.

It felt like an age before I heard the wail of sirens and the pulsing blue lights. But still I refused to move. My hands were wrapped tightly around Cam's, talking gibberish I knew would annoy him. I just needed him to tell me to shut the hell up. That was all I cared about.

'Miss, please come with me,' a voice said from behind me.

I shrugged hands off my shoulders. 'No. I can't leave my brother. I need to make sure he's okay. I have to.'

'The paramedics can't get to him with you sitting here. We'll just go a few meters away. You'll still be able to see the car,' the same voice said softly. I allowed them to pull me back from Cam, my eyes never leaving his still form. 'Are you hurt?'

I shook my head. 'No. I was in my friend's car.' I move my eyes to the police officer guiding me toward her car. 'He'll be okay? My brother?'

'I don't know anything until the paramedics have examined him. I'm sorry.' She sits me in the back seat. 'Why don't you tell me your details, and we can have your parents meet us at the hospital?'

'Hospital?' My eyes widened, flitting frantically from her to Stu's car. Paramedics were swarming around Cam with medical equipment, and I needed to be there. More than anything I needed to be by my brother's side, holding him, telling him it was okay.

The officer held me back before I realized I was moving.

'It's okay. Let them do their job, sweetheart. He's in the best hands.'

'No. No. I need to be there. Be with him. Please.' I didn't recognize the voice crying out. It was raw, it was pained. It sounded nothing like me. Nothing at all.

'You can be. At the hospital,' she says softly. 'There's nothing you can do for him right now.'

~

I broke. Shattered. Gave in.

For one glorious hour, I collapsed under the weight of the pain wrapped around my heart and let it consume me whole-heartedly. I let myself feel the burn of losing Cam more clearly than I have since the day he died.

And now I hate myself for it.

I hate it because the pain is stronger. It's more noticeable. It's heavier. It's frightening and it's panic-inducing. I hurt more than I ever thought I could and I miss him more feverishly than I ever knew.

So I need to forget. I need to put all the bullshit aside, bury the pain and hide the heartbreak, and get on with life. Right after I've stepped through the imposing gate towering above me in the waning light, and stared at his headstone for a while.

I've never hesitated this way before. I've never been so scared to go in there and see his name carved perfectly into the marble or sit next to the grass that covers the space where he's laid to rest.

I don't know how I do it. I just know I do. Somehow my feet move, one in front of the other, and take me to his grave.

A few tiny leaves have fallen from the trees, lining the section of the cemetery he lies in and sitting on top of his headstone. I rub my hand across the top and brush them away, watching as they flutter to the grass, and lower myself next to his grave. I hug my knees to my chest and rest my head on top of them. My eyes trace the letters of his name the way they do every time I come here.

His name. His date of birth. His date of death. The one line that sums his death up perfectly.

The sky has gained the brightest star it will ever have.

My words. They were all I could say when we ordered the stone. And nothing else would have fit him. He was the bright star in everyone's life, so it's only right that's where he ends up. High in the sky, shining over everyone and lighting our way. There was no need to say he'd be missed; we all know he is and he probably knows it too.

'Light my way home tonight, yeah, bro?' I whisper, kissing my fingers and pressing them to the stone. 'Miss you.'

I hold back the tears as I push up from the grass and walk away from him. Selena's house is only minutes away from the cemetery, but I've hidden my emotions for so long they're not noticeable by the time she says goodbye to her parents and we turn toward Leanne's house for her birthday party.

'Is Kyle going tonight?' Selena asks.

I shrug. 'I don't know. Why would I?'

'No reason, I guess. Just that he ran off like his ass was on fire when he realized you'd gone to Layla's the other day.'

'Only because he wanted to empty it over the floor,' I mutter dryly.

So I don't actually care about what he did . . . That much. A part of me is pissed at him, but another part of me is still lolling about in a glowing bubble from him holding me for so long, and both parts know it wouldn't have happened if he didn't empty the vodka all over the floor.

'Good on him,' she replies brashly 'Personally I would have shoved it up your butt, but whatever floats his boat.'

I roll my eyes and push through the open door at Leanne's. 'Whatever. I need a drink.'

'Here we go,' she mumbles.

I ignore her and make my way into the kitchen. Olly's standing by the fridge with his eyes following my every move. His lips curve upward as I approach, and he holds up a bottle of vodka.

'Can I get you a drink, Roxy?'

Like hell you can.

'Thanks, but I think I can pour my own drink.' I take the bottle from him. 'I'm not quite helpless.' I grab a cup and pour it in, mixing it with some coke.

The drink, not the drug.

Olly leans in toward me and puts his mouth by my ear, his hand settling on my hip. 'I can make you helpless.'

I rest the urge to roll my eyes and turn, gripping his collar. 'Try it, Oliver, and we'll see who's really helpless by the end of the night.'

'That sounds like a promise.'

'Oh, it is, but you won't like being helpless.' I glance at his pants. 'In fact, I think nature already did the job for me.' I raise my glass in his direction, a small smile playing at the corners of my mouth. 'Cheers.'

I leave him standing glaring after me, and move through into the front room. A glance around tells me Kyle isn't here yet – if at all, and I relax a little. Both from the freedom his absence gives me and because I haven't seen him since I oh-so-elegantly smeared my mascara across his white shirt.

My drink goes down smoothly – too smoothly – and the others follow. One after another, no thinking, no counting, no anything except the liquid in my cup and the sweet oblivion creeping up onto me. Nothing except the music pounding off the walls and flowing through my body. Nothing except—

'You really don't need anymore,' Selena says through a sigh as I pour another drink.

'Whatever,' I reply, my choice word for the evening. 'Lighten up, Leney. I can still talk, I can still walk, and I can still remember my name.' I turn to her, smiling, the now full cup in my hand. 'When I can't do any of that, then I've had enough.'

I down the drink, feeling it join the already warm puddle in my belly. I don't care what number drink that was. I just care about the swimming in my head . . .

And the blue-grey eyes looking into mine. Well, hello there. 'I don't think we've met,' the owner of the eyes says.

'I think I'd remember you if we did.' I look over him. Light brown hair, strong jaw, fairly firm arms . . . 'Yep. I'd definitely remember you.'

He smirks. 'Then we should introduce ourselves.'

My lips move into a smile that mirrors his but holds more confidence. 'Feel free to introduce yourself, but I don't do names.' I take his hand and pull him into a dancing group of people.

He cups my hips with his hands and draws my body close to him. I slide my hands up to his neck as he lowers his head, turning his face into my hair. He coaxes my body to move and I go with it, let him take control because this is the only control he's gonna have.

The second we leave the control is all mine.

His hands wander, slipping to my back and down to my butt, his fingers probing through the material of my tight skirt. His breaths flutters my hair, his lips ghosting my ear, and I move my face toward his.

'Fucking hell,' Kyle's voice says behind me.

I groan. 'You have got to be kidding me.'

'What?' the guy in front of me asks.

My arms fall from his neck and Kyle's hand clamps on one of them.

'You're leaving,' Kyle orders.

I snatch my arm and glare at him. 'Again? Really? Are you my fucking keeper?'

His eyes are hard and his jaw tight. 'The way I see it you have two options. You leave by my side or slung over my goddamn shoulder. Either way, you're leaving.'

'Who is this dick?' No-Name guy asks. 'Your brother or something?'

'Not her brother,' Kyle responds. 'And you're one lucky jackass he isn't here.' He turns back to me. 'Choose. Now.'

Fine. You wanna play this game.

I grin sassily. 'As tempting as your shoulder is, Kyle, I can still walk. But feel free to hold me up if you want to.'

He drops his head back as I walk past him, putting extra swing in my hips.

'Wait.' I stop in the hallway.

'What now, Roxanne?' he groans from behind me.

I turn to him. 'If you throw me over your shoulder, would you slap my ass? If you would, I might have to reconsider my answer.'

His eyes flash with something between annoyance and heat, and tingles run through my body with the knowledge that I'm affecting him.

Men.

This is what I can control.

And not even Kyle is immune to it.

'Get your ass outside,' he warns. 'Don't fuck me around, Rox.'

'Spoil sport.' I pout, walking outside. His car is parked in the drive, the only one there. 'Let me guess; you want my ass in your car so you can haul me home?'

'And it's a gold star for you,' he replies, holding open my door.

'I'm getting good at this.' I flash him another grin as I climb in and he shakes his head.

This is fun.

He pulls out of the driveway. 'I have no idea what to do with you, girl. I really don't.'

My smile widens, and I shift in my seat so my body is facing him.

'Don't say it,' he says gruffly. 'Don't say what you were about to.'

'What?' I blink innocently.

His eyes shoot a warning glance in my direction. 'You know exactly what I mean. You're just making a complete idiot of yourself.'

'So why do you keep turning up here and saving me like I'm a damsel in distress? I gotta say, your armor isn't up to much, Sir Knight.'

'Because if I turn up and take you away, no one else has the pain of listening to awkward, drunken sentences like that.'

'Or . . .' I open the door when he pulls up outside my house. 'You don't want anyone to have me even though you don't want me yourself.'

I slam the door behind me and *fuck*. I didn't mean to say that out loud. At all. Uh-uh. Damn. Why did I say it out loud?

Oh yeah. Because it's the truth. Isn't it?

'And what the fuck does that mean?' he yells, following me into my back yard.

Well, might as well carry on and blame it on my 'awkward drunken sentences' in the morning.

I spin, my hair flying around my shoulders, and put my hands on my hips. My eyes are dead on his in the darkness.

'What I mean is you've turned up to these parties twice now. Both times you've got pissed off when I've been dancing with a guy even when it's my right to. I'm single, I have no commitments or promises to any guy and I can do what the hell I like.'

'I'm just doing—'

'Bullshit!' I punch the air, stamp my foot, and jab my finger in his direction. 'Bull. *Shit*! You're not doing this for Cam. I don't believe that for one fucking second, Kyle. You get too angry and protective for it to be for him.'

'I've known you our whole lives. Of course I'm gonna protect you from the jackasses you insist on hanging with. I care about you, for fuck sake!' He runs his hands through his hair and turns, looking away from me.

'Of course,' my voice quietens, a sad tinge almost creeping

in. 'I forgot. You've known me forever. I'm Cam's baby sister. How stupid of me to forget.'

'It's not that.' He sighs.

'Then what is it? I am Cam's baby sister. That's all I've ever been to you.'

'Before? Yeah, that's all you ever were. Now? No, Roxy. You're not just my dead best friend's little sister.'

My heart stops and whatever words I had ready to respond with lodge in my throat, leaving my mouth open as I stare at the back of his head.

'What?' I whisper.

'You're not just his sister, okay? Fuck. I wish you were but you're not. You're so much fucking more than just Cam's baby sister.'

'Kiss me.'

The words leave without my permission. They burst from my lips, not a plea but a demand. I'm not asking him to kiss me.

I'm telling him.

Kyle stops, his head turning to the side. His profile is illuminated by the moonlight, and I hate that he's not facing me. I hate that all I can see is the back of him.

'What?'

'If I'm not just Cam's kid sister, then kiss me. Now. Turn your ass around and walk up to me and kiss me like you damn well mean it, Kyle Daniels.'

'Rox . . .' He turns. 'You're drunk. You have no idea what you're saying.'

'I'm not . . .' I pause as he faces me, his eyebrow raised. My arms shoot into the air in surrender. 'Okay, I'm drunk. But that doesn't mean I don't know what I'm saying. I know exactly what I'm saying. I know what I want and I want you to kiss me.'

He takes slow steps toward me, almost stalking me, and my heart finds its beat again, thumping against my chest. I walk backward and my back hits the side of the shed. I swallow as

he moves toward me in the darkness, never taking my eyes
from his.

'You really want me to kiss you? Right here?'

'Right here.'

'Right now?'

'Right now.'

Kyle stops in front of me and flattens his hand against the
shed wall. I can see the heat in his eyes even in the darkness,
and I can feel that same heat emanating from his body into
mine. There isn't a single part of our bodies that is touching
but it doesn't matter.

I can't breathe. My stomach is clenching in excitement and
my heart is pounding against my ribs. Blood and adrenaline
rush around my body, and I'm hyper-aware of everything.

Of me. Of him. Of our bodies. Of our breathing.

'Against the shed wall?' he clarifies in a hot whisper.

'I'm already against it.' When did my voice get so breath-
less?

'I know.' He dips his head lower. 'I'm just trying to figure
out exactly what you're asking me. "Kiss me" is kinda vague.'

'And also kinda clear.'

'Depends who you ask.' His fingers brush against my hip,
sending shivers and tingles across my skin through my clothes.
'And you're asking me to pin you against your shed wall and
kiss you. Right?'

Yes.

'Right?'

'Yes.'

'You don't know what you're asking, Roxy. You really don't.'
He shakes his head, moving back from me.

My hands shoot out and grab his shirt, stopping him from
turning away. 'I know what I'm asking, Kyle. Don't treat me
like I'm stupid. You said I'm not just Cam's kid sister, now
prove it.' I look him right in the eyes, both showing him I'm
serious and challenging him. 'Or just tell me you don't want
to kiss me and go.'

Before I can say another word, his body flattens against mine and pushes me firmly into the wall. His lips crash onto mine, his fingers curl around my waist, and cups the back of my neck. I slide my hands up his chest and around his neck, my fingers sinking into the hair at the back of his head.

Soft. Hot. Hard. Probing.

All these words flit through my mind but none come close to the way I feel as he sweeps his mouth across mine, kissing me in a way I've never been kissed before. His tongue flicks across my closed lips, slipping between them when they part, and moves across mine, exploring every part of my mouth, feeling me, touching me, possessing me. It's primal yet loving, tightening every muscle in my body and turning my legs to jelly at the same time.

Intense.

The way this feels, the way we cling to each other, the way our lips caress and our tongues battle, it's intense. It's intense and consuming and it's owning me, taking me over. It's making me and ruining me, because I know nothing will ever top this.

No kiss will ever feel the way this one does.

'Like that?' he whispers, his lips brushing mine with his words.

I nod. 'Like that.'

'Good.' He pulls me even closer and puts his knee between my legs, closing every inch of space between our bodies. His hand presses flat against the arch of my back, curving my body into his, his thumb brushing across my cheek.

I open my eyes, looking straight into his, and hold my breath. I can't calm the frantic pace of my heart or the speed of my breathing and I sure as shit can't stop the goose pimples erupting over every inch of my skin.

'Rox,' Kyle whispers, tilting my head back slightly. I don't speak; I look at him with my lips slightly parted, my eyes wide and my cheeks flushed, waiting for whatever he's going to say next.

He doesn't say a thing.
He kisses me again.
And I'm lost.

LEABHARLANN
CO. CILL DARA

Chapter Ten – Kyle

Shit.

I never meant to do that.

I was supposed to drag her from that damn party and shove her through her front door, not have her turn those bright blue eyes on me and play me the way she plays all her guys. And I wasn't supposed to hold her against her shed while I kissed her. And God did I kiss her . . . but I couldn't help it. Ever since I've been back I've wanted to kiss her as much as I've wanted to sort her out. And last night I lost it.

It was that spark in her eye – the determination and resolution when she demanded I kiss her – and it was the slight gasp in every word she spoke through her parted lips when I moved closer. It was the knowledge we were close, so close, and it was down to me. The choice was mine. Kiss her or walk away.

There was no way I could have walked away. I couldn't have turned around and left her there, her hair loose and tumbling round her shoulders with her cheeks flushed, any more than I could have stayed away from that party when Selena called me.

And I feel like a fucking teenage girl sitting here replaying those moments in my mind. It's not like it was my first kiss or even just a casual kiss with some girl I barely know. It was different because it was Roxy.

The girl I've kept assholes away from our whole lives.

I can't believe how much has changed in two little weeks. Fourteen days doesn't seem long enough to go from seeing her as a sister to kissing her like my life depends on it.

'Fuuuuuuck.' I dig the heels of my hands into my eyes. 'What the hell did I do that for?'

'Do what?' Iz asks from my doorway.

I tilt my head to the side and look at her. 'Nothing.'

'You're such a bad liar.' She laughs. 'It's almost like the time you and Cam were four and promised Mom you didn't eat her freshly baked cookies. She would have believed you if you didn't have chocolate around your mouth and crumbs down your shirt.'

'Yeah, alright,' I grunt. 'I just . . . I don't feel like talking about it to you.'

'And what's wrong with me?'

'Is anything right with you?'

Iz narrows her light brown eyes and crosses her arms across her chest. She studies me, her eyes flitting to each of my features, and a small smile tugs at the corners of her mouth.

'Don't do your body language shit on me!' I sit up straight.

'You're guilty but confused. No, wait.' She tilts her head to the side. 'Aha. You're confused because you should be feeling guilty, but you're not. You think you've done something bad, but it felt good at the time. And now you want to talk to me but you're incredibly freaked out I've worked out how you're feeling by the way you're sitting.' Her smile evolves into a grin.

Bitch.

'Am I right?'

I sigh. 'Yes. You're right.'

'Oh, this is good.' She kicks my door shut and bounces across my room, jumping onto my bed next to me. She tucks her legs under her and stares at me. 'So. What did you do?'

'I can't believe I'm saying this,' I mumble. 'Uh . . . I . . . Um . . .'

'Yes?'

'Um.'

'Spit it out, Ky!'

'I kissed Roxy!'

The words spill from me, and I hang my head back as soon as I've said her name. Iz's mouth drops open.

'You did . . . what?'

'Don't make me say it again,' I plead and tap my temple. 'I'm already fucked up in here, don't make me be the same way out here too.'

'No, I know what you did. I just . . . You shocked me. Kind of.'

'Shocked you? Not the great Dr. Iz who can tell someone's feelings with a mere glance?'

'Shut it.' She shoves my arm. 'Obviously I could tell there was some serious tension there but I didn't realize it was quite that strong. So . . .'

'Here we go. Do I have to pay you an hourly rate for this session?'

'Half price,' she replies without missing a beat and winks. 'Seriously though, bro. You're guilty because . . . Why?'

I lean back and bend my knees, staring out of my window. 'She's Cam's sister, isn't she? Like . . . His baby sister. The one girl he loved more than anything.'

'And if he wanted anyone to kiss her, surely it would be you?'

'Yeah, but he made me promise I'd protect her, Iz. I'm doing a stellar job at it. How am I meant to protect her from the dicks she insists on hanging with if I can't even protect her from myself?'

She doesn't speak for a moment, letting my question hang in the air between us. And it does hang – heavily. Like no one really wants to answer it.

'Who says you have to protect her from you?' she whispers. 'Besides, the best way to protect someone is to have them by your side.'

Ain't that the truth?

'I dunno. If I were Cam, I'd want to punch me.'

'But you're not Cam, are you?'

I drag my eyes from the window to hers, and hold her gaze. 'It would be easier if I was. Then I wouldn't be stuck in this shitty place where I have no idea what to do. No idea how to make sense of what I feel.'

'So talk to him.' Iz shrugs like it's simple.

'He can't exactly talk back. Have you forgotten—?'

'He's dead, I know. But, Ky, death doesn't have to mean he's gone. Because he's not, not really. He's still here – that's obvious by the way you're feeling.' She slides off my bed and stuffs her hands in the pockets of her shorts. 'Call me crazy, but I bet if you went to his grave and just let it all out you'd feel better. After all, there's no one to answer you back, is there?'

~

'I'm a dick, aren't I?' I ask the marble headstone in front of me like it'll answer. If it could, it would agree. If it could, it'd probably create a stone fist and slam into me.

It's silent here. There are no people, no birds, no wind. It's just me, my words, and my dead best friend. It's just the sick feeling in my stomach when I think about the last time we were sitting together.

'Shaving cream? In her shampoo? Again?' Cam had looked at me.

I shrugged. 'It's the best one, and you know it.'

'Do you ever think we should grow up and stop the pranks?'

'Yeah, one day, but that isn't anytime soon.' We both grin. 'Come on. Let's do this one more time.'

'You know this is on you, right?'

We stand and I hold my arms out. 'Always is, man. Always is.'

And now I'm sitting next to his dead body, expecting responses that'll never come.

Did I want Roxy back then? Was there a small part of me that recognized something the rest of me didn't? Have I secretly always wanted Cam's sister to be more than that?

'You'd know the answer, wouldn't you? You always fucking did. You knew shit before everyone else did.' I run my fingers through my hair and let out a long breath. 'What do I do, man? How do I protect her when the only reason I wanna do it is for a selfish one? If you could see her now . . .' I let out a sad laugh. 'You'd have her locked in a basement somewhere 'til she sorted her shit out, y'know? She's bad, real bad, but I dunno what to do. I can't keep rocking up to these parties and dragging her away.

'I could talk to her, I guess. Talk her down instead of yelling at her ass. But we both know how well that works. She's stubborn as fuck and does whatever the hell she wants to. Worth a shot though, right?' I shrug. 'Option two – fuck me this is like finals all over again – keep dragging her out of those goddamn parties and show her what she's doing. How she's wasting her life. Agreed?'

I wait for a moment in silence, still expecting that answer. Still expecting his voice to laugh at me and tell me to shut the hell up.

'And the last option . . . the last chance . . . walk away from her.' I swallow even at the thought. 'I turn around and leave her alone, hoping it'll knock some sense into her. Drastic, but sometimes that's all she'll react to, isn't it? Like the shaving foam in the shampoo bottle. That was always a pretty damn dramatic reaction.'

His name stares back at me, taunting me, and I chew the inside of my cheek.

Three options. Three chances. Three attempts at getting it right.

Three different opportunities for her to kick my ass.

'Better get started then, eh?' I stand and pat the top of his stone. 'See ya later.'

Odd how we talk to dead people like they can still hear us. I guess a part of us wants them to hear us, wants to believe they can.

I know I want to believe he can hear me and agree with me.

My feet take me in the direction of the café, and I try to figure out what I'm gonna say. Unsuccessfully. What do you say to the girl you pinned up against her shed wall and kissed the hell out of?

Certainly not 'Hi, how are you today?'

I shake my head and push open the café door. Roxy's standing behind the counter, the twins in front of her, and she's laughing with them. There's a lightness to that laugh.

Her blue eyes find mine when the twins turn around. My gaze collides with hers across the café, holding her eyes to mine. She swallows, her lips parting, and I walk toward her.

Chapter Eleven – Roxy

'Mm mmmm.' Marie leans against the counter and gives a little shiver. 'Mmmm.'

I flip the coffee machine on and glance at her over my shoulder. 'Can I help you?'

'Not you, honey,' she replies with a sigh.

'I guess you haven't seen him,' Isla squeezes in next to her sister.

'Seen who?'

'The hunk of a man staying at your aunt's place! Oh!' They both fan themselves with their hands.

I place their coffees in front of them and ring up their order. 'Hunk of a man? I'm listening.'

'He's . . . Oh, he's got me all flustered!' Marie sighs again.

'He's tall,' Isla says dreamily. 'Tall and big and his hair! Goodness me, I could run my fingers through his hair all day long.'

I don't think I've seen these two quite this giggly over a man . . . Well, ever, and that's surely saying something.

'Who is he?' I hand them their change.

'Haven't the foggiest, dear. He did say he'd be meeting us here for coffee, though. So if you see that man come on in, you make sure you notify us immediately!' Isla waggles her finger at me. My lips twist in a wry smile.

'Like I'd notice before you two ladies.'

Marie nods. 'You know, Isla, foxy Roxy has a point there.'

'Foxy Roxy?' I snort. 'You two are getting worse. Go drink your coffees and keep an eye out for this hunky man. Go on.'

The door opens and they both turn with lightning speed.

'Mm, it's not our man, Marie, but he's certainly a hunky one.'

I roll my eyes and laugh. When I look up Kyle's standing in the doorway, one hand resting on the door. There's a light shadow along his jaw, and as I lift my eyes to his, my heart thumps. He's looking at me the way he did last night – intensely, like there's nothing else he can see but me. I swallow as he steps toward the counter.

'Ladies.' He looks at Marie and Isla. 'Don't you look lovely this morning?'

'Oh, you charmer you!' Isla swats his arm, giggling.

'Just tellin' it as I see it.' Kyle winks.

'Well . . .' Marie's eyes flit between me and him. 'I think we should go have a seat, Isla.'

'Right you are, Marie. Facing the door this week, though. We don't want to miss our young man.'

Kyle raises an eyebrow when they've sat down. 'Their young man?'

'Some guy staying at my aunt's bed and breakfast,' I answer dismissively. 'Coffee?'

'Please.'

I turn and busy myself with the machine and his mug. I'm trying not to focus on his gaze firmly attached to my back or on our kiss last night. In fact, all I'm trying to focus on is making this coffee without—

'Shit!' I cry, dropping the mug of milk. I grab a cloth and bend down to mop it up. Kyle's laughing quietly behind me, and I glare at him when I stand up again.

He ignores my icy look and leans forward on the counter. 'Something on your mind, Roxy?'

'Aside from how I wish I'd hit you with the milk instead? No.'

'Sarcasm to your defense again.'

I put his coffee in front of him – with milk. 'Any reason you're here this morning?'

His lips curve to one side. 'I'm having a coffee.'

'Of course you are.' I put one hand on the counter and tilt my head to the side. 'But why are you here?'

His eyes flick to the twins, and they look back at their mugs instead of us. He leans toward me and lowers his voice. 'Can we talk about this when you've finished?'

I glance at the clock. 'That's not for another half an hour.'

Kyle curves his fingers around his mug and lifts it to his mouth. His brown eyes study me over the top of the white ceramic, and my breath catches in my throat at the glint there.

He says quietly, 'I'll wait for you.'

There's double meaning there.

I shake off the thought and head toward Mr. Yeo's table. One kiss and I'm analyzing his every word. Fucking hell.

'How was it?' I ask the old man hidden behind the paper.

'Awesome,' he replies. 'That's what you kids say these days, isn't it?'

I laugh. 'That's it.'

'Good. You tell your mama it's the best she's ever given me.'

'She tried a new recipe today. I'll be sure to let her know it's a success.' I take his plate and head into the kitchen to put it in the sink.

'Well?' Mom asks.

'He loved it.'

'Who knew all I needed was a bit of black pepper?'

I shrug a shoulder. 'Not me.'

'Roxy . . .'

I stop before I walk from the kitchen and slowly turn to her. 'Yeah?'

'Are you okay? You seem a little . . . off.'

'Yeah, I'm fine, Mom. I didn't sleep well last night, is all.'

'Okay, honey. You can go when Selena turns up. I didn't need you both last weekend, so go and get some sleep.'

I nod and walk back into the café. The twins are talking to a tall man with graying hair. Surely this can't be the 'hunk' in Aunt Bonnie's bed and breakfast?

'Psst,' I hiss at Kyle, leaning in close. 'Who's that?'

He turns to me and his face is much closer to mine than I thought it would be. I flinch in surprise but he doesn't move away.

'That's their young man.' The twist in his lips shows just how amused he is.

I peer at the man. 'My house is younger than him.'

Kyle chuckles. 'Play nice, Roxanne.'

'Don't. Call. Me. Roxanne.'

'Or what?'

'Sorry I'm late!' Selena runs through the café. 'I couldn't find my apron.'

I push off the counter. 'Don't worry about it. You could have used mine. I'm going now anyway.'

'You . . . What?'

'Mom said she didn't need me so I can leave early.' I shrug and untie my apron, stashing it beneath the counter. 'Have fun.'

'Pfffft.' Selena pours a cup of coffee, and I grin.

'Behave yourself, you two,' I shoot at the twins as I stroll toward the door. They both turn to me and their eyes twinkle when they see Kyle on my heels.

'We'll say the same to you two,' they say in unison with a giggle.

They get worse.

Kyle holds the door open. 'What are we doing?' I ask him.

'Wanna go up to the gorge?'

'Just us?'

He turns to me, smirking. 'Who else?'

I shrug and walk to his car. I hear him laugh behind me, and he approaches.

'Why, Hughes,' he murmurs into my ear, 'are you nervous around me?'

'Don't be fucking stupid, Daniels.' I shove him away. 'Let's go before I change my mind.'

'Why would you change your mind?'

'Not because I'm nervous around you, that's for sure.'

He laughs again. Damn him. I am nervous around him. It's

a feeling I'm not used to. I'm used to knowing what's going to happen, but Kyle keeps me guessing. I'm used to being in control when I'm not around him. He makes me lose control. I love it and hate it at the same time.

The car is suffocating as we drive toward the gorge. I train my eyes on the passenger side window and watch the wooded areas I've grown up in pass me by. I try to name all the flowers I see in an extreme attempt to distract myself from Kyle, but it isn't working.

I can't stop thinking about kissing him last night. How his hand felt twined in my hair, how his body felt pressed up against mine and how his lips covered mine. I felt every single touch down to my bones. I still do. I can still feel the burning of my skin when he touched me.

The air is cooler out here, and it's a relief to get out of the car and walk through the trees. It's a relief to be here, hiding. Even if the person I know I need to hide the most from is right behind me.

'Why do you always pick the jerks?'

I stop and rest my hand against a tree. 'What do you mean?'

'The guys I see you with every weekend. They're all assholes, Rox. You're not blind or stupid. You know they are.'

'I know.'

'So why do you go for them?'

'Because they don't expect any more than I'm willing to give.'

'Which is a quick fuck.'

His words sting. But they're the truth. 'Yep.'

The ground crunches under his feet as he walks over to me. 'Why? Why don't you find a nice guy?'

I turn and meet his gaze. 'Because they want more from me than I can give.'

'Like what?'

'A relationship.'

Kyle stops right in front of me and puts his hand next to mine on the tree. 'Why can't you give them that?'

Because they're not you.

'I just can't. I go for the jackasses because they don't care if I play them. They're looking for what I am; something that doesn't mean anything. It's easy. Simple. I can fuck them over and they don't give a shit.'

'So why did you kiss me last night?'

I was drunk. I don't know. I was drunk. I don't know.

Great. I can't think of more than two excuses and even then they're both crap.

I swallow instead of saying anything.

'Well?' he prompts. 'Last time I checked, I wasn't a jerk.'

'Depends who you ask.'

He raises his eyebrows. 'Am I a jerk?'

'No.' I sigh. 'You're not.'

'So I'll ask you again. Why did you kiss me last night if you only kiss jerks?'

I narrow my eyes at him. 'Why did *you* kiss *me*?'

'For the same reason I'm about to again. Because I want to.' He bends his head and presses his lips to mine before I can respond.

It feels the same as last night but so different.

This is sweeter. Every brush of his lips against mine feels like he's tasting me and savoring me. It feels like he's using each touch to memorize the feel of my mouth. It's not hard and it's not soft.

This kiss is as raw as the one last night, but in different ways. Last night was an explosion of pure need. This is a wave of emotion full of honesty and sincerity.

'Why?' I whisper.

Kyle pushes my hair from my face and cups the side of my head, his thumb brushing over my cheek. 'Because someone has to show you you're worth more than you've made yourself believe. And it's hard not to punch every guy that touches you. I'm not about to let someone else kiss you that way.'

'Why, Kyle Daniels, are you *jealous*?'

'Yes.'

His answer shocks me. It's the way he said it so simply, like I should have known – like I shouldn't have had to ask at all.

'Why?'

He runs his fingers through to the ends of my hair and steps back. 'I don't know why. Just like you don't know why you can't give a nice guy a relationship.'

Ouch. I deserve that.

I drop onto the ground next to him. 'So you came into the café to find out that I can't give a nice guy a relationship, and that you're jealous of any guy who kisses me.'

'Apparently so.'

'You know why you're jealous.' I look at the floor.

'And you know why you can't give a nice guy a relationship.' In other words, why I can't give him one.

'We're not talking in general now, are we?'

'No,' he replies quietly.

I look at the gorge running past in front of us. The water is quick, crashing against the small rocks breaking its path. It's almost as if the water knows exactly where it's heading before it hits the rock. It's a head-on collision, a wreck.

The way Cam's life ended. The way mine is heading.

Difference is, I'm in control of mine.

He wasn't.

'I don't want to talk about this anymore.' My voice is quiet, almost drowned out by the gorge. 'Can you take me home?'

'In a minute.' Kyle turns to me and twists his body toward mine.

'Why—'

He pulls my face toward his again. I know I should push him away – I should end everything here and now. I should get up and demand he takes me home right this fucking second.

But I won't.

I've spent too many endless nights over the last few years wondering what *this* would feel like. I've spent too many hours staring into space in a girly haze, wondering what it would be like for him to see me as something other than his best friend's sister.

Now I know. I know what it's like to have our lips locked and for him to look at me as someone more than what I always have been.

And I'm afraid I'm helpless against it.

Chapter Twelve – Kyle

Roxanne Hughes is the worst kind of headfuck. *And she doesn't even know it.*

She knows the effect she has on guys. Of course she does – she has enough of them falling at her feet – but she has no idea what she does to us. She has no idea that one smile and blink of her eyes grasp our attention. One touch steals it to the point of no return. And I'm done for.

I'm not naïve. I know exactly what she and everyone else does. Her shit attitude is her way of coping with Cam's death. Hell, she'll tell that to anyone who will listen, but I'm the only one who knows how to tear that crap apart and make her really grieve for him. I'm the only one who knows what's really hiding behind those beautiful blue eyes.

And, hell. I need to tear apart that shitty attitude and put her on her ass long enough to make her realize she doesn't need those jackasses she insists on seducing however many times a week. I need to make her see what she needs is right in front of her. She needs a nice guy who can make her love herself the way he loves her.

I could come to love her so, so easily. Maybe I already do in a tiny corner of my brain. Maybe there's a part of my body I haven't listened to yet that calls out for her.

'Cause, God fucking dammit, the guy she needs is me.

She's needed me her whole life and I'm not about to let that change now. I couldn't give a flying crap if she needed me in a different way then. She needs me now more than ever, and I should have been here six months ago when her whole world fell apart.

She'll never forgive me for that, but y'know what? That's okay. I won't forgive my sorry ass for it either. I should have been here to hold together what was left of her shattered heart.

Now though, now I'm home. Now I'm here and I have just over two months to find all those shattered pieces and put them back together in a way only I know how.

I need to make her see she needs me.

Because I know I need her.

'She doesn't seem to care about anyone other than herself. Well, you've seen that.' Myra rubs her hand down her face.

'I think she does care,' I say carefully. 'She just doesn't know how to deal with it. I think she just misses him so much she has to fill that void somehow.'

'She ain't ever gonna fill that void. No amount of rebellion will fill the gap left by Cam.' Ray sighs. 'And she won't listen. We let it get too far before we stepped in and now we're paying for it. We should have lassoed her butt and grounded her to make her stop.'

Iz snorts. 'She would have found a way to get out. Okay, so she was once quiet and cute, but she's always been determined. We all know Roxy has always found a way to get what she wants when she wants it, everyone else be damned.'

'You're right, Iz,' Myra agrees. 'What was once one of her best traits is now her worst enemy. I just . . .' She pauses and closes her eyes. Ray reaches over and takes her hand in his, and I feel the stab in my chest at seeing her in so much pain. She's like a mom to me and this is breaking my damn heart.

Iz reaches over and takes Myra's hand, too.

'I just wonder if we'd paid more attention to her pain if she'd have done this.' Myra opens her eyes and they're brimming with tears. 'No parent should have to bury their child. The day we lost Cam, half of my soul was brutally ripped out. Of all the people, *my* boy was taken. My beautiful, bright boy. My world was destroyed. I asked so many times why it was him. I didn't understand why he had to go. He was so young, so ready for what life had to throw at him, and none of us realized what it was throwing was a curveball. And one hell of a curveball. I was so caught up in my own pain I forgot she was hurting too.'

'Myra—'

'No. For so long I've tried to keep it inside to keep strong for her, but it hasn't worked.' She shakes her head, tears pouring down her cheeks. 'She saw the crash and she was the one there when he died. She had that moment and her alone. If he had to spend that with anyone, I'm glad it was her. He loved her more than I've ever known someone to love another person. But we all forgot that. We hurt so much we forgot she was the one who watched him die. Our last memory of him alive is a happy one, but hers is watching that life drain from him. Roxy has suffered so much.'

'Myra Hughes, you listen to me right now!' Iz slaps the table. 'That God awful day you *all* lost him. Not just you, not just Roxy. You all lost him, okay? You all had – and still do have – a right to grieve for him in whichever way you feel necessary. Sophia Loren once said that having a child was letting a piece of your heart walk around outside your body, or something like that anyway, and if shutting yourself off was the way of dealing with losing that part of your heart forever, then damn.

'You deserve that. And that's okay. You're allowed to cry and you're allowed to think of no one but yourself. If I even feel half the pain you do, then again, damn! You are allowed to hurt and you don't ever feel guilty for that.

'Roxy didn't pick the right way to grieve. And she isn't even grieving. She's fighting against it – she's sending herself into oblivion God knows how many times a week because she doesn't want to remember. Not because of anything you and Ray did or didn't do. She picked this path. She picked forgetting over grieving and it isn't a long term solution. I'd imagine it works great for a while, but now it must be getting tedious, even for her.'

'I just don't know what we're supposed to do.' Myra breaks down. She leans onto the table and buries her face in her arms. Her shoulders shake, and for a moment, the only sound is the echo of her sobbing around the café.

I walk around the table, and wrap my arms around her neck.
I hug her. I don't know what else to do. This woman who
treated me like her own for my whole life, the one who was
there when I couldn't talk to my own mom about girl stuff,
she's heartbroken. She's lost one child and in her mind, she's
losing another.

'We're back now,' I reassure her. 'You know we'll help.'

'Kyle's already dragged her away from what – two parties?'
Iz looks at me.

I release Myra, grin, and nod. 'Boy did she kick off. So fun.'

My cell buzzes in my pocket. Roxy.

'Hey,' I answer.

'Kyle.' She giggles. 'I need a flavor. No. That's not right. I
need a . . . A . . .'

'A favor?'

'Yes!' She giggles again. 'I'm, um, kind of stuck in Portland.
And I kind of am a little dunk.'

'You mean drunk.'

'That's it! See. You always know what I mean.' Another giggle.

Iz, Myra and Ray all look at me.

'So you want me to drive to Portland and haul your ass back
here?'

'No hauling needed. I'm coming willingly this time. Coming.
Hah!' Another giggle. Jesus . . . She must be really drunk.

'Where are you?' I sigh.

'I am . . . I'm at McDonalds. Mmm, burger.'

'Is Selena with you?'

'No, silly. She's at home. Boring boring booooring!'

'Okay. Are you alone?'

'No. I have this little Transformers guy from my Happy
Meal.'

I don't know if I should laugh or not.

'It's Bumbleybee. He's cuh-*rap*.'

'Okay, Roxy. Stay wherever you are and I'll come find you.'

'Stay here? Right here?'

'Yep. Right where you are.'

'What if I need to pee?'

Is she for real? 'You can go anywhere as long as you don't leave the restaurant.'

'Okay.' She hangs up as abruptly as she called.

I stare at my phone and look at Myra. 'Looks like I'm going to give your wayward daughter a ride home from Portland.'

~

'What took you so long?'

Roxy's sitting in a booth in the back corner, her back to the window and her feet up on the seat. She's holding a tiny toy I'm guessing is Bumblebee, and her eyes are focused on it.

'Hour long drive, remember?' I pick her feet up, sit next to her, and rest her legs over my lap.

'And you drove it just to get me.'

'Looks that way, doesn't it?'

She spins the small doll. 'Because it's what *Cam* would have wanted.'

I ignore the bitterness in the statement and focus on the sadness she thinks she's hidden from me.

'No,' I reply. 'I came because you asked me to.'

Blue eyes meet mine. 'Why?'

'Roxy, you have to know by now I'll always do whatever you ask me to.' I put my finger upon her open mouth to stop her replying. 'Because it's what *I* want to do. Not for Cam. For me. Okay?'

She nods, closing her mouth, and I drop my hand.

'Bumblebee was his favorite,' she whispers. 'I ordered the stupid meal because I wanted him, but it's not right. Cam should be sitting across from me and he should have stolen the damn toy before I had a chance to get it out of the plastic packet.'

'Like you used to do until you got all the Furbys that time.'

'Exactly like that.' Roxy's lips twitch despite the sniff she gives. 'I bought it, thinking if I got Bumblebee I could give him to Cam. Then I sat down and remembered. I remembered he won't ever be around to take him.'

'Roxy,' I whisper, sliding up the seat and wrapping my arms around her. She curls into me as tears begin to fall from her eyes.

'How could I forget, Kyle? How could I forget he's dead? Fucking *dead*!'

I sink my hand into her hair and hold her tighter. She shakes, and her tears soak through my shirt. I have no answer for her.

'Let's go.' She sits up and mascara streaks her cheeks. 'I want to go home.'

'Hang on.' I stroke my thumbs under her eyes. Seeing her cry breaks me. Her eyes are wide as I try to get rid of the black streaks. They're wide and wet, shining under the harsh lights of the restaurant. Another tear drops out and I catch it with my thumb, swiping it away. I bring my lips to her forehead and touch them to her skin, leaving a gentle kiss there, before getting up and sliding her along the seat.

'Come on,' I say. 'Let's get you home, Roxanne Jane Hughes.'

She scowls but lets me pull her up. 'Fine, Kyle Michael Daniels.'

I grin. I like the way my full name rolls off her tongue. I also like the way my tongue rolls off hers . . .

She fiddles with the radio as I pull away from the parking lot. And she fiddles with the radio. And again. And again. I grit my teeth at the constant buzzing and searching as she twiddles the dial for forty-five minutes. I have no idea how I put up with it for so long.

'Roxy. What are you doing?'

She drops her fingers like the radio is burning her and looks at her hands in her lap. 'Um. I don't want to go home,' she whispers.

'But you said—'

'I want to go home to Verity Point, but not to my house.'

'Your mom is worried sick about you, you know.'

'When isn't she?' she snaps. 'I don't want to go home.'

Fucking hell. I thought the girls at college were firecrackers, but Roxy would give them a run for their money. Her temper fires up quicker than a bush fire in the outback.

'Want me to pull over then? Sure you'd be comfy on the side of the road.'

'I take back what I said before. You're not always a jackass, but when you are you're a prize one.'

'Great. I'm right up your street, then.'

'What happened to "I'll do whatever you ask"?'

'I take back what I said before,' I throw her words back at her. 'I'll do whatever you ask when I feel like it.'

'You just climbed another rung on the jackass ladder.'

'Awesome.' I pull up outside my house and turn to her. 'Does that mean I'll get to fuck you one day?'

She opens her mouth to reply but no words come out. Instead she stares at me, her whole body frozen with shock. Good. That's the response I was hoping for.

I get out of the car, slam the door, and walk around to her side. I yank her door open. 'Are you getting out or you sitting in my car all night?'

'I can't believe you just said that.'

'I'm sorry – is that right reserved for fully trained jackasses?'

Roxy climbs out of the car with fire in her eyes and jabs a finger in my chest. 'You're a real prick sometimes, you know that?'

'Yep.' I grin slowly. 'And you love it.'

'I don't. I fucking hate it.' She storms past me.

'Only because I'm the only person that can shut you up.'

She pauses on my doorstep. 'I've been shut up many ways, Kyle. *Many* ways.'

She's fucking with me again. She knows it and I know it. I don't know what it is but she just can't help herself. No matter what happens we always end up back here, both of us fighting. The problem is, I love pissing her off. If she's pissed off she's not hiding from me.

My long strides swallow up my front yard and I stop behind

her. I wrap my arm around her waist and pull her back into me. Her back slams into my chest, and I reach up and pull her hair to the side. My lips move close to her exposed ear, and she shivers.

'I've told you before. Don't fuck with me, Roxy. Don't even try it. Stop playing your little games with me, because you won't win.'

She swallows and takes a deep breath, her back heaving against me.

'Oh – and I can shut you up. And you know I can do it fucking good. Keep giving me your shit and I just might have to remind you of that.'

She really does take a deep breath this time, and her whole body goes tight. My fingers are splayed over her taut stomach, and she turns her face into mine. Her eyes are bright in the darkness when they meet mine, and her voice is breathy.

'Is that a threat?'

'No. It's a promise.' I release her stomach and push my front door open. 'Get in.'

'You're not taking me home?'

'Roxy, you asked me not to so I'm not going to. You can stay here tonight. And quite frankly, I'm reaching the point where I don't care if you stay in my sister's room or mine, so get your ass in and go and find her before I make your fucking mind up for you.'

Her staying in my room would be disastrous since I have nothing but kissing her in my mind and a growing hard-on inside my pants.

She scoots inside and I follow her up the stairs, knocking on Iz's door at the top.

'What do you want?' my sister calls through.

'Present for you.'

'If it's another stink bomb you can suck it.'

I glance at Roxy and smirk. 'No, but she's definitely a ticking bomb with her temper.'

She smacks me. I grin.

Iz opens the door and looks at Roxy. 'I guess we're having a sleepover. Good job I raided Kyle's stash of candy.'

'Bitch,' I mutter, turning to my room before I change my mind about Roxy's sleeping arrangements.

Chapter Thirteen – Roxy

'Mothereff,' I mutter, looking at the mug of coffee attached to the end of Iz's arm. 'My head hurts.'

'That's because you were hammered last night,' Kyle wanders into her room.

'Dude, we could have been naked in here!' Iz cries at him

He smirks and points to me. 'Take it.' Then at her. 'Leave it.'

'Go fuck yourself,' I mutter. Yep, I'm still sore from last night – yet another fight between us.

'Still giving me shit, Rox?' His eyes twinkle.

'I'll give you shit until you realize you can't shut me up for longer than five minutes.' I chuck the covers off, sit up, and take the mug from Iz.

Kyle's eyes flick to my legs and travel up my body. 'There are alternatives to shutting you up, now I think about it.'

'Can you just control it for five minutes?' Iz shoves him toward her door. 'Take your sexually active mind and go and get yourself off or something.'

He laughs as she slams the door behind him, and Iz shakes her head at me.

'How do you put up with that?' she asks me.

'I play him at his own game. It works for a while.' I shrug and sip the hot coffee.

It works until he touches me and whispers something in my ear. Then he unravels me, tearing me apart until it takes everything I have to step away from him. Last night was particularly testing. I cried, we fought, then he turned on the sexy. And fuck, can he turn on the sexy.

There's nothing more dangerous than a guy who knows how to turn you on with his words alone.

Kyle knows exactly what to say and when to say it. Hell, he knows *how* to say it; from the speed he talks to the inflections he puts on words.

He's such a bastard.

'He's such a horny teenage boy it scares me,' Iz mutters. 'Anyway. Finish that coffee, get dressed, and let's get out of this house.'

I glare at her, and she grins.

Yes, boss.

~

'You've got hearts in your eyes.' Selena smirks.

'You need to lay off the cartoons, idiot.' I roll my eyes.

'She's right,' Iz agrees. 'You have a crush on my brother.'

I turn to her. 'Says the one who's had her eyes glued to Si's butt for the last half an hour.'

'He has a nice ass. What can I say?'

'Dude. That's my cousin!' Selena makes a gagging noise.

'I have to listen to my brother and Roxy bitching at each other ten times a day. I never thought I'd say this.' Iz looks at me. 'But I almost wish you'd just go away and get it over with.'

'So many things are wrong with that statement,' I reply. 'Mostly you telling me I need to sleep with your brother. Which, by the way, isn't going to happen.'

Selena grins and glances at Kyle. 'Oh yes,' she says dryly. 'Because sleeping with him would be absolutely fucking horrific. Who in their right mind would be attracted to that body and those eyes?'

I narrow my own eyes. 'I never said I wasn't attracted to him.'

'No need to be pissed off because she's pointing out what most other girls in this town think,' Iz whispers in my ear.

'I am not pissed off!'

She grins.

'Come on, Rox,' Selena says with amusement. 'Just go over there, run him down, and slap your lips on his. I bet he has a killer kiss.'

My cheeks flush, and I know it's given me away when her eyes widen.

'Clearly I missed something! You kissed him?'

'He kissed me,' I correct her. 'So I told him to, but whatever. I was drunk.'

'And that was it? Just once?'

'Just once.'

'Liar, liar, pants on fire!' Iz sings. 'You're lying!'

'I am not!' I protest. 'Once.'

'Then why are your eyes flicking to the right? And why are you touching your nose?'

'I thought eyes went to the left.' Selena frowns.

'Depends what hand you write with,' Iz tells her. 'Left is for lefties, right for righties. Don't ask me why. Point is, you, Roxy Hughes, are a big fat liar!'

'Twice!' I lie again, sitting on my hands. 'Twice, okay?'

'Your mouth is twitching.'

'Three times!' I throw my arms in the air. 'I can't believe you're interrogating me about kissing your brother.'

And now that I'm looking at him I think about kissing him again. His body against mine, his lips against my ear, his breath across my skin – I'm wondering what skin on skin would feel like. I'm wondering what it would be like to have sex with someone I actually care about and who cares about me.

I'm wondering what it would be like to have sex with someone because I actually want to. Because it's an all-consuming, demanding need to do it. Because if I don't feel them, if I don't give in to the screaming inside my body whenever he's around, I'll go crazy.

Kyle will break my jackass rule. No doubt about it.

'Hey . . .' Iz says slowly.

'Hm?'

'Wanna do something crazy?'

Selena and I look at each other. 'Like what?' Selena asks.

Iz pulls her keys from her pocket. 'Let's run off to Portland and get a tattoo.'

'That's your crazy idea? I have two.'

'So get a third.' I shrug. My eyes flick to the guys playing football. Okay. Kyle. 'Let's go.'

~

I hide my hand in the sleeve of my lightweight cardigan as we join Kyle, Ben and Si for dinner. The bandage covering Selena's star on her foot is exposed by her sandals, and Iz's bandage on her thigh is poking out from the bottom of her shorts.

'Where did you go?' Si looks at us.

'Nowhere,' Selena replies.

'Nice try.' His eyes flick to her foot and Iz's leg. 'Another one?'

'Three. I have three, Si. I'm not exactly a walking coloring book.'

Kyle's lips curve up. 'You got tattoos?'

'One each.' I touch my hand.

'What did you get?'

I smile and shake my head.

'Good luck,' Iz mutters and grabs a menu. 'I couldn't even get it out of her. She wouldn't let us see.'

'Why not?' Kyle tilts his head to one side, and I shrug.

'I just don't want to share it yet.'

He gets up and walks around the table.

'What are you doing?'

'I want to see it.' His eyes are twinkling playfully.

'No.' I get up and walk backward around the table. 'It's mine.'

'Show me.'

'No!' I half-shriek as I just escape his grasp and run across the café. I yank the door open and round the side of the café, laughing. My stomach is clenching with how hard I'm laughing at him, so hard I almost miss him stopping in front of me.

Almost. There's no way I could miss his lips taking mine.

He holds my face to his. 'Back there. You smiled like you haven't in a long time. I haven't heard you laugh like that either.'

'So?' I open my eyes to his.

'So I liked it,' he mumbles, curving his hand round my head. 'I like this Roxy. Always have.'

Warmth spreads through my body. I reach up on tiptoes and kiss him – the first time I've kissed him. He always comes to me, but this is my moment. His words have reminded me I'm worth more than I think.

I grasp onto his collar with my bandaged hand and press our bodies together. His fingers splay out on my back and I revel in his touch. He reminds me I didn't die that night. A part of me, a big part, is still living.

'Birds,' I whisper. 'Five birds.'

'Can I see?'

Slowly, I peel the bandage from my left wrist and hand. There, on the side of my hand and wrist, are five tiny birds in flight. Each one with their own meaning, each as important as the other.

'Any reason for the birds?'

I look at the red rimmed tattoo. 'They all mean something to me. One for grief, one for moving on, one for acceptance, one for freedom, and one for . . . love.'

Kyle takes my hand in his and rubs his thumb across the skin above the tattoo. His eyes raise from my hand, and his gaze holds me.

He whispers, 'It's perfect.'

'Yep.'

He's silent for a moment, just stroking my hand, and then he pulls me to him. I wrap my arms around his waist as his go around mine, and I breathe in his distinctive scent. *Calvin Klein* is suddenly my new favorite smell.

'Let's go,' he says into my hair.

'We're having dinner.'
'So? We haven't ordered. Let's go.'
'Where?'
'Who cares?'

Chapter Fourteen – Kyle

'The gorge,' she whispers. 'Let's go there.'

I take my arms from her waist and grab her hand. 'Quickly. Before anyone notices us.' I tug her after me.

She giggles. 'Like anyone will care.'

'My sister.'

'Least of all her.' Roxy's blue eyes are shining with a happiness I really haven't seen in a while. 'She told me this morning I should sleep with you.'

'You should.' The words blurt out before I can stop them, and she freezes.

'You're not a jerk.'

'Exactly.' I pull her into the woods. Toward me. 'I know how to do something other than fuck a girl like she's worthless.'

'Even if she is?' Her voice is quiet.

'Roxy.' I tilt her face up so her eyes are on mine. 'Nothing about you is worthless. You are worth everything.'

She swallows, blinks harshly, and threads her fingers through mine when she pulls away. 'I knew you'd play the field at college.'

Hey there. 'Are you calling me man whore?' I smirk and let her pull me along.

She shrugs. 'Fraternity,' is all she responds. Like that's a good reason. Actually . . . I remember Braden and Aston before their asses were tamed.

'I'm no man whore.' I close the short distance between us and wrap my arms around her shoulders from behind.

'I don't believe you.' Her cheeks twitch with her smile and her face turns into mine.

I move my lips to her ear. 'You don't need to be a man

whore to know how to make love to someone well enough. You just need the right girl.'

My carefully chosen words have an effect I wasn't expecting. She swallows again and lets out a deep breath with a tremble. Huh. Seems Miss-Casual-Fuck isn't quite so okay with the idea of something realer.

'You win,' she breathes out. 'Point taken.'

I grin and release her. Not because I want to – but because she can't walk with my arms around her. If I could, I'd keep her against me all damn day. It'd certainly make it easier when trying to talk her down from her little antics. She's gonna try to run a mile.

'Did you bring me here deliberately?' She looks at me with raised eyebrows.

'Where?' I glance around and notice the pool Cam pushed her in a few years ago. 'Ah. No.'

'I don't believe you.'

'Seriously. I was too busy looking at various parts of your body.'

She barks out a laugh and slaps my chest, making me grin. 'Prove it.'

What is it with this girl and challenging me at every turn?

'You asked for it.'

I spin her into a large tree near to us and meld our bodies together. My lips crash into hers, and I sink into the softness of her body. I half expect her to push me away, but she doesn't. She grabs the sides of my shirt, winds her fingers in the material, and holds me to her. Her tongue flicks out against mine, teasing me, and she grazes my bottom lip with her teeth.

I cup the back of her head with one hand and slide my other across her back and down. My fingers curve round her ass, pulling her hips into mine. She makes a small whimpering sound in the back of her throat and I swear to God, all the blood in my body rushes down to my dick. My erection presses into her stomach. She shifts against me, moving ever closer, and knocks my hand from her head. Her hands guide mine to her thighs, and I get it.

Her tongue dives into my mouth as I lift her with only the tree supporting her. Her legs wrap around my waist, her feet locking at my back, and she grabs the back of my head. I run my hands along her thighs, my thumbs teasing at the apex of them, and she pushes herself into me.

I want this girl. Fuck, I do. I want her more than I've ever wanted anyone else in my life, and if she was anything less than everything to me, I'd take her up against this tree in a split second.

But she is. She's everything. And when I do have her it'll be somewhere I can explore every inch of her body the way it should be explored.

'Roxy,' I whisper against her jaw. 'We have to stop.'

She lets a long, shaky breath escape from between her swollen lips. 'Why?'

I lower her to the ground slowly and push her hair from her face with a kiss to her forehead. 'We just do, okay?'

I'm not about to tell her we have to stop because I'm worried one time is all it will take to make me fall in love with her.

'Protect her.'

'What do you mean?'

'If anything happens to me—'

'Don't be a dick, Cam. Nothing's going to happen to you.'

'Nah . . . You don't know what's round the corner, man. One day you could be all happy and shit, and the next lying on a hospital bed while your family says goodbye.'

'That's some deep shit.'

'Fuck off. I'm just sayin', alright? Roxy means the world to me, you know that. So if anything happens to me, ever, make sure you look after her little ass. She'd be lost without me.'

'Alright.'

'Promise me, man. Promise me you'll be there for her. You're the one guy I trust her with.'

'I promise. I'll always look out for her and protect her little ass.'

*

We were fourteen and it was like we both knew. Even then. Like he knew he wouldn't be around for her. Like I knew I'd eventually fall in love with her. And what a tidy fucking package it looks, eh?

He dies. I come riding in to save the day. She cries on my shoulder. We fall in love.

Maybe if it was a movie. Maybe even a book. But this shit is real and it's never gonna fit in a pretty little box. I was six months too late to save the day, she kicked my ass before she cried on my shoulder, and we either argue or make out. If only it was as easy as it looks to anyone outside.

'Right,' Iz shakes her hair out. 'I'm going to the café. Myra mentioned something about a job.'

'You have a job,' I say dumbly.

'In Miami, moron. Funnily enough, this is Oregon.'

'Alright. I get it.'

'See you later!' She opens the door but pauses before she walks through it, flicking a sassy glance over her shoulder. 'Don't do anything I wouldn't!'

'Free reign then,' Roxy mutters at the slam of the door.

I laugh and pat the sofa behind me. She raises an eyebrow.

'Why are you sitting on the floor?'

'Scamp kept dropping his ball on the floor instead of my lap. I couldn't be bothered to bend down every time so I'm on the floor.' I grab the blue ball and nod to the sleeping terrier in the corner. 'Stupid animal.'

'Hey. He's adorable. Until he humps my leg.' She sits behind me. I lean my head back to look at her.

'You know dogs take after their owners, right?'

'Yeah, I can see it. Your dad is kinda cute.'

I laugh and grab her legs. They hook over my arms and she bends forward, her hair tickling the bare skin on my shoulders.

'Your hair tickles.'

'Put a shirt on then,' she fires back with a grin.

'You don't really mean that.' I tickle her legs. She says nothing. 'Roxy.' She grins wider. 'Do you?'

'No,' she finally gives in. 'It would solve the problem though.'

'Who said there was a problem? I'd like your hair to tickle me in all kinds of places.'

'Kyle!' She slaps my chest and I laugh. I love winding her up.

'What?'

'Pig.'

'Eh, it's better than jerk.'

Her legs tighten. 'Do we have to go there again?'

I wish we didn't. 'As much as I hate talking about the pricks you've been spending nights with, yes.'

'In case you've forgotten, I haven't spent the night with anyone except your sister since you came home.'

I turn to face her. I know my face is like stone – my jaw is tight. 'I should fucking hope not. But it's not the only problem,' my voice softens at the end.

She draws in a sharp breath and her eyes shoot daggers at me. 'You've been speaking to my parents.'

I'm not saying anything. She knows it's true. No point confirming or denying it.

'I can't believe this.' She pulls her legs up and moves to the other side of the sofa.

'I spoke to them because I wanted to know.'

'Then talk to me instead!'

'I've tried. And every time you tell me to fuck off because you don't care. Well here's some news for you, Rox, *I care!*'

She shakes her head. 'Because you always want to talk about Cam. I've done that, okay? I've done what you wanted. The memories, the movie night . . . I can't take any more than that.'

'Fine. No talking about Cam. Will you talk now, about you?'

Nothing. She says nothing. I climb up on the sofa next to her and grab her hands.

'There's nothing to talk about,' she says weakly.

'Besides the drinking and drugs.'

'I hardly use drugs.'

'Hardly isn't good enough. It should be fucking *never*, Rox. Never.'

She takes her hands from mine and runs them through her hair. 'There's no way to talk about this without bringing him up, is there?'

'Looks like you have to pull on some big girl panties and get the hell on with it, then.'

'I'm not—'

'Seven months,' I interrupt her. 'Seven months and you still can't talk about it? I'm not an expert on grief but you're taking the piss. You don't want to talk about him. There's a damn big difference between can't and won't.'

'I was there the moment he died. Of course I won't talk about it. I don't want to remember that moment.'

'If anyone had to be there it should have been you. You were the love of his life. In his eyes no one even came close to his baby sister. But you're not the Roxy he loved.' Her heart is breaking in her eyes and I hate I'm the person doing this to her. But she has to listen. I need to talk her down from her games. I'm probably going about it all wrong, but it's hard to substitute what I want to say with what's right to say. 'The Roxy he loved never would have done everything you have since he died. She would have been there with her parents, getting through it together.'

'The Roxy he loved died when he did.'

'Bullshit. She's still in there. I see her when you're with me. When it's just us, she's there. Now this is the new Roxy – the person you think you want to be. She lives for nothing but all the shit you're destroying yourself with.'

She stands. 'Destroying myself?'

I look up at her. 'You are, aren't you? How many nights can't you remember? How many names of guys do you know? How much can you drink in one go?'

'That's nothing to do with you.'

'Yeah it is. It's everything to do with me.'

'You're not my brother!'

My gaze flick to her lips and back to her eyes. 'Obviously I'm nothing close to your brother.'

Her eyes harden. 'And it makes sense.' She turns and walks from the room.

'Wait. What makes sense?' I jump up from the sofa and go after her. 'Roxy!'

She stops at the door, her head down, her fingers holding tightly to the handle. 'Everything since you've been back. Taking me from the parties, taking me to the gorge, holding me when I cried . . . kissing me . . . I get it.'

'I'm glad you get it. I don't.'

She opens the door forcefully. 'Everything was to stop me destroying myself, wasn't it? It was for my parents and for the promise you made Cam.'

I stare at her in disbelief as she walks to her car. 'Not true. Not one damn bit, Roxy.'

She opens her car door and looks at me. 'We both know it's true.' She gets in the car and starts the engine.

'Roxy!' I step outside when she pulls away. 'Roxy!'

Her car disappears and Scamp yaps inside. I shut the door and lean against it.

How can she really think that? How can she think everything was for everyone else?

And I get it. I get what she thinks.

I spoke to her parents. I made a promise to her brother to always look out for her. Now I am, and she doesn't think I actually care about her the way I do. She thinks the week since she demanded I kiss her has all been a bunch of crap.

And when she looked at me just then, before she got in the car – when she looked at me her eyes weren't shining in anger. They were shining because she was crying. The last week has been as real to her as it has to me.

I'm shoved away as the door opens.

'Okay, so Roxy just flew out of here like her ass was on fire and you're standing with a face like a smacked one. What the hell happened in the twenty minutes I've been gone?' Iz kicks a toy toward the dog and stares at me.

Fuck.

I rub my hands down my face and look at my sister. Concern is glaring from her eyes.

'I fucked up, Iz. I fucked up royally.'

Chapter Fifteen – Roxy

Everything. Everything has been a great big lie to him and now I don't know who my heart hurts more for. Cam or Kyle. I don't know whether it hurts more for the love lost or the one never had. I don't know which it's supposed to hurt more for.

My mouth is dry and my head is banging. I went straight to Layla's after leaving Kyle's yesterday, and a part of me regrets it when I think of him. Until I remember he cares only because he's obligated to. Because he promised he would.

But it felt so real. Every touch and every kiss from him felt as real as the ones I gave. There was that twinkle in our eyes with every smile we shared. Maybe I should have told him the reason I haven't been with anyone since he got home isn't because he stopped me, rather because the only person I want to be with is him. Maybe it wouldn't have made a difference.

Maybe it would have.

'Please smile.' Iz hands me a dress from the rack. 'Between you and my brother I think I'm getting depressed.'

I smile sadly and hang the red dress back up. 'I'm fine.'

'Right. And I'm the president. You're not gonna tell me what happened are you? I bugged him all day yesterday and he's refusing.'

'I don't want to talk about it.'

'Roxy.'

'Iz, please. I just . . .'

She looks at a dress and shakes her head. 'It's none of my business. I know that. But you two are my favorite people in the world. Kyle pisses me off something chronic sometimes, but he's still my brother. I don't need my major to know you care about each other. Hell, I don't need it to know you've cared about him for a lot longer than anyone realizes.'

I open my mouth and close it again.

'I also don't need it to see something big happened. I just want you to be happy. Both of you. And all this to-ing and fro-ing is giving me a headache.'

'Okay.' I grab a pair of light skinny jeans from the rail and put them over my arm. 'Can we forget about it now? It's your birthday.'

'As long as you promise to talk to him tonight.'

Great. I grit my teeth. 'Fine. I'll talk to him later.'

'Thank you.' She smiles. Her eyes travel to the jeans over my arm. 'Jeans?'

I finger the hem of them. 'I just don't feel like dressing up too much tonight.'

'Smile, Rox. He's an ass sometimes, but he's a loveable ass.'

'That's the problem,' I whisper to myself when Iz heads into the dressing room.

~

I wriggle my toes in my heeled shoe boots and put the final clip in my hair. Selena has spent the last thirty minutes curling it, and there's about twenty slides holding it to one side. If it wasn't for the face of make-up and fancy hair, no one would guess I was going to a party. For the first time in ages, I'm dressed like the Roxy I used to be.

'You're the only person I know that can pull off double denim,' Selena announces when I stand.

'It's because the pants are white,' I reply and adjust the jacket. 'You have to look twice to tell they're denim.'

'Still. I'd look like an eighties reject if I tried it.'

I look at her head of curly hair and grin.

'Already do, darling,' Iz sings from the corner of the room. She stands and smooths out the crinkled pale pink material of her strapless dress.

'Holy shit. If my cousin doesn't drag you into a corner tonight I'm booking him for an eye test,' Selena bursts. I giggle into my hand, more so when Iz blushes.

'If your cousin tries to drag me into a corner I'll—'

'Willingly follow for him to have his wicked way!' I finish with a dramatic flair.

'Shut up!' Iz throws her pillow at me, and I catch it.

'I don't hear you denying it. Did you, Leney?'

She shakes her head. 'No denial heard here, Roxy.'

'We have you all worked out, Ms. Daniels.'

'You two.' Iz points her finger at us threateningly before throwing her arms in the air. 'You're incorrigible.'

I tilt my head to the side with a sassy smile on my face. 'It's why you love us.'

'Right.' She rolls her eyes, but she knows it's true. Despite her being two years older than us, the three of us have been through thick and thin together. 'At least you've cheered up.'

'She hasn't seen Kyle yet.' Selena catches the lip gloss I throw at her. 'Hey, thanks.'

'She's right. Who knows what kind of mood I'll be in then?' I'll probably be reminded of the sting in my chest.

'We should move and find out,' Iz replies. 'The sooner you two kiss and make up, the sooner we can all be happy and get drunk.'

'I'm not getting drunk,' I reply automatically. They both look at me, Selena more shocked than Iz. 'What? I don't want my parents on my butt about my drinking. My dad will have his eye on me tonight, and I don't feel like having yet another argument about my supposed "bad girl" behavior.'

'You've always been pretty badass, if I'm honest.' Selena opens the door.

'Yeah, I mean, no one expected quiet little Roxanne Hughes to be such a hot cookie.' Iz shrugs.

I roll my eyes. 'Puh-lease. I was never quiet – I just had a lot of shit I kept inside. Now I'm letting all that noise out.'

'That's what she tells her one-nighters,' Selena stage-whispers to Iz.

Despite my annoyance at that comment, I smile and elbow her. 'Bitch.'

'True though.'

'I never told them much of anything.' I link my arm through hers and we turn in the direction of the village hall. 'Does anyone feel like we're ten again? I mean, wasn't that the last time we had a party in the village hall?'

Iz shrieks a laugh. 'Wasn't that my twelfth birthday? I seem to remember us all using those fake tattoos you put on with water. Cam walked in on us putting them on our asses and insisted on telling everyone.'

'We all had our asses viewed that night,' Selena muses.

'What – are you putting those on your butts?' Cam had laughed like a crazy child.

'Oh my God!' Iz yelled. We all scrambled to put our pants back up as he ran away. We could hear him yelling to anyone who would listen we were tattooing our butt, and all three of us went back out with red faces.

'You put a tattoo on your butt?' Kyle looked at us all. 'Really?'

'They did. Furby ones.' Cam cackled.

'Go away!' I shouted. 'Stop being so mean.'

'We're not being mean,' Kyle protested. 'I'm only asking, Roxy.'

'Well don't, ratface,' Iz shoved him.

We turned to walk away. All we heard was the count to three and our pants were pulled down. Our butts were on show to everyone in the hall, and all Cam and Kyle did was laugh at us.

My lips twitch. 'He was such a shit. Him and Kyle – they were the worst. And before you went to high school, Iz, they paid some kid who'd just moved from Utah to set off the fire bell.'

'That was them?!' Iz stops.

I nod. 'I was there when they did it and I was given detention every night until I told Principal Gough who it was.'

'Did you?'

'Yep. He kept me after school every day for two weeks and I told him as I walked out the door on the last day.'

'Man,' Selena whistles. 'I bet he was pissed.'

'Not as pissed as Kyle and Cam were.' I push against the village hall door. 'They thought they'd got away with it. Man, that was a sweet moment.'.

We're the last to arrive – like anyone is surprised – and we stop when we see the place. It's only Iz's twentieth, but this could rival her sweet sixteenth, and will need some topping for next year. Silver and pink ribbons hang from the ceiling. A DJ is set up in one corner, and in another are tables laden with all kinds of food. In the center of the food table is a four tier, pale pink cake with silver butterflies and dark pink flowers. Her parents have transformed the dreary old hall into something fan-fucking-tastic.

'Wow,' the three of us say in unison.

Selena and I stand by as everyone in Verity Point comes and wishes Iz a happy birthday. I play with the ends of my hair and smile as I watch one of my best friends surrounded by people that love her.

There's so much love and joy in this room it's almost bursting. It feels corny, like it should be in a movie, but it's true. We all suffered a tragedy months ago, my family the most, but we all suffered. We all loved Cam and we all had our hearts broken when he died, but now . . . Now I'm reminded of what Verity Point is.

It's a community. A place where there's always someone with a kind word, a joke to put a smile on your face, a hand to hold. When times get tough we stick together. We get out the super-glue, glue our hands, and link our fingers. We laugh together, we smile together, we cry together.

So many times I've berated living in a tiny village just off the Columbia Gorge. So many times I've cursed the lack of amenities here. So many times I've bitched and moaned about our tiny, wood surrounded community.

But watching my best friend swamped in love, I realize how much I adore this place.

Two familiar hands settle on my waist, and my heart skips a beat involuntarily.

'What are you doing?' I hiss at Kyle as he tugs me away from everyone.

'I want to talk to you,' he says in my ear. He takes my hand and pulls me outside.

'You've already made yourself clear.'

His strong hands spin me into him. My fingers rest against his chest and I look up at him.

'No. I haven't. Not by a long fucking shot, Roxy.'

I step back from him. 'Kyle, this is your sister's birthday. Do we really have to argue here?'

'The only person arguing is you.'

I cover my eyes with my hand. My heart has gotten over its stuttering and is thudding dangerously loud in my chest. If I don't get away from him, the tears threatening in the back of my eyes might just spill over.

'I'm not arguing with you. Not tonight. Can we just pretend to get along for your sister's sake?'

He sighs, his features illuminated by the waning sun. 'After all these years, you think we need to pretend? After the last *week*, you think we need to?'

I don't answer that.

'Exactly. This isn't a game, okay?'

'I never said it was.'

'Good, because you'd be wrong. You know you're good at being wrong, don't you? Even when you think you're right.'

I narrow my eyes at him. 'What the fuck does that mean?'

He takes a lock of my hair between his finger and thumb. 'Rox . . . When you left the other day, you said I didn't care. You said everything was a lie. You were wrong, okay? I do care – and not because of your parents or Cam. I care because *I care.*' He reaches up and moves a curl from my face. I flick my eyes from the floor to his gaze. 'I care because it's you.'

'Okay,' I say quietly. I step back from him and walk into the hall. There's a lump in my throat as I swallow. He cares because it's me. Cam's sister. That's all. I wish it wasn't true, but is. I can't kid myself anymore.

My eyes scour the hall. My parents aren't here yet – Mom will be closing the café still. Thank God. I find Selena by the drinks table.

'No,' she says as I approach.

'One,' I beg. 'Come on, Leney. I'm behaving tonight.'

Her eyes flit across my face for a mere moment before she gives in. 'Fine. But I'm pouring.'

'*Fine*.' I cross my arms and watch as she puts a smidge of vodka in a glass. 'You're taking the piss, Leney.'

'Give her a little more,' Iz insists as she wraps an arm around my shoulders. 'Don't be boooooooring, Leney.'

I grin smugly.

Selena puts a little more alcohol in my glass and tops it up with coke. *There we go.* I've suddenly changed my mind on my no drinking policy for the night. The more I can drink before my parents arrive, the better. There's not enough vodka for it to burn my throat as it goes down, but a few Selena-Measures and I'll be good.

The party goes on around me. The twins seem to have coerced their fancy-man from the weekend to hang around, and even old Mr. Yeo is chilling in a corner. Iz is flirting with Si in another corner, Selena is dancing with Ben, and everyone is wrapped up in their own thing. And I'm sitting in the corner, watching people come and go, watching people take drink after drink.

Watching Kyle lean against the wall, his feet crossed at the ankles, his arms folded across his chest, and his eyes focused on me.

Shivers snake through my body. His gaze is hot, and I'm pretty sure it's the cause of my shivers. The party is still going but, after three sneaky drinks, all I can see is him. All I can feel is him. For the hundred people between us, there may as well just be us.

The effect he has on me is incredible. A tiny part of me has always belonged to him, but now it feels like all of me does. He's branded into every part of my body, his stare searing into my skin and spreading heat through me. For so long I laughed at the girls that said they had The One. For so long I've imagined it was bullshit, imagined Kyle as a girlish crush. And I was wrong.

I was so wrong. Every single fucking time.

I'm the first to admit I can be naïve. I can be stupid and impulsive and thoughtless. But I've never been so right about anything in my life.

Kyle Daniels is my One. He is The One. Capital fucking letters and all.

I slam my empty glass down on the table. The need to get away from this place, from his penetrating gaze, is more than I can take. I can't fight the thread pulling me to him anymore, so I leave the hall and I step into the night. *Home.* My heels click against the sidewalk as I head toward my house.

'What is it about you?' His voice drifts to me through the night. 'What is it about you that keeps me coming back no matter how many times I try to walk away?'

I stop. 'My brother.' I call the words over my shoulder.

'No. Not Cam. In fact, I think he'd kill me if he knew what I was thinking right now.'

My feet come to a standstill. *Walk, you motherfuckers!*

'I've tried to work it out since I got back. Every day I've sat and tried to figure out what it is, the reason I can't stay away from you, and you know what? I can't. I don't have a goddamn fucking clue, Rox. Except you. Whatever it is, you keep me coming back over and over again.'

Breathe. 'Go back inside, Kyle.'

Tap. Tap. Tap. Tap. Tap. He stops behind me. 'I've tried. Fuck, Rox! Don't you think I've tried to walk away from you? Don't you think I've tried to stop this crazy shit in my head? I've succeeded, so many times, but not this time. This time I don't wanna stop it.'

I take a deep breath, not wanting to hear this. I can't hear this. 'You're lying.'

His hand settles on my waist. 'Am I? Am I lying about the times I've thought about holding you in my arms until you're begging for more? Am I lying about the times I've held your body to mine and wished there were no clothes between us? Am I lying about needing to make love to you so bad I'm going fucking crazy with need?'

Heart. No beating. Lungs. No breathing. Mind. No thinking. 'Kyle.'

Lips ghost my neck. 'I've tried, Rox. I've tried so fucking hard, but it's you. I can't fight this shit anymore. All of it is true. Every goddamn word.'

'You're drunk.'

'Am I lying about falling for you? About your eyes being the ones I look in and your lips being the ones I kiss every day? Am I lying about your body being the one I hold, one, two, three, fucking ten times a day? Am I hell!' His voice echoes through the empty woods. 'Do you know what it did to me to see you crying and knowing I'd put those tears there? I know, babe. I know you feel the same, so why don't you just admit it and put us both out of our misery?'

I can't do this. I can't stand here and listen to him. I should run. I know. But I don't.

'Why?' I turn and yell at him although he's right in front of me. My voice seems to echo in the empty village. 'Why, Kyle? I'm nothing special. I'm nothing to scream from the rooftops about!'

'You are to *me*.' He sinks his fingers into my curled hair. 'I told you you were everything to me. I wasn't lying about that either. Rox, babe, believe me, for the love of God.'

I press my lips to his. It could be the small amount of alcohol or it could be his words. I don't know and I don't care. I just know I want him. I need him. Four years of a crush and I can't give up now. I don't give a shit about our past or the pain we share. I just care about the guy I'm holding onto like he's all I have left in this world.

'Get on my back.' He smiles slowly.

'You're kidding.'

'Get on before I put you on.' Kyle grins like a little kid and I stand behind him. My hands on his shoulders and his on my thighs help boost me up. I laugh. Hard.

'I feel like a six year old again.' I wrap my arms round his neck.

He laughs and jogs through the woods. I cling to his back, stifling my giggles the whole way, and wonder how I can go from not wanting to be near him one minute to needing him the next. It doesn't seem right how quickly my feelings change – how quickly my mood changes around him.

His hand dips into my pocket, and he produces my house keys. The key flits into my front door and we step inside. He locks it from the inside before he whispers into the silence, 'Tell me now if I'm wrong about how you feel and you'd rather a jackass than me, tell me now.'

I sink my fingers into his hair, gripping it. 'You're the only jackass I want,' I mutter against his lips.

I sweep my mouth against his and run up the stairs, sliding my jacket from my arms. Thundering steps tell me he's following me, and I can't help the laugh that leaves me when I throw my jacket to the side and run into my room. I'm not used to being chased. Every step, every pound against the wood, it sends a thrill through my body I can't explain.

Kyle catches me just inside the door. His lips are hot and forceful against mine, teasing and pulling at every part of me. I walk backward with him attached to me, and we fall onto my bed, smiling against each other's lips. Every part of my body is on fire where he's touching me and I need more. *Always more.* I'll never get enough where he's concerned – I've wanted him for years, and I don't know if I'll ever stop wanting him.

My breasts are exposed as he pulls my shirt over my head. His lips leave a blazing trail across my skin, and I pull his mouth to mine again. The need to feel his skin against mine overcomes me and I slip his shirt up his back. This is hot. It's passionate.

It's filled with that burning need escaping me, the one I'm sure will never be satisfied.

His shirt lands on my floor at the same time my fingertips creep below the waist of his jeans. His lips push into my neck, making every part of my skin tingle, leaving every kiss and every touch to shoot downward. My core aches, desperately, frantically, insatiably. He's doing this to me and I have to wonder if he knows. If he knows just how my body craves him.

I undo the button on his jeans and push them over his butt. There isn't a part of my body not crying out for him right now.

One of his hands slips beneath my bra while the other slips beneath the lace covering my core. His thumbs tease both my nipple and my clit, flicking and rolling until I'm so wet he'd slip inside me with ease.

And he does. Before I can curl my fingers around him, our jeans are on my floor and he's wrapping my legs around him. I take him, long and hard, clenching as he pushes ever deeper. Yet it's not enough. I need every part of him.

My hands pull his head into mine and our mouths crash together. I flick my tongue across his lips until they meet mine. His tongue dives into me as deeply as his dick is in me. I need to feel every inch of him. I need to feel like he's owning me completely and utterly.

I need everything he has to give to me.

And he gives me it. He gives me every bit of himself. Every stroke of his tongue, every probe of his fingers, every pound of him inside me. He gives me all of him until I can't take anymore.

My body clenches around him, clinging him to me, and I cry out. I let go of all the feelings building inside me and I shout into his shoulder. One, two, three, four – he pounds into me until he groans into my shoulder. Our bodies slump together, our fingers pressing to the other's skin, and we hold each other.

He was right. There is a difference between fucking and making love. And the way he slides to the side, pulling me against him like he can't bear to let me go, lets me know that this was making love.

I snuggle into his chest, happiness taking hold and forming my lips into a smile. Kyle holds me tight, his chest rising and falling against mine, and his heart pounding beneath my cheek, our legs twined together.

It wasn't just physical love. For the last weeks I've been trying to convince myself that it's just a crush, but it's so much more.

Tonight, real love happened, too.

Chapter Sixteen – Kyle

I slide out of Roxy's bed slowly, making sure I don't wake her, and kiss her forehead. She's sleeping so peacefully. Her hair is tumbling over her shoulder and her lips are parted as she breathes deeply. I hesitate before slipping my clothes back on.

I don't want to leave.

I want to climb back in that bed and wrap my arms around her and never let go. I'm trying not to think of what her reaction will be when she wakes up alone – but I know neither of us want to explain to her parents in the morning why I'm here. My phone says it's three a.m., and I know it's too late to go where I want to, but I'm going anyway.

I hold my breath at the click of her door and creep through the house, deliberately not looking at Cam's bedroom door. A part of him still lives in that room. A part of KyleandCam lives in that room, and it's a part I'm not ready to face yet.

I jog back through the woods and toward the cemetery. A shiver of guilt is snaking its way into my mind, but I'm clinging to the fact I know he'd rather it be me than anyone else.

If anyone had to fall in love with Roxy, he'd rather it be me.

I have to hold onto that thought.

The cemetery is closed, the gates locked, so I scale the railings on the wall that surrounds it. It takes me all of five seconds to jump over them, and I make my way to his grave. Even in the darkness it's easy. I've been here so many times in the last month, it's unconscious.

I blow out a long breath as I drop in front of Cam's gravestone. So many things I want to say are rattling around in my mind. So many words and excuses that just won't come out.

So I sit here. I sit here in silence, noise equaling a rock concert in my head, and I stare at his name carved into the marble. So many things are wrong here yet so many are right at the same time. Roxy and me, it's so wrong but so right. Everything over the last few weeks has been building to this moment. Every word, every look, every touch, every kiss. They've all snowballed until tonight and it exploded between us.

There was no way I was letting her walk out of that fucking party without me. There wasn't a chance on this goddamn Earth she was going anywhere without listening to what I had to say.

She has this incredible skill of hearing but not listening, and I know that's what she did when I dragged her outside. She heard but only listened to what she wanted to – to what she believed – so when she left she was always going to listen because I was going to make it so. She was going to listen and she was going to understand me.

More importantly, she was going to damn well believe me and every word I said.

Now I'm sitting in front of my best friend's grave, wondering what he'd say. He wouldn't slap me on the back or laugh with me. He wouldn't ask for details or high five me.

He'd ask me what the fuck I was thinking sleeping with his sister. He'd go ten shades of apeshit, then he'd give me an ear battering using every cuss word he'd ever heard. Then, and only then, would he tell me he's glad it was me.

Because that's it. He'd always want it to be me. He trusted me with her and he believed I'd always keep her safe.

But it doesn't stop the guilt, and it doesn't stop a part of me feeling like I took advantage of him not being here. Like I planned the whole thing. It doesn't matter how many times I say I didn't.

Coming home, I never planned to sleep with Roxy. I never planned to do anything but pull her ass into line. The second time we met, I knew something more would happen. She was more than Cam's sister. She was more than anything I'd ever felt, and she still is. She's so much I don't even have the words for it.

I stay here until the sun begins to rise. It casts orangey hues across the sky that sneak through the leaves of the trees, bathing the cemetery in a dull light, and I stand. Then I say the only words I can. The only words that'll ever comfort him.

'Sorry, man. Guess I went and fell in love with your sister.'

Chapter Seventeen – Roxy

Empty.

I sit upright and look around. He's gone. His clothes are gone. My stomach clenches and my heart pounds once painfully. Of course. I cover my eyes with my hands when my phone buzzes.

I dive over the edge of my bed, feeling for it like a woman possessed.

Didn't think you'd want to explain last night to your parents.

I smile and breathe a sigh of relief. This is Kyle, I remind myself. Kyle.

That could have been awkward, I reply.

Don't think the worst, Rox. I meant what I said last night.

I want to believe it. So I do. I believe it because it's Kyle, and I trust him with my life.

The house is silent, so I get dressed quickly and slip downstairs. I avoid Cam's door. I have to go and see him but I can't handle being around his things this morning. It's almost as if I have to explain myself to him . . . Even if I don't have the words to do so.

Verity Point is quiet as I wander through the village. The cemetery has just opened and I meander through the rows of headstones until I reach my brother's. I sit slowly, holding my thighs to my chest, and read the headstone over and over until I feel like I can speak.

'I wish you were here,' I whisper. 'I wish you were here so you could tell me what to do. You're supposed to be here to hit him. Maybe you wouldn't hit him because it's Kyle, but whatever.

'It would be easier if you were still here. If you were I could ask you if Kyle really does care about me because of me. I think he does, but you'd know. Then I could ask you if you mind. I feel like I did when I was six and needed your Action Man to marry Barbie because I'd lost my Ken doll. You minded then and I guess you do now, too. Just don't do any freaky haunting crap, alright? I know what you're like. You'll go all Nearly Headless Nick on me – you did say once if you'd be a ghost you'd be him, but that would just scare the crap out of me.' I laugh quietly at the memory and swipe my cheek.

'I just miss you, y'know? I miss you being here for everything and kicking my ass every five seconds. I miss you treating me like a kid and warning off every guy who tried to date me, and I miss you going all big bro on him when you find out I dated him anyway. You were never angry at me, and while I hated you pulling that shit with other guys, I don't mind anymore. I know you were just looking out for me. I wish you could do that now. I wish you could give Kyle a shake and give him your big bro chat.

'I guess it was inevitable, though. You never told him how I felt. Hell, Cam, you shouldn't have even known. You only do because you read my diary two years ago – which, by the way, I'm still pissed about – but you never said anything. You never teased me about it. I didn't get it, but now I think I do. If your sister was gonna fall in love with anyone, it's only fitting she falls for the one guy you trust around her.

'I want you to tell me I'm wrong. I want you to walk through the trees next to me and yell at me, dammit! I want you to tell me I'm stupid for sleeping with him and I want you to kick his ass! I want you to be here. Like you should be. With me! I want my brother back. I'd do anything to get you back. Nothing feels right anymore.

'Except Kyle. He's all that feels right without you here. He fills a part of me that was lost when you died. He heals a bit of my heart that broke the same night. I'm in love with him, Cam. I don't know exactly when or how it happened but I am.

And I feel guilty. I need to know it's okay and you don't mind, but you can't ever tell me that. Can you? I need you to tell me you're happy, you'd rather us be together. I need to know so much but you'll never be able to tell me.'

Tears pour from my eyes. They blur my vision but I can still see his name perfectly on the headstone like a cruel joke. I can barely breathe for the pain raging inside, for the ever-present breaking of my heart.

'You were my best friend and my brother. Why did you have to go and die on me, huh? Why did you have to leave me? Don't you see I need you? I feel so fucking lost without you I think I'm going crazy over it. Dammit, Cam! Tell me it's okay!'

I bury my face in my arms and let it out. My whole body wracks with each gut-wrenching sob I take, and I leave every tear to soak into my clothes. Every breath is harder to take than the last and every tear fatter than the last.

Until I look up.

A bird is perched on top of his gravestone. It's sitting there perfectly, looking around until its eyes land on me. I sniff and wipe my tears with a deep breath. I touch my tattoo. The bird tweets once and takes flight.

It's my heart talking, the dreaming part of me, but I'll take it.

I'll take that as my brother's blessing.

Chapter Eighteen – Kyle

'The zoo?' Roxy turns to face me slowly, playing with her plait over her shoulder.

I kill the engine and grin at her. 'What's wrong with the zoo?'

'Nothing is wrong with it. I'm just surprised.'

'What? You think I don't like the zoo? I loved it when we were kids.'

'Hey, I never said that.' She slams the car door as she gets out. 'Don't twist my not-said words.'

I laugh and wrap my arm around her shoulders. 'I'm messin' with you, Rox.'

'Mhmmm.' She tries for annoyed but it's ruined by her arm sliding around my waist.

I pay the entry fee for us both and Roxy opens the map. I grin as her brow furrows over it.

'Here.' I point to the yellow arrow labelled *Entrance* and *Exit*.

'I knew that.' Roxy flips the map round.

'Sure you did.' I pull her into my side and lead her along the path in the Great Northwest section. 'I can't believe you don't know your way round here after all this time.'

'You realize we've seen a lot of these in the wild, right?' She looks up at me, ignoring my last words as we pass the bears.

'So?'

'I'm just saying.'

'Shush,' I say into her hair. 'Can we have one day without arguing?'

'Fine,' she fake-huffs and mumbles, 'As long as we go to the penguins after this.'

I turn my face away and smile. Of course we'd see the penguins. Zoo trips used to be one of our summer highlights every year – we'd all go together. We lost Roxy more than once only to find her at the penguins.

'Where's Roxy?' Myra had looked around frantically, panic in her eyes.

'Penguins,' Cam and I deadpanned in unison.

Myra sighed. 'Of course she is. One of these days, I'm gonna set up a flamin' ice rink in our yard so she can have a pet penguin.'

'What about the water?' Cam asked.

'Yeah, they need to swim,' I added.

'Dudes gotta eat,' we both said with a nod.

Mom rolled her eyes. 'She was kidding, boys.'

'Damn,' I muttered.

'Hey, Mom, Dad? Since we're not getting Roxy a penguin because you were joking, any chance of a lion instead?' Cam asked hopefully.

'Pushing it, son,' Ray chuckled.

'That sucks!'

I ran round the corner to the penguin enclosure, ignoring my mom telling me to wait, and smiled at an eleven-year-old Roxy. She was standing against the glass, her hands pressed against it, and her face a vision of wonder as she watched them swimming.

We walk through the Northwest section, dodging shouting kids on summer break, and as we enter the Pacific Shores section I let Roxy lead me past the polar bears.

It's okay. I didn't want to see them anyway.

She skips out of my hold toward the penguins and presses her body against the glass window. Her hands are flat against the glass, her face almost touching it, and her head moves side to side as she watches the penguins swim and roll underwater. She's more excited than the kids around her, and a smile creeps onto my face as I watch her. *Such a child.*

The kids squeal in excitement when a penguin swims right up against the glass, and Roxy laughs. A real laugh. One I've barely heard from her.

I come up behind her as the group of children and their parents move on. My hands rest on her hips and I press a kiss to her bare neck. She turns her face into me and grins.

'I love penguins.'

'I know.' I laugh. 'You'd stay here all day if I'd let you.'

A penguin comes up to the glass and taps its beak where her hand rests. Roxy moves her fingers along the glass, and the penguin follows them. It breaks the water's surface and drops back under, splashing us over the top of the glass. Roxy squirms at the cold water, pushing her back against me, and I wrap my arms around her stomach. I watch her as she plays with the penguin through the glass, smiling, happy, carefree.

This is the Roxy I know. This is my Roxy.

'I think I'd like to work with penguins,' she says softly, her head tilted to one side, her hand still moving on the glass. 'Or for them. Conservation or something. Maybe even be a zoo vet, you know? Could you even imagine getting close to these animals? It would be amazing.'

'What would you have to do to do that?'

'I don't know. Major in biological science, I guess.' She drops her hand.

'Why don't you do it?'

She shrugs. 'Too late this year, isn't it?'

'So apply for next year.'

'Where though?'

'Berkeley.'

'With you?' She turns and raises her eyebrows.

I shrug. 'Or UCLA. There's loads in California.'

'Dunno.' Roxy starts to walk.

I let her waist go and grab her hand instead.

'I have time to think about it. I'll do some research over the summer. See the best courses. Maybe I'll go to Miami with Iz.'

Fuck that. She's not going to Miami.

I need to convince her to come to California with me. Pronto. We wander around the zoo casually until lunchtime when we go to the BearWalk Café and order lunch. She plays with the cutlery in front of her until the clinking drives me crazy.

'What are you thinking, Rox?' I touch her fingers.

She looks at her hand, her eyes full of sadness, and sighs. 'I'm thinking this is the first time I've ever been here without Cam.'

She's right. For both of us.

'Feels weird, huh?' My voice is quiet.

'Yeah.' She laughs quietly. 'Remember when we saw the monkeys and he tried to be one in the play area? I think I was like seven. He watched them climbing from tree to tree and wanted to be one. He shoved a banana in his mouth and tried to move along the monkey bars . . .'

'. . . Then he fell down and choked on the banana,' I finish, my own lips curving. 'It wasn't funny at the time, but when I think about it now, he looked like a right idiot.'

'I was always surprised you didn't copy him.'

'Hey, I was an idiot, but I wasn't a stupid one. That move was always going to end in tears.'

'Yeah well, it made me laugh.'

I slide my fingers between hers and squeeze her hand. 'And Cam lived for nothing if not to make you laugh.'

Roxy smiles sadly at the truth of my words. Their relationship was so unconventional. I think I've only ever heard them argue once or twice – Iz and I manage that in a week.

'Yeah. He always had the answer to everything, didn't he?' Her eyes drift up to mine. 'He knew everything. It scared me sometimes, you know. Makes me wonder if he knew about everything that would happen after he died.'

'Maybe,' I reply, holding her gaze steadily. 'Maybe he wanted it to happen.'

She blinks slowly. 'Maybe.'

~

'Okay, you've been in a shitfuck of a mood since we left the zoo. What's wrong, Rox?' I throw my arms to the sides and stare at her back.

She's been a little down since lunch, and I get that after our conversation, but ever since we got back in my car she's all but ignored me. She hasn't touched me, hasn't laughed, hasn't spoken, and since we got to the gorge she hasn't done anything except look out the goddamn window at God only knows what.

This time, I haven't even done anything. Which makes a change.

Roxy pulls the band from her hair and combs her fingers through the braid, releasing it in a cascade of black waves that fall down her back.

'What is this?' she asks into the gentle breeze.

'What's what?'

'This.' She turns to face me and pauses. '. . . Us.'

I tilt my head to one side. 'I don't get what you're asking.'

'This!' She repeats, throwing her arms up. 'Everything. I don't even know how to describe it. The last couple of weeks, the other night . . . Today. What is this?'

Ah. I get it.

I run my fingers through her hair, pushing it away from her face. 'This is a relationship.'

My lips twitch at the way her eyes widen.

'What? You still didn't believe me when I said I cared?'

She doesn't answer.

'I more than care, Rox. Get that, will you? "This", as you describe it, is us. You and me.' My hands frame her face and hers settle on mine. I bend my head toward her and brush my lips across hers.

'Why? Don't you have anyone back in Cali waiting for you?'

I laugh.

'What's so funny?' she demands.

'The fact you're only asking me this after we've had sex.'

Her mouth opens and closes before she speaks. 'Shut up. Do you?'

'No. There hasn't been anyone at college. There's only you. Always you.' I run my thumb across her lips. 'Shouldn't I be asking you that question?'

'No one,' she replies instantly. 'Not since you got back.'

'Why?'

She raises her eyes to mine, curls her face into one of my hands, and whispers, 'Only you. Always you.'

I pull her into my chest. She wraps her arms around me, and her face buries into the side of my neck. She shudders. Her fingers splay out on my back, and I kiss her hair.

'He wouldn't mind.' My words are spoken into her hair. 'He told me once if you had to be with anyone, he'd rather it be with me.'

Roxy holds me even tighter. 'If I have to be with anyone, I'd rather it be with you, too.'

'So stop.'

She pulls away slightly. I hold her jaw gently.

'The drinking. All that shit . . . Stop it, Rox. You don't need it.'

Her eyes drop to the floor. 'It's hard. I've tried before. It's just . . . there. It helps me forget it hurts. Makes it better. Sometimes I even forget he's died, and for a few blissful moments it's all okay. It's hard to say no when an escape is dangled in front of you.'

'I'll be your escape. Not the drinking.' No other guys goes without saying. I'd like to see another guy try it. This girl has branded herself into my skin and my heart in a way I never saw coming. 'Just me. I'll be your escape when you feel like you've got nowhere to run to. I'll be your hideout when it feels like everyone is watching you, and I'll be your rock when you feel like everything around you is crumbling.'

'I'll try. I can just try. I can't promise you any more than that.' Her blue eyes are shining when she looks back up, and I nod. She reaches up and wraps a hand around my neck and pulls my face down. Her lips touch mine firmly, like she's sealing the promise with this kiss. 'Thank you,' she whispers against my mouth, releasing me. She gets out of the car, sits on the ground and looks out at the gorge.

'For what?' I follow her and drop down next to her.

'For today. I felt like the old Roxy again.' She turns her gaze to mine. 'I feel like the old Roxy whenever I'm around you.'

'She's my favorite,' I admit. 'So I do things to make you feel like her. That's the Roxy I know. My Roxy.'

Her lips twist at the corners. 'Your Roxy?'

I leap at her and push her back onto the ground. My eyes meet hers. 'Didn't I make that clear?'

She shakes her head, amusement dancing in her eyes. 'Not. At. All.'

'C'mere.' I press and hold my lips on hers. My arm snakes around her waist and her fingers sink into my hair as I flick my tongue against her mouth. I can taste the lingering traces of the candy she was eating in the zoo on her lips. I kiss her deeply, sweeping my tongue along hers and around her mouth in an attempt to make her as lightheaded as she makes me.

'Mmkay,' she mutters when I pull away. 'It's clear. I think.'

'My. Roxy.' I punctuate the words with more kisses. 'Okay?'

She nods slowly and smiles. 'Your. Roxy.'

Chapter Nineteen – Roxy

The twins leave their table and I wipe it down with a smile on my face. The smile that's been there since yesterday.

'Where've you been hiding?' Iz asks as she leads Selena into the empty café.

I grin and walk back to the counter. 'Everywhere and nowhere.'

Selena narrows her eyes. 'Where did you disappear to Saturday night? And why did Kyle disappear at the same time?'

Iz looks at her. 'The same time?'

They both turn to me. 'Oooooooh.'

'Seriously?' I put a hand on my hip. 'We were talking.'

'The language of luh-*urve*.' Selena slides onto the stool in front of the counter as Iz giggles.

'How old are you two?' I raise my eyebrows.

'Come on,' she whines. 'Spill it!'

'Ew. Brother.' Iz winces. 'Not too much spilling.'

'Says the one I caught making out with my cousin.'

I almost drop the glass I'm holding and gape at Iz. 'You what?'

'I might have kissed Si a little.'

Oh, now she looks out the window.

'A little?'

'Okay, okay! A lot. For a long time. Whatever.' She waves her hands. 'This isn't the point. The point is how successful was your "talk" with Kyle?'

I smile and look down. 'I'm going to be vague and go with very.'

''Kay. No more.' Iz puts her fingers in her ears. Selena grins, and I shrug.

No one needs to know any more than that. Saturday night belongs to me and Kyle. It's so much more than just one night.

'But I'm kinda pissed, because it looks like I missed something pretty damn interesting.'

'Me kissing Si is not interesting in the least.'

Selena looks at me. 'Kissing is an understatement. They were as close to sexy time as someone can be with clothes on.'

'Hey, you can have sex with clothes on, y'know,' Iz interjects.

I raise my eyebrows. 'And you've done this?'

Her lips curve. 'The guy didn't look the prettiest under the shirt, okay? But he could kiss like hell, so I thought I'd give him a chance.'

'And?' I lean forward.

Iz whistles. 'It was so fucking worth that chance.'

'Right. And Si?'

She holds a hand up. 'Drunk.'

'Off three drinks?' Selena questions.

'Three very strong drinks,' she protests. 'Give me a break, girls. I'm allowed to kiss a guy.'

'Iz, the way you were kissing him very nearly became indecent exposure.'

I raise my eyebrows.

'Well, wouldn't that have given the oldies a shock?' Iz laughs and turns to me. 'Where did you go, anyway?'

'Somewhere exposure wouldn't be indecent.' I wipe the counter. 'In fact, it was positively decent.'

'I think I'm going to be sick.'

~

I sit on my hands. This is near impossible.

Verity Point is so out of the way, there are no other towns for miles – just the odd farm – so there are plenty of places to hold outside parties and bonfires and shit.

Tonight it's a bonfire.

Tonight I'm surrounded by alcohol and I can't touch a drop.

It's harder than I thought. This is another thing that doesn't feel right without Cam. Nothing feels right without him.

I can't keep using him as an excuse.

No. It's not an excuse. It's the truth. Drinking makes me forget he's not here. Sitting away from everyone while drinking makes it hurt a little less – as if I can simply pretend he's somewhere with the guys. As if I can pretend he wasn't never here. Wishful thinking will be the death of me one day.

Someone sits behind me and legs stretch to either side of me. I turn my face into Kyle's and grip my thighs tighter. He runs his fingers down my arms and finds my hands. They link through mine and pry them from my legs, settling them around my waist. I squeeze his hands and curl into him as much as our position will allow.

'Everyone's looking at us,' he whispers in my ear. Amusement laces his tone.

'What? Have they never seen two people in a relationship before?' I reply loudly.

'Course we have,' Olly shouts from somewhere. 'We're just not used to the girl being a slut.'

Fucker. 'Big words from the boy who never got lucky with his little dick.'

Everyone laughs around us, but it's Kyle I'm focused on. His whole body is tight, his grip on me about to break my fingers.

'You know I'm about to go and break his arm, don't you?'

I shake my head. 'Can't hit him for being right,' I say sadly.

'Rox . . .'

'No. He's right. I was. I'm not afraid to admit that. Olly's just pissed off because I never let him get any.'

'Then how do you know about the size of his dick?'

My lips curve into a smile. 'He has small hands.'

Kyle lifts our hands and opens his. His fingers stretch out and his hand is twice the size of mine. He nods. 'Hm.'

I laugh silently. He drops my hand and turns me in his arms so I'm facing him. His free hand slides through my hair, and brown eyes find mine in the faint light of the fire.

'All the same, the next guy that talks to you that way is gonna find himself in a hell of a lot of pain.'

I run my thumb across his jaw. 'I can handle these assholes, you know.'

'I know,' he murmurs, moving his face closer to mine. 'But I'm afraid they can't handle you.'

'Can you? Handle me?'

'I can handle you and then some, Roxanne. Do you need a reminder?'

'You'll need to do some handling if you call me Roxanne again.'

He kisses me and grins against my mouth. 'You know I'll remember that, right?'

'Why wouldn't you?' I roll my eyes.

Kyle laughs, and it shakes my whole body. I smile and snuggle in closer to him, and his arm snakes round my body even tighter. For a moment, I forget Cam isn't here. I forget it hurts. I forget everything except Kyle.

Sitting here with him now feels crazy. Being with him is like a dream and I'm afraid he'll slip through my fingers if I don't hold on tight enough. I'm afraid one day I'll pinch myself and wake up and realize this whole thing has been another girly swoon in my own mind.

'How do you feel?'

His words pull me back to reality.

'In other words, do I want a drink?' I mumble into his chest.

He hesitates.

'Yes. I do.'

'Why?'

'Is this an episode of Dr. Phil?'

'Hey.' He pokes my side. 'Don't shut me out. If you feel like shit I wanna know.'

I take a deep breath. 'I'm waiting for Cam to appear and

rip it out of you, or for the two of you to play some prank on one of the dicks over there.' I nod to the corner. 'I'm waiting for something that isn't going to happen.'

He whispers something under his breath and holds me tighter. I squeeze my eyes closed. My heart hurts – like really hurts. It clenches with every beat, and my stomach tightens as a sliver of pain travels through my body, taking all of me over. My eyes burn and my bottom lip quivers. Shit.

Is this grieving? Proper grieving? It must be. This must be what I've hidden for so long. What I've been running from. What I've refused to accept.

Grief is waking up every morning with a spark of hope only for that spark to be put out and replaced with a heavy heart. It's holding onto memories and wishing for new ones. Grief is watching the door and watching for that person to walk through again, it's listening for their voice in a silence you know will never be broken, and it's waiting for them to come running round a corner they'll never turn.

And grief is the slow breaking of your heart every time you realize they're never coming back.

'Don't forget, Roxy.' Kyle kisses my head and whispers in my ear, 'Remember with me.'

'I can't.' My eyes fill with tears.

'You can.' His fingers stroke my hair. 'Let's go.'

'Where to?'

'Where no one can find us.' He stands and pulls me up with him.

'The gorge?'

'Exactly.'

His strong arm goes around my body and twists me into him. I slide my arms around his waist, trying to ignore the eyes I can feel burning into our backs. The urge to turn and say something is so strong. But that's something the new Roxy would do. I'm the old Roxy. I think.

It hits me like a punch to the stomach.

I don't know who I am.

I don't know who I should be or who I think I should be. I'll never be the person I was, but I don't know who I will be, either.

I really am lost.

'I'm gonna take three guesses where they're going!' Olly hollers across the field.

Before I can open my mouth, Kyle yells back, 'You're gonna need more than that. You gotta know what to do with a girl before you can guess right, Olly!'

I snort and bury my face into Kyle's side. Again, everyone laughs, and I feel like turning and showing him the smug grin spreading across my face.

'I had two choices.' Kyle shrugs and we head up the path leading to the gorge. 'I either punched him or made him look like an absolute dick in front of the girl he's been trying to impress all night.'

I bite my bottom lip. 'The latter was definitely funnier.'

'Glad you think so.' He squeezes me.

We're silent for the rest of the walk to the spot he found with Cam. I'm certain this is my new favorite place. The seclusion combined with nature's sounds makes it somewhere that shouldn't exist.

It reminds me there's perfection amidst heartbreak and despair.

I step away from Kyle and walk to the edge of the small stream rushing through. The orangey light from the almost-set sun creeps through the trunks of the trees on the other side, and dusk hangs over us. I know if I look up I'll see the stars faintly twinkling and the moon hanging in the sky, bathing the area around it in a bright white light.

'The first time me and Cam found this place we walked the length of this stream. It stems from the mountains – further up than we went the first time I brought you here. There's a tiny fall and water pools at the bottom of it. I was busy thinking how nice it was, but not Cam. No, he decided that pool would be the perfect place to throw you in.'

I glance over my shoulder. 'What did you say?'

Kyle stuffs his hands in his pockets and shrugs a shoulder. 'I told him to wait because there was probably a bigger pool of water we hadn't found yet.'

'Bastards,' I mutter fondly. 'You two have always been out to get me.'

'It was kind of his prerogative as your big brother.'

'Yeah? What was your excuse?'

'I think I wanted you to like me.' He grins.

A small laugh leaves me. 'Obviously it worked.' I run my hand down the tree next to me, feeling the rough bark against my fingers. 'He used to steal my diary every now and then. He thinks I didn't know but I did.'

'I didn't know that.'

Thank God.

'How else do you think he knew exactly when and where to find me when I started dating?' I turn to face him. 'He found out from my diary until I started a second one to throw him off the trail.'

Kyle laughs. 'He thought he'd scared everyone off.'

'Nah, Cam wasn't that scary.' *Wasn't. Wasn't.* 'I hate saying that.'

'Saying that?'

'Wasn't. Talking about him like he's not here. I know he's not, but it doesn't seem normal.' I look down and Kyle walks up to me.

'You really haven't talked about him to anyone except me, have you?'

I shake my head. 'Would you? Would you talk about Iz if it was her?'

He stops and thinks, like it's the first time this has occurred to him. 'No,' he says slowly. 'I don't think I could.'

'It hurts to think about him as if he's not here. He hasn't really gone anywhere, you know? He's still here in Verity Point. He's in every corner we turn and in every doorway we walk through. His idiocy lives in our minds and the tricks you guys played are all over town. But him . . . He's still in our hearts. He'll never go. He's not *here*, but he is. That makes no sense, I know, but only his body is dead. Everything else about him is still alive. I have to keep him alive somehow. I can't face being without him.'

Chapter Twenty – Kyle

Her words ring through every part of my body. He's still alive as long as we remember him. Cam's still alive as long as we hold a piece of him inside.

It's just like Iz said. Dead doesn't mean gone.

I wrap my arms around Roxy's waist from behind her and rest my chin on her shoulder. 'I get that. I feel it too, y'know? He's still here. I'm waiting for him to grab me and shove some fire snaps in my hand to throw on the sidewalk, or I'm waiting for his text to tell me he's got some great plan.'

'The plan was usually to piss me off,' she whispers and smiles.

'Oh, yeah. Nine times out of ten. We only did about half of them, otherwise we'd have been winding you up forever.'

'Jesus, if all the times you hid my stuff and filled my shampoo with shaving foam was only half of it, I'm glad you didn't do more!'

'The shampoo thing was Cam's idea. At least it was at first.' I grin remembering her shriek when she realized what we'd done. 'But now I think about it, you looked good in that towel.'

Roxy elbows me with a small laugh. 'Would you believe the shit he gave me for running out of the bathroom like that? He didn't speak to me for like two days.'

'Oh I believe it.' I pull her down to the floor and lie back, taking her with me. Her head rests on my chest and her arm lies over my stomach. I hold her close to me, breathing her in, and smile.

'He was so protective of me,' she muses, drawing circles on my side. 'What do you think he'd say if he saw us now?'

'I think he'd punch me and call me a dick, but he'd get over it.'

'I think he'd be okay with it.' Her voice is small and nearly broken.

'You know what? He would be. He told me once. Besides, this is the best way for everyone.'

She tilts her head back and looks at me. 'How is it?'

My lips curve to one side and I brush some hair from her face. 'This way I get to keep my promise *and* make you happy. As long as you're happy, I'm happy, and in the end that's all that really matters.'

'He'd call you a pussy for saying that.' Roxy laughs but cuddles in tighter to me. I look up at the sky with a smile on my face.

'Ah, well. Can't say I give a shit.' I laugh with her.

If you'd asked me a year ago if I'd have been here with Roxy, feeling the way I do, I'd have laughed at you. I never thought I would ever see her as more than just Cam's sister, but here we are. I feel for her more than I thought I'd ever feel for anyone. More than I ever thought possible – and I know why.

I know her. I know every little quirk and habit she has, how she likes things done, how to tell her mood from just a glance, and she knows me the same way. She knows me as intimately as I know her and it works.

We both share so much pain. We both had our hearts broken, and it's strange to think it's the pain that's pushed us together. It's ironic we managed to find happiness in a time where there is none.

Perhaps this was always meant to happen and we're the healing the other needs.

Perhaps we were always meant to find beauty in our pain.

~

A body shifts next to me and I instinctively hold it closer. Roxy's gentle giggle reaches my ears as she climbs on top of me.

'What are you doing?' I open my eyes to hers. She's sitting on me, her knees either side of my hips and her hands on the ground next to my head.

'Good morning.' She beams and drops her lips to mine.

I place my hands on her hips and take her kiss. 'Apparently it is,' I mutter. 'Why are you on top of me?'

'Are you complaining?' She wriggles, rubbing herself over my dick, and I feel it harden. I push my hips up.

'Does it feel like I am?'

She runs her tongue over her lips and shakes her head. That movement combined with the glint in her eyes does nothing to help the erection digging into her pants. Because of course she's wearing a skirt and the only thing separating us is her underwear, my underwear, and my jeans. She bends her head forward, her hair falling around us, and rests her forehead against mine.

Her lips are soft and sweet when they press against mine. I wrap my arms around her body when she lowers herself and lays on top of me. Every part of us is touching as she flicks her tongue between my lips. Her fingers slide through my hair as her other hand creeps beneath my shirt and tickles my stomach.

'Rox. We're outside.'

'Don't care,' she mutters against my lips.

'What if I do?'

'We would have done a lot more than just kiss up against that tree the other day if I'd had my way.'

Don't I know it.

She presses herself onto me and every part of my body responds. My brain thinks about what's under her skirt, my hands want to remove what's under there, and my dick wants to *be* under the skirt and inside her. Right inside.

So fuck outside.

I slide my hand up her spine to cup the back of her head and pull her face against mine. This time I kiss her. I kiss her hard, holding our mouths together, and graze my teeth along her bottom lip. She loops her legs around mine and runs her hand across my chest. I ease my fingers up her bare thighs and inside her skirt, taking her ass while holding her lips to mine.

Her exposed skin is too tempting as she sweeps her tongue. She wriggles again, and my hands shift down. I'm straining against my jeans as my fingers touch the wet, tender area between her legs. If I wasn't so fucking caught up in the way she's kissing me, I'd have to grit my teeth to restrain myself.

Because right now all I want to do is flip her on her back, tear away the scrap of lace she thinks passes as underwear, and fuck her the way our bodies are begging me to.

Roxy traces her fingers down my stomach to my waistband, and her fingers fiddle with the button on my jeans for a second before she pops it open.

'Impressive.' I kiss along her jaw and down her neck.

She grins. 'Efficient, actually.'

'I like your efficiency.'

'So do I,' she whispers, creeping her hand lower.

The flick of her fingertips against the head of my cock makes me buck my hips. She wraps her hand around me and rubs her thumb across the tip. I need to be inside her. Now.

I let go of her and reach into my pocket for a condom. Roxy takes it from me and rolls it onto me without looking. Her eyes are focused on me as she guides me toward her.

She jumps when I sit us up and kiss her, and I laugh into her mouth.

'Bastard,' she mumbles.

'Mhmm.'

My fingers splay in her hair and across her ass as she lowers herself onto me. She tenses for a second but doesn't stop until she's taken all of me and I hiss a breath. She's wet and tight and *fuck, she's squeezing.*

She giggles out breathlessly. 'Payback.'

'Bitch.' I drop kisses along her collarbone as she raises herself up and falls back again, grinding her hips the whole way.

'Mhmm.' She finds my mouth with hers and moves her tongue against mine in time with the movements of her body. She's crazy. She's crazy and she's driving me crazy. With every squeeze of her core, every flick of her tongue, every sharp breath combined with a tiny moan, she's driving me to the brink of insanity. She's making me need her so fucking badly I don't know if she'll ever be able to get rid of that need. I don't know if I'll ever not need to hold her body against me, over me, under me, and do this to her.

I drop us back and move my hips against hers. She buries her face into my neck and we're both breathing fast. It doesn't matter that we're hardly skin on skin. I can't feel anything but her. All I can feel is the burning temptation and desperation to take her to the edge the way she's taking me. And I will.

I'm determined to take her to the edge and tip her the fuck over.

I have no idea how much time passes until she falls. Until we both do. I'm completely lost.

'Shit,' Roxy breathes. 'What's the time?'

'After that, that's what you have to say?' I smirk as she gets up.

'No, really. What's the time?'

I sort myself out, tuck the condom back into its wrapper and into my back pocket, and dig my phone out. 'Half nine.'

'Fuck! I have to work at ten!'

Her eyes are wide, surrounded by smudged make-up, and her hand is covering her mouth. It's priceless and I can't help but laugh.

'Kyle!' She shoves my arm. 'Don't laugh. This is your fault.'

'Hey – how is this my fault?'

'You . . . You seduced me!' she sputters.

I laugh again and pull her into me. I brush my lips against her swollen ones. 'Watch it, you, or I'll do it again.'

'Not a very scary threat,' she mumbles, stepping back and wiping under her eyes. 'Let's go.'

I follow her through the trees. 'Who said it was a threat?'

She shoots me a glance and carries on walking. Without

another word she detours at the last minute. I run up behind her and link our fingers, wrap our arms around her waist, and kiss the base of her neck.

'Do you have to go to work?' I mumble into her skin.

'Yes.' She squeezes my hand. 'Mom is already gonna wonder where I am when she goes to wake me up.'

'What are you gonna tell her?'

'I'm undecided.'

I smile to myself as we reach her house and walk round the front. Roxy untangles herself from me, kisses my cheek, and turns to her house. She calls that goodbye?

'Hey!' I yell.

She stops and spins back, her eyes widening as I walk toward her purposefully. I grab her, cupping her head and bending her backward. A squeal leaves her as my lips drop to hers, but she doesn't fight me. She clings to my shoulders and kisses me back with a nip to my bottom lip.

'That was a movie kiss,' she mumbles.

My lips twitch and I touch my nose to hers. 'Tell that to your mom.'

Roxy stands and looks at her house. Myra's face is poking out from the corner of the curtain and there's a smile on her face – the first real smile I've seen since getting back.

'I don't think I need to tell her anything,' Roxy muses. 'Perhaps some explaining, but no telling.'

I laugh and kiss her cheek, and swat her behind gently as she walks to her house.

Ray opens the door and points a finger at me, a frown on his face. 'What you doing keeping my girl out all night?'

'Dad,' Roxy groans. 'Really?'

'Who do you think you are?' he insists.

Another laugh leaves me, and I salute him. 'You don't scare me, old man!'

'Dammit.' He shrugs. 'Worth a try.'

~

I grin at Iz as she walks around the kitchen and makes lunch. She keeps glancing at me and every time my grin widens a little more. She's going mad trying to work out why I'm doing this – trying to work out what I know. Winding her up is probably my favorite thing ever.

Next to kissing Roxy.

Iz rounds on me, pointing the butter knife in my direction. 'Alright, I'll bite. Why the fuck are you looking at me like that, you little creep?'

There we go. I don't say anything, just smile at her. God, this is fun.

'Kyle.'

Grin.

'Kyle!'

I scratch my nose.

'Kyle!'

'I was just wondering if you enjoyed making out with one of my best friends.'

'Funny, I was wondering the same thing.' She waves the knife.

'I do. Very much.' I wink at her.

She screws up her face. 'Mmph.'

'Si. Why Si?'

'Seriously? You want to know how my brain works?'

Not really. 'I just never pictured you two . . . You know. Flicking each other's tonsils.'

'God, a frat house is doing nothing for you, is it?'

'Good job I'm moving out next semester.' I shrug. 'Seriously. Why Si?'

Iz smiles slowly, the corners of her lips seeming to reach her eyes. 'Because he has this solid chest that could make a girl weep and an ass so tight it hurts to look at it. And judging by—'

'Alright, alright!' I hold my arms up. 'I do not need my sister's evaluation on the size of my friend's dick.'

'And judging by the way he kisses, he probably fucks like a porn star.'

I snort loudly. 'A sorority is doing nothing for you, is it?'

'Good job I don't give a flying, tap-dancing monkey then, isn't it?' She takes a bite from her sandwich.

'I actually need to ask you something.'

'Aside from the sexual attraction I have to your friend?'

'It probably doesn't bother me nearly as much as my attraction to Roxy bothers you.' So I'm bluffing. I'm the one who has a poker face – Iz couldn't bluff her way out of a kindergarten class. They'd figure her out in seconds.

'Whatever. What do you want?'

I tap my fingers across the table. How do I ask her what I haven't even fully thought about myself?

'How . . .' I pause and, crap . . . Spit it out. 'How do I convince Roxy to come to Berkeley with me next month?'

Iz stops with her mouth still full and stares at me. Slowly, she chews and swallows. 'Did I hear you right?'

'I dunno. What did you hear?'

'You want Roxy to move to Berkeley. With you.'

'At least you don't need your ears cleaning out.'

'Goddammit, Kyle! This shit is serious.' She slaps the table.

'I know, Iz, alright? I know.' I run my hands through my hair. 'I just . . . I can't leave her here. Not now.'

My sister sits opposite me, her eyes flicking over my face, and smiles.

'Fuck off with your psychobabble.' I glare at her.

'You love her.'

Goddamn psycho body language skills.

'You do.' Her eyes widen. 'You actually do.'

'No need to look so surprised,' I say dryly.

'I'm not. I don't think. I just.' She tilts her head slightly. 'I dunno. You really want her to go to Berkeley with you?'

My head bobs slowly. 'It's Roxy, y'know? How am I supposed to go back there without her?'

'It's not that far.'

'If I can't walk there in half an hour, it's too fucking far, Iz.'

She sighs and rubs her face. 'I don't know. Have you tried

asking her? See if she'll apply there when she decides she'll go. She'd get in – she's smart, Ky. She's just a little off course.'

'I know. And of course I haven't asked her – if I had would I be asking you?' I raise my eyebrows, and Iz shrugs. 'Exactly. I just . . . I love her, Iz. Fuck. I don't even know. I just want her to come to Berkeley with me.'

'Well, you have to ask her,' she reasons. 'But what if she doesn't?'

I say nothing. Let her use her psycho-shit and work this out herself.

'Kyle Michael Daniels.' Iz says my name slowly and carefully, injecting as much question into it as she can. 'Don't tell me you'll stay here if she doesn't go.'

I tap my fingers against the table again and whistle.

'You've wanted to be a doctor since . . . well, forever. You can't seriously say you'd give that up? I know it's Roxy, but . . . Seriously? You would?'

I meet her eyes, the ones that are the exact shade of mine. 'I know I have, but she's more than a dream, Iz. Roxy is everything and she's real. Without her there is no dream. So, yes. If I have to I'll stay here. With her. For her. I'd do anything and everything for that girl.'

Chapter Twenty-One – Roxy

I start my laptop and open my internet browser. *What under-graduate courses do you need to be a vet?* On impulse, I type *Berkeley* after the question. UCLA was on my original list . . . I know it's Southern California, and Berkeley is Northern, but whatever. This is only research, after all.

Basic science courses and advanced courses in animal biology and behavior, among other things. Easy pickings. Science has always come naturally to me – and these science classes would lead to working my dream job.

But I don't have to make any decisions now. In fact I should go back to Google and look at other colleges around the country. I don't. I put the computer to sleep mode and get up.

The house is always quiet when Mom and Dad are at work. I wander across the hall and my hand hovers over Cam's door handle. Slowly, I turn it and walk inside. My feet take me to his bed and I perch on the end of it. The smell of him is almost gone. There's no lingering trace of his *Davidoff*, and my stomach twists. His room should smell like it, so I get up, grab the cologne bottle, and spray it. The fresh scent brings a smile to my face.

This is comfort. This is where he's alive the most. This is where I remember most of him and Kyle.

'You'll get caught,' I'd warned them. I was perched on Cam's desk with my legs swinging beneath me.

'Who cares?' My brother shrugged carelessly.

'Everyone will know it's us anyway,' Kyle muttered. 'No one else has the balls to pull the crap we do.'

'Okay, you have a point. But how do you expect to exchange all the whipped cream for shaving foam?'

They just grinned.

'Okay, one, I feel the need to tell you that you two have an unhealthy obsession with that stuff. And, two, I am not being a part of this stupid plan.'

'Roxy,' Cam whined. 'You have keys to the café.'

'Mom will kill you!'

'No, she won't.' Kyle grinned and tugged on a lock of my hair. 'You'll be the one switching them.'

'Uh, hello? Did you miss point two? I'm not doing it. No. Chance.'

'Fine. But you can get us in, right?' Cam gave me puppy dog eyes. They were the worst ever but I could never resist them.

'I can't get you in. Mom will fire me then kick my ass. Publicly,' I stress.

'Then how—'

I got up and walked to his door. My hand rested on the handle as I peered at them over my shoulder. 'I can't get you in but I can't stop you stealing my keys. The ones I just happen to keep in the top drawer of my nightstand when I'm not working.'

Kyle and Cam looked at me, their smiles wide enough to break their faces and their eyes dancing with mischief.

My lips twitch now with the memory. They did steal my keys and did it without getting caught. I never asked how they got the shaving foam in whipped cream cans and they never offered. They took the shit for it though, maintaining I knew nothing about it. And if I'm honest, I didn't actually know when they did it.

They really did steal my keys.

I was like their silent partner in everything they did – unless I was their victim – and no one ever found out. I think I miss the three of us together almost as much as I do Cam himself.

It's so hard to have such a huge part of your everyday life ripped away from you.

It's so hard to say goodbye to someone you thought would be there forever.

~

Some people are devils in disguise.

They're all too willing to tempt you into something you have a weakness for. They seem to know when you're having a bad day and just creep up on you with a solution. An antidote. An escape.

But it's always the wrong one. They're always short term and they don't ever make it better. Nothing about a short escape from a devil can help you move forward in the way you need.

And this is how I feel right now looking at Layla.

'C'mon, Roxy. I need the money and you need this.'

I look at her red hair and her wide, brown eyes. She looks desperate. I'm not.

'I don't want it, Layla. I don't need it, okay? You'll have to find someone else to buy it off you.'

'Roxy!'

'Here.' I pull out my cell and give her the number of a guy I met in Portland a few months ago. 'He's always looking for drugs. Call him.'

'He's in fucking Portland.'

I shrug and turn. 'You either want money or you don't.'

You either want the escape or you don't. Right now, I don't. I don't need them to make me forget how much it hurts. I need to grit my teeth and bear it.

My family deserve more than what I've been doing to them.

I walk in the direction of my house, dragging my feet. I'm finally noticing the true hollowness of Verity Point without my brother and the jokes he used to play with Kyle. And I'm wishing I hadn't blown my chances of going to college in September. Now I'm stuck here for another year.

I put my key in the door and twist it. Hands land on my shoulders and I scream.

'It's me.' Kyle laughs.

'Oh my god. You dick. You scared the crap outta me.'

He laughs again and follows me into my house. 'Sorry. I thought you would have heard me coming.'

I shake my head. 'No. I was in my own little world.'

'Can I ask you something?'

'You can ask.'

'Did you get any?'

I stop. 'Any what?'

'You know what I'm on about.'

'No, I really don't.'

'Ben just saw you with Layla.'

Of course he did. And of course he had to tell Kyle, because why wouldn't he?

My lips thin and annoyance spreads through my body. 'And you naturally assumed I bought alcohol or drugs from her.'

'No . . . Kind of. I just wondered,' he says warily.

That annoyance quickly changes to anger, and I chew on my lip. I stare at him for a second before turning away.

'It's nice to know you have so much belief in my ability to say no.' I storm up to my room. The stairs creak as Kyle follows me.

'Hey, I didn't say that!' He puts his foot between the door to stop me closing it in his face.

'You meant it.'

'No. I didn't.'

'Bullshit.' I turn to look at him. 'You knew I'd been with her and thought I'd give in. Well, I didn't! She said she needed money, so I gave her the number of someone else who'd buy drugs from her. Ben conveniently left out that part, didn't he, huh?'

'He was just telling me what he saw.'

'He obviously didn't see enough then, did he?' I'm almost shouting. I can't believe he really thinks this. I can't believe he'd assume I'm so weak I have to give in whenever temptation is dangled in front of my face.

It actually hurts he thinks I'd go and do that after I promised him I wouldn't.

'I said I wouldn't do that. I told you I'd try my best not to do all that shit and you don't even think I can stop, do you?' My eyes meet his and he steps forward.

'Rox.'

I move away from his outstretched arm. 'You don't think I can, do you?' I repeat. 'Admit it. You didn't believe it so you rushed over here to ask if I bought anything. You didn't ask if I walked away. You automatically assumed the worst.'

Kyle's shoulders slump and he runs a hand through his hair. I'm right. We both know it.

I take a deep breath, my stomach clenching. 'You can go now,' I whisper and turn away from him.

'What?'

'Please go,' I whisper again. 'I don't know if I can be around someone who thinks so little of me right now.'

'Is that what you think?'

'At least I can admit what I think.'

'Yeah, let's ignore the fact I thought that because I care about you, shall we?'

'Don't throw that in my face. You don't believe I can stop drinking and shit and that's that.'

'How many times? I didn't say that!'

I cover my face with my hands and a lump forms in my throat. 'No, you didn't, but you meant it. So go. Please.'

'This isn't over, Rox. Call me when you've calmed the fuck down.'

He leaves my room and his footsteps are heavy on the stairs. I cross my room and slam my door, falling against it, tears build in my eyes.

One week ago he asked me to stop the way I've been acting, and already he's given up on believing in me.

I don't want to listen to him talking reason. I don't want to listen to him trying to dig himself out of what he *didn't* say, because what he did say is enough.

He knows me better than anyone – maybe even better than Iz and Selena – but he doesn't know me well enough to trust me to keep my word.

Tears drip down my cheeks and I lean my head back against the door.

'Fuck you,' I whisper.

Chapter Twenty-Two – Kyle

Three days.

It's been three goddamn, stupid days since she made me walk out on her and I'm running out of options. I'm running out of things to do to make her stop and keep her that way. I don't know what else I can do. I don't know what else I'm supposed to do.

Whatever progress I'd made, whatever convincing I'd done, I've fucked it all up by speaking first and thinking after. I'm back at square one, except this time I have a lot more to make up. I have to convince her I believe in her and that I know she can do this.

Shit, I need her to do this. For her. For me. For us. She has to do it. She has to accept Cam's gone so she can move on. Every time she drinks she's holding onto something that doesn't exist. She needs to step back from it and hold on to what does exist.

The memories. The good times. The future.

I know she'll never forget that night. She watched him crash and watched him die only an hour later, but she can't let that be her focal memory of him. The only way she'll be able to ease the pain is by thinking of the good times we all had together. She'll only ease the pain by remembering.

I'm the person that could help her remember.

And I've fucked that up.

I've destroyed everything we've had between us. I should have known better than going round there and asking like that. Roxy's temper flares up without a second's warning. I should have known she'd react that way . . . The same way I did.

Speak first, think later.

Impulsively.

But everything about us has been impulsive. Every fight, every kiss, every time we've had sex . . . They've all happened in a crazy spur of the moment that wrapped us up before we'd even had a chance to think about it. So of course this would be too.

I shouldn't have expected it to be anything but, I conclude as Si walks through my front door.

He smacks me round the head. 'Get your fuckin' ass off your sofa and in my car.'

'What for?'

'Party. We need to cheer you up, you miserable dick.'

'I don't need cheering up. I'm chirpy as fuck. See?' I fake-grin.

He laughs. 'Look, man, Roxy will be there. Go see her, chat a little then go wherever you guys go when you sneak off and do whatever.'

'It's gonna take a bit more than a damn chat to get her to go anywhere with me willingly right now.' I lift myself from the sofa and follow him out to his car.

Hey – she isn't coming to me anytime soon, so I'm gonna have to go to her.

'Ben really starred, huh?' Si glances at me.

'Nah, it was me. He was just telling me what he saw – I'm the one that assumed shit. I should have just asked her properly instead of half-accusing her, or better yet, not said a fuckin' word.'

He shrugs. 'You only did it 'cause you care about her.'

'Yeah? Do me a favor and tell her that will you?'

'I would if I didn't think she'd rip my balls off.'

'Nice to know you value your balls over our friendship.'

We grin at each other but mine is still half-hearted. Dread is settling in my stomach and I know why. Roxy and party go hand in hand too well, and I'm afraid of what I'll find there. I'm afraid I'll find her drunk, maybe high, or maybe even with another guy.

And I wonder why she thinks I don't believe in her.

Fuck.

Music booms from the house Si pulls up to and I don't even care enough to see where we are. Seeing her is all I care about. I push my way through into the house and look in each room as we go past. Si does the same, and we find her in the kitchen.

She glances up as we enter and her blue eyes crash into mine. They're heavy. Sad. Soft. Angry. Hard. They're a mixture of so many things, making my stomach twist in guilt for a moment before she turns away.

'Ouch,' Si mutters.

'Thanks for that.' I take the beer he hands me.

'Anytime. What you gonna do?'

'Same thing I did before when I wanted her to talk to her. Piss her off.'

'Don't be a prick, Ky,' Iz says, coming up behind me and standing next to me. 'I think she's pissed off enough at you.'

'Hey – she told *me* to go. I fucked up, alright? She just didn't listen to me when I tried to explain.'

'You two are both stubborn as shit and that's your problem. Neither of you will listen to the other nor will you give in. You'll just stand here on either side of the kitchen, mad and upset, until the other one leaves.'

'Thanks for your evaluation. Do I pay you now or later?'

'Sometimes I wonder why I bother helping you, you ass.'

I rest my arm over her shoulders and squeeze her. 'I know, Iz. I'm sorry.'

She shrugs out of my hold. 'It's not me you need to apologize to. It's the girl over there who's wondering if she should just give up on you.'

Hit me where it hurts why don't you, sis. Just punch me in the gut. It'd be easier to deal with.

Until I see her throw a shot back with Selena.

'Yeah.' I nod in her direction. 'Really looks like she's wondering. Looks like she already fucking has.'

'No,' Iz muses, leaning against the wall. 'She's given up on giving up. She thought you believed in her, now she thinks you don't, so in her eyes she has nothing to give up for.'

'She should give up for herself,' Si interjects. 'She should do it because if she doesn't, she's gonna go the same way as Cam.'

The truth hurts. Like a fucking bitch.

Iz looks past me to speak to Si. 'You're right, but that doesn't mean she can see that.' Her voice gets quieter. 'Kyle was her reason. He was her rock. He's the only person that knew Cam the way she did, the only person that could understand even a fraction of her pain. We all know that, Si. We're not stupid. None of us can do for her what he can.'

'Still here, y'know.' I watch as Roxy does yet another shot.

'And now . . .' Iz trails off, ignoring me. 'Now, she thinks she's lost him.'

A guy approaches her and she smiles at him. I chew the inside of my cheek as they start up a conversation, and I can feel Iz and Si watching me carefully. Even Selena is glancing at me across the room.

My jaw tightens when he leans in to her. Every part of my body goes on high alert. Who the fuck does this guy think he is hitting on my girl this way? Because she is. No matter what she says, she's fucking mine.

My fingers tighten on the side of the counter at that thought. There isn't a part of me that doesn't want to go over there and kiss the fuck out of her in front of everyone here.

'I think this is my cue,' Iz mutters. She crosses the room and steps between Roxy and the guy. He moves back and lets Iz take him into the front room. A bottle slams onto the table next to me. I glance at Si.

Seems I'm not the only one that has issues tonight.

My eyes travel back to Roxy. They burn into her back, following her wherever she moves to in the kitchen, tracing the lines of her body. They shoot daggers at any guy who looks like he's approaching her, and eventually they get the message.

She's off limits. She's off limits to every motherfucker that isn't me.

'Here we go,' Si says with too much amusement.

I look away from the guy who's now approaching Selena and see Roxy storming toward me. Wordlessly, she grabs the front of my shirt and drags me after her. I shoot a look to Si over my shoulder, and he's laughing.

Roxy pushes the back door open and pulls me into the yard. She looks me over angrily, her hands on her hips. 'What the fuck are you doing?'

'I'm pretty sure that's meant to be my line, isn't it?'

'I'd tell you not to be so stupid but you obviously came out with your jackass hat on tonight.'

'Rox.' I sigh. 'Can we go and talk about this? Away from here. Please.'

Her shoulders drop and she shrugs a little. 'I don't know if I want to. I'm so fucking mad at you.'

'So mad you decided to drink tonight.'

She looks up at me. 'I figured you had so little belief in me anyway it wouldn't matter.'

The hell? 'Wouldn't matter?'

'Yep. You think I'm gonna go do it anyway, so who cares?'

Who cares? Who cares?

'I fucking care!'

I want to grab her and shake her. I've tried everything and if this doesn't work, if I can't make her believe me, then I have no choice but to do the one thing I thought I could avoid. I want to beg her not to make me do it, but as every second passes without her speaking, I know I'm gonna have to.

I'm gonna have to take the biggest risk of my life.

I'm going to be walking away from her by the end of the night.

Chapter Twenty-Three – Roxy

He looks the way I feel. Angry and confused and hurting.

'But you still don't believe in me,' I say softly.

'Jesus, Rox. I do, okay? I do.' He frames my face with his hands. 'I know you can do it.'

'What if I can't? What then, Kyle? Will this happen again and again until we finally get it?' I step back. 'What if this is me now?'

'This isn't you. We know it.'

'No, we don't. We think we do. I don't know who I am. Do you get that? I don't know if I'm the old Roxy or the new Roxy or someone entirely different. Right now I think I'm the new Roxy and you hate her. You hate everything she is and everything she does and this,' I gesture between us, 'this wouldn't work.'

'I could never hate you. You know that.'

'No, I don't.' I swallow. 'You said yourself the person I was before is your Roxy. This person isn't, is she? Maybe we're just kidding ourselves. You don't want this Roxy, do you?'

'Fucking hell, Rox. I want *you*. I don't get how we've gone from a simple misunderstanding to you deciding I don't want you!'

'But you don't want *this* Roxy!' I yell, not caring there are faces pressed against the windows watching us and that everyone in the yard is quiet and listening in. 'This could be the person I am. It probably is. I guess . . .' I pause for a moment. I need to hold these tears back. Why does the truth have to hurt so much? Why does it have to break my heart even more?

Why can't the truth be beautiful for once?

'You guess what?'

I drop my eyes to the floor. 'I guess if you don't want the person I could be, then you don't really want me at all.'

I can't look up. I don't want to see his eyes as he realizes what I'm saying is true. Because it is. He said it himself – the old Roxy is his Roxy. I'll never be her again, not even if I try hard.

'The Roxy I know respected herself, she respected others, and she looked down on the kind of person you are right now. The Roxy I know? She had the most beautiful smile I've ever seen and never failed to make my day, even when she was just my best friend's kid sister. That's the Roxy I want – the Roxy you're trying to hide,' he replies softly.

'I can't be the person you want me to be.' My eyes fill and my heart cracks. Not just a little, it's a booming crack I feel right through my body. It's a shattering motion that could destroy my composure in seconds.

'Can't, or won't?'

I shake my head.

'Then I guess . . . I guess I'm done here.'

Now I look up.

'If you want to destroy yourself this way, Rox, I can't stand by and watch it. I can't spend another night across a house from you while you drink yourself into oblivion. Keep it up and you'll be the one getting into a car because you're too drunk to think straight. Your parents will have to bury another child.' He starts walking. Backward. Away from me. 'If you wanna fall, you can, but I'm not going with you. I'm not going to watch you do this to yourself anymore.'

He's going.

He's really going.

'I was right. You don't believe in me at all.'

'Oh, I believe in you. The problem is that you don't. You don't believe in you, you don't believe in me, and you sure as shit don't believe in us. If you believed in us you wouldn't be here drinking tonight. And I wouldn't be walking away from us.'

'Like you don't care. You wouldn't be walking away like you don't care.' My voice breaks on the final word. My stomach knots and I feel sick. He's walking away.

But isn't this what I was trying to get him to do?

Yes.

No.

I was trying to get him to see what I see.

I didn't think it would end this way.

I didn't think it would hurt so much.

'I care, Rox. I care about you too much – so fucking much it hurts. You think I wanna do this? You think I wanna turn my back on you and leave you here? I don't, but you don't believe. You don't believe and I can't believe in us if you don't.'

He turns and walks away.

'Kyle,' I call his name. *No no no. Don't go.* 'Kyle!'

'You've made it clear, Rox.' His voice is sad. *Fuck don't do this!* 'You said yourself you can't be my Roxy. In fact, you couldn't have said it any more times.'

He disappears around the corner. I hold my hands against my stomach and bend down. The tears in my eyes threaten to escape and I shake my head.

He's right.

I said I can't be his Roxy anymore.

I said I can't try.

I said I don't believe in us.

He's right, and I'm wrong.

I'm naïve and impulsive and that's my stupidity. I don't think before I do things. I let my temper control me and now look at me. I'm standing here staring at a black hole where he should be.

'What the fuck are you all looking at?' I yell at the people staring at me and run away from the house. I don't want to be here. I don't want to be anywhere near here. There's only one place I can be right now.

Cam.

I run toward the graveyard, holding my tears in the whole

way, and crawl through a hole in the bushes. My feet take me
to Cam's grave and I collapse on the floor there.

I let them go. I let the tears spill over and fall to the ground,
and I rest my head against the headstone.

'I fucked it, Cam. I finally got what I wanted and I fucked
it all up. Now I'm worse than I was before, because I still have
neither of you, but this time I have twice the broken heart.' I
hold onto the cold marble. 'I've made a mess of everything,
and it's all my fault.'

The tears are falling hard and fast I'm alone. I'm so alone
in everything, and I know it's all my own doing.

'What am I supposed to do?'

~

It should be raining. The sky should be dark and grey to match
my mood, but it isn't. It's blue and bright and fucking sunny.

At least it's quiet in the café. I don't know if I could deal
with having to be all sugar and sweetness today – I can barely
smile.

'Well don't you look happy today?' My cousin's voice travels
across the café. I glare at her as she sits in front of me. 'I heard
about what happened.'

'No laptop?'

'Finished last night. I'm having a day off.' She shifts in her
seat. 'Nice try, by the way. Are you okay?'

'Fine.' I grab a mug and flick the coffee machine into action.

'Right. I get it. You don't want to talk about it.'

I sigh and pour her coffee. 'I don't know, Lou. I don't know
what I want to do.'

She takes the mug from me and looks at me sympathetically.
'Apart from go home and have a good cry?'

I swallow and nod slowly. 'That's pretty much it.'

'Why don't you just apologize? You both made a mistake.'

'It's not that easy.' I rest my elbows on the counter and lean
forward. 'I mean, yeah, we both said shit we shouldn't have,

but it's done now. It wouldn't work. He's walked away and I'm okay with that.'

Louisa raises her eyebrows. 'Wow. That's what you're telling yourself, huh?'

I have to tell myself I'm okay with it. If I don't, I don't know what I'll do.

'Roxy,' she says softly. 'Do yourself a favor and ask Aunt Myra if you can leave early. Just go home, cry, and go to sleep. You're allowed to do that, you know. She'd understand.'

I shake my head. 'No. I don't want to do that. I just . . .'

'Roxy, baby, go home.' Mom comes out from the kitchen. 'Lou, can you help out until Selena comes in later?'

'Are you paying me?' Louisa grins.

'Depends how good you are,' Mom teases her.

'Okay. I'll take over.' She turns to me. 'See? Go home.'

Mom strokes my hair. 'You'll feel better. We'll talk later, okay?'

It doesn't look like I have a choice. I untie my apron and hand it to my cousin.

This is one of the times I'm glad Verity Point is so small. Sure, half the people that live here are probably watching me walk home right now, but at least I can get there quickly.

I close my bedroom door behind me, lean against it, and look around my room aimlessly.

Even being here reminds me of Kyle. Everything is him, from the photo on my dresser to the lingering scent of him on my pillow. I can't stay here any longer. I can't be in this room for another second.

I stuff some clothes into a backpack and get out of the house. If there's no belief, there's no reason to stay.

Chapter Twenty-Four – Kyle

'Are you sure you're okay?'

'Iz, I'm fine. Just go, will you?'

She sighs. 'Okay. I'm going to the café.'

I'm not replying to that. I know why she's going, and I already have too much Roxy on my mind to be able to think about anything else. And knowing how she's hurting is the last thing I need.

Seeing the look on her face as I walked away near damn killed me. Her eyes held a sadness and shock I've never seen before. The pain in her voice when she called after me made me feel like the biggest dick in the world, but I had no choice.

I still have no choice.

This is my last option. Walking away from her, breaking both our hearts, it's all I have left to convince her to stop. One stupid little misunderstanding – one that we're both to blame for – and she jumped straight back into her old ways.

Yet I still can't believe I actually walked away from her.

If I'd been another guy, I would have punched me in the face by now. Shit, who am I kidding? I wanna punch me in the face anyway.

I get up and take the stairs to my room. Fuck everything today. Fuck everything that doesn't involve following my sister to the café to grab Roxy and apologize till I'm blue in the face.

Nothing I do can save us from this fall-out. I'm not stupid. The only thing that could is her coming to me, not the other way around. If I go to her the way I want to I'm forgiving her for everything she's done. I'm forgiving her for giving up on herself, on us, and right now that's out of the question.

I never stopped believing in her. I never stopped believing in us. Not even for a minute.

Maybe I could have tried harder to make her believe me. Maybe I could have been honest with her. "I care about you" is such an understatement. It's the understatement of the goddamn fucking millennium!

If I could go back I would. If I could tell her how I really feel, if I could stay in her room instead of walk away, I would. I'd do everything differently and we wouldn't be here right now. She wouldn't have a broken heart, she wouldn't have had those tears in her eyes on Friday night, and she wouldn't have had to watch me go.

The irony of this situation is that everything I've done this summer was to mend her broken heart . . . And now I've broken it all over again.

I never honestly thought I'd have to walk away from her. I thought – although I never planned it – us just being together would be enough. I thought I would be enough to make her stop the way she's been acting. I thought everything between us would be enough to make her give up the bad girl act.

Because she's not. No matter how many times she tells me she's not the person she was, that she's a different person now, I know otherwise. I've seen the person she was before Cam died. I've seen that smile and heard that laugh and seen that sparkle in her eyes. I've heard that teasing sarcasm and wit and seen that playful eye roll.

I've also seen the hurt and confusion. If she really didn't have any of the old Roxy left, she wouldn't have been hurt when I walked away. She wouldn't have cared. She can try to convince us both otherwise, but she's still my Roxy.

But that wasn't the Roxy I fell in love with.

I fell in love with the person she is right this second.

The Roxy that's lost and hurt, confused and alone, and most of all, heartbroken. Yet she's the Roxy that's not afraid to grab you by the balls and twist them. The one that's playful, sexy, and challenging one minute, then she's soft and gentle and quiet the next. She's a mixture of so many things, so many contradicting things, and I fell in love with all of those things.

I didn't walk away from the bad girl Roxy.

I walked away from the mixture of good and bad, the mixture of her past and present self.

I walked away from the girl I fell in love with.

And that makes it worse. That makes this whole clusterfuck of emotions running through me stronger. It makes it so much fucking worse because now I'm not thinking I need to stay away for her own good. I'm thinking I need to get off my ass and go and get my girl back.

I have to remind myself walking away from her was my third and final option. I didn't expect it to hurt this way. I didn't expect us to fall in love and tear our own hearts out.

I guess the third time isn't always so lucky.

'Kyle!' Iz screams through heavy steps on the stairs. She flies through my bedroom door. 'Kyle!'

I jump up and look at her. 'What? What's wrong?'

'You have to do something.' She swallows and blinks harshly, but I can see the tears brimming in her eyes.

'What?'

'No one's seen or heard from her for four days. She's gone.'

And just like that, everything stops. My heart pauses and my breathing ceases. Every muscle in my body tightens and I stare at my sister, hoping to fuck I'm thinking something different to what she means. Hoping the twisting and turning feeling in my stomach isn't telling me what I'm suddenly so scared of.

'Who?'

Iz puts her hand over her mouth.

'Iz. Tell me who!' I yell. Fuck. Please don't say it. Please don't say her name.

A tear spills from my sister's eye.

Please.

'Roxy. She's missing.'

'Missing?' I repeat. My fingers come up to my head and sink into my hair. 'What do you mean, she's missing?'

'She disappeared on Saturday afternoon. Myra called everyone in case Roxy was hiding there. She thought she'd be with Selena, but she isn't. She hasn't heard from her either.'

'Layla?' I choke on her name.

Iz shakes her head. 'Hasn't seen her since before . . . You know.'

I nod. I know. 'Why didn't she tell us? I've been sitting here feeling sorry for myself and she's been fuck knows where!'

'She didn't want to worry us. She thought she might have just taken off for a day or two to calm down. Apparently Roxy did that just after Cam died, but now she's worried. She's never disappeared for four whole days before.'

I sink back to the bed and bury my face in my hands. 'Has she called the cops yet?'

'No. She wanted to talk to us first . . . See if we might know where she is.'

'Let's go then.'

'Wait,' Iz calls, running after me. 'Kyle! That's not all.'

'What? How can it get any fucking worse than the girl I'm in love with being God knows where?' I yell. 'How?'

My sister grabs me and holds me in a way she hasn't since we were little. I clench my whole body, biting back the tears burning in the backs of my eyes.

I'm real fucking mad she's gone and no one knows where she's been. But I'm worried. And I'm scared. I've never been so scared about anything in my whole life. I thought I was scared of losing her before, but that fear was nothing compared to the one running rife through me right now.

The fear I could lose her for good.

She could be anywhere. With anyone. Doing anything.

I need to know Roxy is okay.

Nothing else matters except for that. Nothing else ever matters.

'Myra's broken down,' Iz tells me when she releases me. 'Really broken down. She's locked herself in the bedroom and is refusing to leave. She's just . . . God, Ky. She's just crying.

She can't fight anymore and I'm worried about her. She won't let Ray in. She won't talk. All she's doing is crying.'

I don't answer her. I pull the door open with all my strength and run toward her house. My feet pound against the asphalt as I run faster than I ever have.

Without Cam here, the only person that can be the strength in that family is me. I'm the only person left that can hold it together – and that's exactly what I'm going to do.

I burst through their front door and up the stairs, only just registering Iz panting behind me. Ray's leaning against Roxy's door, his shoulders hunched and his fists clenched at his side.

I spent half of my childhood looking up to this man as my second dad. I've seen him in every mood, from raging mad to laughing his ass off, but I've never seen him look so vulnerable. I've never seen him so broken.

I tear my eyes from him and bang on Myra's door. Once. Twice. Three times.

'Open the door, Myra!'

Nothing.

'C'mon, it's me.' Bang. 'Please.'

Nothing.

Bang bang bang. 'I swear, I'm not going anywhere until you open it! If I have to sit here until you open it then I will!'

Nothing. Nothing except the sounds of desperate sobs creeping through the gaps around the door. Nothing except the sounds of complete and utter despair.

Of surrender.

Of heartbreak in the purest, rawest sense of the word.

'Fine,' I call through. 'I'll just sit here until you come out.'

I turn my back to the door and slide down it. Ray turns and hits me with destroyed, pale blue eyes full of questions. I meet his gaze and hold it steadily despite the shaking of my body.

'You lost your son, but you still have me.'

Chapter Twenty-Five – Roxy

I stare at the penguins, my body pressed against the glass the way it has been so many times before. The chill of it calms me. One of the penguins follows my finger's movement round the glass.

We're not so different, me and the penguins. Both of us are trapped in a place we don't want to be. There's no way of escaping, instead we're destined to live this way until some miracle happens. But they didn't choose this. I did.

I chose to trap myself. I chose to let my grief rule me, acting before thinking, speaking before pausing. And now I'm just like a penguin.

Cold. Alone. Trapped.

Stuck in an endless circle I'm not sure I have the power the change.

'Excuse me,' a voice says behind me. 'I'm going to have to ask you to leave. The zoo closed fifteen minutes ago.'

'Oh. I'm sorry. I didn't realize.' I push off the glass and head toward the exit.

The roads of Portland are filled with traffic from people rushing home to their perfect families for their perfect dinners after work. The streets are laden with couples going for an early dinner, children begging their parents for candy before they have their McDonalds treat, and teens joking, waiting to hear where the next party is.

I push through all of these people, my mind intent on getting back to the motel I've been staying in. There I can drink until Layla gets me and we go to her cousins to drink again. There I can forget all the shit of this year and just be. I can drown in a never-ending sea of vodka and not remember. No memories. No feelings. No anything.

Because forgetting is all that matters. Being numb is all that really counts when you hurt too much to feel anymore.

I walk into my tiny room, the bang of the door against the doorframe sounding too final. But then everything else in the last few months has been final, so why not that too?

I sit on the bed and unscrew the cap on the vodka bottle. I bring it to my lips, relishing the burn as it goes down.

I've lost everything, even the thing I should have been able to hold on to. I never should have let Kyle go. I never should have let him walk away from me on Friday night. I should have chased after him, grabbed him and told him I was talking crap, that I need him.

I should have swallowed every stupid ounce of pride in my body and told him I'm in love with him.

Now it's too late. A fuck up of my own making. A disaster of my own doing.

I don't even want to think about him. I can't think about him. I don't want to think about his lips on mine or his fingers through mine. I don't want to hear his laugh in my ear or his voice teasing me. I don't want . . . I don't want . . .

I want everything. I want every single thing I threw away.

A part of me wants him even more than I want Cam. My heart cries out for them both. It's broken for the two guys in my life that were always there, but my soul screams for Kyle. It's my soul that's hitting me round the head with my own stupidity, stinging me with my own words, cutting me with my own cruelness.

And it's too late. He's gone. I'm gone.

A knock on the door pulls me from my reverie, and I put the now half-empty bottle on the nightstand. I shove some notes in the pocket of my pants and join Layla outside.

She says nothing as we get into her car and drive to her cousin's apartment. The differences between her and Selena are absolute. Selena wouldn't be taking me to a party like this to get wrecked – she'd be following me, making sure I was safe. She wouldn't be giving me my escape, she'd be fighting it. Iz too. Both of them would be holding me back and slapping me.

But they're not here. They're in Verity Point, doing who knows what, and I'm here, forgetting and numbing and sinking into an empty space.

Alex's apartment is a constant party venue. Since he lives in one of the seedier, run down areas on the edge of the city, no one cares what he does. I'm almost certain he lives beneath drug dealers and above a whore.

Eyes follow me as I pour a strong drink and down it. They follow me as I have another, and another, and they follow me into the writhing mass of drunken bodies grinding together. They're inquisitive and threatening and appreciative all at the same time.

It's the threatening look that makes me pause. I don't know where it's coming from but it sends a spark of fear down my back. I look around the apartment, and unable to find it, I have another drink.

I'm probably imagining things. Scaring myself.

The night wanders on. I drink again and again, losing myself to the alcohol and the music the way I have for the last few days. Yet it's still there.

The look. The feeling of my every movement being watched. Of being stalked.

My eyes find the corner of the room, finally pinpointing the place it's coming from, and stare into a pair of dark brown eyes. I don't recognize them or the light hair or the stubble on his chin. I have no idea who he is.

But the way he's looking at me, the way he holds my gaze so intensely I'm afraid to turn away, tells me he knows me.

I swallow and turn my back to him. I'll give it half an hour, then I'll leave and head back to the motel. There isn't a single part of me that's comfortable here, and I don't want to stay any longer than I have to.

I'm drunk, not stupid.

I weave through the people here, slowly making my way to the door, and hope he doesn't notice me going in the dim light of the apartment. A big hope. I open the apartment door, unnoticed by the people crowded in the hallway, and slip out onto the street.

It's eerily quiet, and I wobble a little as I walk unsteadily. The urge to look over my shoulder overcomes me at the same time as the feeling that I'm being followed does. Out of fear, I don't look. I won't look. I can't look.

I look.

The guy from the party is behind me. Following me. Quickly.

I snap my head back around and take a deep breath. Oh God. What do I do? Do I run? That would look obvious. But I can't just walk like this. Fuck. Why am I out of town where there's nowhere to hide? If I were downtown I could walk into a restaurant or something.

'Roxy.'

Shit. Keep walking. Keep walking. Pretend he's got the wrong person.

Footsteps behind me increase in volume and speed, and before I can think, a hand clasps round my arm.

'Nice try, but I know it's you.'

The vodka gives me false bravado, and I turn to look at the guy. 'Who the hell are you?'

'You don't remember me? I shouldn't be surprised,' he sneers, his face morphing into anger. 'You don't remember any of the guys you fuck, do you?'

My eyes widen and I try to pull my arm from his grasp. 'I . . . don't know what you mean.'

'Not all guys like being used.' He leans closer to me, the beer on his breath making my nose wrinkle. 'Any idea what that's like?'

'I really don't know what you're talking about.' I try again to pull my arm away as panic bubbles in my throat. I'm suddenly stone cold sober, only aware of this guy in front of me. I step back and he moves with me.

'I couldn't believe it when I saw you here tonight. Seems like the perfect opportunity for you to know what it's like to be used, don't you?'

Breathe, Roxy.

'I don't . . . Please let me go,' I beg, tugging my arm back for a third time. He grips my other arm and pulls me toward him. My body goes on red alert at the movement, and when he shoves me back against the wall, my throat constricts. I struggle against him but he isn't loosening his grip, even through my begs and pleas. I open my mouth to scream and—

'Shut up,' he hisses, clamping his hand over my mouth. I bite down on his skin. Hard. He cusses at me, bringing a fist toward my face, colliding with my upper cheek. I trap my tongue between my teeth to stop myself screaming out, and this time I act instinctively, bringing my knee up to his pelvis.

He groans when I make contact with his balls and loosens his grip on me. I snatch myself from his grip and run like hell, my speed fueled purely by the adrenaline sprinting through my body. I don't dare to look behind me for a second. My hand is against my cheek, holding the throbbing there as if it can stop it.

I don't stop running until I get back to the motel and lock myself in the room. I lean against the door until I stop panting and the fear subsides. But I'm still shaking frantically, and I can't believe what almost happened.

Is that what I've caused?

I cross the room to the mirror and drop my hand from my face. My cheek and eye are red, and I know they'll bruise tomorrow, but I'll take a black eye over what could have happened any day.

The bed creaks as I sit on it, and I look at my reflection in the mirror. Flyaway hair, bruising face, chapped lips from running . . . What could have happened . . .

Have I really given myself a reputation that bad?

I know the answer is yes.

Chapter Twenty-Six – Kyle

Slowly, the door in front of me opens, and Myra steps out. Her hair is pulled into a bun on top of her head, her face is red and puffy, her eyes dull and lifeless. She's swirling in pain. I can feel it. I can touch it.

It's the strongest kind of pain, the most devastating. It's the kind that takes everyone else down with you.

'You're still there,' she says quietly.

'Yeah.' I rub my neck and stand. 'Should really get a carpet up here. Wood floor isn't all that great to sleep on.'

'You should have gone home.'

'I told you I was staying until you came out,' I remind her softly. 'Wanna talk?'

She takes a deep breath and tears roll down her cheeks. 'I . . .' I grab her as her legs buckle, and that shows me just how weak she is.

She's given up on everything.

Myra clutches at me and buries her face in my shoulder as she cries. It's the same cries as yesterday – hard and filled with unimaginable pain. Cries that make me want to join her.

I hold her the way I held Roxy when she broke down. I hold Myra until she's exhausted and can't cry anymore.

'Let's go downstairs.' I wrap an arm around her waist. 'Have a hot drink and some toast and you'll feel better.'

'I'm not hungry, Kyle. I just want my baby girl back.'

I swallow harshly. *You and me both.* 'A hot drink at least. Tea.'

She hesitates, but gives in. She knows I'm not giving in.

I sit her at the kitchen table and turn my back as Ray comes in. 'Is Iz still here?'

'No, son,' Ray answers. 'She left late last night after making sure I was okay.'

Three cups it is then.

I join my second parents at the table. 'I can't believe she's disappeared.'

'You were our last hope,' Ray says sadly. 'We thought she might be with you.'

'No. I haven't seen her since Friday night.' Guilt snakes through me. Fuck.

'She left on Saturday. Myra sent her home from the café early and when we got back, she was gone. Didn't think much of it. It's not exactly a surprise when she takes off – she did it a few times after Cam died – but Selena always knew where she was, and she always came back. Five nights is the longest she's been gone, and we're the last people to see her.'

'Have you called the police?' I look at Myra and nudge the mug closer to her. 'Drink.'

'No,' she answers in a small voice, lifting the mug. 'I thought . . . I thought she'd come back by now. I'm too scared to call them. I'm too scared something bad has happened to her.'

'Isn't it better to know?'

'No. Cam, and then her . . . If anything has happened to her . . . I don't know what I'd do, Kyle.' She shakes. 'I can't lose both of my babies. I can't.'

Tears glisten in Ray's eyes as he pulls her close and looks over her shoulder. I shake my leg to keep my own composure. Someone here has to be strong and it has to be me. I need to be the glue that holds them together.

I owe my best friend that.

'Right.' I stand. 'Where are the keys to the café?'

'What?' Ray asks.

'Someone has to open the café. You need that café to live. If it isn't open, you aren't making money. I've been there enough time when it's opened to know how it works.'

'Kyle, you don't have to.'

'No, I do,' I say firmly and hold out my hand. 'I'll call the girls. Iz and Louisa can cook and I'll stay out front with Selena. I'll even put an order in for you.'

'Kyle.'

'Keys.' I give my hand a shake for good measure. 'You two need each other and I need to do something useful, so let me have them.'

~

'She's really that bad?' Louisa asks from across the counter.

I nod. 'She's too scared to call the cops. I think that says it all, don't you?'

'Poor Aunt Myra,' she whispers. 'I can't believe Roxy would do this. She hasn't exactly thought of anyone since Cam died, but I didn't think she'd be this selfish.'

'I guess she felt like she has nothing left.' I swallow. 'I'm partly to blame. I walked away from her, Lou. I thought it might be the kick she needed – I didn't think she'd run off to fuck knows where. I took a risk and it wasn't worth it.'

She punches me in the arm. Hard.

'The hell was that for?'

'This is *not* your fault!' she yells. 'This is no one's fault. It's not even Roxy's. This is a fuck up none of us saw coming. You didn't know she'd do this when you walked. And y'know what? I'm glad you did. Walking away from her was the best damn thing you could have done, Kyle. Eventually, she'll get the kick she needs, and we all know you'll be waiting for her.'

'How do you know that?'

'Because your heart breaks in your eyes every time someone says her name.'

It breaks everywhere else too.

'Fine. Don't you have cooking to do?'

'Yep. I'm just taking a moment to think this would be a really good story.'

I shake my head and direct her toward the kitchen. 'Go.'

The bell above the door rings as the Stevens sisters come in. 'Is she back yet?'

'No. We still haven't found her.'

'Oooh dear,' Marie fusses.

'I wish we could do something to help,' Iyla adds.

'You can,' I smile at them sadly. 'You can hope.'

Chapter Twenty-Seven – Roxy

I'm trying to fight the pounding in my head and throbbing in my cheek by staring at the blank screen of my cell phone. The afternoon sun is glaring through the dirty window, illuminating my bed and dancing off the screen.

I haven't switched the phone on since I left Verity Point. It's stayed in the drawer of the nightstand, off, probably collecting messages. Such a huge part of me wants to turn it on to see them, but I know they'll make me go back and I can't.

I head out of my motel room and walk downtown. The fresh air helps to clear my head, and when my legs get sore from walking, I detour to McDonalds and order a Happy Meal. I open the box and pull out the toy. Optimus Prime.

Kyle's favorite.

Sigh. I tuck the tiny figure into my pocket and stare out the window as I eat. If it's not Cam, it's Kyle, and vice versa. One of them is always in my head and hurting my heart. Time flies as I sit here, letting the world pass me by.

And I'm wondering if I'm numb always. Is there too much pain inside me that I really can't feel anything anymore? No. I can still feel – it's why they encompass my every waking moment, stealing my thoughts.

I stare at my cell again and turn it on, switching it to airplane mode before any messages come through. It's got to the point I don't even know the date. Last night was a wake-up call, a kick up the ass, but that doesn't change the fact I've spent all day every day in a state of oblivion since I left home.

Shit. The date.

I go to my calendar, and I'm taunted by the red dot on the

space showing five days ago. Taunted. Warned. Threatened. It stares at me and I blink at it, frozen in this spot. I don't know how I missed that.

I don't know how I missed being late.

~

Run. That was my first thought as I left McDonalds, two days ago now. Run and hide and get out of Portland. I can't drink now – how can I? How can I do that knowing there could be something . . . a *baby* . . . growing inside me? I can't. No way.

I left the restaurant, stopped by a drugstore and the motel, and got the bus back to Verity. I packed my bag full of food, grabbed a blanket from the hotel and left. For the last two days I've been hiding out at the gorge trying to clear my head.

I need to run, and this is the only place I have to hide.

My hand grazes over the tree trunks while I walk around aimlessly. The rough bark is much like my thoughts; chopping and changing every second. I can barely think straight for all the craziness in my head.

I know hiding isn't the answer, and I know I can't hide up here forever, but I can't go home without knowing. It would be easier if I could talk to someone about this, but I can't. If I'm too scared to answer myself there's no way I can answer someone else right now.

Besides, the one person that needs the answer isn't around. The one person that deserves the truth and would hold me as I wait isn't here. That's something I only have myself to blame for.

I pushed him away. I pushed him away with the same force I held him to me with so many times. I'd do anything to pull him back to me right now. I'm just too stubborn to apologize.

I'm too stubborn and afraid and guilty to grab my phone and dial his number. I'm too chicken to give him the truth he deserves. The truth he needs.

The truth that's both our faults. It's the age old cliché as always – caught up in the moment and forgot to use protection. I've never forgotten before – *ever* – but I did with Kyle. I forgot to reach into the drawer in my nightstand and grab the little foil packet.

If I had I wouldn't be here now. I wouldn't be hiding out like a fugitive, bathing in my own guilt and fear. I'd be in Portland still, probably, wondering what the hell to do. Wondering whether to come home or not.

Now the white box taunts me as the corner of it pokes out of my bag. It begs me to rip off the plastic wrapping and get the answer I'm so desperately craving. But I won't. I won't because I keep hoping I'll get the courage to call him . . . even though I know it's not gonna happen.

My cell screen blinks at me as I check through the calendar one more time like it could be possible I've miscounted one hundred times. I haven't.

Silence.

That's all that's here.

It lets me think. It makes me think.

I've accepted no one is going to find me up here. It really is the perfect hiding place. There's no prying eyes, no whispers, no anything.

I didn't go home last night. I wanted to, but I'm not ready to talk to anyone yet. I'm not ready to tell everyone what's going on.

Hell, I need to find out for myself still.

The little white box stares at me again. The words burn into my brain, searing into my memory, and it's just begging me to pick it up.

It's the only way I'll get my answer. I'm a week late now. I either I am or I'm not.

I don't know what I'll do if I am.

I don't know how I'll tell Kyle.

I grab the box and pull off the plastic wrapping. My fingers run around the edges of the box, my eyes following their path.

I could know in five minutes. I could have the answer I've

been waiting for. I could put an end to my wondering and my worrying and find out for certain.

I could.

I don't know if I will. I don't know if I'm still ready to know, as crazy as the not knowing is driving me.

Maybe I will.

Maybe I won't.

Chapter Twenty-Eight – Kyle

I slam my phone down on the sofa. Another call reaching voicemail. At this point I have to ask myself if the only reason I'm calling her is to hear her voice, like that means she's okay.

'When did you last see her?'

'Ten days ago,' Ray answers. 'She'd had a rough night so we let her leave work early on Saturday.'

'A rough night? How?'

'We broke up,' I offer quietly. Guiltily. Myra reaches forward and grasps my hand, squeezing my fingers with what little strength she has left.

Ten days and she's finally accepted calling the cops is our only option, no matter what the outcome is.

'Okay.' The officer scribbles something on her pad. 'And you say her brother died at the beginning of the year? Cameron?'

Myra nods.

'Ah, I remember that,' the other cop says, shaking his head. 'Terrible crash.'

We're all silent for a moment. Like we need him to tell us that.

'And you think her disappearing act is related to that?'

'Of course it is.' My sister walks through the front door. 'Everyone knows that.'

'Iz,' I warn.

'And you are?' The officer raises his eyebrows in her direction.

'Her best friend and a psychology major, more than qualified to answer questions on her state of mind.'

'Iz!' I stand. 'Go home.'

'My best friend is missing and you want me to go home?'

'Yeah. I'll call you later. Please, Iz.'

She sighs heavily. 'I came to get the café keys. I'll open today.'

'On the side in the hall,' Ray tells her.

'Thanks.' She grabs the keys, glances at us all, and slams the door behind her.

I sit down and look at the cops. 'I'm sorry about my sister. She's worried about Roxy.'

'It's fine,' the older officer answers. 'So to summarize, you kids broke up, she left work, then disappeared. And she definitely went of her own choice?'

'Yes,' Myra answers.

'The combination of those things, and her brother's death, caused her to run, correct?'

Run.

'That's correct.'

'Do you have any idea where she would hide?'

Hide.

'I know,' I say slowly. 'I know where she is.'

Of course. There's only place she'd go.

Our spot.

I push past the officers, get of out of the house and run like I'm possessed. Branches catch my shirt but I don't care. I can't believe I didn't think of this straight away. I should have known.

The gorge is where I took her to hide when she needed to run.

I gave her the escape and the hideout.

Now I need to be her rock.

I need to fix this and take her home. Where she belongs.

I pause at the small clearing. She's sitting against a tree, her knees bent up, and she's looking at something in her hands. She puts her legs down and I get a glimpse of what's in her hands.

A white stick.

What is . . .?

Oh shit.

'Something you wanna share, Rox?'

Chapter Twenty-Nine – Roxy

Oh no.

Slowly I raise my eyes and swallow. Kyle's standing between two trees, his hands resting on each of them, and his eyes steady on me.

'How did you find me?'

'Doesn't matter.' He walks toward me and I try to hide the test. It's pointless. He's already seen it. He knows what it is.

'Um,' I stutter.

'Why didn't you tell me?'

'I don't know yet,' I whisper. 'I'm still waiting.'

He takes a deep breath and sits on the ground next to me, looping his arms around his knees. 'I'm waiting with you. Then you can tell me what motherfucker gave you that black eye.'

He doesn't ask whose baby it would be if it's positive. He doesn't doubt for a second it'd be his.

I nod slowly and pull the test back out from my sleeve. The little hourglass is spinning in the bottom corner of the screen and every turn seems like an hour instead of a second. My hand is shaking as I hold onto the test. My heart is pounding with fear, spreading it through my body. I feel sick. I can't breathe. Until—

'Negative,' I breathe out.

I drop the test as relief hits me. My hands rub down my face and I let out a long breath. Kyle's eyes are burning into the side of my head, and I know it's time to be honest with him.

'Why didn't you tell me?' he asks softly.

'That night . . . The first time we had sex, on Iz's birthday, we didn't use protection.' I stand and walk a couple of steps. 'I drove to Portland the next afternoon and got the morning after pill when I realized, and I thought it was taken care of. I didn't think about it anymore, like, at all. I completely shut it out. On Saturday, when I left work . . . I went to Portland with Layla. You didn't believe in us anymore, so I had nothing left to believe in, and I practically drank the week away. That's how I got this.' I touch my cheek and relay to him what happened that night.

'He didn't do anything to you, did he?'

'Not apart from this. I kneed him in the balls and ran like hell.' I take a deep breath and continue before he can stop me. 'But this . . . I only realized I was late two days ago. I didn't tell you because I was scared. Maybe it would have been different if we didn't break up . . . But I couldn't just call you up and be all, "Hey, I know you just walked away from our relationship, but just so you know, I could be having your baby," could I? That's why I didn't tell you. I was hurting and I was scared.'

The ground crunches beneath his feet. Kyle grabs me and pulls me into his chest, wrapping his arms tightly around my body. I circle his waist with my arms and bury my face into him as tears drip from my eyes.

'Fuck the break up,' he says into my hair. 'It doesn't matter anymore. I wish you'd told me, Rox. You wouldn't have had to run and hide and do that test alone. You have to know I would have been here.'

I shake my head. 'I thought you didn't care. What if it had been different?'

'It wouldn't have mattered!' He pulls back and lifts my face so he's looking in my eyes. 'I would have been here either way for whatever. The break up is all bullshit. Everything I said is crap. It means nothing, okay? Forget it ever happened. I don't care about that anymore. I just care you're okay. That's all that matters to me. I've been so fucking worried about you, you can't even imagine.'

He presses his lips to mine, and I sink into his hold, feeling a tiny piece of my heart mend.

'I really thought you didn't care,' I whisper in a thick voice, dropping my eyes.

'Oh, Rox.' He laughs and strokes my cheek with his thumb. 'I more than fucking care about you. I love you.'

Hold your horses. My eyes snap up to his. A small smile is playing on his lips, his eyes clear and raw.

'Wha?' is all I manage.

'I love you. *I* love you. I love *you.* The old you and the new you. Every part of you. I fell for the person you are right now and I wouldn't have you any other way. You don't have to change to be the person I want you to be because you're already there. You're already her.'

I swallow, his words sinking in, and run my fingers through his hair. 'Really?'

'Yep.' He nods. 'I. Love. You. Are we clear?'

'Not quite.' I step closer and let my lips curl into a smile. 'We're missing something.'

'We are?'

I wind my hand around his neck and pull his face down to mine. I touch our lips together firmly, and he brings our bodies together. His arms wrap my waist and mine wrap his neck until there's no space between us.

'Kyle?' I whisper.

'Roxy?'

I open my eyes to his and stare at him for a moment. 'I love you too.'

~

'I'm sorry. For last week.' I run my finger up and down his arm.

'Me too,' he replies.

'I should have listened to you. I shouldn't have gone mad at you when you asked me if I'd bought from Layla.'

'I shouldn't have asked you, Rox. I should have trusted you.'

'Yeah, maybe, but I should have believed you enough to know you didn't ask to piss me off.'

'It would have been a success if that was my aim,' he mutters into my hair.

'Shut up.' I smile. 'I'm sorry for being a bitch to you too. I was just trying to make a point, I guess.'

'Well it worked. Although I don't think it was quite the outcome we were expecting.'

I shake my head. 'I didn't actually think you would walk away the way you did,' my voice trails off.

'Hey.' Kyle holds me tighter to him and I turn my face to look at him when he puts his fingers in my hair. 'I was bluffing. Do you really think I could have walked away from you like that? I was always going to come back to you. Always.'

'Then what took you so long to get here?' I tease.

'I only just realized where you were. I've been living at your parents for the last few days looking after your mom and running the café with the girls.'

'Looking after my mom?' my voice quivers.

'She broke down when you disappeared.'

Tears burn my eyes. 'I'm sorry. I shouldn't have run away.'

Kyle pulls me tight. 'Shit, Rox. You scared the ever-loving life out of me. I've never, ever felt that way before and I hope I never have to again. I was so fucking scared you were gone. Really gone.'

'I'm sorry,' I repeat.

'As soon as I realized you were here I left your house like my ass was on fire. Would you believe I got up here in less than ten minutes?' He raises his eyebrows and smirks.

I grin. 'Impressive. Did you have Red Bull for breakfast or something?'

'No. I just needed you.'

I curl into him, feeling every part of our bodies touching.

After everything we're here. Heartbreak from death and heartbreak from love. And I'm sitting here, his arms around me, and wishing we didn't have to move.

'Please don't ever do that again.' His voice is thick with emotion, and I hug him tightly.

'I promise. Never again.'

'Good. I love you too much to feel like that again.'

'As long as you promise to never walk away like that again.'

He opens his eyes to mine. 'I promise. Only you.'

'Always you.'

Our lips linger together for a long moment.

'We have to go now, don't we?' I ask in a small voice.

'Yep.' He sighs. 'I text your mom so she knows you're okay, but she'll want to see you. She's so worried about you, Rox.'

I swallow. Guilt hits me hard. 'I know. I've been so horrible to her, and Dad.'

'As much as I hate to, I have to agree with you. You've been pretty fucking awful.'

'You know, I can be mad at you again if you want.'

Kyle laughs and helps me stand. 'Just because you're not mad at me anymore doesn't mean I won't still tell you as it is. Besides, you don't stay mad at me for long.'

I glance at him. 'That can be changed, you know.'

He grabs me from behind and wraps his arms around my shoulders. 'No, it can't be. We usually end up *very* close after you've been mad at me, so you won't let it last too long.'

Damn him for being right.

'And as much as I hate to let you go, you do have to go and talk to your mom . . . and the police.'

Uh-uh. I did it this time, didn't I?

'Stay.' I stop and turn. 'Please. Even if you're just in the house.'

'You have to do this, not me.'

'I know that.' I fist the front of his shirt and rest my forehead against his chest. 'But it's gonna hurt, isn't it? I'm gonna have to remember it all. I'm gonna have to be honest about how much I've been hurting. And . . . We're gonna talk about the night he died.' My chest tightens. 'You're the only person I've spoken to about it.'

He strokes my back and takes a deep breath. 'Okay, but I'm staying upstairs. This is your talk with your parents – you guys have a lot to sort out. I'm only staying because I know you'll need me after.'

We're both thinking about the day I broke down in the woods and told him about the night Cam died. There's no way I could have stayed sane if it wasn't him holding me after.

'Thank you,' I whisper.

Kyle kisses the top of my head. 'Come on. Let's take you home.'

I walk back with him, his arm wrapped around my body. Nothing is scaring me more than the conversation I know I'm about to have with my mom and dad. This is going to be as hard as walking away from the hospital.

Except this time I'm not numb. By the time we left the hospital, I'd gone through every emotion I could and I was exhausted. I'd cried and screamed and hit the walls. I'd screamed even louder and sobbed even harder and given everything into trying to break the wall. When we left, I had nothing left to give. I had nothing left to feel.

This time I have it all.

I have the pain and the anger. I have the sadness and the guilt. I have the grief and the regret.

This time, I have Kyle.

I can't help but wonder how different the last few months would have been had he come back for the funeral. If he'd been here we would have had each other like we do now.

If he'd been here, I might have been going to college this year instead of next.

'Ready?' he squeezes my shoulders.

I nod and we turn the corner. I'm as ready as I'll ever be, at least.

'Roxy.' Mom runs to me as soon as Kyle opens the door, and I fall into her embrace. Dad's arms go around us both, and they're both crying.

It hits me now, between both my parents, how selfish I've

been. They've needed me as much as I've needed to forget, but I didn't think about them. All I could think about was myself, my own pain, my own guilt.

I lost my brother, but they lost their son.

That day we all lost a member of our family. We all lost our best friend, our light, our joker. We all lost our star.

'I'm sorry,' I cry into Mom's shoulder. 'I am so, so sorry.'

'You're here now.' Dad kisses the side of my head. 'Everyone is exactly where they should be.'

Chapter Thirty – Kyle

Roxy's bedroom door opens and she walks in slowly. Her eyes are ringed in red and there's tear stains on her cheeks. She gives me a small, sad smile that damn near breaks my heart, and I hold my arms out to her. She runs across the room and falls onto my lap, burying her face in my neck. I squeeze her as tight as I can without hurting her and kiss her neck. Her body shudders as she lets out a long breath.

'Okay?' I ask softly.

She nods. 'As okay as I can be, I guess. We talked, got everything out, and there was a lot of apologizing and crying. They've gone to open the café now. I think we all need a bit of space.'

'Good. Do you feel better?'

She nods again but doesn't say anything. I sigh and rest my cheek on top of her head, squeezing her a little, holding her a lot. For a long time.

'Thank you,' she whispers after a while, looking up at me.

My lips curve on one side. 'For what?'

'For being here. You were kinda late – okay, six months late – but I seem to remember you never come on time.'

'I'm always on time,' I mutter. 'It's not my fault if you're always early.'

'Kyle!' she squeals, her lips parting.

'What?' I grin. 'You left that wide open for my interpretation.'

'It's not the only thing I've left open for that.'

My jaw drops. 'Roxy!'

Her eyes twinkle, and she mock pouts. 'What?'

'It's a damn good job you're stuck with me, you know that? I'm certain no one else can handle you.'

'It's not my fault if I'm a handful.'

I creep my hand between us and cup her breast. 'And a very nice handful you are too.'

She laughs, the sadness in her eyes now replaced with a sassy spark. 'I'm not the only handful here, Daniels.' Her hand goes down and her fingers curl over my dick. It twitches at her touch and gets hard the second I see her lidded eyes staring down at me.

'Handful?' I push her round until she's lying on her back on her bed. 'I think you mean handfuls, Roxanne.'

'One and a half if you're lucky,' she murmurs.

'Forgotten already, have you?' I run my nose along her jaw and my breath covers her neck.

She shivers. 'Forgotten what?'

'That's my ego you're bruising.' I touch my lips to her collarbone.

'You have plenty spare.' She slides her hands beneath my shirt and runs them across my back, her fingers dipping just beneath my jeans and circling to the front.

My jaw twitches when they reach the button. 'My ego isn't my fault. There's this girl I know. She's amazing, sweet, and she's damn beautiful. And she's just about the sexiest thing I've ever seen, and she wants me. Can you blame me for having a big ego when I get to be the envy of almost every guy who has ever laid eyes on her?'

My lips hover over hers, and I feel her smile although we're not touching.

'You're in the wrong place then. There's no sweet girl here.'

I laugh. 'You're sweet and spicy, Roxy. Just how I like it.'

'Yeah? I left the sweet in the hall. Just the spicy here.' To make her point she unclasps the button deftly and hooks her fingers inside the waistband of my boxers.

'Good job you did.'

I finally touch my lips to hers. She sighs against my mouth and wriggles beneath me. She tugs me down and snatches her hand from my pants just before my hips hit hers. Her legs go round my waist, holding me to her, and the action presses me against her.

My dick hardens even more when she pushes her hips up. I run my hand down her thigh, and it's so fucking hard not to rip her clothes off right now. Every movement she's making beneath me is precise and perfectly executed. She knows exactly what she's doing – there's no way she can't feel the way my cock is pressing into her through both of our jeans. Every arch, every shift, every wriggle, it's all deliberate.

She pulls her lips away and kisses along my jaw to my ear. 'Looks like I'm open for your interpretation again.'

I smile and dip my hand in the back of her jeans, cupping her ass.

Interpret I fucking shall.

~

'I can't even take the blame for that one.' I shake my head. 'That was all Cam's idea.'

'C'mon!' Roxy says in disbelief. 'You expect me to believe it was all Cam's idea to steal everyone's dressing gown cords and tie them to the top of the bunk beds so you two could bungee jump from them?'

Ah, that was fun.

'Yep.'

'I don't believe it. You had some say in it.'

'He came up with it, and my say was it'd be fun.' I grin at her and squeeze her hand. 'Cling filming your door? That was all me, baby.'

'Of course it was. Every stupid fucking prank you two ever played on me was your idea!'

No arguing with the truth. 'I told you before. I wanted you to like me.' I wink.

'I actually think I hated you until I was fourteen.'

'Then what? You woke up one day and decided I wasn't an asshole?'

Her lips curl. 'Who said I've decided that?'

'Don't make me whip out the jackass, Hughes.'

'I happen to like your jackass, Daniels.' She swings our hands between us. 'No, I just decided I kinda . . . *liked* . . . you.'

I don't miss the inflection on the word 'liked' . . . Maybe I should have stolen her diary like Cam tried to get me to several times.

'Liked, huh?' I spin in front of her and stop. 'How much did you like me?'

She purses her lips.

'Roxy . . .' I smirk and look down at her, glad her black eye has finally faded. 'Did you have a crush on me when you were fourteen?'

Her tongue snakes out and across her bottom lip, and the slight flush of her cheeks answers my question.

'No,' she blatantly lies. 'You were my brother's asshole best friend.'

'You're a terrible liar.' I start walking again and pull her with me.

'I'm so not lying!'

'You so *are*.'

She mutters something under her breath. 'Fine. I had a crush on you when I was fourteen.'

'And fifteen, and sixteen, and seventeen, and eighteen . . .' I tease her.

'God, I know. What was I thinking?'

'You were thinking very smartly.'

'Does that make me a genius now?'

I smile and stop, not caring we're in the middle of a street in Portland. I pull her into me and push some hair from her face.

'Why would you be a genius?'

'You're just trying to make me say it again, aren't you?'

'Maybe.'

'You're such a girl.'

'Watch it.' I start walking again. 'You wouldn't want anyone here to see how much of a girl I'm *not*.'

'Promises, promises.' She sighs. 'Hey, Kyle?'

'Yes, Roxy?'

She tugs on my hand and stands on her tiptoes so her lips are by my ear. 'I love you.'

My lips twitch the way they do whenever she says it. 'Smart girl.'

Roxy slaps my chest. 'Ass.'

I drop her hand, wrap my arm around her shoulders, and pull her into me. 'I love you too.'

I'll never get tired of hearing it or saying it. So what if falling in love with her wasn't my plan? Somehow we got here and I wouldn't change this for the world.

Maybe she has a point with the 'girl' stuff.

'Smart guy.' She curls into me.

'Debatable.'

'It's amazing how much jackass you put into one word.'

I grin. 'Just trying to get in your pants again, babe.'

She laughs. 'I'm not wearing pants.'

'In your pants, up your dress, either one works for me.' I shrug. 'Admittedly the dress would be easier.'

Roxy runs her fingers through her hair and looks up at me. Her lips are curved on one side, her eyes wide and shining in amusement.

'You just want me for my sex.'

'And your hands. And your mouth. Oh, and your boobs. Definitely for your boobs.'

She laughs again, louder, and pokes me in the stomach. 'You're crazy.'

'I could go for a really cheesy response to that, but I think I'll settle for a, "You're just realizing this?"'

'Mild or mature?'

I raise an eyebrow at her. 'You what?'

'For your cheesy response. Mild or mature?'

'Now who's the crazy one?' I tap her nose. 'For the record, it would have been extra mature.'

A giggle leaves her and I can't help but laugh with her. Since she spoke to her parents a few days ago it's like a huge weight has lifted off her shoulders. You can see it in everything she does; she's more playful, more teasing. Even when she's at work she's happier.

Walking away from her was the best thing I could have done. It killed us both but now she's like the girl I remember her being. Sure she's older, more mature, and a hell of a lot fucking sexier, but the way she laughs and jokes makes her more like the Roxy I grew up with.

She's not perfect. She's stubborn as shit and challenges me at every turn, but I kinda like it.

I just hope she won't challenge me now.

'Let's get food.'

'From where?'

'Wherever you want, Rox.'

'McDonalds.'

I stop. 'Are you fucking serious?'

She looks up at me. 'What?'

'I just told you we can get dinner wherever you want, and you pick *McDonalds*?'

'What's wrong with Maccy's?' she demands.

'Nothing. I just . . .' I shake my head. 'Never mind.'

'I don't do fancy restaurants. I'd rather have a burger and fries.'

'Okay, strange girl. If you want fast food, Maccy's it is.'

We turn off the street and walk in the direction of McDonalds. I can't believe she picked fast food. It's not exactly the place I imagined when I pictured myself asking her to come to Berkeley with me.

I pictured actual waiters, not Ronald fucking McDonald.

We order our food and Roxy finds a table while I wait for it. I didn't know girls ordered large meals, and I say as much when I sit down.

'Psh.' She scoffs. 'I'm not a stick. If I want to eat crap food, I will. I'm hardly going to get fat from one large burger and fries, am I?'

If I wasn't already in love with her, I definitely am now.

'I'll just have to do a little more exercise.' She shrugs, pauses, then points a fry in my direction. 'And before you say anything, mister, that exercise has been considered and accepted.'

Yep. I love this girl.

'And here I was with a book full of ideas to convince you.' I sigh.

'There might be a part of me that still needs convincing.'

'Right here?'

She throws a fry at me. 'You're insatiable, Daniels.'

'Maybe, maybe not.' I smirk. 'I don't think I will ever get enough of you. That's all.'

'Too much of me isn't necessarily a good thing.'

'Depends who you ask. And what you're doing too much of . . .'

'I think I can guess where this is going.'

I grin. I could sit here forever and banter with her, back and forth constantly. I'll never get tired of her smart-ass remarks, her sarcasm, or her teasing comments. And I'll never get tired of being able to follow through with that banter afterward.

'I need to ask you something,' I say slowly.

'Uh-oh.' Roxy puts her milkshake down. 'What did I do this time?'

I laugh. 'Nothing. I just need to ask something.'

'Well stop babbling and ask me.'

I nudge her under the table, and she kicks me back. 'Have you thought about what'll happen when I go back to California in a few weeks?'

The small smile lingering on her lips fades, and she drops her eyes. 'No.'

'I have.'

She nods quietly. I take a deep breath, staring at her. Here goes nothing.

'I want you to come with me.'

Her eyes snap up. They're wide in shock, and her lips are parted. 'What?'

'Come with me. To California.'

'You live in a frat house, Kyle.'

I shake my head. 'Mom and Dad saved up money for our college funds. We had the choice of it paying our tuition or renting an apartment for a year when we hit sophomore year. We both picked an apartment. And we have our trust funds from our grandparents – not much there, but enough to get started with somewhere to live.'

'And you've not touched a dollar of it?'

'Nope. We were told when we were eighteen about the funds, and Iz and I both decided the same thing. It makes sense – we have a place to live and when we finish college we can stay, but if we go, we already have the money to find another apartment.'

She looks down again and dips a fry repeatedly into the ketchup. 'I guess. So you're moving into an apartment when you go back?'

'Yep.'

'And you really want me to come with you?'

'You were going to go to UCLA anyway, right? Live with me in Berkeley, then move there next year. There are loads of places in California offering the courses you need.'

Including Berkeley. But I'm not going to tell her I know that . . . Or that I searched Berkeley specifically.

'I know.' She looks up again, her eyes meeting mine. 'Berkeley does too.'

My lips twitch.

'I just looked for . . . I don't know. Weighing up my options, you know?'

I nod and let my lips lift up at the corners. I'm not sure who she's trying to fool.

'It's a good school,' I comment, wanting to see how far she'll take this.

'Right. And I mean, I wanna go to a good school.'

'Yep.'

'And the weather would be a nice change to Oregon.'

'Definitely.'

'But it's a lot to think about.'

I grab her hand across the table and hold in my amusement. 'Moving with me would be totally beneficial. You'd get to see the college and the area and decide if it's where you want to go.'

'I suppose. But don't you have a rabid fan base down there would who chew me up and spit me out?'

The thought makes me laugh loudly. 'I can think of about four girls who have an attitude to rival yours, and none of them are in my supposed fan base, so I think you're safe on that side.'

We get up and throw our wrappers in the trash before leaving.

'Good to know.' She muses.

'Roxy.'

'What?'

'Stop being a dick and answer the question.'

'I'm sorry. What was the question again?'

Pain in my ass. I stop and pull her to me. 'Come to Berkeley with me.'

'That's an order, not a question.'

'You're making this hard for me deliberately, aren't you?'

Her eyes twinkle with amusement, her lips turned up at the corners. 'Maybe,' she says quietly.

'Do you want an epic declaration of love? McDonalds' roof looks easy to climb on.' I make to move, and she shrieks and grabs my shirt.

'No! No, no epic declarations needed today, thank you.' She laughs. 'Ask me again.'

'Fine.' I tuck her hair behind her ear. 'Roxy, will you come to Berkeley with me?'

She wraps her arms around my neck and squeezes. 'Only if you promise to give me an epic declaration of love when we get there.'

I smile into her hair. 'I think I can do that.'

'Then yes. I'll come with you. To check out the area,' she adds in a teasing lilt.

'But of course.' I kiss her softly.

Just like walking away, the question was worth the risk.

Chapter Thirty-One – Roxy

It's funny how things change.

Your life can change in the time it takes you to blink – for better or worse – and there's nothing you can do to change it. You have to take the curveballs life throws at you and take the hit. You have to take the fall and pull yourself back up, however hard it might be, however you can.

You might not always pick the right way, but that's okay. No one is perfect and no one can be expected to get it right all of the time. Making mistakes doesn't necessarily matter; it's acknowledging them and making it right that matters.

I never knew what would happen to Cam so I couldn't change it. I've accepted that now. I'll always have a lingering piece of guilt inside for letting him get in the car with Stu, but I have to remind myself that it was *his* choice. Cam's. Not mine. For all I knew, we'd have a safe drive and we'd all get to where we were going in one piece. I couldn't have guessed how that night would end.

You can't change what you can't predict.

My life, the way I've been dealing with that night, is one thing I can change. I can stop drinking, doing drugs, sleeping with the wrong guys. I can stop going to parties until I'm ready to.

I've faced up to my mistakes now and I've apologized for them. I can't do anything but stop myself making them again, and that's easier when you have someone by your side who believes in you. When you have someone who understands you, who gets you, it's easier.

Kyle knows my pain because he feels it too. I hate the fact

losing Cam is the thing that brought us together, but that's another thing I can't change. Of course I'd give up Kyle for Cam if I had the choice, but I think if Cam had the choice he'd have it this way.

He'd rather have me happy and in love than loving from afar. Even if the person I love is his best friend.

I still can't bring myself to say 'was' a lot of the time. In my heart he's my brother. He'll always be my brother the way he'll always be Kyle's best friend. We haven't stopped loving him just because he's dead. He's still alive inside of us, and that's what matters.

Although I would have really liked him to be around when Kyle pulled his walking away stunt.

I hate him for that, but it's the best thing he could have done. He was all I had then, and I didn't know how low I was until I hit the bottom. His walking away hit me harder than I ever thought it would, and I don't think I realized how I really felt about him until he did that. How I do feel about him.

And the truth of it is I'm completely and utterly, heart-wrenchingly, skin-tinglingly, unquestionably in love with him.

He knew what I needed when I didn't. He knows when to hold me, when to tease me, when to laugh at me, when to drive me to the brink of insanity and when to bring me back. He knows how to wind me so tightly and hold me there until I'm ready to unravel, and he knows how to touch me until it tells me he loves me without words.

Kyle doesn't just tell me he loves me. He shows me. He makes me feel it and makes me believe it with everything he does.

The last few weeks have been a clusterfuck of bullcrap. We've hit just about every wave possible since he came home and we've sunk more than a few ships in this whirlwind. We've fought and we've made up, and then we've fought some more.

When you fight over every little thing, you know you're truly in love. It proves your love is worth fighting for and it proves how much you care.

If I have to fight with him every single day for the rest of my life to prove to him every single part of me loves him, then I fucking well will.

~

'You're going to California? With my brother?' Iz stares at me like I'm completely crazy.

'That's what I just said.' I pick the petals off a daisy.

'He's a nightmare to live with. Leaves his socks everywhere then goes mad because he has none to wear.'

'He'll soon start washing them. Every sock I see on the floor I'll chuck in the trash.'

Iz laughs. 'That'll go down well.'

'It'll teach him to pick them up,' I muse, looking toward him playing football with the guys.

'When did you decide this?'

'Huh? Oh, last week.'

'And you're only just telling me?' She shoves me. 'I'm pissed, Roxy. You've kept this quiet for a week?'

I shrug. 'We had to talk to our parents first. Mom was unsure, but Dad got it right away and he's worked on her. She finally came round this morning. Said she's choosing to focus on the fact I'll be closer to prospective schools than living with a *real boy*!'

We both laugh, and Iz sighs. 'I can't believe my best friend is going to move in with my brother. And you're both younger than me! What's that all about, huh?'

I glance at Si then back at her. 'I can think of a guy who wouldn't mind keeping you company at night.'

She bites her lip. 'One kiss, Roxy. We kissed once, and now you're all acting like we're in love. I rarely see him at college. It's a complete fluke he ended up in Miami like I did, and being on the football team, he has like a thousand little fan girls screaming his name every week.'

I cover my mouth with my hand. 'That's some stamina.'

Iz buries her head in her arms. 'Okay, I'm not gonna deny, I'd like to have a go at that stamina. Look at the guy.' She motions in his direction. 'He's all muscle and fitness, and like I told Kyle, he could probably fuck like a porn star.'

'You said that to Kyle? For real?'

She sighs happily. 'Best moment of my life.'

My lips curl up. 'So fuck him. There's still two weeks of summer left. Get it out of your system, then when you're cheering his games, don't let him forget it.'

'Hmm.' Her eyes flick to his butt and back to me. 'I have a hunch that cheering might be out of place at a football game.'

We both erupt in giggles.

'What are you two tittering about?' Kyle sits behind me and wraps his arms around my shoulders.

'Nothing you'd want to hear,' Iz replies quickly. 'Besides, I think we're done with that conversation, don't you, Roxy?'

'Yes, Iz.' I bend my head down so my mouth is covered by Kyle's arms. 'For now.'

'I feel for you, Roxy,' Si says as he sits in front of us. 'Living with this dick.'

'Oh, c'mon, Si. It won't be that bad,' I reply. 'After all, I'll have sex on tap.'

Kyle snorts into the back of my head as Si grins.

Yep. Girls can play the sex comment game, too.

'She's got you there, man,' Kyle says. 'Just think, while you'll be out finding some poor chick to fuck, all I have to do is go home.'

My eyes slide to Iz's and I raise my eyebrows. She gives me a look of stone. I grin. Our exchange goes completely unnoticed by the guys. Unsurprisingly.

'. . . not that many girls,' Si responds.

'I'm calling bullshit on all that!' Iz cries, dragging her attention back to the conversation. 'You forget, Si Jason, that I am at every single one of your home games, and you never leave the parties after without some blonde bimbo on your arm.'

Si turns his face toward her and smirks. 'I'm surprised you

notice. Aren't you usually too busy being chatted up by the rest of my team?'

'Yep. What can I say? They could teach you a thing or two about taste in girls.'

'Burn,' Kyle whispers into my ear.

'I know plenty of tastes in girls, Iz. In fact, every single one.'

'Oooh,' I whisper back.

'Really? Judging by the way they circle you, I'm shocked you can tell one taste apart from the other. Don't they all taste like slut?'

'She wins,' we whisper together, then laugh quietly.

'What if I like the taste of slut?'

'Then that proves my theory of you being the only boy on your football team.'

'Give it up, dude.' Kyle laughs and looks at Si. 'You're not gonna win this one. We gotta go play again, anyway.'

Both guys get up to go back to their game. Si bends down and whispers something in Iz's ear before walking away with a shit-eating grin on his face, leaving her gaping after him.

'Okay, what did he say?' I demand when she's regained some composure.

She swallows. 'He told me I should remember exactly how much of a man he is from our kiss, and if I've forgotten he's more than happy to give me a reminder I'm not gonna forget anytime soon.'

I smile slowly, amusement radiating out of me, then sigh. 'Why did you two have to go to school in Miami? This is something I'd love to see.'

'Just . . . Don't,' she mutters as Kyle comes running back over.

'What?' I frown when he grabs my hands. '. . . Are you doing?'

'You're playing football.' He pulls me up.

I dig my feet into the ground to the sound of Iz's laughter. 'I'm doing *what*?'

'Playing football.'

'Dunno what you're laughing at,' Si says to Iz as he pulls her up. 'You're playing too.'

'Fuck no. I cheer, not play!' She fights against his hold, and he laughs, dragging her toward the guys.

'Really, Iz? You think you can make me let go of you?'

'I'm so cheering for you to lose when we get back to college, you cock.' She sniffs and he lets go of her.

'Come on,' Kyle drags me over. 'Come play.'

'I don't play football.'

'You do now.'

I let him pull me over, knowing I have no choice but to. He's stronger than me anyway . . . And I really wanna see Iz try to play. She picks the ball up and looks at Si.

'What do I do with this?'

'You throw it . . .' He smirks.

She throws it against the side of his head.

'Fucking hell!' Si grabs his head.

A satisfied smile creeps onto Iz's face. 'You know, I have quite the aim. I might be good at this after all.'

'You would be if the aim wasn't at people's heads!'

'Hey – don't underestimate me. I can apparently throw a ball, plus I'm fast, strong, and I'm agile. I might just surprise you.'

'You're not a fucking race horse, Iz,' Kyle shoots at her.

'You know any race horses that can throw a ball?'

'Well. No.'

'Shut it then, before you get a ball to the side of the head too.' She puts her hands on her hips. 'Alright, you've dragged us over here, now what are we doing?'

Kyle's hands clamp onto my shoulders and he steers me across his yard, and Si does the same to Iz.

'Stand here. When you catch the ball, throw it,' Kyle tells me.

'Throw it where?' I raise my eyebrows.

'Either at Mark or Ben, okay?'

'Um, okay. I'd rather no one threw the ball to me, if I'm honest.'

He laughs as he backs off, and Iz and I share a wary look. *What the fuck are we doing here?* The ball goes flying through the air, and we both stand where we are, not moving at all, just watching it move.

We have been coerced into this, after all.

And I have no idea what they're doing or if we're even supposed to be doing anything.

'Roxy!' Ben yells my name, and before I can blink, I see the ball come flying at me. And Kyle.

Kyle comes flying at me and knocks me to the ground.

'Oomph!' I take a deep breath and smack his arm. 'What the hell did you do that for?'

'It's my job to take down the unsuspecting girl who's doing nothing but standing and looking pretty.'

Right. 'I think you've changed that rule.'

'Maybe a little. But only so I can do this.' He cups my neck with his hand and touches his lips to mine, his other hand resting on my side.

'Mhmm. Can we keep this rule?'

'Most definitely,' he replies, lowering his mouth to mine again.

Definitely the best game of football I've ever played.

Epilogue – Kyle

Roxy walks through our apartment, her eyes calculating every inch of space. It's not the biggest place, but it's the perfect size for two people. She managed to get a job in a café downtown before we left Oregon. I told her we'd be fine until after Christmas between our savings, but she insisted she'd go crazy sitting here by herself all day, so I let her get on with it. Besides, it'll be good for her to meet some of the people round here.

Here.

I still can't believe she's here. In California. With me.

Being mine.

'I think we need to paint, but other than that, it's cool.'

I walk up to her and wrap my arms around her waist. 'Is that your expert opinion?'

She nods with a small smile on her face. 'The color on the walls here doesn't match the furniture, and the bedroom could do with a repaint. And a bit of color in the bathroom would be nice. White is boring.'

'Is that right?'

'Yep. Some photos too, and some other little bits, and it'll be perfect.'

'You sound like you're staying here for the long haul.'

'How do you know I'm not?' She raises her eyebrows at me and puts her hands on my chest.

I bend my face toward hers. 'I was under the impression you were moving to LA next year.'

'Don't be a dick,' she mutters, sliding her hands up and around my neck. 'We both know I'm staying in Berkeley. Someone needs to wash your socks.'

'And someone needs to keep your ass in check.'

'You know, I like the way you keep my ass in check.'

I touch my lips to hers and smile. My hand slides down to her body, cups her ass, and I pull her hips to mine. 'I think it needs keeping in check now. In our bedroom.'

She laughs and kisses me, her lips soft against mine. I walk backward, tugging her with me, and kiss her more firmly. Her tongue snakes against my mouth, and she nips my bottom lip, making me grow hard. I move to pick her up and . . .

The fucking buzzer goes.

I sigh and push the button. 'Yes?'

'Let us in!' Megan yells through the intercom. Roxy raises an eyebrow.

'Who's us?'

'Me and Maddie!'

'Do you have to come up right now? Can't you come back later?'

'We want to meet your girlfriend!' Maddie shouts. 'Let us up now, Kyle, or we'll ring all these buzzers until someone does!'

'I have no doubt about it,' I mutter dryly. 'Okay, come up.'

I release the button and look at Roxy.

'Rabid fan base?' she asks.

'Two of the girls who have attitudes to rival yours. This should be fun,' I finish when there's a knock at the door. I open it. 'Roxy, meet Megan and Maddie.'

'Um, hi?' Roxy says uncertainly.

'She's real pretty,' Megan says.

'Yeah.' Maddie looks at me. 'How did you manage that one, Kyle?'

Here we go. 'She's smart and clever.'

'I don't doubt it,' she says. 'I'm wondering what she's doing with you, though. That's definitely a blip in the intelligence.'

I give her a gentle shove with my elbow. 'Be nice, you two.'

'We'll be nice to her.' Megan grins. 'You're a different story.'

Roxy smiles at her from her position leaning against the wall. 'That happens a lot, huh?'

I wrap my arm around her shoulders. 'Yeah, you girls are always mean to me. Especially you.' I poke Roxy's side and she slaps my stomach.

'You make it too easy,' she replies. 'Taking candy from a baby would be harder.'

'I like her!' Maddie announces. 'She's gonna fit in well here.'

'Hey, are you going to Berkeley?' Megan asks her.

'Next year,' Roxy answers. 'I got dragged down here by Kyle this year. I was hoping for another year of peace before I got stuck with him again, but no such luck.'

'Oh, you know each other from before then?' Megan looks between us.

'Yeah, she's crushed on me since she was fourteen,' I offer.

'Not that it means anything,' Roxy adds. 'Because he's crushed on *himself* since he was about ten.'

My lips twist. Damn girl.

'You know, I was worried about taking your girl into a frat house,' Maddie admits. 'But I think she'll handle herself just fine.'

'Hell, if she can deal with Kyle, she can take our guys.' Megan grins.

'I'm nowhere near as bad as Braden and Aston!' I argue. They both give me a look. 'Okay, only on Saturdays.'

'And it's Saturday today,' she reminds me. 'So shut it. Hey, why don't you guys come to the frat house tonight?'

'I don't know . . .'

'Come on, you know no one will believe us if we say you have a girlfriend,' Maddie teases.

'Oh, ha ha ha.'

'Let's go.' Roxy looks up at me. 'We have nothing else to do.'

I can think of plenty of other things we could do.

'Sure?' I pull her closer to me, and she nods.

'We don't have to stay long, do we? We've still got unpacking to do.'

'Hey! I have an idea.' Maddie's eyes twinkle. Oh no. I know her ideas. 'We'll take Roxy for coffee and you can unpack!'

'I hope you like Starbucks,' I murmur to Roxy and kiss her before the girls grab her from me.

'Love it,' she whispers back. 'Be good and unpack for me.'

'It's not the thing I was planning to unpack, but whatever.' I kiss her again and Megan whisks her off.

'We'll bring her back in one piece!' Maddie yells over her shoulder.

'And with a whole new impression of you!' Megan giggles.

Roxy smiles at me and shrugs as they lead her down the stairs.

I watch her go with a smile on her face. If anyone had to turn up and take her away, I'm glad it was those two. They're crazy as hell but have the sweetest hearts, and even though I know they'll tell her everything they know about me, I don't care.

I just want her to be happy here.

I walk past the bathroom and see our toothbrushes on the side, and my face breaks into a grin.

Yep. She'll be happy here, if only because I'll bend over backward to make it so. My eyes are drawn to the picture of me, her, and Cam after a football game, and I nod to it.

'Promised you I'd look after her, didn't I?'

Find your next delicious read at

THE
Book
BAKERY

The place to come for cherry-picked monthly reading recommendations, competitions, reading group guides, author interviews and more.

Visit our website to see which great books we're serving up this month.

www.TheBookBakery.co.uk

🐦 BookBakeryUK
📘 TheBookBakeryUK

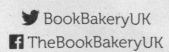